NAKED HEAT

NAKED HEAT

RICHARD CASTLE

HYPERION

NEW YORK

Trade paperback edition ISBN: 978-1-4013-1108-7

Hyperion books are available for special promotions and premiums. For details contact the HarperCollins Special Markets Department in the New York office at 212-207-7528, fax 212-207-7222, or email spsales@harpercollins.com.

Original book design by Shubhani Sarkar

FIRST TRADE PAPERBACK EDITION

10 9 8 7 6 5 4 3 2 1

THIS LABEL APPLIES TO TEXT STOCK

We try to produce the most beautiful books possible, and we are also extremely concerned about the impact of our manufacturing process on the forests of the world and the environment as a whole. Accordingly, we made sure that all of the paper we used has been certified as coming from forests that are managed, to ensure the protection of the people and wildlife dependent upon them.

To the real Nikki Heat,
with gratitude.

NAKED HEAT

ONE

Nikki Heat pondered red lights and why they seemed to last so much longer when there was no traffic. The one she waited for at Amsterdam and 83rd was taking forever to change. The detective was rolling on her first call of the morning and probably could have lit up her gumball to make her left turn, but the crime was long since done, the medical examiner was on scene, and the body wasn't going anywhere. She used the interlude to peel back the lid of her coffee to see if it was drinking temp yet. The cheap white plastic cracked, and she ended up holding half the lid with the other half still seated on the cup. Heat cursed aloud and chucked the useless half on the passenger-side floor mat. Just as she was about to take a sip, desperately needing a caffeine jolt to lift her morning fog, a horn honked behind her. The light had finally gone green. Of course.

With an experienced hand tilting the cup so the momentum of her turn wouldn't slop coffee over the rim and onto her fingers, Nikki steered left onto 83rd. She had just straightened the wheel passing Cafe Lalo when a dog darted out in front of her. Heat slammed the brakes. Coffee sloshed onto her lap. It was all over her skirt, but she was more concerned about the dog.

Thankfully, she didn't hit it. She didn't even scare it. The dog, a small German shepherd or husky mix, boldly stood there in the street right in front of her, not moving, just staring at her over its shoulder. Nikki smiled at it and waved. And still, it just stood there. That stare unnerved her. It was challenging and intrusive. The eyes were sinister, piercing under dark brows and a permanent frown. As she examined it, something else seemed off about the dog. Like it wasn't a dog at all. Too small for a shepherd or husky, and the coloring of its rough coat was tan mottled by gray. And the muzzle was too thin and pointed. It was more foxlike. No.

It was a coyote.

The same impatient driver behind her gave another horn blast and the animal left. Not in a panic run, but a trot, displaying wild elegance, potential speed, and something else. Arrogance. She watched it reach the other curb, where it stopped, gave her a backward glance, complete with brazen eye contact, and then dashed off toward Amsterdam.

For Nikki, an unsettling way to start her morning: first the scare of almost hitting an animal; then the creepy look. She drove on, blotting herself with napkins from the glove box, wishing she had chosen a black skirt this morning and not gone with the khaki.

———

It never got any easier for Nikki to meet a corpse. As she sat behind the steering wheel at 86th and Broadway, parked behind the OCME van, observing the silent movie of a coroner at work, she once again reflected that maybe that was a good thing.

The medical examiner was crouched on the sidewalk in front of the shared storefront of a lingerie shop and the newest gourmet cupcake bakery. A duo of mixed messages, if there ever was one. She couldn't see the victim he was working. Thanks to a citywide garbage strike, a waist-high mound of refuse started in the gutter and encroached on a good bit of the sidewalk, obscuring the body from Heat's view. She could whiff the two days of trash rot even in the morning chill. At least the mound formed a handy barrier to keep the looky-loos back. There were already a dozen early risers up the block and an equal number behind the yellow tape down at the corner near the subway entrance.

She looked at the digital clock flashing time and temperature on the bank up the street. Only 6:18. More and more of her shifts were starting like this. The downturn in the economy had hit everyone, and in her personal observation, whether it was the city cutbacks in policing or merely the sort of economy that fueled crime—or both—Detective Heat was meeting more corpses these days. She didn't need Diane Sawyer to break out the crime stats for her to know that if the body count wasn't up, the rate was at least quickening its pace.

But no matter what the statistics, the victims meant something to her, one at a time. Nikki Heat had promised herself never to become a volume dealer in homicides. It wasn't in her makeup and it wasn't in her experience.

Her own loss almost ten years ago had shredded her insides, yet in between the scar tissue that formed there after her mother's murder, there still sprung shoots of empathy. Her precinct skipper, Captain Montrose, told her once that that was what made her his best detective. All things considered, she'd rather have gotten there without the pain, but someone else dealt those cards, and there she was, early on an otherwise beautiful October morning, to feel the raw nerve again.

Nikki observed her personal ritual, a brief reflection for the victim, forging her own connection to the case in light of her own victimhood and, especially, to honor her mom. It took her all of five seconds. But it made her feel ready.

She got out of the car and went to work.

Detective Heat ducked under the yellow tape at an opening in the trash heap and stopped short, startled to see herself staring up from the cover of a discarded issue of a *First Press* magazine poking out of a garbage bag, between an egg carton and a stained pillow. God, she hated that pose, one foot up on her chair in the precinct bull pen, arms folded, her Sig Sauer holstered on her hip beside her shield. And that awful headline:

CRIME WAVE
MEETS
HEAT WAVE

At least someone had the good sense to trash it, she thought, and moved on to join her two detectives, Raley and Ochoa, inside the perimeter.

The partners, affectionately team-nicknamed "Roach," had already been working the scene and greeted her. "Morning, Detective," they said almost in unison.

"Morning, Detectives."

Raley looked at her and said, "I'd offer you a coffee, but I see you've already worn yours."

"Hilarious. You should host your own morning show," she said. "What do we have here?" Heat made her own visual survey as Ochoa filled her in on the vic. He was a male Hispanic, thirty to thirty-five, dressed in worker's clothes, lying faceup in a pile of garbage bags on the sidewalk. He had ghastly flesh tearing and bite marks on the soft underside of his neck. More on his gut where his T-shirt was ripped away.

Nikki flashed on her coyote and turned to the ME. "What are all these bite marks?"

"Postmortem is my guess," said the medical examiner. "See the wounds on the hands and forearms?" He indicated the victim's open palms draped at his sides. "Those weren't caused by animal bites. Those are defense wounds from an edge weapon. I say knife or box cutter. But if he'd been alive when the dog got to him, he'd have bites on his hands, which he doesn't. And take a look at this." He knelt beside the body, and Heat dropped to a squat beside him as he used a gloved finger to indicate a piercing of the man's shirt.

"Stab wound," Nikki said.

"We'll know for sure after the autopsy, but I bet that's our COD. The dog was probably just a scavenger working the trash." He paused. "Oh, and Detective Heat?"

"Yes?" She studied him, wondering what other information he had for her.

"I enjoyed your article in this month's *First Press* immensely. Kudos."

A knot formed in Nikki's stomach, but she said thanks and rose up, moving quickly away to stand with Raley and Ochoa. "Any ID?"

Ochoa said, "Negative. No wallet, no ID."

"Uniforms are canvassing the block," said Detective Raley.

"Good. Any eyewitnesses?"

Raley said, "Not yet."

Heat tilted her head to scan the high-rise apartments lining both sides of Broadway. Ochoa anticipated her. "We've set up a check of facing residences to see if anybody saw or heard anything."

She dropped her gaze to him and smiled slightly. "Good. Also see if any of these businesses spotted anything. The bakery is a good bet to have staff around in the early-early. And don't forget security cams. That jewelry store across the way might have picked up something, if we're lucky." She side-nodded up the block to the man holding five leashed dogs on a sit command. "Who's he?"

"That's the guy who found the body. Made the 911 call at 5:37."

Nikki looked him over. He was about twenty, had a slim figure, tight jeans, and a theatrical scarf. "Let me guess. AMDW." Working a precinct on the Upper West Side of New York, she and her team had pet codes for some of the types who lived and worked there. AMDW was their acronym for actor-model-dancer-whatever.

"Close, Detective." Ochoa consulted a page from his notebook and continued, "Mr. T. Michael Dove, in the drama program at Juilliard, came upon the body while it was being bitten. He says his dogs made a mass charge and the other dog took off."

"Hey," said Heat, "what do you mean close? He's an actor."

"Yes, but in this case AMDW is actor-model-dog-walker."

Nikki opened her blazer to cover her hand from onlookers while she gave him the finger. "Did you get his statement?" Ochoa held up his notebook and nodded, affirming. "I guess we're covered here, then," she said. And then she thought of her coyote. She looked up the block at the AMDW. "I want to ask him about that dog."

Nikki regretted her decision immediately. Ten paces from the dog walker, he called out, "Oh, my God, it *is* you! You're Nikki Heat!"

Onlookers farther up the sidewalk pressed forward, probably just wondering what the sudden commotion was more than knowing who she was, but Nikki took no chances. She instinctively lowered her gaze to the pavement and turned sideways, adopting the pose she'd seen in the tabloids, of celebrities ambushed by the paparazzi on their way out of restaurants.

She stepped close and tried to clue the AMDW into the decibel level she wanted him to adopt by speaking in a low one herself. "Hi, yes, I'm Detective Heat."

The AMDW not only didn't pick up on the tone, he got more effusive. "Oh. My. God!" And then could it get worse for her? "Can I have a picture with you, Miss Heat?" He held out his cell phone to her two detectives.

"Come on, Ochoa," said Raley, "let's see what's happening with Forensics."

"Is that . . . Roach? It's them, isn't it?" called the witness. "Just like in the article!" Detectives Raley and Ochoa looked at each other, made no attempt to mask their disdain, and kept walking. "Oh well," said T. Michael Dove, "this will have to do, then," and he held his cell cam out at arm's length, leaned his head beside Heat's, and snapped the picture himself.

Like most people raised in the say-cheese generation, Nikki came factory-programmed to smile when her picture was taken. Not this time. Her heart was sinking so fast she was sure the pic came out looking something like a mug shot.

Her fan examined his screen and said, "Why so modest? Lady, you've got the cover of a national magazine. Last month, Robert Downey, Jr., this month, Nikki Heat. You're a celebrity."

"Maybe we can talk about that later, Mr. Dove. I'm really sort of focused on what you might have seen concerning our homicide."

"I can't believe this," he said. "I am an eyewitness for New York City's top homicide detective."

Nikki wondered if a grand jury would indict if she put a cap in him. Dropped him right there. But instead she said, "That's not really so. Now, I'd like to ask—"

"Not the top detective? Not according to that article."

That article.

That damned article.

That damned Jameson Rook for writing it.

It had felt wrong to her from the beginning. Last June, when Rook got his assignment from the magazine, it was to profile an NYPD homicide squad with a high rate of case clearance. The department cooperated because they liked the PR of cop success, especially if it personalized the force. Detective Heat was underwhelmed by the fishbowl aspect when her squad was chosen, but she went along because Captain Montrose told her to.

When Rook began his one-week ride-along, it was supposed to be in a rotation with the entire team. By the end of his first day he had changed his focus, claiming he could tell a better story using the leader of the squad as the eyes to cover the entire picture. Nikki's eyes saw his plan for what it was, a thinly veiled ruse to hang out with her. And sure enough, he started suggesting drinks, dinner, breakfast, offering backstage passes to Steely Dan at the Beacon and black tie cocktails with Tim Burton at MoMA to kick off an exhibition of his sketches. Rook was a name dropper, but he was also actually connected.

He used his relationship with the mayor to stay on ride-along with her weeks beyond his initial commitment. And over time, in spite of herself, Nikki started to feel, well, intrigued by this guy. It wasn't because he was on a first-name basis with everyone from Mick to Bono to Sarkozy. Or that he was cute, or looked good. A great ass is just that, a great ass and no more—although not to be discounted completely. It was . . . the total package.

The Rook of him.

Whether it was Jameson Rook's charm offensive or her passion for him, they ended up sleeping together. And sleeping together again. And again. And again . . . Sex with Rook was always smokin' but did not always represent her best judgment, she reflected in hindsight. However, when they were together, thinking and judgment took a backseat to the fireworks. As he put it the night they made love in his kitchen after dashing to his place through a torrential downpour, "The heat will not be denied." Writer, she thought. And yet, so true.

Things began to unravel for her around the stupid article. Rook hadn't shown her his draft yet when the photographer showed up at the precinct to shoot pictures, and the first clue was that they were all of her. She held out for team shots, especially of Raley and Ochoa, her stalwarts; however, the best she could get out of the shooter were a few group photos with her team arranged behind her.

The worst of it for her were the poses. When Captain Montrose said she had to cooperate, Nikki indulged a few candids, but the photographer, an A-lister with a bulldozer approach, started posing her. "This is for the cover," he said. "The candids won't work for that." So she went along.

At least she did until the photographer was directing her to look tougher peering through the bars in the lockup and said, "Come on, show me some of that avenging-my-mother fire I've been reading about."

That night she demanded Rook show her the article. When she finished reading, Nikki asked him to take her out of it. It wasn't just that it made her the star of the squad. Or that it minimized the efforts of her team, turning the others into footnotes. Or that it was destined to make her so visible—*Cinderella* was one of her favorite movies, although Nikki thought she'd rather enjoy it as a fairy tale than live it. Her biggest objection was that it was too personal. Especially the part about her mother's murder.

To Nikki, Rook seemed blinded by his own creation. Everything she mentioned, he had an answer for. He told her that every person he profiled freaked before publication. She said maybe he should start listening to them. Argument on. He said he couldn't edit her out of the article because she *was* the article. "And even if I wanted to? It's locked. It's already typeset."

That was the last night she saw him. Three months ago.

She thought if she never saw him again, it would be just fine. But he didn't go quietly. Maybe he thought he could charm his way back to her. Why else would Rook keep calling Nikki even in the face of serial no's and then a stonewall of no replies? But he must have gotten the message, because he'd stopped reaching out. At least until two weeks ago, when the issue hit the newsstands and Rook sent her a sonar ping in the form of a signed copy of the magazine plus a bottle of Silver Patrón and a basket of limes.

Nikki recycled the *First Press* and re-gifted the booze at a party that night for Detective Ulett who was taking advantage of the early retirement buyout to trailer his boat to Fort Leonard Wood, Missouri, and start drowning worms. While everyone got lit on tequila shooters, Nikki stuck to beer.

It was to be the last night of her anonymity. She had hoped that, as Mr. Warhol predicted, her fame would only last fifteen minutes and be done, but for the past two weeks, everywhere she went, it was the same. Sometimes stares, sometimes comments, always a pain. Not only was the recognition aspect unpleasant for her, but each sighting, each comment, each cell phone picture, became another reminder of Jameson Rook and the busted romance she wanted to put behind her.

Temptation had gotten the better of a giant schnauzer, who started licking milk and sugar from Nikki's hem. She smoothed its forehead and attempted to steer T. Michael Dove back to the mundane. "You walk the dogs around this neighborhood every morning?"

"That's right, six mornings a week."

"And have you ever seen the victim around here before?"

He paused dramatically. She hoped he was just beginning his Juilliard drama work, because his acting was all dinner theater.

"No," he said.

"And in your statement you said he was being attacked by a dog when you arrived. Can you describe the dog?"

"It was freaky, Detective. Like a little shepherd but sort of wild, you know?"

"Like a coyote?" asked Nikki.

"Well, yeah, I guess. But come on. This is New York City last time I looked."

The same thought Nikki had had. "Thanks for your cooperation, Mr. Dove."

"You kidding? Am I ever going to blog about this tonight."

Heat stepped away to take a cell phone call. It was Dispatch reporting an anonymous tip on a home invasion homicide. She made her way to Raley and Ochoa as she talked, and the other two detectives read her body language and started to get ready to roll before she even hung up.

Nikki checked the crime scene. Uniforms had started their canvass, the remaining stores wouldn't open for a couple of hours, and CSU was busy running a sweep. There was nothing more for them to do there at the moment.

"Got another one, fellas." She tore a page off her notebook and handed the address to Raley. "Follow me. Seventy-eighth, between Columbus and Amsterdam."

Nikki got herself ready to meet a new corpse.

The first thing Detective Heat noticed when she pulled off Amsterdam onto 78th was the quiet. It was just past seven, and the first rays of sun had cleared the turrets of the Museum of Natural History and were beaming golden light that turned the residential block into a placid cityscape begging to be captured in a photo. But the serenity was also odd to her.

Where were the blue-and-whites? Where was the ambulance, the yellow tape, and the knot of gawkers? As an investigator, she had grown accustomed to arriving on scene after the first responders.

Raley and Ochoa reacted, too. She could tell by the way they cleared their coats from their sidearms as they got out of the Roach Coach and then clocked the surroundings on their walk over to meet her. "This is the right address?" Ochoa said without really asking.

Raley turned a swivel to scope out the homeless guy picking through the uncollected trash for recyclables up at the Columbus end of the street. Other than that, West 78th was still. "Kind of like being the first one to a party."

"Like you get invited to parties," came the jab from his partner as they approached the brownstone.

Raley didn't come back at him. The act of stepping onto the curb put an end to the chatter, as if an invisible and unspoken line had been crossed. They single-filed between a gap somebody had forged in the row of trash bags and refuse, and the two men flanked Detective Heat when she paused in front of the next-door brownstone. "The address is the A-unit, so it's that one there," she said in a hushed tone, indicating the garden apartment a half story below street level. Five granite steps led down from the sidewalk to a small brick patio enclosed by a metal railing trimmed by wooden flower boxes. Heavy drapes were drawn behind the ornate wrought-iron bars covering the windows. Intricate stone-carved decorative panels were set into the façade above them. Under the archway created by the stoop stairs leading to the apartment above, the front door stood wide open.

Nikki hand-signaled and led the way to the front door. Her detectives followed in cover mode. Raley watched the rear flank, and Ochoa was an extra set of eyes for Heat as she put her hand on her Sig and took the opposite side of the doorway. When she was sure they were in position and set, she called into the apartment. "NYPD, if there's anyone in there, let's hear it."

They waited and listened. Nothing.

Training and working so long together as a team had made this part routine. Raley and Ochoa fixed eye contact on her. They counted her head nods to three, drew weapons, and followed her inside in Weaver stances.

Heat moved quickly through the small foyer and into the hallway, followed by Ochoa. The idea was to move fast and clear each room, covering each other but being careful not to bunch up. Raley lagged slightly to watch their backs.

The first door on their right gave on to a formal dining room. Heat rolled into it with Ochoa in tandem, each sweeping an opposite side of the room. The dining room was all clear, but a mess. Drawers and antique hutches gaped open above tossed silverware and china that had been raked out and smashed on the hardwood floor.

Across the hall they found the living room in the same state of disarray. Upended chairs rested on shredded coffee-table books. A snow of pillow feathers coated broken vases and pottery. Canvas flags drooped out of frames where someone had torn or slashed the oil paintings. A pile of ashes from the fireplace blanketed the hearth and the oriental rug in front of it, as if a critter had tried to burrow out through there.

Unlike in the front of the apartment, a light was on in the adjoining room toward the back, which, from where she stood, Heat made out to be a study. Nikki hand-cued Raley to hold his place and spot them as she and Ochoa once again took position on opposite sides of the door frame. On her nod, they rolled into the study.

The dead woman looked to be about fifty and was seated at the desk in an office chair, with her head tilted way back as if frozen in the windup to a huge sneeze. Heat signed a circle in the air with her left hand to tell her partners to keep alert while she navigated her way through the office debris scattered on the floor and went to the desk to check for any pulse or breathing. She released her touch from the corpse's cold flesh, looked up, and gave them a head shake.

A sound from across the hall.

They all spun at once when they heard it. Like a foot crunching broken glass. The door to the room where it came from was closed, but light was shining on the polished linoleum under the crack. Heat worked out the likely floor plan in her head. If that was the kitchen, then the door she'd seen at the back end of the dining room would also lead to it. She pointed at Raley and signed for him to go around to that door and wait for her move. She pointed to her watch and then made a chop on it to indicate half a minute. He checked his wrist, nodded, and went.

Detective Ochoa was already spotted at one side of the door. She took the opposite and held up her watch. On her third nod, they burst in large and loud. "NYPD! Freeze, now!"

The man sitting at the kitchen table saw three guns coming at him from two doors and shrieked as he thrust both hands high in the air.

As the flash of recognition hit her, Nikki Heat called out, "What the hell is this?"

The man slowly lowered one of his hands and pulled the Sennheiser buds out of his ears. He swallowed hard and said, "What?"

"I said, what the hell are you doing here?"

"Waiting for you," said Jameson Rook. He read something he didn't like on their faces and said, "Well, you didn't expect me to wait in there with her, did you?"

TWO

As the detectives holstered up, Rook breathed a sigh. "Man, I think you took ten years off my life there."

Raley came back with, "You're lucky you still have a life. Why didn't you answer us?"

Ochoa piled on. "We called out to see if anyone was here."

Rook simply held up his iPhone. "Remastered Beatles. Had to get my mind off the b-o-d-y." He made a wince face and pointed into the next room. "But I found that 'A Day in the Life' wasn't the most uplifting diversion. You guys crashed in on me at the end, just on that big piano bong. For real." He turned to Nikki and smiled meaningfully. "Let's hear it for timing, huh?"

Heat tried to ignore the undercurrent, which to her ear wasn't very much under anything. Or maybe she was more sensitive to it. As she scanned Roach for reactions and didn't see any, she wondered if things were more raw for her than she'd thought, or if it was just the shock of seeing him there, of all places. Nikki had crossed paths with old lovers before, who didn't? But usually it was in a Starbucks, or a chance glimpse across the aisle at the movies—not at a murder scene. One thing she was sure of. This was an unwelcome distraction from her job, something to be pushed aside. "Roach," she said, all business, "you two clear the rest of the premises."

"Oh, there's nobody here, I checked." Rook raised both his palms up. "But I didn't touch anything, I swear."

"Check anyway" was Nikki's answer to that, and Roach left to sweep the remaining rooms.

When they were alone, he said, "Nice to see you again, Nikki." And then that damn smile again. "Oh, and thanks for not shooting me."

"What are you doing here, Rook?" She tried to remove any hint of the playfulness that she used to hang on his last name. This guy needed a message.

"Like I said, waiting for you. I was the one who called in the body."

"Not what I'm trying to get at. So let me ask the same question another way. Why are you at this crime scene to begin with?"

"I know the victim."

"Who is she?" All the years on the job, Nikki still found it hard to go to the past tense when referring to a victim. At least not at the hour of discovery.

"Cassidy Towne."

Heat couldn't help herself. She half turned to look into the study, but from where she was standing, she couldn't see the victim, only the post-tornado effect of office supplies scattered around the room. "The gossip columnist?"

He nodded, affirming. "The buzz saw herself."

She immediately started calculating how the apparent murder of the *New York Ledger*'s powerful icon, whose "Buzz Rush" column was the ritual first read for most New Yorkers, was going to ratchet up the stakes on this case. As Raley and Ochoa returned and deemed the apartment clear, she said, "Ochoa, better reach out to the MEs. Give them a courtesy heads-up that we have a high-profiler waiting for them. Raley, you call Captain Montrose so he knows we're working Cassidy Towne from the *Ledger* and he doesn't get blindsided. And see if he can put a hustle on CSU and also get some extra uniforms here, like, now." The detective could already project that the quiet, golden block she had enjoyed a few minutes ago would soon be transformed into a media street fair.

As soon as Roach left the kitchen again, Rook stood and took a step toward Nikki. "Seriously. I've missed you."

If his step closer was meant as body English, she had some nonverbal cues of her own. Detective Heat turned her back to him, got out her reporter's-cut notebook and a pen, and put her face to a new page. But she knew herself well enough to know the chill message she wanted to send was as much to herself as to him. "What time did you discover the body?"

"About six-thirty. Listen, Nikki . . ."

"How close to six-thirty? Do you have a more accurate idea of the time?"

"I got here exactly at six-thirty. Did you get any of my e-mails?"

"Got here, as in 'in the room to discover her,' or got here, as in 'outside'?"

"Outside."

"And how did you get in?"

"The door was open. Just as you found it."

"So you walked right in?"

"No. I knocked. Then called out. I saw the mess up the hall and went in to see if she was all right. I thought maybe a burglar had been here."

"Did you ever think someone else could have been in here?"

"It was quiet. So I went in."

"That was brave."

"I have my moments, you may recall."

Nikki looked as if she was focused on a notation but really she was replaying the night in the hallway of the Guilford last summer when Noah Paxton used Rook as a human shield, and how, even though he had a gun in his back, he still put a body slam on Paxton that gave Heat a clean shot. She looked up and said, "Where was she when you found her?"

"Right where she is now."

"You didn't move her in any way?"

"No."

"Did you touch her?"

"No."

"How did you know she was dead?"

"I . . ." He hesitated and continued. "I knew."

"How did you know she was dead?"

"I . . . I clapped."

Nikki couldn't help herself. The laugh shot out of her with a mind all its own. She was angry at herself for it, but the thing about a laugh like that was you couldn't take it back. You could only work to suppress the next one. "You . . . you clapped?"

"Uh huh. Loud, you know . . . to see. Hey, don't laugh, maybe she was asleep, or drunk, I didn't know." He waited while Heat composed herself. And then a chuckle of his own fought its way out. "It wasn't like applause. Just . . ."

"A clap." She watched the way the corners of his eyes crinkled when he smiled, and she started to thaw in a way she didn't like, so she threw the switch. "How did you know the victim?" she said to her notepad.

"I've been working with her the past few weeks."

"You're becoming a gossip columnist now?"

"Oh, hell, no. I sold *First Press* on the idea of doing my next piece for them on Cassidy Towne. Not so much the titillating gossip thing but profiling a powerful woman in a historically male-dominated business, our love-hate relationship with secrets, you get the idea. Anyway, I've been shadowing Cassidy for the past few weeks."

"Shadowing. You mean like . . ." She let it fall off. This took Nikki down an all-too-uncomfortable road.

"Like the ride-along you and I had, yes. Exactly. Without the sex." He paused to read her reaction, and Nikki did her best not to let it show. "The editors got such a good response to my piece on you, they wanted to follow up with another like it, maybe turn it into an occasional series on kick-ass women." He studied her again, got nothing, then added, "It was a nice article, Nik, wasn't it?"

She tapped the tip of the ballpoint twice on the pad. "Were you here to do that today? Shadow her?"

"Yeah, she got an early start every day, or maybe just continued from the night before, I could never tell. Some mornings I'd show up and she'd be at her desk in the same clothes as the day before, like she'd been working there all night. She'd want to stretch her legs so we'd walk up to H&H for some bagels and then next door to Zabar's for the salmon and cream cheese, and then come back here."

"So you did spend a fair amount of time with Cassidy Towne over the last few weeks."

"Yep."

"Then, if I need to ask you for cooperation, you may have some information about who she saw, what she did, and so forth."

"You don't need to ask, and yes, I know tons."

"Can you think of anyone who would want to kill her?

Rook scoffed. "Let's dig around this mess and find a New York phone book. We can start with the letter A."

"Don't be smart."

"Shark's gotta swim." He grinned, then continued. "Come on, she was a mud-slinging gossip columnist, of course she had lots of enemies. It was in the job description."

Nikki could hear footfalls and voices entering the front and put away her notes. "I'll have you give a statement later, but I don't have any more questions for you now."

"Good."

"Except one. You didn't kill her, did you?" Rook laughed, then saw her expression and stopped. "Well?"

He folded his arms across his chest. "I want a lawyer." She turned and left the room and he called after her, "Kidding. Mark me down as a 'no.'"

Rook didn't leave. He told Heat he wanted to stick around in case he could be helpful with anything. She had the push-pull thing going: wanting him away from her in the worst way because he was such an emotional disruption; but then seeing the benefit of his potential insights as they went over the wreckage of Cassidy Towne's apartment. The writer had been to plenty of crime scenes with her during his ride-along last summer, so she knew he was scene-friendly, at least trained enough not to pick up a piece of evidence in his bare hands and say, "What's this?" He was also a first-person witness to the most profound element of his magazine story, the death of his subject. Mixed feelings or not, she wasn't going to begrudge Jameson Rook that professional courtesy.

When they went into Cassidy Towne's office, he returned her unspoken favor in kind, keeping out of her way by standing over near the French doors that led out to the courtyard garden. For Detective Heat it always began by slowing down and studying the body. The dead didn't talk, but if you paid attention, sometimes they did tell you things.

In getting a feel for Cassidy Towne, Nikki read the power Rook was talking about. Her suit, a tasteful, navy pinstripe over a French-blue blouse with starched white collar, would work for a talent agency meeting or premiere party. And it was expertly tailored to her, accenting a body that had seen regular gym time. Heat hoped that when she reached fiftysomething that she'd keep it that together. Nikki saw some tasteful David Yurman on Towne's ears and neck, potentially ruling out robbery. There was no wedding ring, so unless that had been stolen, Heat could also rule out marriage. Potentially. Towne's face was slack in death, but angular and attractive, what most would call handsome—not always the highest compliment to a woman, but according to George Orwell, she had had about ten years since forty to earn that face. Not making a judgment, but letting instinct talk to her, Nikki regarded her impression of Cassidy Towne, and the picture that emerged was of someone suited for battle. A hard body whose hardness seemed to run deeper than just muscle tone. A snapshot formed of a woman who was, at that moment, something she probably never was in life. A victim.

Soon CSU was there, dusting the usual touch points for prints, taking photos of the body and the roomscatter. Detective Heat and her team worked in tandem, but more big-picture than close-up. Wearing their blue latex gloves, they walked here and then there and then back again in appraisal of the office, the way golfers read a green before a long putt.

"All right, fellas, I've got my first odd sock." The detective's approach to a crime scene, even one in this much disarray, was to simplify her field of view. She pared everything down to getting inside the logic of the life that was lived in that space and using that empathy to spot inconsistencies, the small thing that didn't fit the pattern. The odd sock.

Raley and Ochoa came across the room to join her. Rook adjusted his position at the perimeter to follow quietly from a distance. "Whatcha got?" asked Ochoa.

"Work space. Busy work space, right? Big newspaper columnist. Pens everywhere, pencils, custom notepads and stationery. Box of Kleenex. Look at this beside her here." She stepped carefully around the body, still cast backward in the office chair. "A typewriter, for God's sake.

Magazines and newspapers with clippings snipped out of them, right? All that stuff makes lots of what?"

"Work," said Raley.

"Trash," said Rook, and Heat's two detectives turned slightly his way and then back to Heat, unwilling to acknowledge him as part of this exchange. Like his season pass had expired.

"Correct," she continued, more focused on where she was going than on Rook now. "What's with the wastebasket?"

Raley shrugged. "It's right there. Tipped, but there it is."

"It's empty," said Ochoa.

"Right. And with all the tossing this room took, you'd think, OK, maybe it spilled out." She crouched near it and they went with her. "No clips, snips, Kleenex, or crumpled paper anywhere around it."

"Maybe she emptied it," said Ochoa.

"Maybe she did. But look over there." She side-nodded to the armoire that the columnist had used as a supply closet. It had been rifled, too. And among the contents scattered on the floor was, "A box of waste-can liners. Simplehuman, sized for this can."

"No liner in this can," said Raley. "And no liner on the floor. An odd sock."

"An odd sock, indeed," said Heat. "On the way in, I saw a wooden bin for trash cans in the little patio."

"On it," said Raley. He and Ochoa headed toward the front hall. Lauren Parry from the medical examiner's was making her way in the door as they went out. In the tight space between the tipped furniture, she and Ochoa ended up doing an impromptu dance step getting around each other. In her quick glance over, Nikki caught Ochoa lingering to check Lauren out as he left. She made a mental note to warn her girl-friend later about rebounding men.

Detective Ochoa was still fresh from a marital separation. He had hidden the breakup from the squad for about a month, but those kinds of secrets don't keep in such a tight working family. The laundry sitch alone gave him away when he started showing up in dress shirts with telltale "Boxed for Your Convenience" creases on their torsos. Over an after-work beer the week before, Nikki and Ochoa were the stragglers at the table, so she took the opportunity to ask him how it was going.

A gloom settled over him and he said, "You know. It's a process." She was happy to leave it at that, but he finished his Dos Equis and half smiled. "You know, it's kind of like those car ads. What happened to the relationship, I mean. I saw one on TV in my new apartment the other night and it said, 'Zero interest for two years.' And I went, yep, that was us, all right." Then a sheepishness came over him about opening up like that. He left some money under his empty glass and called it a night. He didn't bring it up again, and neither did she.

"Sorry not to be here sooner, Nikki," Lauren Parry said as she set her plastic examination cases on the floor. "I've been working a double fatal on the FDR since four a . . ." The ME's voice trailed off when she spotted Rook leaning a shoulder against the connecting door leading to the kitchen. He pulled one of his hands out of his pocket and gave her a wave. She nodded and smiled at him, then turned to Heat and finished her sentence. ". . . four A.M." With her back to Rook, she was able to sneak a what-the-hell? face to Nikki.

Nikki lowered her voice and muttered to her friend, "Tell you later." Then, at full volume, she moved on. "Rook found the victim."

"I see . . ."

While her BFF from the ME's office set up to perform her exam, Heat filled her in on the discovery details the writer had provided in their kitchen interview. "Also, when you get a moment, I noticed a blood smear over there." ME Parry followed Heat's gesture to the same doorway she had just entered. Beside the jamb, the floral Victorian wallpaper showed a dark discoloration. "Looks like she might have tried to get out before she collapsed in the chair."

"Could be. I'll swab it. Maybe Forensics can cut a patch so we can lab it; that would be better."

Ochoa returned to report that both trash barrels in the patio hutch were empty. "During a garbage strike?" said Nikki. "Find the super. See if he disposed of it. Or if she had private pickup, which I doubt. But check anyway, and if she had it, find the truck before they barge it to Rhode Island or wherever it goes these days."

"Oh, and get ready for your close-up," said Ochoa at the door. "The news vans and shooters are lining up in front. Raley's working with the uniforms to move them back. Word is out on the scanners. Ding-dong the witch is dead."

Lauren Parry rose up from Cassidy Towne's body and made a note on her chart. "Body temp indicates a prelim TOD window of midnight to three A.M. I can do better after I run the lividity and the rest of the course."

"Thanks," said Nikki. "And cause?"

"Well, as always, it's preliminary, but, I think, obvious." She gently moved the office chair so that the body leaned forward, revealing the wound. "Your gossip columnist was stabbed in the back."

"No symbolism there," said Rook.

––––––––

When Cassidy Towne's assistant, Cecily, reported for work at eight she broke down in sobs. Forensics gave Nikki Heat the OK, and she righted two of the chairs in the living room and sat with her, resting a palm on the young woman's back as Cecily leaned forward with her face in her hands. CSU had closed off the kitchen, so Rook gave her the bottle of water he had in his messenger bag.

"Hope you don't mind room temperature," he said, and then shot an oops look at Heat. But if Cecily made the connection to her boss's state in the next room, she didn't let on.

"Cecily," Nikki said, when she finished a sip of water, "I know this must be very traumatic for you."

"You have no idea." The assistant's lips began to tremble, but she kept it together. "Do you realize this means I have to find a new job?"

Nikki's gaze slowly rose to Rook, who stood facing her. She knew him well enough to know he wanted his water back. "How long had you been with Ms. Towne?"

"Four years. Since I graduated Mizzou."

"University of Missouri has an intern program with the *Ledger*," Rook injected. "Cecily transitioned from it to Cassidy's column."

"That must have been quite an opportunity," said Nikki.

"I guess. Am I going to have to, like, clean all this up?"

"I think our crime scene unit is going to be busy here for most of the day. My guess is the paper will probably let you take some time off while we do our thing." That seemed to mollify her for the moment, so Nikki pressed on. "I need to ask you to think about something, Cecily. It may be difficult at this moment, but it's important."

"'K . . ."

"Can you think of anyone who wanted to kill Cassidy Towne?"

"You're kidding, right?" Cecily looked up at Rook. "She's kidding, right?"

"No, Detective Heat doesn't kid. Trust me."

Nikki leaned closer in her chair to draw Cecily's attention back. "Look, I know she was a lightning rod and all that. But over the past days or few weeks, were there any unusual incidents or threats she got?"

"Oh, every day, like literally. She didn't even see them. When I sort her mail at the *Ledger*, I just leave them there in a big sack. Some of them are pretty random."

"If we gave you a ride there, could we see them?"

"Uh, sure. You'd probably have to get the managing editor to sign off, but fine with me."

"Thanks, I'll do that."

"She got calls," said Rook, "her *Ledger* extension forwarded to here."

"Oh, right, right." Cecily looked around at the mess. "If you can find it, her answering machine has some nasty shit on it. She screened." Nikki made a note to locate it and have the messages gone through for leads.

"I know something else that's missing," said Rook. "No filing cabinets. She had big filing cabinets in the corner near the door."

The idea of a filing cabinet hadn't occurred to Nikki. Not yet, anyway. Score one for Rook.

"There should be two in there," affirmed the assistant. She leaned forward in her chair to venture a look into the study but decided against it.

Heat made a note about the AWOL filing cabinets. "Other things that might be helpful would be her appointments. I assume you have access to her Outlook calendar." Cecily and Rook shared a look of amusement. "Am I missing something?"

Rook said, "Cassidy Towne was a Luddite. Everything was on paper. Didn't use a computer. Didn't trust them. She said she liked their convenience, but it was too easy for someone to steal your material. E-mail forwards, hackers, what not."

"But I do have her planner." The assistant opened her backpack and handed Nikki the spiral-bound datebook. "I have old ones, too. Cassidy had me hang on to them for documenting business meals and for tax prep."

Nikki looked up from a recent page. "There are two sets of handwriting in here."

"Right," said the assistant. "Mine's the one you can read."

"No kidding," said Nikki as she turned pages. "I can't make out her handwriting at all."

"Nobody could," she said. "Just part of the joy of working for Cassidy Towne."

"She was tough?"

"She was impossible. Four years of J-school to be the next Ann Curry, and where do I end up? Nanny to that thankless bitch."

Nikki was going to ask later, but with that opening, it seemed the perfect time. "Cecily, this is a routine question I ask everyone. Can you tell me where you were overnight, say between eleven P.M. and three A.M.?"

"In my apartment with my BlackBerry turned off so my boyfriend and I could get some sleep and without getting called by Her Highness."

———

On the short drive back to the precinct Nikki left voice mail for Don, her combat trainer, to rain check her busted morning jujitsu workout with him. The ex–Navy SEAL was probably in the showers by that time, no doubt having found another sparring partner. Don was a no strings, no worries guy. Same for their sex, when they had it. They both had no trouble finding other sparring partners there, either, and the no-strings relationship made for a mutually workable life design. If workable was your deal.

She had taken a hiatus from sleeping with Don during the time she was with Rook. Not a decision she made, it just worked out that way.

Don never seemed bothered, nor did he ask about it when they resumed their occasional night sessions when summer ended and Jameson Rook was out of her life.

Now there he was again, Jameson Rook in her rearview mirror. Her ex-lover, riding shotgun with Raley, the two of them sitting wordlessly at the stoplight in the car behind her, looking out opposite windows of the unmarked like an old married couple with nothing more to say. Rook had asked to pool with Nikki back to the Twentieth, but when Ochoa said he wanted to accompany Cassidy Towne's body down to the OCME, Heat told Raley to play chauffeur for the writer. Nobody seemed thrilled with the arrangements but Nikki.

Her thoughts drifted to Ochoa. And Lauren. He fooled no one with his duty sense to stay close to the high-profile victim, calling it due diligence to see the delivery through from crime scene to morgue. Maybe she should butt out and leave Lauren to find her own way. When Ochoa had approached to suggest his plan, Nikki saw the masked smile on her friend's face as Lauren eavesdropped. As Nikki turned onto 82nd and double-parked in front of the precinct, she thought, hey, they were adults and she wasn't the den mother. Let them have whatever happiness there was to be found in this work. If a man is willing to ride with a corpse just to be with you, that's more effort than you get from most.

———

The coroner's van took a nasty pothole on Second Avenue, and in the back, ME Parry and Detective Ochoa took some air and came down hard on the seats flanking Cassidy Towne's body bag. "Sorry," came the driver's voice from up front. "Blame last winter's blizzards. And the deficit."

"You OK?" Ochoa asked the ME.

"Fine, I'm used to it, believe me," she said. "Are you sure this doesn't weird you out?"

"This? Nah, fine. No sweat."

"You were telling me about your soccer league."

"I'm not boring you?"

"Please," Lauren said. And after the slightest hitch, she continued, "I'd like to come see you play sometime."

Ochoa beamed. "For real? Nah, you're just being polite to me because I'm a live person in your day."

"True . . ." And they both laughed. His eyes fell away from hers for a second or two, and when he looked up she was smiling at him.

He gathered his courage and said, "Listen, Lauren, I'm playing goalie this Saturday, and if you're—"

The tires squealed, glass shattered, and metal crunched. The van crashed so hard to a sudden stop that its rear tires lifted and slammed down, tossing Ochoa and Lauren. The back of her head smacked the side wall of the cargo bay as the van came to rest.

"What the hell . . . ?" she said.

"You all right?" Ochoa unbuckled his belt to cross to her, but before he could get out of it, the rear doors flew open and three men in ski masks and gloves were filling it, holding guns on them. Two were Glocks, the third guy had a nasty-looking assault rifle.

"Hands!" shouted the one with the AR-15. Ochoa hesitated, and the shooter put a round in the rear tire underneath him. Lauren screamed, and even with all his range experience, the muzzle blast made Ochoa jump. "Hands, now!" Ochoa raised his high. Lauren's were already up. The other two masks belted their Glocks and went to work unlatching the hardware securing the gurney holding Cassidy Towne's body to the floor of the van. They made quick work of it, and as the rifleman adjusted his position to keep his aim on Ochoa, his crew rolled the gurney out of the cargo bay and wheeled it somewhere to the side of the vehicle where Ochoa had no view.

Behind them southbound traffic on Second was bunching up. The lane immediately behind the shooter was at a stop; the other lanes were crawling around the blockage. Ochoa tried to memorize all the details for later, if there was going to be a later. Not much to go on. He saw one passing driver on his cell phone and was hoping it was a call to Emergency when the crew returned to slam the cargo doors.

"Come out, and you're dead," called the AR-15 through the metal.

"Stay in here," said Lauren, but the detective had his weapon in his hand.

"Don't move," he told her and kicked the door open. He jumped out on the opposite side of where they had taken the gurney and did a cover roll behind the rear wheel. Underneath the van he could see broken glass, fluid streaming from the engine, and the wheels of the dump truck they had T-boned.

Tires burned rubber, and Ochoa booked it around the van in shooting position, but the big SUV—black, no plates—sped off. Its driver cut a sharp, evasive turn to put the dump truck between himself and Ochoa. In the seconds it took the detective to run up to the truck and brace, the SUV had turned off onto 38th Street for the FDR, the East River, or who knew where?

Behind Ochoa a driver called out, "Hey, buddy, can you move this?"

The detective turned. Sitting out there in the traffic lane was Cassidy Towne's gurney. It was empty.

————————

Detective Heat returned to the bull pen from dropping off Cassidy Towne's phone message cassettes and datebook for analysis by Forensics. Raley strode to her as soon as she walked in. "Got an update on Coyote Man."

"Do you have to do that?" Heat objected to giving victims nicknames. She understood the economy of it, the shorthand it created for a busy squad to quickly communicate, sort of like naming a Word file something that everyone could easily reference. But there was also a dark humor component to it she didn't like. Heat also understood that—the coping mechanism on a grim job was to depersonalize it by making light of the dark. But Nikki was a product of her own experience. Recalling her mother's murder, she didn't want to think the homicide crew on that case had had slang for her mom, and the best way to respect that was not to do it herself. . . . And to discourage it in her squad, which she had always done, albeit with spotty success.

"Sorry, sorry," said Raley. "Re-set. I have some information on our deceased male Hispanic from this morning. The gentleman who you speculated may have been attacked by the coyote?"

"Better."

"Thank you. Traffic found an illegally parked produce truck a block from the body. Registered to . . ." Raley consulted his notes, "Esteban Padilla of East One Hundred and Fifteenth."

"Spanish Harlem. You sure it's his truck?"

Raley nodded. "Positive match to the vic in a family photo taped to his dashboard." Just the sort of detail that always made Nikki's stomach take an elevator plunge. "I'll do a follow-up."

"Good, keep me up on it." She gave him a nod and started to her desk.

"So you really think that was a coyote, huh?"

"Looked it to me," she said. "They do get into the city every now and again. But I have to go with the ME on this one. If it was a coyote, it came after the fact. I can't think of any coyote that would steal a man's wallet."

"Wile E. Coyote would have." Rook. Smart-assing from the old desk he used to sit at. "Of course, he would have gotten some ACME dynamite first and blown his nose and hair off. And then stood there blinking." He demonstrated. "I watched a lot of cartoons as a youngster. Part of my unsupervised upbringing."

Raley looped back to his desk and Heat stepped over to Rook. "I thought you were going to write a statement and go."

"I wrote it," he said. "Then I tried to make an espresso out of this machine I gave you guys and it's NG."

"We, um, haven't made a lot of espresso drinks since you left."

"Clearly." Rook stood and dragged the machine from the back of the desk toward him. "God, these things are always heavier than they look. See? It's not plugged in, the water reservoir is down . . . Let me set it up for you."

"We're good."

"OK, fine, but if you decide to use it, don't just put water in. It's a pump, Nikki. And like any pump it has to be primed."

"Fine."

"Do you want some help with that? There's a right way and a wrong way."

"I know how to—" She ended that thread of conversation right there. "Listen, let's forget all about . . ."

"Steamy deliciousness?"

". . . coffee, and look at your statement. Deal?"

"Done." He handed her a single sheet of paper and sat on the edge of the desk, waiting.

She looked up from the page. "This is it?"

"I tried to be concise."

"This is one paragraph."

"You're a busy woman, Nikki Heat."

"All right, look." She paused to collect her thoughts before she continued. "I was left with the distinct impression that your weeks— weeks—in the company of our murdered gossip columnist would mean you had more knowledge than this." She dangled the page at its corner between her thumb and forefinger so that it sold flimsy. The air-conditioning kicked on and it even waved in the breeze, a nice touch.

"I do have more knowledge."

"But?"

"I'm bound by my journalistic ethics not to compromise my sources."

"Rook, your source is dead."

"And that would release me," he said.

"Then pony up."

"But there are others I talked to who might not want to be compromised. Or things I saw, or confidences I was given access to that I wouldn't want to write down and have taken out of context at someone's expense."

"Maybe some time to think about this is what you need."

"Hey, you could put me in the Zoo Lockup." He chuckled. "That was one of the great take-aways from my ride-along, seeing you break down the newbies in Interrogation with that hollow threat. Beautiful. And effective."

She assessed him a beat and said, "You're right. I'm a busy woman." She took a half step and he blocked her.

"Wait, I have a solution to this little dilemma." He paused long enough to let her complete a rather unsubtle watch check. "What would you say if I told you we could work this case together?"

"You don't want to hear what I'd say, Rook."

"Hear me out. I want to see through this critical new angle of my Cassidy Towne piece. And if we were a team, I could share my leads and insights about the victim with you. I want access, you want sources, it's win-win. No, it's better than win-win. It's me-you. Just like old times."

In spite of herself, Nikki felt a tug on a level she didn't control. But then she thought, maybe she couldn't control the feeling, but she could control herself. "Do you have any idea how transparent you are? All you want to do is dangle your sources and insight so you can spend time with me again. Nice try," she said and moved off to her desk.

Rook followed her. "I was kind of hoping you'd like this idea, for two reasons. First, beyond—yes—the pleasure of your company, it would give us a chance to clear the air about whatever happened between us."

"That's only one reason. What's the other?"

"Captain Montrose already approved it."

"No . . ."

"He's a great guy. Smart, too. And the pair of Knicks tickets didn't hurt." Rook extended his hand to shake. "Looks like it's you and me, partner."

While Nikki stared at his hand, her phone rang and she turned away to answer. "Hey, Ochoa." Then her face lost color and her exclamation of "What?!" made heads turned in the bull pen. "Are you all right?" She listened, nodding, and said, "All right. Get back here as soon as you can after you make your statement."

When she hung up, she had an audience of the bull pen around her desk. "That was Ochoa. Somebody stole Cassidy Towne's body."

A stunned silence followed, which was broken by Rook. "Looks like we're teaming up just at the right time."

Heat's look didn't match his enthusiasm.

THREE

t's not easy to stun a roomful of veteran New York homicide detectives, but this did it. The brazen daylight assault on a coroner's van and the theft of a corpse en route to its autopsy—right under the nose of an armed cop—was a first. It smacked more of Mogadishu than Manhattan. When the speechlessness in the bull pen gave way to low muttered curses, and then to actual conversation, Raley said, "I don't get why somebody would want to steal her body."

"Let's get to work and speculate on that." Detective Heat was going to ask for her squad to gather around for a meeting, but, except for Ochoa, who was in a car on his way back from giving his statement at the Seventeenth Precinct, where the jacking took place, all hands were present.

Detective Rhymer, a cop from Burglary who had drifted into the bull pen after the news spread to his division, asked, "Do you think it's possible the body snatchers were Cassidy Towne's killers?"

"First thought, of course," said Nikki, "but her COD was a stab wound. This crew had an AR-15 and plenty of other firepower. If they were her killers, wouldn't they have been more likely to just shoot her?"

Raley added, "Yeah, and even if they worried about the noise from a gunshot, if they wanted the body, three guys like that would have just taken it this morning when they did the deed."

"Doesn't sound like this crew does a lot of worrying," said Heat.

There were nods of agreement, and then wheels turned in the silence as they considered motives. Detective Hinesburg, who had a knack for irritating Nikki with her personal habits, snapped a bite out of an apple. A few heads turned her way while she munched and slurped, oblivious to the looks she was getting. "Maybe . . ." She paused, chomping some more, and then, after she finally swallowed, continued. "Maybe there was evidence on the body."

Heat nodded. "All right. That could work." She walked over to the whiteboard and wrote, "Hiding evidence?" She turned back to them. "Not sure what, but it's a start."

"Something in her pockets? Money, drugs, jewels?" said Raley.

"Embarrassing photo?" added Hinesburg, followed by another bite of her apple.

"All possible, too," said Heat. She logged all of those on the murder board as well, and when she was done, she faced the room again. "Rook, you spent a lot of time with her recently. After everything you observed about Cassidy Towne, do you have any idea why someone would steal her body?"

"Well, maybe, given the number of people she trashed in her column, I dunno . . . to make sure she was dead?"

They all laughed in spite of themselves, and when Heat stepped to the whiteboard, she continued. "Actually, he's not far off. Cassidy Towne was one of the city's most feared and hated muckrakers. That woman had the power to make and break lives, both of which she did at her own pleasure."

"And for it," Rook added. "Cassidy enjoyed what she could make people do, for sure. As well as making them pay for what they did to her."

"But that's more a reason to kill her, not to steal her. Unless there's something on her body that would give up the killer." Nikki uncapped her marker again. "Like if it was a crime of passion and there was a fight and there's skin under her fingernails. This could be a crew for hire to get rid of that evidence."

Raley said, "Or like the ring marks you found that connected the Russian who killed that real estate guy, Matthew Starr."

Heat printed the words "Skin?" and "Marks?" "If that's the case, we're still looking at an enemies list. And, if what Rook says is true, an enemies list too large to clear with shoe leather. I sent some uniforms to the *Ledger* city room Midtown to get her hate mail. It took two of them to lift the sack."

Hinesburg muttered, "How many uniforms does it take to . . ."

"Hey, hey," said one of the uniforms standing at the back.

Detective Ochoa had returned from his ordeal. "I feel bad about this, guys," he said as he took his usual seat in the semicircle facing the whiteboard. "First her trash gets stolen, and now she does. And on my watch."

"You're probably right," said Raley. "Show of hands. How many think Ochoa should have taken an armor-piercing round to save a DB?" Ochoa's partner raised his own hand as a demo and soon everyone's hand shot up.

"Thanks, guys," said Ochoa. "Touching."

Heat asked, "Any news to bring us, Oach?"

"Not much. Fortunately we're getting good assist from the One-Seven. They determined the dump truck used to block the ME van was a stolen, but they're working that, along with interviewing witnesses and the van driver now that he's regained consciousness. They're also generating a sheet of crews that favor ski masks and AR-15s."

"So here's what we'll do," said Detective Heat to the room. "Proceed on two fronts, still work the Cassidy Towne murder scene but hit the body snatch hard. I have a feeling it's a case of find the body, find the killer." As the meeting broke up, she said, "Roach?"

"Yo," they answered in near-unison.

"Knock on some doors along Seventy-eighth. Start in the upstairs of her building and work out from there. Any sound, any detail, any relationship . . ."

"Looking for another odd sock," said Raley.

"You got it. And while you're en route, fill in Ochoa on our male Hispanic."

"Coyote Man?" said Ochoa.

"I'll give you a pass on that one since you survived today. Yes, Coyote Man. Rook and I will start building a set of likelies into a manageable enemies list."

"You and Rook," said Ochoa. "You mean, like . . ."

"I'm ba-a-ack," answered Rook in the old, familiar singsong.

As they were preparing to go, a delivery box arrived from the Columbus Café. Rook told everyone to help themselves to a sandwich. He popped for it as a welcome-back gesture. As Raley grabbed a tuna on white and turned to go, Rook called him back, holding up a large cup. "Got this 'specially for you, Rales."

Raley took it from him. "Oh, uh, thanks."

"And I know how you like it sweet, so there's extra packets of honey in the bag just for you, Sweet Tea."

Hearing the despised nickname a former partner had stuck him with because of his love of tea with honey irritated Raley enough. Hearing it from Rook after he'd divulged it in his article set him on edge. The skin was mottled white around Raley's lips as he tightened them. And then he relaxed and set the cup back down. "Not thirsty, I guess" was all he said before he showed a confused Rook his back and then left.

———

Detective Heat got into her unmarked car with Rook belted in beside her. She asked where they were going, and he only winked and put a shush finger to his lips and instructed her to take the West Side Highway south. She wasn't crazy about the arrangement, but he had spent all that time with Cassidy Towne and maybe some of his insight could come to something useful. And besides, without any leads yet, the price to pay for needing Jameson Rook was to actually have to spend time with Jameson Rook.

"How about this?" he said as he and Nikki Heat rolled along beside the Hudson.

"How about what?"

"I'm talking about the flip-flop. The switcheroony. It's still a ride-along, except this time, instead of a journalist's ride-along with a cop, it's a cop's ride-along with a journalist."

She paused and then looked over at him. "Have you noticed, I'm the one driving?"

"Even better." He powered down his window and breathed in the clean fall air. As he surveyed the Hudson River, Nikki watched the wind rustle his hair and remembered how it felt to have a handful of it. She thought of grabbing it and pulling him to her the first night they had sex, and could almost taste the limes from the margaritas they had improvised in her living room that night. He turned back and caught her staring and she felt her face grow flush. She turned away so he wouldn't notice, but she knew he had. Damn him. Damn that Jameson Rook.

"What's the deal with Raley?"

"What do you mean?" God, she was glad he was going off-subject, away from the two of them.

"Did I somehow piss him off? I've been getting a vibe off both your guys, but Raley truly gave me the stink eye just now."

She knew what it was for her, same as she knew what it was for Raley and Ochoa. Ever since Rook's piece about his summer ride-along experience with her squad hit the October issue of *First Press*, Nikki had been battling the negative attention the article gave her. So many colleagues felt left out and were either jealous or hurt. The fallout was not pleasant and it was in her face every day. Even Raley and Ochoa, the strongest allies on her team, harbored their own bruised feelings about getting footnote status in what turned out to be, unhappily for Heat, a love letter to her. But Nikki wasn't up for getting into their resentments about Rook's article any more than she wanted to open that can about her issues, which ran more personal. "Ask Raley" was all she said.

He let it drop while he did some texting, then said, "We're all set. Get off the highway at Fourteenth and head south on Tenth Avenue."

"Thanks for the notice." They were right on top of the exit. She shoulder checked and jacked the wheel to get them in the feeder lane before they blew past it.

"Skills," he said.

As she nosed onto Tenth Avenue, she asked, "Are you sure this source you're taking me to is willing to talk to me?"

"Affirm." He held up his iPhone. "That was the IM. We're all good."

"And will this require a special series of knocks? A password? A secret handshake?"

"You know, Detective Heat, you mock me and it hurts."

"Skills," she said.

Just two minutes later they got out in the parking lot of the Apple Shine 24/7 Car Wash. Rook came around to meet her. She tipped her sunglasses down her nose and looked over the top of them at him. "You're kidding."

"You know, a little red hair and you could be that CSI guy."

"I swear, Rook, if you're wasting my time here . . ."

"Hey, Jamie," came the voice from behind her. She turned to see Rook's mob buddy, Tomasso "Fat Tommy" Nicolosi, across the lot, holding open the glass door to the wash lobby and waving them over. Rook gave her a self-satisfied grin and walked to meet him. She followed, making a casual sweep of the lot for any hood pals.

Inside the lobby of the Apple Shine, Fat Tommy gave Rook a bear hug and a double-clap on his back, then turned to Heat with a smile. "Nice to see you again, Detective." He extended his hand and she shook it, all the while wondering how many beatings and worse he had used it for over his decades in The Life.

A livery driver in the requisite black suit and red tie came out of the restroom and sat down to read the *Post* behind them and they could see Fat Tommy's face tighten. "It's a beautiful day," said Rook. "Would you rather talk at one of the outside tables?"

The mobster made a cautious appraisal of the busy corner where Tenth met Gansevoort. "I don't think so. Let's use the office."

They trailed him around the counter and into the room marked "Private."

"Are you losing more weight?" asked Rook as Fat Tommy closed the door. The hood had gotten his nickname in the early 1960s when legend had it that during one of the racket wars he took three slugs in the stomach but survived because of his gut. Nicolosi was still heavy enough to tilt his El Dorado to one side when Rook first met him, but now he was more afraid of cholesterol than brass jackets. Heat noticed he was wearing a similar track suit to the one he'd worn when she was introduced to him at the construction site in the summer, and it did seem a little loose on him.

"Bless you for noticing. Five more pounds. Check it out, Fat Tommy's tipping it at one seventy-three."

Rook tugged at some excess velour. "You lose any more, I'm going to have to tie a ribbon on you just to find you."

Tommy laughed. "You gotta love this guy. Don't you love this guy?" Nikki grinned and did a bobble head. "Sit, sit." As they took seats on the couch, he eased into the chair behind the desk. "By the way, that was some nice article Jamie wrote about you. Real nice. Didn't you like it?"

"It was . . . memorable, for sure." She turned to Rook and gave him the ready look.

Rook picked up on it. "We really appreciate the courtesy of this meeting." He waited for the protocol of Fat Tommy dismissing it with a wave and continued. "I'm working with Nikki on that murder from this morning, and I told her you had some information that might be helpful."

"You didn't tell her?"

"I gave you my word."

"Good boy." Fat Tommy removed his oversized sunglasses, revealing his basset-hound eyes, which he set on Nikki. "You know my business. I keep my hands clean, but I know people who know people who aren't the most upright citizens." Heat knew he was lying. This cordial little man was as bad as they come but was a master at insulating himself from anything prosecutable. "Right, just so you understand. Anyway, I got a call recently from somebody inquiring about what it would involve to take out a hit on Cassidy Towne."

Heat sat herself up a little higher on the couch. "A contract hit? Somebody called you to make a hit on Cassidy Towne?"

"Not so fast. I didn't say someone asked for a hit. Someone asked what it would take. You know, there are stages to these things. So I'm told." She started to speak, but he held out his palm and continued. "And—and nothing ever came of it."

"That's it?" she said.

"Right, it ended there."

"No, I mean that's all you have?"

"Jamie said you wanted help, so I'm giving it. What do you mean, is that all?"

"What I mean," she said, "is I want a name." He put his elbows on the desk and looked to Rook and then back to her. Heat turned to Rook. "Did he tell you the name?"

"No," said Rook.

"He doesn't know it."

"I want it," said Detective Heat, holding the mobster's stare.

A long silence followed. Through the walls they could hear jet blowers blasting water off a car. When they stopped, Fat Tommy spoke quietly. "I want you to know I'm only giving you this because you're with him. Understand?"

She nodded.

"Chester Ludlow." He put on his sunglasses.

Nikki felt a skip in her chest. She was going to write it down, but she thought she could remember the name of an ex-congressman.

"We good?" asked Fat Tommy as he rose.

"We're good," said Rook, who also stood.

"Almost good," said the detective, who remained seated. "I want something more from you."

"She's got balls, this one."

Rook's turn to head bobble.

Nikki rose. "This morning a crew, three shooters and a driver, jacked the coroner's van and stole the body of Cassidy Towne."

Fat Tommy slapped his thigh. "Holy crap, somebody ripped off the meat wagon? What a town."

"I want them. Two of my friends were on that van and the driver is in the hospital. Not to mention a body was stolen."

Fat Tommy opened up his poor-me hands. "I already made it clear, I don't do that kind of work."

"I know. But like you said, you know guys who know guys." She stepped close to him and put a finger point on his chest for each word. "Know some guys." Then she smiled. "I'd appreciate it. And it'll make it nicer when we see each other next time, Tommy. Hey, and congrats on the weight loss."

He turned to Rook. "You gotta love the balls."

Out in the lobby they shook hands again. Rook said, "By the way, Tommy, I didn't know you owned this place."

"I don't," he said. "I'm just here getting mine washed."

Heat called the precinct for an address on Chester Ludlow as soon as they got back in the Crown Victoria. When she hung up, she said, "What's Chester Ludlow's beef with Cassidy Towne?"

"She was the reason he's not a congressman anymore."

"I thought that was his doing, given the scandal."

"Right, but guess who broke the story that started it all caving in on him?" She pulled out of the car wash parking lot, and Rook said, "I want to know how you like my sources now."

"Fat Tommy? I want to know why you didn't notify the police."

"Hello, I think I did."

"After she died."

"You heard Tommy. It wasn't going to happen, anyway."

"Except it did."

———

Chester Ludlow wasn't at his Park Avenue town house, or at his penthouse office above Carnegie Hall. He was where he spent most of his time these days, enjoying the snooty insulation of the Milmar Club on Fifth Avenue, across from the Central Park Zoo.

When Heat and Rook stepped onto the marble floor of the reception area, they trod the same ground that New York's mega-wealthy and social elite had for over a century. Within those walls Mark Twain had toasted U. S. Grant at his New York welcoming gala, when the general settled on East 66th Street after his presidency. Morgans, Astors, and Rockefellers had all danced at masked balls at the Milmar. They say Theodore Roosevelt famously broke the color code there by inviting Booker T. Washington to cocktails.

What it lacked in relevance, it made up for in grandeur and tradition. It was a hushed, opulent place where a member could be assured of privacy and a strong highball. The Milmar stood now as an idealized fortress of postwar New York, the city of John Cheever, where men wore hats and strode out into the river of light. And, as Jameson Rook discovered, they also wore ties, one of which he chose from the coat check before he and Nikki Heat were allowed into the saloon.

The host delivered them to the corner farthest from the bar, where the large format portrait of Grace Ludlow, matriarch of the political clan, stood in grand judgment of all she surveyed. Under that portrait, the once-great hope, now the errant son, Chester, read the *Financial Times* by window light.

After they greeted each other, Rook sat beside Ludlow in a wing chair. Nikki settled opposite him on a Louis XV canapé sofa and thought this sure wasn't the office at the car wash.

Chester Ludlow neatly folded the pale salmon pages of his newspaper and picked up Heat's business card from the silver plate tray on the coffee table. "Detective Nikki Heat. That has a ring of excitement."

What do you say to that? Thank you? So, instead, she said, "And this is my associate, Jameson Rook."

"Oh, the writer. That explains the tie."

Rook ran the flat of his palm down the borrowed neckwear. "Wouldn't you know? The one day you don't dress for the club."

"Funny thing about this place, you can get in without pants but not without a tie."

Considering the disgraced politician's undoing by sex scandals, Nikki was surprised by his comment and the size of his laugh. She looked to see if any of the members were annoyed, but the few sprinkled about the spacious, vaulted room didn't seem to even notice.

"Mr. Ludlow," she began, "I have some questions I'd like to ask you concerning an investigation we're conducting. Would you like to go someplace more private?"

"Doesn't get any more private than the Milmar. Besides, after the fairly public year that I've just had, I don't believe I have any more secrets."

We shall see, thought the detective. "This brings me to what I'd like to talk to you about. I suppose you've heard that Cassidy Towne has been murdered."

"Yes. Please tell me it was painful and unpleasant."

Rook cleared his throat. "You do realize you're talking to a cop."

"Yes," he said, and then flipped Nikki's card to read again. "And a homicide detective." He placed the card neatly on the sterling tray. "Do I look worried?"

"Do you have a reason to be?" she asked.

The politician waited, more for the effect of working an audience, and then said, "No." He reclined in his chair and smiled. He was going to let her do the work.

"You had a history with Cassidy Towne."

"I think it's more accurate to say that she had one with me. I'm not the one with the daily muckraking column. I'm not the one who aired my sex life in public. I'm not the parasite leeching off the misfortune and misadventures of others without so much as a care for the damage I might be doing."

Rook jumped in. "Oh, please. Do you know how many times people get caught at something and then blame the media for reporting it?" Nikki tried to catch his eye to back off, but this pushed a button on his panel and he couldn't stay out of it. "A journalist might say she just did the raking. You were the one doing the . . . mucking."

"And what about the days when there was nothing to report, Mr. Rook? The days upon days when there was no news, nothing new to the scandal, but that bottom-feeder printed speculation and innuendo, unearthed from 'unnamed sources' and 'insiders who overheard.' And when that wasn't enough, why not rehash events to keep my pain in the public spotlight?" Now Nikki was glad for Rook's intervening. Ludlow was coming off his cool. Maybe he would get sloppy. "Yes, so I had some sexual adventures."

"You got caught visiting S and M parlors in Dungeon Alley."

Ludlow was dismissive. "Look around. Is this 2010, or 1910?"

Heat did look around. In that room, it could have been either. "If I may," she said, deciding to keep the pressure on, "you were a congressman who got elected on a family values platform and were exposed for doing everything from pony play to torture games. Your nickname on Capitol Hill was the Minority Whipped. I'm sure it didn't sit so well that it was Cassidy Towne who blew the whistle on you."

"Unrelentingly," he hissed. "And with her, it wasn't even politically motivated. How could it be? Look at the joker they put in there to succeed me when I resigned. I had a legislative agenda. He has lunches and listening tours. No, with that bitch it was all for the ink. All for selling papers and advancing her sleazy career."

"Makes you glad she's dead, doesn't it?" said Nikki.

"Detective, I haven't had a drink in sixty-four days, but I may open a bottle of champagne tonight." He reached for the glass of ice water on the coffee table and took a long drink, emptying it to the cubes. He replaced it, getting his feet under him again. "But as I'm sure you know from your experience, the fact that I have a strong motivation in no way implicates me in her murder."

"Clearly, you hated her." Rook was trying to restart him, but Chester Ludlow was back in full command.

"Past tense. It's all behind me now. I did the sex rehab. I did the alcohol rehab. I did the anger management. And so you know? I not only won't have that champagne tonight, I didn't need to satisfy my anger at that woman by acting upon it."

"You didn't need to." Heat went for it. "Not when you can farm out your violence to other people. Like, say, taking out a mob hit on Cassidy Towne?"

Ludlow was smooth. He reacted but not much. It was as if someone had told him his linen blazer was out of season. "I did no such thing."

Rook said, "We have other information."

"Oh, I see. I never figured you to be the unnamed sources type, Mr. Rook."

"I protect them. That's how I'm sure to get credible information."

Ludlow stared at Rook. "It's Fat Tommy, isn't it?"

Rook only gave him a blank stare, not about to give up a source, and especially not about to throw in Fat Tommy.

Nikki Heat reloaded. "So I take it you are admitting you contacted Tomasso Nicolosi in your solicitation for a hit?"

"All right," Ludlow said. "OK, I did make an inquiry. It was a relapse in my therapy. I started to fantasize and toyed with what it would take, that's all. I may not write laws anymore, but I do know there isn't one against asking a question."

"And you want me to believe that just because Fat Tommy didn't set you up, you didn't take your business to someone else?"

Chester Ludlow smiled. "I decided there was a better way to get revenge. I hired a private investigator from a top security firm to do a little dirt digging on Cassidy Towne. Turnabout, you see?" Or hypocrisy, she wanted to say, but she thought better than to break his flow. "Look into a certain Holly Flanders." He spelled the last name for her, but Nikki didn't write it down, didn't want to take dictation from this man.

"And why should I look into her?"

"I'm not going to do your work for you. But you will find her intriguing in light of this case. And, Detective? Be careful. She bought a handgun ten days ago. Unlicensed, of course."

After the trust-fund politician alibied himself at home with his wife all night, Heat and Rook left him. As they crossed to the lobby, a wisp of an old woman perched on a love seat looked up from her daiquiri. "Congratulations on your lovely magazine profile, young lady." Even with her smile, Grace Ludlow looked more fearsome than she did in her painting.

While Rook undid his borrowed tie at the coat check, he said, "Ludlow's family has so many resources and is so well connected, he could have easily made all of this happen." The tie tangled on him and Nikki stepped in to help with the knot.

"But here's what I don't get," she said. "Say it were him. Why steal the body?" With both wrists brushing his chest, Nikki was close enough to breathe in the scent of his cologne, subtle and clean. She looked up from the knot and met his eyes, held them briefly and then stepped away. "Looks like you're going to need scissors."

———

Heat called in from the front steps of the Milmar to see if anything had turned up about her missing victim. Nothing. While she was on, Nikki ordered a check on a Holly Flanders. She also retrieved a voice mail from Roach and started walking to the car. "Let's take a ride. The boys have turned something for us."

On the drive across the park, Rook asked her, "OK, this is bugging me. How is it you know about pony play?"

"Does that excite you, Rook?"

"In a happy-scared way, yes. And no. Leaning to yes." He frowned. "You know?"

"Oh, trust me, I know. I know all about happy and scared." She smiled a wicked smile but kept her eyes on the taxi in front of her. "Just like I know my lollycrops from my posture collars." She didn't have to look to know he was staring at her to see if she meant it.

Traffic Control had to move sawhorses to let them onto West 78th. The number of news vans had doubled, with every station staking out turf for the live shots that would be coming starting on the four P.M. casts, still hours away. It gave Nikki's stomach a twist that the lead wouldn't be the murder but the theft of the body. They met up with Raley and Ochoa in the subbasement of Cassidy Towne's brownstone, in the office-workshop of her building superintendant.

They introduced him to Nikki, and as Rook appeared in the door, he smiled. "Hey, Mr. Rook."

"JJ, hi. Sorry about what happened."

"Yeah, it's going to be a big cleanup," said the super.

"And, also. You know."

"Ms. Towne, right. Horrible."

Nikki addressed her detectives. "You have something for me?"

"First of all," said Raley, "no private trash pickup."

"That's like the worst joke," chimed in JJ. "Owner of this building isn't going to spring for that. Can't even get budget for paint. Or to get a new rolling bucket, look at the wheel off that thing. Pitiful."

"So you're still on the trash," she said, trying to keep things on course. "You said first. What's the second?"

Ochoa picked it up. "JJ says that he recently had to change the locks on Cassidy Towne's apartment."

That got her interest. She cast a glance at Rook.

"That's right. It was a couple of days ago," said Rook.

The super corrected him. "No, that was the second time. Had to do it twice."

"You changed them twice?" said Heat. "Why was that, JJ?"

"I have locksmith training, so I was able to do it myself on the side for her. You know, off the books. Works out good for the both, you understand? Saves her a little coin, puts a little jingle in my pocket. It's all good."

"I'm sure it is," said Nikki. JJ seemed like a nice guy but a talker. To interview talkers, she had learned, you needed to keep things concrete, move in steps. "Tell me about the first time you changed the locks. When was that?"

"Just two weeks ago. Day before my man here started." JJ indicated Rook.

"Why? Did she lose her key or something?"

"People are always losing things, aren't they? Heard on talk radio yesterday about cell phones. You know where most people lose their cell phones?"

"Bathrooms?" asked Rook.

"No more calls, please." He extended a hand and gave Rook a shake.

"JJ?" said Heat, opening her notebook to signal a sense of importance. "Why did Cassidy want you to change her locks two weeks ago?"

"Because she said she felt like someone had been coming into her apartment. Lady wasn't sure, but she said things were just off in there. Little things moved around where she didn't put them, stuff like that. Said it creeped her out. I thought, maybe she's just paranoid, but, hey, it's money in my pocket, so I rekeyed them for her."

Nikki made a note to have Roach check for the exact date, just for the time line. "And what about the second time? Did she feel like somebody was still getting in?"

The super laughed. "Didn't need a feeling. Some dude kicked the door in on her. Right in her face."

Heat immediately turned to Rook, who said, "I knew she had the door fixed, because JJ was working on it when I came over to meet her for dinner. I asked her why, and she told me that she locked herself out and she had to break in. It seemed weird, but if Cassidy Towne was nothing else, she was full of surprises."

"Hoo, tell me," from JJ, who shook hands again with Rook.

Heat turned to Roach. "Is there an incident report on this?"

"None," said Ochoa.

"Running a double-check now," added Raley.

"When was this, JJ?"

He turned to his workbench, looked at some busty babe tool calendar, and pointed to a day with an orange grease pencil mark on it. Heat wrote down the date and asked, "Do you know what time of day this was?"

"Sure do. It was one in the afternoon. I was about to have my cigarette when I heard it. I've been trying to cut back, those things are bad for you, so I put myself on a schedule."

"You say you heard it? You mean you actually saw it happen?"

"Saw it after it happened. I was up the sidewalk, no smoking in here, and heard the shouting and then, boom. Dude kicked that door right in."

"And did you see who did it? Could you describe him?"

"Sure can. You know Toby Mills, right? The baseball player?"

"Sure do. You say he looked like Toby Mills?"

"No," said JJ. "I'm saying it was Toby Mills."

———

The Yankees were up a game in the Division Series, but without the services of starting pitcher Toby Mills, who was on the disabled list with a pulled hamstring he'd suffered in a heroic sprint to cover first base in Game One. Mills got the out for the win and a complete game, but also got the DL for an indefinite period and had to enjoy the rest of the ALDS as a spectator. On the drive back across the Central Park transverse to the pitcher's town house on the Upper East Side, Heat said, "OK, Jameson Rook, A-list magazine journalist, now I have a question for you."

"I have a feeling this isn't going to be about the pony play, is it?"

"I'm trying to fathom why, if you were flying in close formation with Cassidy Towne for an up close magazine profile, you didn't know about Toby Mills kicking her door down."

"Simple. Because I wasn't around when it happened and because she didn't tell me." He shifted toward her in his seat. "No—more than that. She lied to me about it by saying she did it herself. And I'll tell you something, Nik, if you knew Cassidy, you could see her doing it. I mean she wasn't just strong, she was . . . she was a force of nature. Things like locked doors didn't stop her. I even wrote that little metaphor in my notes for the article."

She drummed her fingers on the steering wheel. "I do take your point. And she not only lied to you, there was no police report."

"An odd sock."

"You don't get to say that, all right?"

"Odd sock?"

"That's ours. I don't want to hear that from you again unless you're sorting your fluff-and-fold." The light changed at Fifth Avenue and she drove out of the park, past the rows of embassies and consulates. "What sort of problem did she have with Toby Mills or vice versa?"

"Not much that I know of currently. She used to write about his wild-child days when he first got to the Yankees, but that was history. Last week she did run an item that he had moved to his new digs in the East Side, but that's hardly the stuff scandals are made of. Or assaults."

"You'd be surprised, writer boy, you'd be surprised," she said with a superior grin.

As they stood at the intercom at the front door of Toby Mills's town house, Nikki Heat's smile was a distant memory. "How long has it been?" she said to Rook.

"Five minutes," he said. "Maybe six."

"Seems like longer. Who the hell do they think they are? It was easier getting into the Milmar and you didn't have a tie." She mocked the voice from the little speaker: " 'We're still checking.' "

"You know they can probably hear you."

"Good."

He nodded upward. "Probably see you, too."

"Even better." She squared herself to the security camera and held up her shield. "This is official police business, I want to see a human being."

"Seven minutes."

"Stop that."

And then in a low mutter he said, "Odd sock."

"Not helping."

A crackle of static and then the man's voice returned to the intercom. "I'm sorry, Officer, but we're referring all inquiries to Ripton and Associates, Mr. Mills's representative. Would you like that phone number?"

Nikki pressed Talk. "First of all, it's not Officer, it's Detective. Homicide Detective Heat of the NYPD. I need to speak directly to Toby Mills regarding an investigation. You can make that happen now, or I can come back with a warrant." Satisfied with herself, she released the button and winked at Rook.

The tinny voice came back. "If you want to get a pen, I can give you that number."

"OK. That's it," she said. "This is officially a mission for me. Let's see about a warrant." She pivoted from the door and stormed to the sidewalk, and Rook came along. They had almost reached Madison, where they had parked across from the Carlyle, when Rook heard his name called out.

"Jameson Rook?"

They both turned to see Cy Young contender Toby Mills on the sidewalk in front of his town house, beckoning them to come back.

Rook turned to Nikki, gloating. "Whatever I can do to help, Detective."

FOUR

"I'm Toby," he said when they got to the front door. Before Nikki could introduce herself, he said, "Could we take this inside? I don't want to draw a crowd out here, if you don't mind."

He held the door for both of them and followed them into the foyer. The baseball star was in a white polo shirt and jeans and was barefoot. Nikki couldn't tell if his slight limp was from being shoeless or from his sore hamstring. "Sorry about the mix-up out there. I was taking a nap and they didn't want to wake me." To Rook, he said, "And then I saw you and said, 'Oh, man, I can't send Jameson Rook away mad.' And you're with the police?"

"Hi. Nikki Heat." She shook his hand and tried not to be the typical fan. "A pleasure, really." So much for playing cool.

"Well, I thank you for that. Come on in. Let's get comfortable and see what I've done now to have the police and the press pounding on my door."

There was a spiral staircase to the left, but he led them to an elevator on the back wall of the entryway. Beside it, a man who looked like a secret service agent, in a long-sleeved white shirt and maroon pattern-less tie, sat at a desk watching a split screen of four security cams. Toby pushed the elevator call and, as he waited, said, "Lee, when Jess gets here, would you tell him I'm taking our guests up to the den?"

"Sure thing," said Lee. Nikki recognized his voice from the intercom, and he registered her reaction and said, "Apologies for the confusion, Detective."

"No problem."

The elevator showed five floors in the town house, and they got off at the third. They were greeted with a new-carpet smell as they stepped into a circular room with halls branching off in three directions. From what Heat could tell, two of them led to what were most likely bed-rooms, toward the rear of the rectangular property. Mills hooked his multimillion-dollar arm to indicate they should follow him to the near doorway, which put them in a sunny room giving out onto the street below. "Guess you could call this my man cave."

The den was a sports trophy room, done with taste. Mounted baseball bats shared wall space with classic sports photos: Ted Williams watching one fly out of Fenway, Koufax in the 1963 Series, Lou Gehrig enjoying a Babe Ruth headlock. Atypically, it wasn't a shrine to Toby. The only pictures of him were with other players, and none of the trophies were his, although he could have easily filled the room. Heat read this as where he came to escape the hype, not to bask in it.

Toby stepped behind a wet bar of blond wood with turf green inlay and asked if he could fix them something. "Now, all I've got is Colonel Fizz, but, truthfully, it's not just because they sponsor, I like the stuff." Heat could hear the Oklahoma in his voice and wondered what it was like to graduate high school in Broken Arrow and come to all this in fewer than ten years. "I assume you're working; otherwise, I'd offer something more of a bump up."

"Like what? Is there a General Fizz?" said Rook.

"See? There it is. Writer." Toby snapped open some cans and poured drinks over ice. "I'll start you off with the cola. It hasn't killed anyone, not yet, anyway."

"I'm surprised you knew me," said Rook. "Do you read that much of my stuff?"

"To be honest, I read your Africa trip with Bono and the Portofino article about Mick Jagger on his boat. Man, I have to get myself one of them. But the political stuff, you know, Chechnya, Darfur, I can do without, no offense. But I know you mainly because we have a lot of friends in common."

She wasn't sure whether Toby Mills was a natural host or was stalling them, but while they talked she took in the view from the window. A few streets over, she picked out the Guggenheim. Even cropped by the rows of town houses, the distinct shape of the roof gave it away. Up the street, the treetops of Central Park were just beginning to show a hint of autumn. In two weeks, the color would bring out every amateur photographer on the eastern seaboard.

Nikki heard a man talking to Toby, but when she turned he wasn't in the room yet. "Hey, Tobe, I got here fast as I could, buddy." Then he stepped in, a fit-looking guy in a power suit with no tie, moving quickly to Rook. "Hi, Jess Ripton."

"Jameson Rook."

"I know. You guys should clear these with me first. We don't do press without advance clearance."

"This isn't a press interview," said Nikki Heat.

Ripton turned, seeing her for the first time. "You the cop?"

"Detective." She gave him her card. "You the agent?"

Behind the counter, Toby Mills just laughed. An actual "Whoa, ho, ho."

"I'm not an agent. I'm a strategic manager." He smiled, but it did little to soften him or take the clang off his brass balls. "The agent works for me. The agent stays out of the way and collects the checks and we're all happy. I handle public relations, bookings, media, endorsements, every point along the value chain."

"Must be tough to fit all that on a card," said Rook, earning another laugh from Toby.

Ripton sat in the corner easy chair. "So tell me what this is about."

Nikki didn't sit. Same as she didn't take dictation from Chester Ludlow, she wasn't going to honor Jess Ripton's type-A stampede. She wanted to keep this her meeting. But now, at least, she understood the stall. Daddy's here.

"Are you Toby's attorney?"

"I have a degree but no. I'll call the attorney if I think we need one. Do we need one?"

"Not my call to make," she said with a bit of push-back in her tone. Then she thought, what the hell, and left Ripton in his chair to take a bar stool facing Mills. "Toby, I want to ask you about an incident last week at the residence of Cassidy Towne."

The PR handler shot to his feet. "No, no, no. He's not answering any questions like that."

"Mr. Ripton, I am a New York City homicide detective on official

business. If you'd rather have me conduct this interview at the Twentieth Precinct, I can arrange that. I can also arrange for those news
trucks on 78th Street to roll four blocks north for some choice video of
your client's arrival for questioning. Now tell me, exactly what point
would that be along your value chain?"

"Jess?" Toby broke the silence. "I think we should just clear the air
and get this behind us."

Nikki didn't wait for Jess. Toby was willing, so she grabbed the
moment. "An eyewitness says a few days ago you kicked in the door at
that residence. Did you?"

"Yes, ma'am, I sure did."

"And may I ask why you did that?"

"Easy. I was pissed off at that bitch for dickin' with me."

Jess Ripton must have bent over and picked up the face that he'd
lost, because he got back in the mix, albeit with more diplomacy. "Detective, would it be all right if I told the story? Toby's here to correct
me if I miss anything and you can still ask him all your questions. I
think it will go a lot smoother for all of us, and, as Tobe says, we can
put this behind us. Looks like the team is going to advance to the
ALCS next week, and I want him focused on getting his hammy better
so he can be ready for the opener."

"I am a baseball fan," said Heat. "I'm a bigger fan of a direct answer."

"Of course." He nodded then continued as if she had never spoken.
"I don't know if you've noticed, but Toby Mills isn't found in the scandal sheets. He has a wife, a young child, and one on the way. His brand
value is family friendly, and he not only has multiple top-tier endorsements, but a thriving charitable foundation."

Nikki turned her back on the suit and faced the client. "Toby, I
want to know why you kicked in the door of my murder victim."

That got Ripton on his feet. He took the bar stool between her and
Rook and drew it back so he formed the center of a semicircle around
his client when he sat. "It's a simple story, really," said the manager.
"Toby and Lisa just moved into this place two weeks ago. They
wanted to be in the heart of the city he plays in instead of Westchester
County. What does Cassidy Towne do? She prints the story, including the street address, right? So there it is in the *New York Ledger*, a

full half page of her column. A picture of Toby. A picture of this house. And the street address for every nutjob in the world to see.

"Well, two guesses what happened. Toby has a stalker. Last week, a couple mornings after they move into their new dream home, Lisa takes her son for a walk to Central Park. The sailboat pond is, what, a block away? They're crossing into the park, and this stalker rushes up, starts yelling his crazy talk, and scares the crap out of both of them. Her security guy intervened, but the guy got away."

"Do you know the name of the stalker?"

"Morris Granville," said Toby and Jess together.

"Is there a police record of this?" Heat asked.

"Yes. You can check it out. Anyway, Toby was at the stadium when Lisa calls him, crying, and he goes ballistic."

"I tell you, I freaked."

"Do I need to school you about stalkers? Do I need to tell you what happened to John Lennon less than a mile from where we're sitting? So, forget the baseball star crap, Toby Mills is a man. He did what any good husband and father would do when the primal threat comes. He charged over to Cassidy Towne's place to read her out. And what does she do, but slam the door in his face."

"So I kicked it in."

"And left it at that. Game over."

"Game over," echoed Toby.

The manager smiled and reached out to the bar to pat his client's arm. "But we're much calmer now."

Jess Ripton escorted Heat and Rook out to the sidewalk and paused to chat. "Have you found her body yet?"

"Not yet," said Nikki.

"Tell you something. In my career, I've had to handle my fair share of PR nightmares. I don't envy One Police Plaza today. Although, at my fee, I could get over that, if anyone asks." He laughed at his own joke and shook Heat's hand. "Listen, sorry I gave you a slam at first," he said. "It's my protective instinct. It's how I got my nickname." Asshole? thought Nikki. "The Firewall," he said with no small measure of pride. "But now that we're on the right foot, let's keep it that way. Anything you need, call me."

"I'll tell you what I would like," she said.

"Name it."

"Any communication this stalker had with Toby. Letters, e-mails, anything."

Ripton nodded. "Our security boys have all that on file. You'll have copies on your desk by the end of the day."

"You guys have a lot of security cameras. Do you have a picture of him?"

"A couple, unfortunately. I'll include them, too."

He started to go back to the town house, but Rook said, "I've been thinking about something, Jess. I'd been working pretty closely with Cassidy on a profile I was doing of her and she never told me about Toby's door kick."

"Your point?"

"That was the same afternoon he pulled his hamstring," Rook made air quotes, " 'in the game,' right?"

"You're going to have to spell it out for me, Jameson, because I'm not following." But Ripton's look of innocence was unconvincing.

"The math I'm doing suggests maybe he injured himself before the game. Or his stunt contributed to it later. That would have an impact on his contract, not to mention a few family-friendly endorsements, if it came out, wouldn't it?"

"Don't know about any of that. If she chose not to be open with you, that was her choice." He paused and gave the mirthless smile again. "What I do know is we apologized and compensated her for her damage," said The Firewall. "And her trouble. You know how this song goes. She got a little money and a few pieces of gossip I happened to be privy to. That's how we fill the favor bank. Trust me, Cassidy Towne was not unhappy with the results."

Nikki smiled. "I'll have to take your word for it."

———

Nikki Heat heard the hissing and turned from her desk. Rook. Across the bull pen, steaming milk. She resumed her reading, and when she finished a no-foam latte arrived blotterside.

"I primed it," said Rook. "By myself."

"A skill you will, no doubt, find useful." She called, "Hinesburg, you there?"

"Yo," came the voice from the hall. It bugged Nikki that Detective Hinesburg spent so much time away from her desk, hanging out, and she made a mental note to discuss it with her privately.

When the roaming detective entered, Heat said, "I'm looking for that record I asked you to run on Holly Flanders."

"Look no further. Just came in." Hinesburg handed over a manila interoffice envelope and snapped her chewing gum. "Oh, and I screened the calls on Cassidy Towne's answering machine. It produced no leads, although I did learn a few new curse words."

While Nikki finished unwinding the red string from the cardboard button on the interoffice envelope, she said, "Trade ya," and handed Detective Hinesburg the sheet she'd just been reading. "This is the incident report from a stalker assault last week." She made an aside to Rook, "Toby's story checks out, as advertised."

"Are we working this?" asked Hinesburg between gum snaps.

Heat nodded. "Central Park Precinct owns it, but the victims live in the One-Nine. Let's make it a party and join in. Don't get in a turf contest, but stay close. I'm especially interested in any leads on the stalker."

"Morris Granville?" Hinesburg said, scanning the sheet.

"He took a powder. Just let me know if he surfaces. I have some pics coming in later. I'll shoot them to you."

Detective Hinesburg took the sheet to her desk and began reading it. Heat took the file out of the interoffice and gave it a quick scan. "Yesss."

Rook sipped his double espresso and said, "Your winning lottery numbers?"

"Better. A lead on Holly Flanders."

"F-L-A-N-D-E-R-S, as in the Chester Ludlow 'Flanders'?"

"Uh huh . . . ," she said as she turned a page in the file. "A sheet, but not much of one. Twenty-two years old, a few petty this's and misdemeanor that's. Recreational drugs, shoplifting, a little street grifting, now graduated to low-echelon hooking."

"And they say all the good ones are taken. She doesn't seem like much. Here's my theory."

"Oh, God, I forgot. The theories."

"Young woman, nefarious hooker over here." He cupped his left hand and held it up. "Ageing boomer S and M demolished politico over here." He held up his cupped right. "I think she's the tipster who took him down and now he wants payback for her."

"Your theory is interesting, except for one flaw."

"Which is?"

"I wasn't listening." She stood and put the file in her bag. "Let's go meet Holly F-L-A-N-D-E-R-S."

"What about your latte?"

"Oh, right." Heat returned to her desk, scooped up the latte, and then gave it to Detective Hinesburg on her way out.

But Heat's route to the parking lot included a detour. She made her usual side scan of Captain Montrose's office window as she went by. Typically, he was on a call, at his computer, or out making surprise appearances to his officers and detectives in the field. This time, he was hanging up his phone and gave Detective Heat a beckon with his forefinger that stopped her. She knew what it would be about.

Rook waited until they pulled out onto Columbus Avenue before he asked how it went. "With the Cap, it always goes fine," said Nikki. "He knows I'm doing everything to find the corpse. And clear the case. And make the planet safe for a better future. One of the things I like about him is that he knows he doesn't have to hold my feet to the fire."

"But . . . ?"

"But." Out of nowhere a wave of gratitude washed over her for having Rook beside her. She wasn't accustomed to having an ear. No, more than that, a sympathetic ear. The self-sufficiency she prized so much worked, but it never smiled back or cared how she felt. She looked over at him in the shotgun seat, watching her, and an unexpected warmth filled her. What was this?

"But what?"

"He's under pressure. Cap's review is coming up for his promotion to deputy inspector and this isn't the best timing. He was in the middle of phone calls from downtown and from press. People want answers and he just wanted to ask me the most current status."

Rook chuckled. "No pressure on you, or anything."

"Right, well it's always the elephant in the room. This time it was just sitting in his lap."

"You know, Nikki, while I was waiting for you, I was thinking how much Cassidy Towne would be enjoying this. Not the being dead part—that would pretty much suck—but what's happened since."

"You're creeping me out now, you do know that, don't you?"

"Hey, I'm just sharing," he said. "One thing I got to know about her for sure is that she loved having impact. See, that's the discovery for me about what kind of person writes a column like hers. At first, I thought it was all about the salacious parts. The spying, the gotchas, all that. For Cassidy, both the column and her life were all about the power. Who else leaves abusive parents and an abusive husband to go into a business that isn't any kinder?"

"So you're saying her column was her revenge on the world?"

"I'm not sure it's that simple. I think it was more a tool. Just one other way for her to wield power."

"Isn't that the same thing?"

"Similar, agreed, but what I'm getting at—what I looked for in my profile—is her as a person. To me, her story was about someone who survived a life of getting the crap kicked out of her and was determined to control situations. That's why she sent perfectly cooked steaks back to be redone. Because she could. Or screwed actors because they needed her more than she needed them. Or made guys like me show up to work at the crack of dawn and then mosey off to get a bagel. Know what I think? I think Cassidy loved the fact that she was able to get so into Toby Mills's head that he came to her place and kicked down her door. It validated her power, her relevance. Cassidy Towne thrived on making things happen her way. Or when she was at the center."

"Couldn't be much more at the center than now."

"My point exactly, ma'am." He rolled down his window and looked up like a little kid at the cotton-ball clouds reflecting on the towers at Time Warner Center as they rounded Columbus Circle. As they came out of the rotary onto Broadway, he continued. "All things considered, she'd rather be alive, I'm fairly sure, but if you've got to go and you're Cassidy Towne, what's a better legacy than having half the city looking for you while the other half is talking about you?"

"Makes sense." And then she added, "But you're still kind of creeping me out."

"Does it make you scared? . . . Or happy-scared?"

She mulled that and said, "I'm sticking with creeped out."

The gentrification of Times Square in the 1990s had miraculously transformed the once-dangerous and skeevy zone into a wholesome family destination. Broadway theaters got face-lifts and blockbuster musicals, good restaurants popped up, megastores flourished, and people came back, symbolizing, and maybe driving, the comeback of the Big Apple.

But the Skeeve Factor didn't go away. It mostly got pushed west a few blocks, and that's where Heat and Rook were headed. Holly Flanders's last known address after a prostitution bust was a weekly-rate hotel off Tenth and 41st.

The two drove in silence most of the way down Ninth Avenue, but when Heat turned onto Tenth and the streetwalkers started to show, Rook started singing a cold-cut jingle. "Oh, my hooker has a first name, it's H-O-L-L-Y . . ."

"All right, listen," Heat said. "I can put up with your theories. I can tolerate your inflated sense of significance to this case. But if you insist on singing, I need to warn you, I am armed."

"You know, you keep needling me about my significance in this case, but let me ask you, Detective Heat, who got you in to see Toby Mills when you were stonewalled? Who got you in with Fat Tommy so we can now be happily en route to question a woman whose very existence we didn't know of until Fat Tommy led us to Chester Ludlow, which led us here?"

She thought a moment and said, "I should have shut up and just let you sing."

An undercover police car is anything but undercover to most street prostitutes. A champagne-gold Crown Victoria might as well have "VICE" written in Day-Glo lettering on the doors and hood. The only thing more obvious would be to light the gumball and run the siren. Mindful of that, Heat parked around the corner from the Sophisticate Inn so she and Rook could make their approach without lighting up the radar too much. It could only help that the parking spot was behind a mound of uncollected garbage.

In the manager's office a skeletal dude, with a nasty patch of hair missing where somebody had ripped it out, was reading the afternoon edition of the *New York Ledger*. Cassidy Towne's face filled the space above the fold. The headline was in giant font, the kind usually reserved for V-E Day and moonwalks. It read:

R.I.P. = M.I.A.
Murdered Tattler's Body Missing

For Nikki Heat today, there was just no escape.

The dude with the pale skin and bloody patch of scalp kept reading and asked them if they wanted it for an hour or a day. "If you get day, ice and baby oil comes with."

Rook leaned over to Heat and whispered, "I think I know why they call this the Sophisticate."

Nikki elbowed him and said, "Actually, we're looking for one of your guests, Holly Flanders." She watched his eyes dart up from the paper toward the ceiling above his head and then back to her.

"Flanders," he said. "I'm trying to remember." And then, pointedly, "Maybe you can help me."

"Sure." Nikki drew aside her blazer and flashed the tin on her belt. "That help you any?"

The room number he gave them was down a dingy second-floor hall that smelled like disinfectant and puke. There was an outside chance Ichabod Crane was going to call the room and tip Flanders off, so Heat told Rook to stay down there to watch him. He didn't like the assignment, but agreed. Before she left, she reminded him what happened last time he didn't stay downstairs when she told him to.

"Oh, yeah. I have a vague recollection. Something about getting taken hostage at gunpoint, right? . . ."

Behind every door she passed, daytime television blared. It was as if people blasted TV noise to cover life noise and only succeeded in making more noise. Inside one room, a woman was crying and moaning, "It's all I had left, it's all I had left." It sounded like prison to Heat.

She stopped outside 217 and positioned herself off-line with the door. She didn't know how much to put into Ludlow's warning about the handgun purchase, but she checked her coat clearance anyway. Always good policy if you planned to go home that night.

She knocked and listened. A TV was on in there, too, although not as loud. *Seinfeld*, from the bass guitar riff after the laugh. She knocked once more and listened. Kramer was getting banned from the produce market.

"Shut up out there," came a man's voice from somewhere across the hall.

Heat knocked louder and announced herself. "Holly Flanders, NYPD, open this door." As soon as she said the word, the door flew open and a chubby man with braided pigtails ran past her and up the hall. He was naked and carrying his clothes.

The door had a pneumatic closer, and before it shut, Nikki crouched low and clotheslined it open with her left arm as she put her hand on her gun butt. "Holly Flanders, show yourself." She heard Jerry himself getting thrown out of the produce market and then a window sash thrown in the room.

She rolled in low and came up with her Sig Sauer just in time to see a woman's leg disappear out the window. Heat ran to it, pressed her back against the wall, and made a quick look out and then back. A yelp came from below, and she looked down to see a young woman, early twenties, in jeans but topless, lying on her back on a pile of trash.

When Heat holstered her weapon and ran out into the hall, it was crowding with people, mostly women, coming out of their rooms to see what the excitement was. Nikki shouted, "NYPD, back, back, clear the way," which only brought more curiosity-seekers. Most of them were slow movers, too; drugged or dazed, what did it matter? After fighting her way through them, she bounded the stairs in twos and pushed through the glass doors to the outside. A large dent in a black trash bag marked Holly's landing spot.

Heat stepped to the sidewalk and looked right. Saw nothing. Then left, and could not believe what she saw. Holly Flanders being led back to her by the elbow, escorted by Rook. She was wearing his sport coat but was still topless underneath.

When they arrived, he said, "Think we could get her into the Milmar like this?"

An hour later, wearing the clean all-purpose white blouse Nikki kept in her bull-pen file drawer to change into after all-nighters, field scrapes, or coffee mishaps, Holly Flanders waited in Interrogation. Heat and Rook stepped in and sat side by side across from her. She didn't speak. Just looked up over their heads, staring at the slip of acoustical tile that ran above the observation mirror.

"You don't have much of a rap sheet, at least not as an adult," Nikki began, opening Holly's file. But I have to warn you that, as of today, you've taken your game to the next level."

"Why, because I ran?" She finally brought her eyes down to them. They were bloodshot and puffy, rimmed by too much mascara. Somewhere in there, given some good living, and losing the hardness, thought Nikki, was somebody pretty. Maybe even beautiful. "I was afraid. How did I know who you were or what you were doing?"

"I announced myself as police twice. The first time you may have been too busy with your john."

"I saw that guy racing through the lobby," said Rook. "May I say? No man over fifty should wear pigtails." He caught Nikki's shut-up look. "I'm done."

"That's beside the point, Holly. Your main worry isn't the flight or the hooking. In your room, we found a Ruger nine-millimeter handgun, unlicensed and loaded."

"I need that for protection."

"We also found a laptop computer, stolen, by the way."

"I found it."

"Well, just like the other charges, that's not your worry. What's on the computer is your worry. We've been looking at the hard drive and we've found a number of letters. Threatening letters and extortion demands addressed to Cassidy Towne."

This part was getting through to her. The hard pose was crumbling as the detective slowly, quietly, and deliberately tightened the screw with each revelation. "Are those letters familiar to you, Holly?"

Holly didn't answer. She picked at the chips of nail polish on her fingers and kept clearing her throat.

"I have one more thing to ask you about. Something that wasn't in your room. Something we found somewhere else."

The manicure destruction stopped and a puzzled look crossed Holly's face, as if the other things were something she expected and had to cope with. Whatever this lady cop was now referring to seemed a mystery to her. "Like what?"

Nikki slid a photocopy out of the folder. "This is your fingerprint array from your booking on a prostitution charge." She pushed it across the table to let Holly examine it. Then Detective Heat took another photocopy from the folder. "This is another set of prints, also yours. These were taken by our technicians this morning off several doorknobs at the home of Cassidy Towne."

The young woman didn't respond. Her lower lip trembled and she slid the paper away. Then found her spot to stare at again above the Magic Mirror.

"We took these fingerprints because Cassidy Towne was murdered last night. In that apartment. The one with your fingerprints." Nikki watched Holly's face grow pale and then still. And then Nikki continued. "What would a prostitute be doing in Cassidy Towne's apartment? Were you there for sex?"

"No."

Rook asked, "Were you one of her sources, maybe? A tipster?"

The woman shook her head no.

"I want an answer, Holly." Heat gave her the look that said this would go on until she got it. "What relationship did you have to Cassidy Towne?"

Holly Flanders closed her eyes in a slow blink. And when she opened them, she looked at Nikki Heat and said, "She was my mother."

FIVE

Nikki searched Holly's face for a tell. The cop in her lived every waking hour on alert for one. Something to let her know more than what was being said. An indication that this was a lie. Or, if it wasn't, what the woman felt about the information she was giving. Detective Heat worked in a business where people constantly bullshitted her. Nine times out of ten, it was only a matter of how much. Looking for the tell and, especially, being able to read it, helped her figure out the degree of dishonesty.

Hers was a beautiful world.

The feedback on Holly Flanders came across the Interrogation Room table to Nikki from a face clouded by a storm of mixed emotions, but it felt like the truth. Or some version of it. When Holly broke eye contact to chip away at her nails some more, Heat turned beside her and gave Rook an arched brow. The writer should have no trouble reading *her* tell. It said, Well, Mr. Ride-along?

"I didn't know Cassidy Towne had any children." He took a soft tone, sensitive to the girl. Or maybe because he was feeling defensive.

"Neither did she," Holly spat back. "She got knocked up and basically disowned me."

"Let's slow this down here, Holly," said the detective. "Walk me through this because this is pretty new and pretty big to me."

"What's hard to understand? What are you, stupid? You're a cop, figure it out. I was her 'love child.'" She put a stink on the term as years of anger spilled out of her. "I was her bastard, her dirty little secret, and she couldn't wait to sweep me under the rug. She had me placed before my frickin' umbilical fell off practically. Well, now she doesn't need to pretend I don't exist. Or to refuse me any support because she's ashamed of me, like I'm some constant reminder of how she screwed up. Of course you didn't know. She didn't want anybody to know. How can you be the ball-busting queen of scandal when you've got a scandal of your own?"

The young woman wanted to cry, but instead she sat back in her chair, panting off her rant as if she had run a sprint. Or gotten startled awake again from the same nightmare.

"Holly, I know this is difficult, but I need to ask you some questions." To Heat, Holly Flanders was still a murder suspect, but she proceeded with a quiet empathy. If Cassidy Towne was indeed her mother, Nikki had a personal feeling for Holly's position as the daughter of a murder victim. Assuming, of course, she hadn't killed her.

"Like I have a choice?"

"Your last name is Flanders, not Towne. Is that the name of your father?"

"It was the last name of one of my foster families. Flanders is an OK name. At least it's not Madoff. What would people think about me then?"

Detective Heat brought Holly back to her agenda. "Do you know who your father is?" Holly just shook her head. Nikki continued. "Did your mother?"

"She got laid a lot, I guess." Holly gestured, acknowledging herself. "Family trait, right? If she knew, she didn't ever say."

"And you never had any inkling who?" Nikki was pressing the point because a paternity situation could point to a motive. Holly only shrugged, and the tell was a dodge.

Rook read it, too. "You know, I didn't know who my father was, either." Nikki reacted to this disclosure. Holly canted her head to him slightly, showing her first sign of interest. "God's truth. And I know firsthand how you form your life around that missing space. It colors everything. And I can't imagine, Holly, that any normal person, especially one as ballsy as you, wouldn't have at least done some checking to see."

Nikki felt the conversation enter a new phase. Holly Flanders spoke directly to Rook. "I did some math," she said. "You know."

"Counting backwards nine months?" he said with a small laugh.

"Exactly. And best I could figure, that was May of 1987. My m—She didn't have her own column yet, but she was down in Washington, DC, for the *Ledger* all that month digging up stuff on a politician who got busted for banging some ho' on a boat, not his wife."

"Gary Hart," said Rook.

"Whoever. Anyway, my best guess is, she got knocked up with me down there during that trip. And nine months later, ta-da!" She said it with an irony that was heartbreaking.

Heat wrote "DC, May, 1987?" on her pad. "Let's talk about now." She set her pen down to rest against the spirals at the top of her page. "How much contact did you have with your mother?"

"I told you, it was like I didn't exist."

"But you tried."

"Yeah, I tried. I tried since I was a kid. I tried when I dropped out of high school and got myself emancipated and realized I screwed up. Same thing. So, I was like, Fine. F-off and die."

"Then why did you get back in touch with her now?" Holly said nothing. "We have your threat letters on your computer. Why did you reach out again?"

Holly hesitated. Then said, "I'm pregnant. And I need money. My letters came back, so I went to her. Know what she said?" Her lip quaked, but she held strong. "She told me to get an abortion. Like she should have."

"Is that when you bought the gun?" If Holly was playing for emotions, Nikki would call her with business. Let her know this wasn't a jury. Sympathy wouldn't beat facts.

"I wanted to kill her. I picked the lock to get into her apartment one night and went in there."

"With the gun," said the detective.

Holly nodded. "She was asleep. I stood over her bed with the thing pointed right at her. I almost did it, too." She shrugged it off. "After that, I just left." And then, for the first time, she smiled. "Glad I waited."

As soon as the uniform led Holly off to Holding, Rook spun to Heat. "I've got it."

"You can't."

"I do. I've got the solve." He could barely contain himself. "Or at least a theory."

Heat gathered up her files and notes and left the room. Rook drafted off her all the way back to the bull pen. The faster she walked, the faster he talked. "I saw that notation you made when Holly brought up the Gary Hart trip. You're with me, too, on this, am I right?"

"Don't ask me to co-sign on your half-baked, undercooked theories, Rook. I don't do theories, remember? I do evidence."

"Ah, but what do theories lead to?"

"Trouble." She made a fast turn into the bull pen. He followed.

"No," he said. "Theories are little seeds that sprout up into big trees that— Damn, some writer, I'm dead-ending on my own metaphor. But my point is, theories are how you get to evidence. They're Point A on the treasure map."

"Hooray for theories," she said in a flat tone and sat at her desk. He rolled a chair up and sat beside her.

"Follow along. Where was Cassidy Towne when she got pregnant?"

"We haven't established—"

He interrupted. "Washington, DC. Doing what?"

"On assignment."

"Covering a politician caught in a scandal. And who put us on the trail of Holly Flanders in the first place?" He smacked both hands on his thighs. "A politician caught in a scandal. Our man is Chester Ludlow!"

"Rook, as adorable as I find that I-Solved-the-Riddle-of-the-Sphinx look on your face, I would hold on to that theory."

He tapped a finger on her notebook. "Then why did you make the note?"

"To check on it," she said. "If the father of Holly Flanders proves relevant, I want to be able to see who was in DC at that time, and who Cassidy Towne had relationships with."

"I'll bet Chester Ludlow was there in DC. He wasn't in office, but a political dynasty like his, he might have been in a patronage job there."

"He might have been, Rook, it's a big city. But even if he were Holly's father, what sense would it make for him to send us on her trail if it led back to him as a suspect?"

Rook paused. "OK, fine. It was just a theory. Glad we could, you know . . ."

"Dismiss it?"

"One less to worry about," he said.

"You're a big help, Rook. It hasn't been the same here without you." Her phone rang. It was Detective Ochoa. "What's up, Oach?"

"Raley and I are over at the brownstone next door to Cassidy Towne's, with the neighbor. Guy called the precinct to complain that her trash was in his private trash cans." In the background, Nikki could hear the reedy voice of an elderly man speaking in a complaining tone.

"Is that the citizen I'm hearing?"

"Affirm. He's sharing the joy with my partner."

"And how did he discover it was her trash?"

"He monitors," said Ochoa.

"One of those?"

"One of those."

When Detective Ochoa finished his conversation with Heat, he joined Raley, who seized on his partner's return to break away from the old man. "Excuse me, sir."

"I'm not done," the citizen said.

"Won't be a moment." When he was out of earshot, he said to Ochoa, "Man, you hear those wackos on talk radio and you wonder where they live. So which is it, are we hauling trash or waiting?"

"She wants us to hang until Forensics comes over. Mr. Galway probably contaminated the trash bags, but they'll get a set of his prints for elimination and do their thing. Doubtful, but they may find something on or around the patio here."

"Worth a shot," agreed Raley.

"Did I hear you say you were going to fingerprint me?" Galway had inched over to them. His cheeks gleamed from a recent shave, and his pale blue eyes flashed decades of angry suspicion. "I've committed no crime."

"Nobody says you did, sir," said Raley.

"I don't think I like your tone, young man. Has this country gotten so accustomed to wiping its hinder with the Constitution that now the police are free to go door-to-door gathering fingerprints from citizens without cause? What are you building, some kind of data bank?"

Raley had had enough and gestured to Ochoa that it was his turn. The other detective thought a moment and beckoned Galway closer. When the old man moved in, Ochoa said in a low voice, "Mr. Galway, your action as an involved citizen has provided the NYPD critical information in a major murder investigation, and we are very grateful."

"Well, thank you, I— This trash of hers was just one offense. I've made numerous complaints."

Ochoa had siphoned some steam out of him and he stayed with the approach. "Yes, sir, and this time it looks like your vigilance paid off. The clue to Ms. Towne's killer may be right here on your patio."

"She never recycled, either. I called 311 till I was blue in the face." He tilted his head close enough so Ochoa could count the capillaries under his translucent skin. "Smut merchant like that is bound to be a scofflaw, too."

"Well, Mr. Galway, you can continue your service by helping our crime lab technicians eliminate your fingerprints from others on these bags so we have no obstacles to finding the killer. You do want to continue to help us, don't you?"

The old guy tugged at an earlobe. "And this won't go into some black ops data bank?"

"You have my personal word."

"Well, I can't see the harm, then," said Galway, who went up to the top of the stoop to share the news with his wife.

"Know what I'm calling you?" said Raley. "The nut whisperer."

———

With her neat, block capitals, Detective Heat entered on the whiteboard the date and time of Holly Flanders's break-in at Cassidy's apartment. As she capped the dry-erase, she heard her cell phone vibrate on her desktop.

It was a text message from Don, her combat trainer. "Tomorrow A.M. Y/N?" She rested a thumb on the Y on her keyboard but hesitated. And then wondered what that pause was about. Her gaze lifted to Rook across the bull pen, sitting with his back to her, talking to someone on his phone. Nikki circled the key with the pad of her thumb and then pressed Y. Y not? she thought.

As soon as Roach came back to the bull pen, Heat gathered her squad around the board for a late-day progress report. Ochoa looked up from a file he was carrying in. "This just arrived from the One-Seven on the body jacking." The room fell quiet. Everyone gave him their attention, feeling the significance of a lead or even, hopefully, recovering the missing body. "They located the getaway SUV, abandoned. It was a stolen just like the dump truck. Says it was taken from a mall parking lot in East Meadow, Long Island, last night. CSU has it for prints and whatever else they can turn." He read a little more to himself, but then simply closed the file and handed it to Heat.

She looked it over and said, "You left something out. It says that it was your observation of the honor student bumper sticker that gave them the critical lead. Way to go, Oach."

"So I guess you weren't too distracted," said Hinesburg.

"What would I be distracted by?"

She shrugged. "There was a lot happening. The accident, the crew, the traffic, whatever . . . you had lots to think about." Apparently, gossip was getting around about the newly separated Ochoa and his request to ride with Lauren Parry. And it figured Hinesburg would be the one to flog it.

Heat did not like where this was going, someone getting convicted through gossip, and moved to cut it off. "I think we're good for now."

Ochoa wasn't through. "Hey, if you're saying I was distracted from my job by something, say so."

Hinesburg smiled. "Did I say that?"

Nikki interrupted more concretely. "Let's move on here. I want to talk about Cassidy Towne's trash," she said.

Raley was about to speak, but Rook interrupted. "You know, that would have been a much better name for her column. Too late now."

He felt their cool stares. "Or maybe too soon." Rook backpedaled his rolling chair to his desk.

"Anyway," said Raley, putting some hair on it, "CSU is working the scene now. Doesn't look like they'll get much. As for the trash itself, it's weird. Only household waste. Coffee grounds, food scraps, cereal boxes, what have you."

"No office materials," continued his partner. "We were especially looking for anything like notes, papers, clippings—*nada*."

"Maybe she did everything on computer," said Detective Hinesburg.

Heat shook her head. "Rook said she didn't use one. And besides, everybody who uses a computer still prints something. Especially a writer, am I right?"

Since she was addressing him, Rook rolled over to rejoin the circle. "I always print safety copies as I go along just in case my laptop crashes. And also to proof. But like Detective Heat said, Cassidy Towne didn't use a computer. Part of her control thing. Too paranoid about having digital pages scanned, stolen, or forwarded. So she typed everything on that dinosaur IBM Selectric and had her assistant run the copy to the *Ledger* for filing."

"So we still have the mystery of the missing office papers. Her hard copies." She opened a marker and circled that posting on the board.

Raley said, "It sure looks to me like somebody wanted to get their hands on whatever she was working on."

"I think you're right, Rales, and I'll take it a step further. I'm not closing any doors"—Heat used the marker to gesture to the list of interviewees on the board—"but this is starting to feel less like payback for what she wrote and more like stopping what she was writing. Any help there, Rook? You're our inside man."

"Absolutely. I know she had a big project going on the side. That's why she told me she was burning the midnight oil so much; why she was in the same clothes some mornings when I showed up."

"Did she tell you what it was?" asked Nikki.

"Couldn't get it out of her. I assumed it was a magazine piece and maybe she saw me as a rival. The control thing again. Cassidy told me once—and I even wrote it down to quote in the article—'If you have anything hot,'" Rook closed his eyes to summon the exact words, "'you keep your mouth shut, your eyes open, and your secrets buried.' Basically, she was saying if it's that big you don't talk it up or someone might beat you to it. Or sue you to stop it."

"Or kill you?" said Nikki. She moved on to point out two days on the time line. "JJ, Cassidy's building super and resident oral historian, said he changed her locks twice. First time was when she felt like someone had been in her place. Based on our interrogation of her estranged daughter, she's the one who had been in there. It also accounts for her prints. She alibied with a john the night of the murder. We're checking, good luck. As for the other lock change, we interviewed Toby Mills, who admits to the kick-down and says it was in response to Towne initiating a stalker episode. Sharon?"

"Copies of the incident report are on your desks along with a picture of this man." Hinesburg held up a security cam still. "He's Morris Ira Granville, still at large. I copied CPK and the One-Nine."

Heat tossed her marker onto the aluminum tray that ran along the bottom of the whiteboard and crossed her arms. "I don't need to tell you Montrose is getting heavy pressure about the missing body. Roach, I got the Cap's OK to pull some manpower from Burglary to canvass those apartments and businesses around"—she paused to find the victim's name on the other board—"Esteban Padilla's crime scene. That way you can stay on this and the body jacking for now."

"I have a thought," said Rook. "That typewriter Cassidy Towne used. Those Selectrics had a ribbon cartridge that spooled through the type guide a letter at a time. If we had any of her old ribbons, we could look at them and at least see what she was working on."

"Roach?" said Nikki.

"On it," said Ochoa.

"Back to the apartment," from Raley.

A few minutes after the meeting broke up, Rook sidled up to Heat, holding his cell phone. "I just got a call from another one of my sources."

"Who is it?"

"A source." He slipped his iPhone into his pocket and crossed his arms.

"You're not going to tell me who, are you?"

"You up for a ride?"

"Is it worth one?"

"Do you have any better leads? Or maybe you'd like to hang around here so you can sit with Captain Montrose and watch the five o'clock news." Nikki considered that a moment. She dropped a stack of files onto her desk and snatched up her keys.

———

Rook told her to pull up to the curb on 44th Street in front of Sardi's. "Beats hanging out at a round-the-clock car wash, don't it?"

"Rook, I swear, if this is your sneaky way of getting me out for a drink, it won't work," she said.

"And yet, here you are." When she popped the transmission into Drive, Rook said, "Wait. I'm kidding. That's not what I'm doing." When she put it back in Park, he added, "But if you change you mind, you know I'm always game."

Inside at the host podium, Nikki spotted Rook's mother, waving from her table across the room. She answered with a wave and then put her back to the woman so she couldn't see the anger on her face as she spun to Rook. "Your mother? This is your source? Your mother?"

"Hey, she called and said she had information on the murder. Would you turn that down?"

"Yes."

"You don't mean that." He studied her. "OK, you do. Which is why I didn't want to tell you. But what could I say to her? Tell her you didn't want to hear whatever information she had? And what if it's useful?"

"You could have done this by yourself."

"She wanted to talk to the police. That would be you. Come on, we're here, it's the end of the day, what have you got to lose?"

Nikki put on a smile and turned to walk to the table. On her way, still grinning, she quietly said to him, "You are so going to pay for this." And then she let her smile grow as they approached Margaret Rook.

She was seated in a corner banquette, regally situated between the caricatures of José Ferrer and Danny Thomas. It occurred to Nikki Heat that the setting for Margaret Rook was probably always regal. And if it wasn't, she made it so. Even at the poker game in Rook's loft when Nikki met her last summer, his mother's presence had been decidedly more Monte Carlo than Atlantic City.

After hugs and hellos, they sat. "Is this your usual table?" Nikki asked. "Nice and quiet."

"Well, it's before the pre-theater rush. Trust me, kiddo, it will get loud enough when the buses unload from New Jersey and White Plains. But yes, I like this table."

"It's her favorite view," said Rook. He twisted in his chair, and Heat followed his gaze to his mother's own caricature on the facing wall. The Grand Damn of Broadway, as he called her, smiled back from the 1970s.

Mrs. Rook draped her cool fingers on Nikki's wrist and said, "I have a feeling your caricature might have been up there, too, if you had stuck with theater after college." It jarred Nikki that Rook's mother knew this, since she'd never mentioned it to her, but then it came to her. The article. That damned article. "I would like another Jameson," said the actress.

"I'm afraid you're stuck with me," said Rook, probably not for the first time in his life. Nikki asked the waiter for a Diet Coke and Rook ordered an espresso.

"Right, you're on duty, Detective Heat."

"Yes, Jameso— Jamie said you could tell me something about Cassidy Towne."

"Yes, do you want to hear it now, or wait for cocktails?"

"Now," said Heat and Rook in unison.

"Very well, then, but if I get interrupted, don't blame me. Jamie, you do remember Elizabeth Essex?"

"No."

"Look at him. It always irritates Jamie when I tell him stories about people he doesn't know."

"Actually, it only bugs me when you tell them two or three times and I still don't know who they are. This will just be the first time, so go, Mother, go."

Nikki prodded her more gently by giving her what she wanted, an official ear. "You have relevant information to the Cassidy Towne case? Did you know her?"

"Only in passing, which was how I liked it. We all trade in favors, but she reduced the high art to low commerce. When she was new at the paper, Cassidy would invite me to drinks and ask me to trade her house seats for planting items about me in her column. Oh, I made sure I paid for the drinks. It was different with male actors. She would promise a lot of men ink in exchange for sex. From what I heard, she wasn't always good for her end of the bargain, either."

"So is your information about her . . . recent?" Nikki asked with hope attached.

"Yes. Now, Elizabeth Essex—write that name down, you'll need it—Elizabeth is a marvelous patroness of the arts. She and I are on the committee to bring an outdoor program of Shakespeare soliloquies to the fountain at Lincoln Center next summer. This afternoon we met with Esmeralda Montes from the Central Park Conservancy for lunch at Bar Boulud before it gets too cool for the patio seating."

"Where's that coffee?" said Rook. "I could use the caffeine."

"Relax, hon, I'm getting there, it's important to set the stage, you know? So we're on our third glass of a very nice Domaine Mardon Quincy, talking all about the murder and the stolen body, as everyone must be, and Elizabeth, who does not hold her liquor well, reveals, in a moment of wine-soaked melancholy, a rather shocking piece of news I feel duty-bound to share."

Nikki asked, "And what would that be?"

"That she tried to kill Cassidy Towne." As the waiter delivered the drinks, Margaret relished the looks on their faces and lifted her fresh rocks glass in a toast. "And, curtain."

———

Elizabeth Essex couldn't stop staring at Nikki Heat's badge. "You'd like to talk to me? About what?"

"I'd rather not discuss it out here in the hallway, Mrs. Essex, and I think neither would you."

The woman said, "All right, then," and opened the door wide, and when the detective and Rook were standing on the imported Venetian terrazzo in her foyer, Nikki began.

"I have some questions to ask you about Cassidy Towne."

Suspects and interviewees in murder cases have a panorama of reactions to the police. They become defensive, or belligerent, or emotional, or stone-faced, or hysterical. Elizabeth Essex fainted. Nikki was eye-balling her for a tell and the woman became a marionette with severed strings.

She came to as Heat was in the middle of her call for an ambulance, and the woman pleaded with her to hang up, that she would be fine. She hadn't hit her head, and her color was coming back, so Nikki obliged. She and Rook steadied her on the way to the living room, and they settled into an L-shaped sofa set angled to take advantage of the penthouse view of the East River and Queens.

Elizabeth Essex, late fifties, wore the Upper East Side uniform, a sweater set and pearls, complete with the tortoiseshell headband. She was attractive without trying, exuded wealth without trappings. She insisted she was all right and pressed Detective Heat to continue. Her husband would be home soon and they had evening plans.

"Well, then," said Detective Heat, "one of us should start talking."

"I've been waiting for this," said the woman with quiet resignation. Nikki was back to observing responses more familiar to her experience. Elizabeth Essex was vibing a mix of guilt and relief.

"You are aware, I assume, that Cassidy Towne was found murdered this morning?" said Heat.

She nodded. "It's been on the news all day. And they say now her body was stolen. How does that happen?"

"I have information that you attempted to kill Cassidy Towne."

Elizabeth Essex was full of surprises. She didn't hesitate; she simply said, "Yes, yes I did."

Heat looked over to Rook, who knew enough to stay out of Nikki's way on this one. He was busy tracking a jet that was banking around Citi Field on short approach to La Guardia. "When was this, Mrs. Essex?"

"June. I don't know the exact date, but it was about a week before the big heat wave. Do you remember that?"

Nikki held her gaze but sensed Rook shifting his weight on the cushions beside her. "And why is it that you wanted to kill her?"

Again, the woman's answer came without pause. "She was screwing my husband, Detective." But the demure politeness had also quickly fallen away, and Elizabeth Essex spoke from a primal place. "Cassidy and I were on the board of the Knickerbocker Garden Club. I used to have to drag my husband to our events, but suddenly, that spring, he seemed more enthused than I to attend. Everybody knew Cassidy spent her life with her legs in the air, but how would I ever suspect it would be with my husband?" She paused and swallowed dryly and, as if anticipating Heat's question, said, "I'm fine, let me get this out."

"Go on," said Nikki.

"My attorney found an investigator to follow them, and sure enough, they met for several trysts. Nicer hotels, usually. And once . . . once, on our guided visit to the botanical garden, they disappeared from the tour and rutted like animals behind the herbaceous and mixed borders.

"Neither of them knew that I knew, and I didn't blame my husband. It was her. It was the slut. So when our summer banquet came, I did it."

"What did you do, Mrs. Essex?"

"I poisoned the bitch." She now had every bit of her color back, seeming exhilarated with her story. "I did some research. There's a new drug kids are into. Methadrone." Heat knew it very well. It went under the name M-Cat and Meow-Meow. "You know why it's so popular? Access. It's found in plant food." She grinned. "Plant food!"

"That stuff can be fatal," said Rook.

"Not to Cassidy Towne. I got in the kitchen at the banquet and put it in her dinner. It seemed poetic. To die of plant food poisoning at our garden club event. Either I got the proportions wrong, or she just had an incredible constitution, but it didn't kill her. She just thought she had picked up some gut-wrenching stomach bug. You know something, I'm actually glad I didn't kill her. It was more fun to watch the bitch suffer." And then she laughed.

After she settled, Heat said, "Mrs. Essex, can you verify your whereabouts between midnight and four this morning?"

"Yes, I can. I was on a red-eye from Los Angeles." And to bring home the point, she added, "With my husband."

"Then I assume," said Nikki, "that you and your husband have a good relationship?"

"My husband and I have a great relationship. I got divorced and married again."

Minutes later, Heat broke the silence of the elevator ride down and said to Rook, "I'm eager to meet more of your sources. Circus cousins, colorful uncles, perhaps?"

"Don't you worry, I'm just warming up."

"You got nuthin'," she said, and stepped into the lobby.

———

At five-thirty the next morning, Nikki Heat's combat trainer tried to put a choke hold on her and ended up on his back on the mat. She danced a circle around him as he got up. If Don felt it, he didn't let on. He deked a move left but she read it and side-slipped his attack from the right. He barely grazed her as he went by. But the ex–Navy SEAL didn't go flat on the ground this time, instead taking his fall in a shoulder roll, whirling back around on her and taking her by surprise with a back-scissors to her knee on the blind side. They both hit the mat, and he grappled and pinned her until she tapped out.

They sparred again and again. He tried the blindside attack once more, but Nikki Heat didn't have to be shown twice. She raised her leg in an air kick as he swung around at the back of her knee, and with no leg there to stop him, his momentum carried him off balance. She topped him when he went down, and it was Don's turn to tap out.

Heat wanted to finish the session with a series of disarms. She had made it a regular part of her regime since the night the Russian held her own gun on her in her living room. That disarm worked like a page from the manual, but Nikki believed in rehearsal, the goal to avoid a closing night. Don drilled her on handguns and rifles, then finished off with knives, in their own way trickier than guns, which, once you slipped inside the muzzle line, offered cover with proximity, just the opposite of what happened with a shank. Fifteen minutes and twice that many drills later, they bowed and left each other to hit the showers. Don called to her as she was about to enter her locker room. They walked to meet each other again mid-mat and he asked if she felt like company that night. For reasons she couldn't figure, or at least didn't sanction, she thought about Rook and almost declined. Instead she blew it off and said, "Sure, why not?"

––––––––

Jameson Rook came out of the locker room at the Equinox in Tribeca and saw that he had two messages from Nikki Heat. The morning was brisk. Autumn was coming in earnest, and when he stepped out onto Murray Street and put his cell phone to his ear to return her call, he saw steam rising off his damp hair in the glass of the front door.

"There you are," she said. "For a minute I was starting to think you'd changed your mind about our ride-along arrangement."

"Not a bit. I'm just one of the few who actually observes the sign about no cell phones in the locker room at my gym. What's going on? Heat, if you found the body and didn't take me, I'm going to be so pissed."

"I'm a step closer."

"Get out."

"Yep. Fat Tommy called. He gave up the crew that jacked the coroner van yesterday. Be in front of your place in twenty minutes and I'll pick you up. If you behave, you can come to the party."

––––––––

"Two of them are inside," said Nikki Heat into her walkie-talkie. "All we need is for Bachelor Number Three to show up and we can make our move."

"Standing by," said Detective Hinesburg in reply.

Heat, Rook, Raley, and Ochoa were Trojan horsed inside the cargo bay of a uniform supply truck parked on East 19th, across from a cell phone store. Fat Tommy had told Nikki the store was a front for the trio's real business, which was fast-jacking parked delivery trucks while the driver was dollying in his first load. They turned over the merchandise to fences and ditched the vehicles, which were of no interest to them.

"So I guess my Fat Tommy thing paid off," Rook said.

"Neediness is so unflattering, Rook," she said. Behind him, he could hear Roach sniffing in laughter.

"But it is what got us here, right?" Rook was trying, without success, to make that sound not needy.

"Why did he give this up to you, Detective Heat?" asked Raley, all too happy to twist Rook's jock like this. Ochoa was enjoying it, too.

"I don't want to say it," answered Heat.

"Say it," from Ochoa in a low growl.

She paused. "Fat Tommy said it was because I had the balls to get up in his face yesterday morning. He also said not to make it a habit."

"Was that a threat?" asked Raley.

She smiled and shrugged. "More like the start of a relationship."

"On your side rear," came the walkie report from Hinesburg, who was in the vestibule of a coin-op laundry two doors down the block. As soon as she finished the call, a motorcycle thundered by.

"Check him out, Ochoa," said Nikki. She moved aside, and through the ob port he saw a big man in a leather vest hanging from the ape bars.

"Could be my AR-15. He was covered up, but that's definitely the build." He sat back on one of the canvas laundry bags to let Heat have a look as the biker parked on the sidewalk in front of the store and went in.

"All right," said Detective Heat into the mic. "Let's hit them before they decide to take a ride. We'll go on mine in sixty seconds." She looked at her watch and said, "Woof," to sync with the others. "Ochoa, you go last," she said. "I don't want them making you in the middle of the street."

"Got it," he said.

"And Rook?"

"I know, I know, please remain comfortably seated until the captain turns off the seat belt sign." He shifted to let them by and sat on Ochoa's canvas bag. "Ooh, still nice and warm."

"In three, two, go," said Nikki, who was first out the back door, followed by Raley. Ochoa hung in the open doorway, as directed.

Rook could see Detective Hinesburg approaching the store on the opposite side of the street.

There was a brief lull, and Ochoa turned to Rook and said, "I wonder if I should—"

And then came the gunfire. First a heavy round, the AR-15, and then a volley of small arms. Rook moved to the observation port, and Ochoa pulled him back. "Stay down. You trying to get killed?" He shoved Rook down into the middle of the laundry sacks and then bailed out the back with his gun drawn, moving around the protected side of the truck.

There was another volley of fire, repeated rounds from the assault rifle, and Rook looked through the passenger-side window of the van in time to see Ochoa dive for cover in a discount smoke shop. More covering shots and next, the motorcycle fired up.

The biker revved and popped a wheelie off the curb and onto 19th. Heat and Hinesburg jammed it out of the store, bracing for shots, but were blocked by a passing taxi. The biker looked over his shoulder at them, and when he turned back, he was smirking. That was the expression Rook would always remember, right before he swung the laundry bag into the dude and knocked him clean off that hog and right onto the pavement.

A half hour later, the biker was in the jail ward of Bellevue Hospital, nursing a concussion. He was a true badass, not just the AR man but probably the leader, and wouldn't break so easily. His two accomplices faced Nikki Heat in her Twentieth Precinct Interrogation Room. From the looks on them, she figured they were going to take some work. She sat across from both of them, taking her time looking over their arrest jackets. Both had done prison stretches for everything from petty theft to violent robberies and drug sales.

Detective Heat knew she would end up separating these two. But she'd first have to find a weakness in one of them; he'd be the one she cut from the herd. To do that, she had a strategy, and that required that they be together for now while she made her choice. She closed their rap sheets and began calmly. "OK, let's have it. Who hired you for that gig yesterday?"

Both men stared with dead eyes that saw nothing and betrayed nothing. Prison eyes.

"Boyd, let's start with you." The big one, the one with the salt-and-pepper beard, let his eyes fall on her, but said nothing. He acted bored and looked away. She addressed the other one, a ginger redhead with a spiderweb tat on his neck. "Shawn, what about you?"

"You got nothing," he said. "I don't even know why I'm here."

"Don't insult me, OK?" she said. "Less than twenty-four hours ago you and your biker friend jacked a city vehicle, stole a corpse, brandished firearms at a police officer and a medical examiner, put a city driver in the hospital, and yet here you sit, busted and destined for long stretches in Ossining. Is that because I don't know what I'm doing, or is it, maybe, because you don't?"

Inside the Observation Room, Rook turned to Ochoa. "Harsh."

"These guys need more than harsh, you ask me," said the cop.

Nikki folded her hands on the table and leaned forward toward the two men. She had made her choice, decided which of the two was the bitch. You can always break the bitch. She half turned to the glass behind her chair and nodded. The door opened and Ochoa came into the room. She studied their faces as the detective stood behind her. Boyd, the iron beard, acted like he didn't even see him, finding that no-place place to stare at again. Shawn flicked his eyes over and darted them away.

"You good, Detective?" she asked.

"Let me see the necks, left side of both."

Heat asked the pair to turn their heads to the right, and Ochoa leaned across the table, looking at one then the other. "Yeah," he said when he was done. "I'm good." And then he left the room.

"What was that?" said Shawn, who had the spiderweb.

All Nikki said was "Be right back," and she left. But she kept it short, returning in less than a minute with two uniforms. "That one there," she said, indicating Shawn. "Take him to Interrogation 2 and hold him until the DA guy gets here."

"Hey, what are you doing?" said Shawn as they led him out. "You don't have anything on me. Nothing."

The officers held him at the door and Nikki smiled. "Interrogation 2," she said, and they left. Nikki let the quiet do its talking. At last she said, "Your pal always this jumpy?"

He remained stoic, disconnected.

"It doesn't take much to see he's not as together as you, Boyd. But see, here's what you need to be thinking about. Your friend with the neck tat? He's boned. And he knows it. And know what's too bad for you? We want this. We want the name of whoever hired you. And we are in a dealing mood. And you know and I know that Shawn is going to take it. Because the deal will be sweet. And he's . . . well, he's Shawn, isn't he?"

Boyd sat there, a statue breathing.

"And where does that leave you, Boyd?" She flipped open his file. "Pedigree like yours, you're looking at some long time in Ossining. But you know that can be done. Time passes. And besides, your pal Shawn will be able to visit you. Because he'll be out."

Nikki waited. She had to be stoic herself because she was starting to think she'd cut the wrong one from the herd. She worried he was too smart to see Ochoa's tattoo ID as anything but what it was, a ruse. She worried that Boyd might just be a sociopath, and she was, therefore, the boned one in this transaction. Nikki thought about scrapping her strategy and offering him a deal. But it would mean she'd blinked. Her heart fluttered, feeling like a bird against her neck. She was so close, she hated to let it slip away. So she went the other way. Heat got tough and decided to push her game to the brink.

Without another word, she rose and closed the file. Then squared the pages by tapping it on the tabletop. She turned and took measured steps to the door, hoping to hear something on each footfall. She put her hand on the knob, paused as long as she could get away with, and pulled the door open.

Damn, nothing.

Feeling the awful sensation of her strength leeching out of her, she let the door close behind her.

In the Observation Room, she breathed a sigh and met the disappointed gazes of Rook, Raley, and Ochoa. And then she heard, "Hey!" All four of them turned to the window. Inside, Boyd was standing at a crouch at the table, restrained by his manacles.

"Hey!" he shouted again. "What kind of deal?"

SIX

Detective Heat stood on the sidewalk getting her squad ready for their second raid of the day, hoping upon hope that her streak would extend and that, in the next few minutes, she'd claim possession of Cassidy Towne's stolen corpse.

According to Rook, it didn't seem like their suspect had much of a motive. Cassidy Towne had dragged him to Richmond Vergennes's new restaurant the week before for its soft opening. Rook said it felt at the time like it was a payback stroke, like she was getting a freebie meal from a TV celebrity chef in exchange for some mentions in her column. Rook said that while he was there he heard the two of them in a shouting match in Vergennes's office. She came out a few minutes later and told Rook to catch up with her the next day. "It didn't stick with me," he told Nikki, "because she argued with everybody, so it didn't seem like a major deal."

Now, just feet from the front door of that very Upper East Side restaurant, a small army of NYPD was deployed. Translation: It did seem like a major deal.

Heat brought up her two-way. "Roach, you in position yet?"

"Good to go," came back Raley's voice over the radio.

Nikki did her customary last-minute detail check. The small detachment of uniforms was doing its job holding pedestrian traffic back on both ends of the sidewalk on Lex. Detective Hinesburg stood behind her and gave her the nod as she adjusted her shield on the lanyard around her neck. Rook took two steps back to position himself, as agreed, behind the two plainclothes from Burglary who were joining the party.

The squad followed Detective Heat, streaming through the front doors of the empty restaurant in a brisk walk. Nikki had waited, timing this to come down right after the lunch service so there wouldn't be customers to deal with. Rook had sketched her the layout of the restaurant, fresh in his mind from his visit the previous week, and Nikki found Richmond Vergennes exactly where Rook said he would be at that time, presiding over the staff meeting at the big table near the showcase kitchen.

One of the busboys, an illegal, saw her first and made a fast exit to the men's room, and his flight made everyone else turn from their staff meal. Heat flashed tin as she strode toward the head of the table and said, "NYPD. Everyone remain seated. Richmond Vergennes, I have a warrant for—"

The celebrity chef's chair tipped back onto the hardwood floor when he bolted. Nikki peripherally registered a few gasps and clangs of dropped silverware from the staff as she took off into the kitchen after him.

Vergennes tried to slow the cops down by sweeping a stack of oval plates onto the floor behind him as he rounded the break in the counter leading to the kitchen, but Nikki didn't even go that way. The stainless serving station was waist-high, designed to allow diners a view of the superstar chef and his crew at work. Heat slapped a palm on it, kicked her legs to the side, and vaulted into the kitchen, dropping just three steps behind Vergennes.

He heard Nikki stick her landing and knocked a tub of ice chips onto the drainage mats. She slipped but didn't fall, yet it gave him some steps on her. But even though the chef was a weekend triathlete, nobody moves fast in Bistro Crocs. Speed wasn't his issue at that point, however. Raley and Ochoa came through the back delivery entrance from the alley and blocked his exit.

Chef Vergennes stopped and made a desperate claw at the set of Wüsthofs nested in their rack. He came up brandishing an eight-inch cook's knife and the guns came out. In the chorus of "drop its," he let go of the knife as if the handle were on fire. As soon as it left his hand, Heat came from his blind side and scissor-kicked his legs from under him—the same takedown she had practiced just that morning.

Nikki pulled herself up off the deck and read Vergennes his rights as Ochoa cuffed him. They put him in a chair in the middle of his prep area, and she said, "I'm Detective Heat, Mr. Vergennes. Let's make this easy and you just tell us. Where's the body?"

The ruggedly handsome face seen by millions on TV over the years bled a trickle from a small scrape on his eyebrow from the takedown. Behind Nikki, Chef Vergennes saw his entire staff at the counter, staring in at him. He said, "I have no idea what you're talking about."

Nikki Heat turned to the squad. "Toss it."

———

An hour later, after searching his restaurant and finding nothing, Heat, Rook, and Roach brought Richmond Vergennes in handcuffs to his SoHo loft off Prince Street. In police custody, he did not look anything at all like a perennial Zagat favorite and *Iron Chef* candidate. His starched white tunic was soiled, embossed with the grid pattern of the grimy floor mats from his Upper East Side restaurant. A bloodstain the size and shape of a monarch butterfly had dried on the knee of his black-and-white checked chef's pants, another battle prize from Heat's takedown, to complement the cut on his eyebrow, which paramedics had cleaned and Band-Aided.

"You want to save us some trouble here, Chef Richmond?" asked Heat. It was like he didn't hear her. He lowered his gaze and just studied his blue Crocs. "Suit yourself." She turned to her detectives. "Have at it, guys." As they moved off, opening closets, cabinets, anywhere large enough to hide a body, she warned him, "And when we finish searching your loft, we're going to your other restaurant in Washington Square. How much will you lose if we close down The Verge for all your seatings tonight?" He kept his silence, giving nothing.

After they had searched the armoires and closets and a steamer-trunk coffee table in the living room, they put him in a chair in his custom kitchen, a kitchen so large and well appointed, one of the lifestyle cable networks had used it to shoot his series, *Cook Like a Vergennes.* "You're wasting your time." The chef was trying to sound affronted and wasn't pulling it off. A ball of perspiration hung on the tip of his nose, and when he rocked his head to shake it off, his dark hair, long and parted in the middle, fanned in the air. "There's nothing here you'd be interested in."

"I don't know about that," said Rook. "I wouldn't mind finding the recipe for these jalapeño corn sticks." He was helping himself to a sample from the cast-iron corncob forms on the counter.

"Rook?" said Heat.

"What? They're crunchy outside, moist on the inside, and the kick from the pepper . . . Mm, the way it melds with the butter . . . Man."

Ochoa returned from the pantry. "Nothing," he said to Heat.

"Same in the office, and bedrooms," reported Raley as he came in the other doorway. "What's he doing?"

Nikki turned to see Rook's face, contorted into a wince. "Being a nuisance. You know, Rook, this is why we don't let you come along."

"Sorry. I got a little spice issue here. Know what I wish I had? Some sweet tea."

Raley gave Rook a foul look and joined his partner, who was trying to open a locked door at the back of the kitchen. "What's in here?" said Ochoa.

"My wine closet," said the chef. "I have some rare bottles in there worth thousands. And it's temp controlled."

That got Heat very interested. "Where's the key?"

"There is no key, it takes a code."

"OK," she said, "I'll ask nicely. Once. What is the code?" When he said nothing, she added, "I have a warrant."

He seemed amused. "Why don't you use it to jimmy the door?"

"Ochoa, call Demolitions and tell them we need a team with a blast matrix. And evacuate the building."

"Hold on, hold on. Blast matrix? I have a 1945 Château Haut-Brion in there." Nikki cupped a hand behind her ear. He sighed and said, "It's 41319."

Ochoa entered the code on the keypad, and a servo motor whirred inside the lock. He flipped on the light switch and stepped into the large closet. After a short moment, he stepped out and shook his head to Heat.

"Why are you hassling me, anyway?" said the chef. The attempt at peeved bravado had returned.

Nikki stood over him, close enough to make him have to strain his neck to look up at her. "I told you. I want you to give up the body of Cassidy Towne."

"What would I know about Cassidy Towne? I didn't even know the bitch."

"Yes, you did, I heard you fighting," said Rook. "Whoo," he blew air out of his mouth in a huff, "must have gotten a seed."

Vergennes acted as if a distant memory had been jogged free. "Oh, that. We argued, OK? What the hell, you think I killed her because she was pissed I wouldn't comp her a party of twelve at my opening?"

"We have a witness that says you hired them to steal her body."

He scoffed. "I'm done. This is getting crazy. I want my lawyer."

"All right. You can call him after we take you to the precinct," said Heat.

Taking opposite sides of the kitchen, Raley and Ochoa moved in a line, systematically opening and closing custom cabinets, all full of either cookbooks, imported dinnerware, or a Williams-Sonoma's worth of kitchen gadgets.

"For real, my mouth is seriously on fire." Rook stepped to the big Sub-Zero. "Wow, this is some fridge. Gorgeous."

Vergennes called out, "No, don't, that's broken."

But Rook had already pulled the handle. And then he got knocked backward when the body of Cassidy Towne bumped open the refrigerator door as it toppled out and landed on the Spanish tiles at his feet.

The uniformed officer posted at the front door ran in when he heard Rook scream.

Richmond Vergennes was a different man when confronted by the harsh reality of the Interrogation Room. The cockiness was gone. Nikki watched his hands, callused and scarred by years on the cook line. They were quaking. From the chair beside him, Vergennes's lawyer gave him the nod to begin. "First of all, I didn't kill her, I swear."

"Mr. Vergennes, think of how many times in your career you've heard a waiter bring a dish back to the kitchen and tell you the customer says it's cold. That's about half as many times as I've sat here and heard the guy in cuffs on your side of the table say, 'I didn't do it, I swear.' "

The lawyer chimed in. "Detective, we are hoping to be cooperative here. I don't think there's any call to make this difficult." The suit was Wynn Zanderhoof, a partner in one of the big Park Avenue firms that specialized in entertainment law. He was their criminal face, and Heat had seen plenty of him over the years.

"Sure, Counselor. Especially after your client made our lives such a breeze. Resisting arrest, brandishing a weapon at a police officer, obstructing an investigation. And all that comes after the murder of Cassidy Towne. Plus the conspiracy to hijack her body. Plus the numerous charges related to that. I think difficulty is the word of the day for Mr. Vergennes."

"Granted," said the attorney. "Which is why we were hoping to strike some sort of arrangement to mitigate the unnecessary tensions surrounding all this."

"You want a deal?" asked the detective. "Your client is facing a murder charge, and we have a confession from a man in the crew he paid to steal the damn body. What are you going to bargain with, a complimentary dessert?"

"I didn't kill her. I was home with my wife that night. She'll vouch."

"We'll check." There was something that crossed his face when she said that. His dark Cajun looks lost their cockiness. Like the alibi wouldn't hold or maybe something else. What was it? She decided to pick at that and see where it led. "When you say you were with your wife, when was that?"

"All night. We watched some TV, went to bed, woke up. Like that."

She made a show of opening her notebook and poising her pen. "Tell me the exact time you and your wife went to bed."

"I dunno. We watched some *Nightline,* then hit the hay."

"So," said Nikki as she wrote, "you're saying it was twelve o'clock? Midnight?"

"Yeah, or a few minutes after. Those late-night shows are all like five minutes late getting started."

"And what time did you get home?"

"Mm, about eleven-fifteen, I guess."

Something seemed off to Heat, so she pressed. "Chef, I hear all the stories about the restaurant business. Especially for a new restaurant, isn't quarter after eleven kind of early for you to be home?"

She could see she was getting at something. Vergennes was showing nerves, working his mouth like he was looking for a strand of hair with his tongue. "Business was light, so I, ah, knocked off early."

"Oh, I see. What time did you knock off?"

His eyes roamed the ceiling. "Don't remember, exactly."

"No problem," she said. "I'll be checking with your staff, anyway. They'll tell me what time you left."

"Nine o'clock," he blurted.

Nikki wrote it down. "Does it typically take you two and a quarter hours to get to SoHo at that hour from Sixty-third and Lex?" When she looked up from her pad, he was coming unglued. His lawyer leaned over to show him a note he'd scrawled, but Vergennes pushed it away.

"All right, I didn't go straight home." The attorney tried again by putting a hand on his shoulder, but he shrugged it off and said, "I'll tell you exactly where I was. I . . . was at Cassidy Towne's."

Heat wished Lauren Parry had had that body sooner so she could have a more accurate time of death. It was entirely possible that the TOD was before midnight. She followed her instinct to seize Vergennes's moment of weakness and take the leap. "Are you saying you went to Cassidy Towne's and stabbed her?"

"No. I'm saying I went to Cassidy Towne's and . . ." He trailed off, lowering both his head and his voice, mumbling something she couldn't make out.

"Excuse me, I don't hear that. You went to Cassidy Towne's and what?"

Vergennes's face was sallow when he looked up, his eyes unable to hide the misery of his shame. "I went there . . . and . . . I fucked her."

Nikki watched him bend down to dry wash his face with the palms of his hands. When he rose up from his manacles, some of his color had returned. She tried to look at this heartthrob master chef who had conquered Manhattan and put him together with Cassidy Towne, the unofficial arbiter of public scandal. Something in her didn't see them as a couple, although, after years on the job, Nikki could believe just about anything. "So you and Cassidy Towne were having an affair?"

Nikki tried not to paint the picture before she got his answer. The one she saw was a married man trying to break it off, an argument got too heated, and so on. Once again, she went to training and listened instead of projecting.

"We weren't having an affair." His voice was weak and hollow. Nikki had to strain to hear him even in the quiet room.

"So that was your first . . . liaison?"

The chef seemed amused by a private thought. He said, "Sadly, no. It was not our first 'liaison.'"

"You're going to have to explain to me why you don't call this an affair."

The dead quiet that followed was broken by his lawyer. "Rich, I have to advise you not to—"

"No, I'm going to get this out now so they'll see I didn't kill her." He settled down and then came out with it. "I was doing Cassidy Towne for one reason. I had to. I bought this new place right before the economy cratered. I had zero budget for advertising, suddenly people weren't dining out, and if they were, they were skittish about new restaurants. I was desperate. So Cassidy . . . made a deal with me." He paused again and muttered his pitiful, defining words. "Sex for ink."

Heat reflected back on her Sardi's experience with Rook's mother. Apparently, Cassidy didn't restrict herself to actors.

"You have to understand, I love my wife." Nikki just listened. No sense telling him the hundreds of times she's heard that, too, from husbands in that chair. "This wasn't something I came up with. She caught me at a vulnerable time. I said no at first, and she just made it harder to refuse. Said if I loved my wife, I'd . . . sleep with her so we didn't lose our investment. It was stupid. But I did it. I hated myself for it, and you know what's crazy? She didn't even seem into me. It was like she just wanted to prove she could make me do it."

He paused and his face drained again, turning the color of an oyster. "Can't you see? That's why I had those guys steal the body. I woke up yesterday morning and my wife has the TV on and says, 'Hey, somebody killed that gossip bitch.' I thought, Holy Mother . . . I screwed her the night before, now she's dead, and whose DNA are they going to find in her? Mine. So my wife will know I've been banging her? I panic, I'm trying to think, what can I do?

"This food supplier I work with has some connections to some wiseguys for hire, so I call him up and tell him he's got to get me out of a jam. It cost me large, but I got the goddam body."

"Wait, you did this because you were afraid your wife would find out about your relationship?" asked Nikki.

"People knew I was hanging around Cassidy. Your writer pal, for one. Only a matter of time till it came back and bit me, I thought. And Monique's got all the money. I signed a prenup. I'm losing my ass in this economy, the new place is going down; if she cuts me off, next week I'm slinging sauce on ribs at Applebee's."

"So why have the body delivered to where you and your wife live?"

"My wife left yesterday for Philly to work publicity for the Food and Wine Festival. It was all I could think of until I could think of something better." He grew somber after his outburst, the way people did when they'd unloaded their guilt. "Those dudes came by and shook me down for another fifty grand to dispose of her. I don't have that, so they left her with me and told me to think fast."

Nikki flipped to a fresh page of her notebook. "And what time do you claim you last saw Cassidy Towne alive?"

"I did see her alive. It was about ten-thirty. That's when I left her apartment."

Raley and Ochoa were off hunting for Cassidy Towne's typewriter ribbons so when Heat wrapped Vergennes's interrogation and he was led off to be processed for Riker's, she assigned Detective Hinesburg to check out his alibi. The chef said he had paid for the cab home with a credit card around ten-thirty, so there would be a record with the card company and the taxi.

"Blast matrix?" said Rook from his old desk, which he had reclaimed across the bull pen.

Heat welcomed the half smile he was putting on her face, especially in the wake of her disappointment about Vergennes apparently alibi-ing out. She had the body but probably not the killer. "What, you've never heard of a blast matrix?"

"No," he said, "but it didn't take me long to figure out that was just a Heatism. Sort of like the Zoo Lockup, am I right? Some BS term you make up and sling out there to scare the ignorant into thinking there's big trouble coming if they don't comply."

"It worked, didn't it?" Her desk phone rang and she picked it up.

He laughed. "The Heatisms always do."

Nikki finished her call and asked Rook if he felt like a ride. Lauren Parry was ready with Cassidy Towne's autopsy.

As they came into the precinct lobby on their way to the car, Rich-mond Vergennes's lawyer was signing out. "Detective Heat?" Wynn Zanderhoof hurried to intercept her, toting his Zero Haliburton atta-ché, one of those aluminum cases you saw slick hit men and power-suited drug dealers using to carry bundles of cash in every eighties cop movie. "A word, please?"

They stopped at the glass door, and when the attorney just stood there, Nikki got the hint and asked Rook to wait for her at the car. When they were alone, the lawyer said, "You know a murder charge is going to get laughed out of the DA's office."

Heat didn't believe Richmond Vergennes killed Cassidy Towne, but she couldn't entirely rule it out yet and so was not about to let the pressure off. "Even if his alibi checks, that doesn't mean he didn't hire somebody to do it, just like he outsourced stealing the body."

"True. And that's good diligence on your part, Detective." Zander-hoof smiled the kind of empty smile that made her want to check to make sure she still had her watch and her wallet. "But I'm sure your tenacity will also lead you, at some point, to ask yourself why, if my client had someone else kill her, he didn't have them dispose of her re-mains then and there rather than suffer all the risk and attention caused by the incident on Second Avenue yesterday."

He said "incident" in a downplaying way, already jockeying to have charges reduced. Fine, that was his job. Hers was to catch a killer. And as much as she didn't like being jawboned, she had to concede his point. She had as much as arrived at that conclusion herself staring at the time line on the whiteboard not three minutes before. "We'll follow this investigation wherever it leads, Mr. Zanderhoof," she said, giving no ground. No reason to until the chef was entirely ruled out. "The fact remains, your client is up to his neck in this, starting with his affair with my murder victim."

The lawyer chuckled. "Affair? This was no affair."

"Then what was it?"

"A business arrangement, simple as that." He looked through the glass at Rook, leaning on the fender of the Crown Vic, and when he was sure Nikki registered that, his eyes narrowed into a smile she didn't like and he said, "Cassidy Towne was trading sex for print. She certainly wouldn't be the first woman to do that, now, would she, Nikki Heat?"

"You're being awfully quiet." Rook twisted himself sideways in his seat to face her as best he could, given the seat belt and the radio gear between their knees. It was never an easy trip from the Upper West Side to the Office of the Chief Medical Examiner down near Bellevue, and since they had hit the meat of rush hour, it was taking forever. It probably seemed longer than forever to Rook because Heat seemed far away in her thoughts. No, more than that, her vibe was brittle.

"Sometimes I like the quiet, OK?"

"Sure, no problem." He let exactly three seconds pass before he broke the silence. "If you're bumming about Chef Vergennes not being the killer, look at the glass-half-full part, Nikki. We got the body back. Did Montrose say anything?"

"Oh, yeah, Cap's plenty happy. At least the tabloids won't be putting pictures of magicians and disappearing bodies on their covers tomorrow."

"Guess we can thank Fat Tommy for that, can't we?" He searched her for a reaction, but she steadied her focus on traffic, seeming especially interested in anything that was going on out the opposite window from him. "And I'm not trying to claim credit because he was my source. I'm just saying."

Nikki nodded imperceptibly and went back to studying her side mirror like she was somewhere else. Somewhere that didn't feel so comfortable if you were Jameson Rook.

He tried another approach to connect with her. "Hey, I liked that line you hit them with back there in Interrogation. You know, the one about what did they have to offer except a complimentary dessert?" Rook chuckled. "Pure Heat. That's going in the article, for sure. That and blast matrix."

Nikki did engage, but not how he'd expected. "No," she added sharply, "no." Then she checked the side mirror and jerked the wheel, bringing the car to a lurching stop that made everything on the backseat slide off onto the floor. She didn't care. "What the hell do I have to do to get through to you?" She poked her finger in the air, punctuating her words with a stab. "I do not, do *not*, want to be in your article. I do not want to be named, quoted, pictured, or so much as alluded to in your next or any other article. And further, since we seem to have hit a dead end in terms of your so-called secret journalistic sources and insights, I'm thinking this is our last ride. Call the Captain, call the mayor if you want to, I have had it. *No más.* Now do you understand?"

He studied her a beat and grew quiet.

Before he could say anything more, Heat pulled back onto the road and punched Lauren Parry on her speed dial. "Hi, we're two blocks away. . . . Good, see you then."

Between the stoplight and the OCME garage Nikki had second thoughts. Not about her feelings regarding the article and the myriad ways it was screwing with her life. But she worried she'd blistered Rook too much. She could rationalize it, just chalk it up to being pissed after the cheap shot from the slimebag Wynn Zanderhoof, but still, she could have handled Rook a little more deftly and at the same time made her point. She snuck a look at him as he watched the road in wounded silence. A picture memory came to her of Rook sitting right there in that very seat on so many rides, making her laugh the way he did—and then another glimpse of him, sitting there that night in the rainstorm when they couldn't get enough of each other so they spent the night trying. Heat grappled with an overwhelming twinge of regret for losing it with him.

Nikki had no problem being tough. She couldn't abide being mean.

They had the elevator to themselves on the ride up from the second basement parking level, and it was there that she tried to soften her message to him. "This isn't anything about you, Rook, just so you know. It's the whole publicity thing, of having my name and face out there. I kind of have had it with that."

"I think I got your message loud and clear in the car."

Before she could respond, the doors parted and the elevator filled with lab coats and the moment was lost.

"Hey, there, I'm all set for you," said Lauren Parry as they entered the Au-topsy Room. As usual, even behind a surgical mask, you could see her smile. "We did some shuffling to get this workup for you STAT, knowing it's a priority and all."

Heat and Rook finished gloving up and came around to the stainless-steel table that held Cassidy Towne's remains. "I appreciate that, Lauren," said Nikki. "I know how every detective wants it like yesterday, so thanks."

"No problem. I have a bit of a personal interest in this one, too, you know."

"Oh, right," said Heat. "How's the noggin?"

"Hey, I'm hardheaded, everybody knows that. How else does a girl get from the St. Louis projects to all this?" She said it without irony. Lauren Parry lived for her job and it showed. "Nikki, you e-mailed that you wanted a best-earliest TOD, right?"

"Yeah, we have a potential suspect. We just confirmed his taxi ride, so he alibis out at ten-forty-five."

"No way," said the ME. She picked up a chart. "Now, you have to understand this was made a more challenging task because the body had been through a lot. Movement, handling . . ." She looked at Rook and added, "refrigeration. All that made it harder to establish our TOD, but I did it. This was more like the three A.M. range, so cross your ten-forty-five off. Is this the chef who had us jacked?" When her friend nodded, Lauren said, "Well, too bad, but cross him off anyway."

Nikki turned to share a we-figured shrug with Rook, but he wasn't paying attention. She studied him for a few gloomy seconds in the chilly room, felt the after-pain of her outburst, and had to be drawn back by Lauren. "Hello?"

"Oh, sorry. So, three A.M., right."

"Or later, could be a two-hour window after then. Now I'll give you the usual disclaimer that we're still running toxicology, and blah, blah." She paused and turned to Rook. "Isn't this where you usually say if erections last over four hours, call your doctor?"

"Right," he said flatly.

For a medical examiner, Lauren Parry was a people person. She turned from Rook to give Nikki a what's-up? look. She gave nothing back to Lauren, so the ME continued on. "Tox report notwithstanding, I'm still going with the stab wound as COD. But check it out, I have a few things to show you." Lauren beckoned, and Heat followed her around to the other side of the body. "Our deceased was tortured before she died."

Rook came out of his haze and strode to join the other two for a look. "See here on the forearm?" Lauren drew aside the sheet to expose one of Cassidy Towne's arms. "Discoloration from contusion and uniform loss of hair along two matching strips at the forearm and wrist."

"Duct tape," guessed Rook.

"That's right. I didn't catch it at the scene because of the long sleeves she was wearing. The killer not only removed the tape when he was done, but pulled the cuffs down. Thorough job, detail-oriented. As for the tape itself, adhesive residue is at the lab now. Over the counter everywhere, so good luck matching it, but you never know." The ME used a stick pen to indicate points along the body template on her chart. "Taping was on both arms and both ankles. I already called Forensics. Sure enough, the chair tested positive for residue as well."

Nikki made a note. "And what about the torture itself?"

"See the dried blood in the ear canal? There were numerous probes from sharp objects prior to expiration."

Heat suppressed an involuntary shiver at the thought. "What kind of sharp objects?"

"Various needle-like probes. Like, maybe, dental picks. Nothing larger than that. Small wounds but painful as hell. I took some digitals for you with the cam on my otoscope. I'll e-mail them to the precinct. But somebody definitely wanted this woman to be in pain before she died."

"Or talk about something," said Nikki. "Two distinct motives, depending on which." Nikki quickly processed the significance of this torture along with the missing office papers and came down on the side of someone getting Cassidy Towne to talk. This felt more and more about whatever it was she had been working on.

"Other points of interest." Lauren handed a lab report to Nikki. "That blood smear you spotted on the wallpaper? Negative match for the victim."

Nikki showed surprise. "So maybe she injured her attacker before she was subdued?"

"Maybe. There are some defense wounds on her hands. Which brings me to the final piece of info I have for you. This woman's hands were filthy. I don't mean just a little. She's got residual dirt in the creases of her palms, and look at the fingernails." She gently lifted one of Cassidy Towne's hands. "It was hidden by her nail polish, but here's what I found under her fingernails." Each finger had a crescent moon of dirt under the nail.

"I know what that's from," said Rook. "That's from her gardening. She said it was her one escape from her work."

"Some escape for a gossip columnist," said Lauren. "Digging more dirt."

———

Rook was a few strides ahead of Heat getting to the elevator. "Hang on," Nikki said, but he had already pressed the button. The doors opened when she arrived at his side, and she rested a hand on his arm and said to the passengers inside, "We'll get the next one." As the doors curtained closed on their annoyed faces, she added, "Sorry."

"Accepted," said Rook. And they both laughed a little.

Damn, she thought, what was this knack he had to disarm her all the time? She drew him away from the elevators to the southwest windows, where the October sun cut blinding light across them as it got ready to set. "I was a little rough on you. I do apologize for that."

"I'll put some ice on it, I'll be all right," he said.

"Like I said, it's not personal to you. It's the article, which is only you sort of."

"Nikki, you disappeared off the grid. That felt personal. I'm funny that way. If I hadn't had the good fortune to be doing a profile of a murder victim, we might not be lucky enough to be arguing now." She laughed, and he said, "That's right, I killed Cassidy Towne just to get close to Nikki Heat. Hey, there's my title!"

Nikki smiled again and hated it that he could be so cute. "Anyway, accept my apology?"

"Only if you accept an invitation to buy you a drink tonight. Let's be grown-ups and clear the air so I don't have to feel all weird when I see you on the street."

"Or at a murder scene," she added.

"Odds are," said Rook.

Nikki wouldn't be seeing Don until later that night, so she agreed. Rook caught a cab back to his loft to get some writing done, while she took the elevator to the garage to drive back to the precinct and wrap her day.

At her garage level, the elevator doors opened and Raley and Ochoa were there, about to get on. "We miss the autopsy?" asked Ochoa.

Nikki stepped out with them and the doors closed behind her. She held up the file. "Report's right here."

"Oh," said Ochoa. "Good, then." Heat wouldn't have been much of a detective if she couldn't read the disappointment in him. He was, no doubt, hoping for an excuse to see Lauren Parry.

"Got something for you, though, Detective," said Raley. He held up a heavy-duty manila envelope bulging with something square inside.

"You're kidding," she said, daring to feel some energy in the case again. "The typewriter ribbons?"

"Some typewriter ribbons," cautioned Raley. "Her nosy neighbor recycled a bunch of them before the garbage strike, so they're long gone. These are strays he had in his bin. Four of them."

"Nothing in her typewriter," added Ochoa. "We'll run them up to the precinct so Forensics can get on them."

Nikki looked at her watch and then to Ochoa, feeling bad for the guy that his plan to see Lauren Parry had been thwarted by minutes of bad timing. "Tell you what would be a better plan," she said. "As long as you're here, I don't want to have the Padilla case fall through the cracks. Would you go up and see where they are on his autopsy? They're beyond swamped, but if you ask nicely, I bet Lauren Parry will do it as a favor."

"I guess we could ask her," said Ochoa.

Raley knuckle-tapped the manila envelope. "We're going to lose a day with Forensics, though."

"I'm heading uptown, anyway," said Nikki. "I'll drop them at Forensics."

Getting no argument, she signed the chain of evidence form and took the envelope from them. "Let's hear it for nosy neighbors," she said.

Uptown traffic was impossible. Ten-ten WINS said there was a major crash under the UN on the FDR and the work-around traffic was clogging everything northbound on the island. Nikki cut across town, hoping the West Side Highway would at least be crawling. Then she did some calculation and wondered if she should call Rook to rain check. But her gut told her that would just revive the friction she was trying to cool. Another plan.

She was only minutes from his loft. She could stop by, pick him up, and he could come with her to the precinct. They could have a drink around there. The weather was still nice enough for a patio table at Isabella's. "Hey, it's me, change of plan," she said to his voice mail. "We're still on, but call me when you get this." Nikki hung up and smiled, thinking of him writing to his remastered Beatles.

Heat parked in the same loading zone she had parked in once before, the night of the pounding rainstorm when she and Rook had kissed in the downpour and then run through it to his front steps, soaked to the skin and not caring. She put her police sign on her dash, locked the manila envelope in the trunk, and, a minute later, stood at the foot of his steps, pausing, feeling a bit of a flutter remembering that night and how they couldn't get enough of each other.

A man with a chocolate Lab on a leash passed her and climbed the steps. She followed behind and petted the dog while the man got out his keys. "Name's Buster," he said. "The dog, not me."

"Hello, Buster." The Lab eyeballed his man for permission and got up to offer Nikki his chin for a scratch, which she was glad to oblige. If dogs could smile, this one was doing it. Buster looked at her in his bliss and Nikki flashed back on her encounter with the coyote and its defiant stare-down in the middle of West 83rd. She felt a sudden chill. When the man opened the front door, the dog moved by reflex to go with him. She was just reaching for Rook's door buzzer when the man said, "You look trustworthy, come on."

And she followed him in.

Rook had the penthouse loft. The man and his dog rode as far as three and got off. Nikki didn't like the idea of surprising men in their apartments or hotel rooms, having had one poor experience resulting in a tearful flight home from Puerto Vallarta one spring break. Tearful for him, that is.

She reached for her phone to call Rook again, but by then the car was at the top of the shaft. She put her phone away, pulled the metal accordion doors open, and stepped into his vestibule.

Heat approached his door quietly and listened. Nothing to hear. She pressed the button and heard it buzz inside. She heard a footstep, but realized it wasn't coming from inside the loft but from behind her. Someone had been waiting in the vestibule. Before she could turn, her head slammed into Rook's door and she blacked out.

―――――

When Nikki came to, it was in the same blackness she had just left. Was she blind? Was she still unconscious?

Then she felt the fabric on her cheek. She was wearing some kind of sack or hood. Her arms and legs wouldn't move. They were duct-taped to the chair she was sitting in. She attempted to speak, but her mouth was duct-taped, too.

She tried to calm herself, but her heart was pounding. Her head ached above her hairline where it had banged into the door.

Calm yourself, Nikki, she said to herself. Slow breaths. Assess the situation. Start by listening.

And when she listened, what she heard only made her heart pound louder.

She heard what sounded like dental instruments being set out on a tray.

SEVEN

To keep herself from getting swept away in a current of panic, Nikki Heat clung to her training. Fright wouldn't get her out of this alive. But fight would. She needed to be opportunistic and aggressive. She pushed her fear away and focused on action. She repeated silently to herself: Assess. Improvise. Adapt. Overcome.

Whoever was arranging the metalware was nearby. Maybe two yards away. Was her captor alone? She listened, and it seemed so. And whoever it was seemed very busy with the small-sounding tools.

She didn't want to call attention, so, without making overt movements, Heat flexed her muscles, slowly tensing herself against her bonds, knowing she couldn't rip free of them, but testing them, hoping for some sort of give, anything that would betray some area of weakness in the duct tape. All she wanted was a little slack somewhere, anywhere—at her wrist, at her ankle—just a quarter inch of play to give her something to work at.

No luck. She was bound efficiently to her chair at the upper forearms, wrists, and at each ankle. As she ticked off each point of restraint, she replayed her memory of Lauren Parry indicating each place on Cassidy Towne's autopsy template. Her own were identical to that diagram.

So far, the assessment of give sucked.

Then the sorting stopped.

A foot scraped, and she heard two hollow heel strikes on uncarpeted floor as someone came near. The footfalls could have been the heels of a woman's shoe, only they seemed more substantial. Nikki tried to remember the layout of Rook's loft—if that was even where she was. He had rugs everywhere except the bathroom and kitchen, but that flooring was slate. This sounded like hardwood. Maybe this was the great room where he held his poker games.

Cloth rustled beside her, and she could smell Old Spice aftershave right before she heard the voice in her ear. It was a man, forties, she guessed, with a Texas drawl that would have been appealing in other circumstances. It was a crisp, simple voice that would make you feel comfortable about buying the man's church raffle tickets or holding his horse. Gently, calmly, he asked, "Where is it?"

Nikki made a small mumble against her gag. She knew she wouldn't be able to talk, but maybe if the Texan thought she had something to say, he would remove the gag along with her hood and shift the dynamic at least that much. Heat wanted to create an opportunity she could capitalize on.

Instead, he said in his smooth, relaxed tone, "Talking's going to be an issue for you just this moment, isn't it? So let's do this. Just nod if you'll tell me where it is."

She had no idea what the man was talking about, but she nodded. The flat of his hand struck her immediately on the tender spot where her head had met the front door, and she whimpered more in surprise than pain. Heat detected motion and tensed for another blow, but instead she got a strong whiff of Old Spice. And then the voice. Quiet as before, and even more chilling because of its calm folksiness.

"Sorry, ma'am. But, see, you were fibbing, and even in New York City, that dog's not gonna hunt." This Dr. Phil act was all about dominance, and Nikki had a response. She shot her head in the direction of his voice and butted some part of his face. She braced again, but no blow came.

The man simply cleared his throat and took two steps away from her on the hardwood. The hollow-sounding heels made sense to her now. Cowboy boots. She heard a clank of something metal, and the boots approached her side. "Now, I believe you need a reminder about the reality of your situation," he said. Then she felt something like the point of a pencil come to rest on the flesh of her left forearm. "This'll help you along those lines."

He didn't break the skin, but with the needle-sharp point he scored a line along her skin until he reached the duct tape binding her wrist.

He held it there, applying just enough pressure to cause pain without puncturing her. And then he removed it and stepped away, only to come back and stand close to her. Something clicked, and a small motor like a dental drill, or one of those cordless tools they sell on infomercials that cuts nails in half, revved in a high-pitched whine bedside her ear. Nikki jumped and instinctively jerked away from it, but he clamped her in a headlock with his muscular arm. He slowly brought the tool closer and closer to her ear. When it touched the cloth of her hood, vibrating, spinning, chewing fibers, he shut it off. Silence. He put his mouth close to her again.

"You think about that till I get back, now. And when I do, no lies, ya hear?"

She heard the bootfalls again, but this time they went in the opposite direction. When they hit rug, they softened but kept going until they faded away, disappearing into a back room, she guessed. Heat listened, wondering how far the man had gone. Then she bent as far forward at the waist as she could and flung herself upright, feeling her hood inch upward from the momentum of her rise. Before she attempted another flip, she stopped to listen. The boots were approaching again. They clomped when they reached the hardwood, and she felt her slacks rustle as he went by. He paused, and she wondered if he had seen the slight rearrangement of her hood.

Apparently not, because next came the jingle of keys, and then the hard soles crossed the stone of a kitchen floor. From that aural sequence she pictured herself definitely in the great room off Rook's kitchen. She got confirmation when the front door in the entry off the kitchen was unbolted and closed and she heard the teeth of the key insert into the lock. As soon as the tongue of the deadbolt shot, Nikki went to work twisting her head to get the hood off.

It wasn't moving. The cloth was loose but hung too far down onto her shoulders to work off without the use of her hands. She stopped, held her breath, and listened.

The elevator hummed distantly and whined with a slight squeal when it came to a stop. When she heard the metal accordion doors open and close, she went to work wildly shimmying her upper arms. Concentrating her efforts on her right side, she pinched a fold of cloth between her chin and her shoulder, then extended her neck to push upward with the top of her head, slipping the hood up an inch. It was only an inch, but it worked, and so she repeated it until an inch more moved up. After three reps, light started to show underneath the hem. Nikki wished she had access to her mouth to grab it with her teeth, but this would have to do.

She bent for one more flip, and that one succeeded in raising the hood above her eyes, as if she were wearing a hoodie. Nikki shook it off her head and rested while she looked around. Her chair was positioned in open space between the kitchen counter and the oriental rug and the dining table where Rook held his weekly poker nights.

Nikki's heartbeat leveled off, and she went at the task of getting herself to the counter. Careful not to tip the chair over, which would only strand her turtled on the floor, she bucked her body side to side and created enough momentum to shift the chair across the floor a few inches. Heat started to worry she would run out of time before the Texan came back, and she threw more weight into her next motion and started to tip. She almost went over, but managed to get all four feet of the chair down with a slam. It was enough of a scare to settle her into more even movements. Think inch, not inches, she repeated, creating a rhythm. Inch, not inches.

When Nikki reached the counter, which was even with her jawline, seated as she was, she began to rubbing her cheek sideways along its edge. On one of her strokes, her face actually squeaked along the polished granite. The friction made her cheek burn. But it was also causing the ragged edge of the duct tape to catch where it met her skin and curl slightly with each pass. To shut out the pain of the abrasion she thought about the prize that waited on the countertop, inches away: the cordless drill and a half dozen picks and dental tools.

The tape started to give on the left side where she had been working it. Nikki used her tongue, her jaw, and her face muscles to work at it between strokes until she had created a small opening at the corner of her mouth. When she had freed enough tape to create a loose flap, she extended her neck and twisted until her cheek was just above the countertop. Angling slowly, carefully, Nikki lowered her cheek onto the counter and pressed. The tack on the sticky side of the fold of duct tape held to the granite. Keeping her face pressed down hard on the cold surface, Heat swiveled her head left to right, and when she came up, the entire strip of her gag had peeled off and was stuck to the counter.

Her arms and ankles were bound to the chair, but she was not belted down so she was able to rise up and chin her way across the cool granite to the tools. The nearest was a small pick. The drill was farther away, but that was the one she wanted. That was the time saver. She made a lunge for it and slammed her shoulder into the edge of the counter and bounced back into her seat. She torqued herself in the chair until it squared more to the counter and rose up again, not lunging this time but yoga-stretching herself over the smaller tools to the drill.

The handle was cylindrical but had small rubber feet so that the power button presented itself on top. Nikki rested the tip of her chin on the button and pressed once, twice, three times. On the fourth try the drill started to whirr. Her back muscles were crying out, protesting against the strain of holding herself up, contorted, over the counter, but she held steady, concentrating on the handle of the drill as she grabbed it in her lips and then clenched it between her molars.

Evenly distributing her weight between her elbows, she sat herself down gently so she wouldn't knock the drill from her mouth and then leaned over to cut away at the tape that bound her right wrist to the wooden arm of the chair.

Nikki worked fast. By curling her wrist upward, she created tension on the cutting surface, and the fabric peeled apart where the bit of the drill met the tape. Once her right wrist was free, she transferred the drill from her mouth to that hand and was able to cut the bonds on her left wrist even faster. She wanted to get her ankles free so she could move if he came back, but with her upper arms still strapped to the armrests, she couldn't reach down that far, so she began cutting at the right upper. When that came free, she heard something and turned the drill off.

The hum of the rising elevator.

Heat leaned over and, first, cut her right ankle loose, then went to her left. In her rush, she poked herself on the lower shin under her pant leg and winced. But she pushed the pain aside and did her job. She had less than a minute to get loose and had to keep cutting. Her left

ankle came free and she stood up just as she heard the elevator's muffled squeal, signaling its stop at Rook's floor.

Nikki was still attached to the chair at her left elbow when the accordion gate opened. She made the decision to turn off the drill so the
Texan couldn't hear its whine through the door and be warned.

She couldn't find the seam of the duct tape with her nails to peel it
back and the dental tools were all precision points, no good for cutting. The front door key chunked into the lock. In the kitchen there
would be knives. The deadbolt shot open. She picked up the chair and
carried it with her around the counter. The wooden knife holder was
too far to get to. But there. Beside the sink right in front of her: a bottle
opener beside a bent bottle cap. Heat grabbed it as the knob turned
and she heard the front door creak open around the corner in the foyer.

She backed herself and the chair into the great room, crouched down
below the counter to buy a few seconds and some cover, and started to
cut herself free with the sharp point of the opener. The boots stepped
onto the slate kitchen floor and stopped.

Nikki was still cutting at the tape when the Texan bounded over
the counter and landed on top of her.

The force of his tackle knocked Heat sideways under the dining
table. His hands clutched her throat in a choke from behind and she
couldn't do anything about it. Her right arm was pinned under her
side, trapping her hand and the bottle opener under her own weight,
and her left was strapped to the chair, which had been dragged along
like a slipped boat anchor.

She tipped her body backward and rolled on top of him, pinning
him under her back. He responded by strengthening his choke grip on
her throat, but with her right hand now free, she plunged the bottle
opener down. He yelled when the point sunk into his upper thigh, and
his grip loosened. Nikki rolled off him and sprung to her feet, franti-
cally cutting away at the duct tape to free herself. He was on his feet
quickly, out from under the table, lunging at her.

Heat used the damned chair to her advantage, swinging her left
arm outward as he approached. He put up his arms to deflect, but the
wood still smacked him enough to drive him off center. He shot past
her, his near arm getting hooked in the stretcher bar between the chair

legs, and as he flew by, the last strip of duct tape ripped, and the chair went with him. Nikki was free to move.

She didn't wait for him to recover from his fall. Heat lunged for him, but his reflexes were quick. He spun, using the chair to deflect her. Nikki's church key flew out of her hand and across the room, clanging into the radiator before it fell. She thought of going for it, but the Texan was already up and coming at her. Heat sidestepped a few inches, clamping his throat with her right hand as he arrived, jerking his chin up while she palmed the top of his forehead with her left to push down and backward. Her Krav Maga move buckled his knees, and he toppled onto his ass.

Nikki spotted her blazer on the floor under a window and, sticking out from under it, the butt of her gun. She turned to rush for the weapon, but the Texan had obviously also had personal combat training. He spun on his hips and scissored Heat at the knees, locking up her legs and flipping her down hard, face-first onto the floor. From her workouts with Don, she anticipated a grapple from him to tie her up, so she flailed an elbow at his approaching face, caught him in the cheek, and when he recoiled, she broke free, delivering a rib kick on her rise.

The Texan came to his feet, reaching into his sport coat and pulling out a knife. It was a scary piece of business, one of those military-issue combat blades with a knuckle guard and twin fullers, or blood grooves, running along each side. Nikki's unhappy thought was how comfortable it looked in his hand. He looked at her and actually smiled. Like he knew something. Like he was holding The Game Changer.

Training and experience told Nikki that the only fight you want to be in is the one you win—and fast. Don had drilled her on the mantra just that morning, as he had every session: Defend and attack at the same time. And now, here she was, empty-handed in a fight against an experienced assailant with a combat knife.

The Texan didn't give her much time to reflect on strategy. This man was also trained to end fights quickly, and he came for her right away. Having height on Nikki, he lunged at her from above, bringing the point down at her as he stepped in. Defend and attack, she thought, and jumped right in to meet him, slapping his wrist away to the outside while moving in close to deliver a knee to his groin. It doesn't always go like in training, though. He anticipated the knee and countered his body to the side. Not only did Heat miss, he used his free hand to shove her, taking advantage of her momentum to whisk her right past him.

Nikki stumbled but didn't let herself fall. Instead, she spun to brace for his attack, which she knew would be immediate. It was.

This round he came in low and up, going for her belly. Nikki didn't try to slap the arm to the side. It was time to get the knife away from this asshole and now. As he came in, she clutched his wrist, pulling his arm to the outside and not letting go. At the same time, she brought down a hammer fist on the weak spot she had exposed by pulling his arm to the side: his collarbone. Heat felt and heard it crack under the force of her blow, and he cried out.

But his knife had that knuckle guard, so it did not fall even though his grip was weakened. While he was overcome with pain, she reached with both hands to pry it from him, but he brought his fist down on the back of her neck and knocked her to the floor, dazed. She was on her knees on all fours, her vision tunneling to black, when she heard him scramble across the slate of the kitchen. Nikki shook her head and drew a deep breath. The stars started to clear and she got to her feet. Feeling slightly nauseous, the detective stumbled to the wall, felt under her blazer, and got her gun.

He would be out the front door by the time she made it through the kitchen. Counterintuitively, Nikki rushed to the other side of the great room, where there was a portion of the foyer visible through the kitchen entry. She knew that from her poker night the summer before, when she kept eyeing that door, longing for a chance to leave.

When she saw him, the Texan was just opening the door, but pausing to pick something up off the hutch, a large manila envelope. The same one she'd had locked in her trunk. Heat braced on the counter and called, "Police, freeze." He didn't freeze, but slid quickly into the doorway. Nikki fired off one shot in the narrowing sliver of the opening as the door shut behind him.

———

Detective Heat kicked open the door to the stairwell off Rook's penthouse floor and entered with her gun up in an isosceles brace. When she had made sure the Texan wasn't hiding on the landing, she considered his options: up one flight to the rooftop or down seven to the street. Then below her, Nikki heard the bark of a big dog and boots descending the painted concrete steps.

As she flew down the stairwell, two steps at a time, and past the third floor, the dog barked again from inside his apartment. Good work, Buster, she thought, as she raced by. That was when Nikki heard the echo of the door slam come up from street level beneath her.

Heat paused briefly with her hand on the door before she jerked it open and made her defensive exit, gun ready, out onto the sidewalk. The Texan was not there, but he had left something behind. A spatter of blood on the sidewalk, visible in the pool of light shining down from the sodium lamp above the service door.

The sidewalks in Tribeca were busy with the cocktail and pre-dinner crowd. Heat made a quick survey and couldn't see her cowboy, and there were no nearby blood droplets to track. And then the detective heard a woman talking to the man she was walking with. She was saying, "I swear, honey, that looked like blood on his shoulder."

Nikki said, "Police. Which way did he go?"

The pair looked at Nikki. The woman said, "Do you have some kind of ID or a badge?"

Time was wasting. Nikki looked down, but her badge wasn't on her hip. "He's a killer," she said and then she showed them her gun, pointed upward, unthreatening. They both immediately pointed across the street. Nikki told them to call 911 and ran.

"Up Varick toward the subway," called the woman.

Heat ran full-bore north on Varick, dodging pedestrians, looking at both sides of the street and in every vestibule and open storefront she passed. At the triangle intersection where Franklin and Varick met up with Finn Park, she stopped at the corner and scanned the windows of a coffeehouse to see if her man had mixed in with the customers. A diesel pickup truck clattered by, and when it had passed, Nikki jogged across the crosswalk to the concrete island surrounding the Franklin Street stop for the southbound 1 train. Beside a bank of newsstands and plastic boxes full of free handouts for singles clubs and the Learning

Annex she saw more blood. Nikki turned across the square, toward the steps leading to the subway. She saw the Texan illuminated by the light coming from underground. He made her just as his head disappeared down the stairs.

A train must have been due, because the station was full of people waiting to go downtown. Nikki vaulted the turnstile and followed the commotion. People were getting shoved aside along the platform to her left, and that's where she went. She wove her way through the commuters, many of whom were swearing or asking one another, "What's with that guy?"

But when Nikki reached the end of the platform, he wasn't there. Then she heard someone behind her say, "He's going to get killed," and she looked on the track. The Texan was down there in the darkness, climbing across to the northbound side. His right shoulder was tilted lower on the side where she had broken his clavicle, and a line of rusty red traced down the arm of his tan sport coat from the same shoulder, where it looked like he was also carrying her 9mm slug. His free hand clutched her manila envelope, which was now finger-painted with his blood. She braced against the wall, hoping for a shot, but bright light filled the platform, a horn blasted, and a 1 train screeched into the station, blocking her.

Heat raced back to the exit, to beat the passengers getting off the train, and ran up the stairs and across Varick to the northbound station, almost getting creamed by a taxi. The blood drops at the head of the stairs told her she was too late. She went down into the station just to make sure he hadn't doubled back on her as a feint, but the Texan was long gone.

Detective Heat had one consolation prize for her efforts. As she turned to come back up the stairs, something caught her eye on the dirty tiles at the foot of the bottom step. A single typewriter ribbon cartridge.

The couple she had encountered must have made that 911 call, because the street was filled with blue-and-whites and plain wraps when Nikki got back to Rook's block. Detective Heat pressed her way through the onlookers, found a sergeant, and identified herself.

"You were in pursuit?" he asked.

"Yes. But I lost him." Heat gave a description of the Texan and his last-seen to put out on the air, and while one of the sergeant's men did that, she started for the front door, telling him that Rook might be up there. The notion released a strong primal wave of worry coursing through her gut and her vision fluttered.

"You OK? Do you want a medic?" asked the sergeant. "You look like you're going to faint."

"No," she said, pulling herself back together.

Moving through the front door of Rook's loft with a half dozen cops behind her, Nikki pointed out the spray of the cowboy's blood on the jamb as she passed. She led them through the kitchen and past the toppled chair where she had fought her captor and strode to the back of the apartment, retracing the steps the Texan had made before he left the first time. She clung to the hope that his reason for that trip to the back of the apartment was to check on Rook, which could mean he was all right.

When she reached the hall leading to his office, Heat immediately saw the shambles through the open door at the end of it. The cops behind her had their weapons drawn, just in case. Not Nikki. She forgot all about hers and just rushed ahead, calling out, "Rook?" When she got to the door of his office, her breath caught.

Rook was facedown under the chair he was duct-taped to. He had a black pillowcase over his head, just like the one she had been wearing. There was a small puddle of blood collected on the floor under his face.

She got on one knee beside him. "Rook, it's Heat. Can you hear me?"

And then he moaned. It was muffled, as if he had been gagged, too.

"Let's get him up," said one of the cops.

A pair of EMTs came into the room. "Easy," said one of them, "in case his neck's broken." And Nikki felt another twinge in her gut.

They brought Jameson Rook upright slow and easy, by the numbers, and cut him loose. Fortunately, the pooled blood was only from hitting his nose on the floor when he toppled over trying to escape. The EMTs did a check to make sure it wasn't broken, and Nikki came in from the bathroom with a warm facecloth. Rook used it to swab himself clean while he told Detective Nguyen from the First Precinct what had happened.

After he'd left the OCME, Rook had come straight there to his loft so he could type up the day's notes for his article. He grabbed a beer, walked up the hall, and as soon as he arrived at his office, he saw that the whole place had been ransacked. He turned to Nikki. "It was like Cassidy Towne's crime scene, except with electronics from this century. I was just getting my cell phone to call you when it rang, and it was actually you on the caller ID. But as I went to answer, he came up behind me and put that pillowcase over my head."

"Did you struggle?" asked the detective.

"You kidding? Like crazy," said Rook. "But he had the pillowcase around my head real tight and had me in a choke hold."

"Did he have a weapon?" asked the detective.

"A knife. Yes. He said he had a knife."

"Did you see it?"

"I had a pillowcase blindfolding me. Plus, last year I got taken hostage in Chechnya by some rebels. I found that you live longer if you don't ask to see the knife."

"Good call," said Nguyen. "What next?"

"Well, he sat me in this side chair, told me not to move, and started to tape me down."

"Did you ever see him? Even through the pillowcase?"

"No."

"What did his voice sound like?"

Rook thought a moment. "Southern. Like Wilford Brimley." And then he added, "Oh! But not the look-at-that-Wilford-Brimley's-doing-TV-commercials-now Wilford Brimley. Younger. Like from *Absence of Malice* or *The Natural*."

"So . . . Southern." Nguyen made the note.

"I guess that would be easier to fit on the APB than Wilford Brimley's IMDb credits, yes," said Rook. "Southern, it is."

Nikki turned to Nguyen and said with simple authority, "The accent was North Texas."

Nguyen turned an amused side glance to Heat, who smiled and shrugged. He turned his attention back to Rook. "Did he say anything else to you, say what he wanted?"

"Never got that far," answered the writer. "His cell phone rang, and next thing I know he leaves me sitting there and goes out."

Heat interjected, "He must have had somebody outside watching the street who tipped him that I was coming up."

"So we have an accomplice," said Nguyen, making that note.

Rook continued with his story, "While he's out, I try rocking myself over to the desk, where I have scissors and a letter opener. But I tipped over. And there I was, stuck. He came in here briefly and left, then a while after that I heard all sorts of commotion out there. And a gunshot. And then nothing until now."

Rook listened silently as Nikki recounted in detail to Detective Nguyen the story of how she had decided to drop by and pick Rook up, and how she'd gotten ambushed at his front door. And then she described the essentials of the fight in the great room and the pursuit that came afterward.

When she was finished, Detective Nguyen asked if she could come to the precinct to meet the sketch artist. She said she would and he left, leaving Forensics behind for prints and samples.

Waiting for the elevator to arrive and take her and Rook down, Nikki found her badge in her blazer side pocket and clipped it on her hip. Rook turned to her and said, "So. You just came over without my OK? What if I had been 'entertaining' someone?"

They got on the elevator, and as the doors closed, she said, "That'll be the day, you entertain anyone. Anyone but yourself." He looked over at her and laughed, and then she did, too. And when they stopped laughing, they still held eye contact. Nikki wondered if this was going to turn into a kiss, and her mind was racing to figure out how she felt about that when the car reached the lobby and the outer door opened.

Rook pulled the elevator gates open for her and said, "Close call, huh?"

Nikki decided which way to take it. "Yeah. But we'll catch him."

The sketch artist was waiting for them when they got to the First. So were Raley and Ochoa, who took the typewriter ribbon from Heat to run up to Forensics. Raley held up the evidence bag holding the cartridge. "Do you think this is what the Texan was looking for?"

Heat could hear that soft drawl asking, 'Where is it?' and the memory of it made her inner ear tickle. The columnist's ransacked office, the missing filing cabinet, the looted trash, and absent typewriter ribbons . . . Clearly someone was trying to get their hands on whatever Cassidy Towne was working on. And she knew if he didn't get everything he was looking for, he'd kill again.

There were only three remaining sketch artists in all for the NYPD. Nikki's was a detective who did his sketching on a computer using software to cut and paste facial features onto the graphic he was creating. As an artist, he was fast and he was good. He asked Nikki precise questions, and when she was unsure of the most descriptive term she could use to explain some of the Texan's features, he guided her to choices, making use of his experience and his degree in Behavioral Psychology.

The result was a portrait of a lean, groomed man with short gingery-red hair, parted on the left; narrow, alert eyes; a sharp nose; and a look made earnest by thin lips and hollow cheeks.

Heat's sketch result was added to the sheet, with her description of the suspect: early forties, six-one, 165 to 170 . . . (muscular but lean, she thought; more Billy Bob than Billy Ray). Last seen wearing a tan sport coat with bloodstain, dress white Western shirt with pearl buttons, brown dress slacks, and brown pointed cowboy boots. Known to be carrying an eight-inch knife. From the computer database of blades, Heat was able to find a picture of his weapon, a Robbins & Dudley 3-Finger Knuckle Knife with a cast aluminum molded grip.

With that done, Rook waited in the lobby while Heat met with the shooting team from Police Plaza. The meeting didn't take long, and she left it still carrying her gun on her hip.

Detective Nguyen had offered them each a ride home in a blue-and-white, and Rook said, "Look, I know we had plans for a drink, but I'd understand if you wanted to bag it for the night."

"Actually . . ." She looked up at the wall clock in the lobby. It was almost nine-thirty. And then she looked at Rook. "I'm really not up for a bar tonight."

"So, rain check? . . . Or has the fact that we cheated death made us fated to kick it out privately?"

Nikki saw she had a half-hour-old text from Don, her trainer with benefits. "Still good for tonight? Y/N?" She held the phone in her hand and then glanced up at Rook, who looked just as frayed as she must have from an evening with a killer. But the post-trauma fragility she felt wasn't just from her throw-down with the Texan. She was still recovering from the fear throb she'd felt when she walked down the hall to Rook's office afterward, not knowing what she would find in there.

"We could compare notes on the case so far," he said.

She looked thoughtful. "I suppose we could do that. Take a fresh look at the evidence."

"Do you have wine?"

"You know it." Heat put her thumb on her keypad, pressed the N, and said to Rook, "Not your place, though. I'm not much for yellow tape and graphite dust, either." When they reached the blue-and-white, she gave the uniform the address of her apartment, and they both got in.

———

Heat handed Rook a glass of Sancerre while he stood in her living room, in front of the John Singer Sargent poster he'd given her last summer. "You can't hate me too much, you've still got my Sargent prominently displayed."

"Don't flatter yourself, Rook. It's all about the art. Cheers." They clinked and sipped. Then she said, "Let's keep this informal. You relax, enjoy some TV, whatever. I'm going to get a bath and soak some street chase off me."

"Sure, no problem," he said, picking up the TV remote. "Take your time. I think *Antiques Roadshow* is in Tulsa tonight."

Nikki gave him the finger and disappeared down the hall. She went into the bathroom, set her wineglass on the vanity, and opened the taps over her bathtub. She was just reaching for her bubble bath when he knocked on the doorjamb.

"Hey, what if I had been 'entertaining' somebody?" she said.

"With what," he said with a sly grin, "a little pony play?"

"You wish," she said.

"Just wondering if you were hungry."

"Now that you mention it, yes." Funny, she thought, how adrenaline shuts that part down. "Want to order in?"

"Or, if you don't mind, I could scrounge your kitchen. No booby traps, I trust."

"None," she said. "Knock yourself out, I'll just enjoy the fact that I'm soaking while you work."

"Love this thing," he said and stepped to her claw-foot bathtub. He rapped his knuckles on it and the cast-iron bonged like a church bell. "If the asteroid ever hits, this is where you should duck and cover."

A half hour later, Nikki emerged in her robe, brushing her hair. "Something smells good out here," she said, but he was not in the kitchen. He wasn't in the living room, either. "Rook?"

Then she looked down on the rug and saw a trail of cocktail napkins leading to the open window and the fire escape. She went back to her bedroom for her slippers, stepped through the window onto the metal stairs, and climbed them to the roof.

"What are you doing?" said Nikki as she approached. Rook had set up a card table and two folding chairs and lit votive candles to light the meal he had prepared.

"It's a little eclectic, but if we call it tapas we'll never know it's just stuff I scrounged." He pulled a chair out for her. She put her wineglass on the table and sat.

"This looks great, actually."

"It is, if you're not too hungry and can't see the burn marks in the dark," he said. "It's basic quesadillas cut into quarters and then there is smoked salmon with some capers I found in the back of your pantry. Out of sight, out of mind, you know." He must have been nervous because he kept on. "Is it too chilly up here? I brought the blanket off the couch if you need it."

"No, it's nice tonight." Nikki looked up. There was too much ambient light to see any stars, but the view of the New York Life Tower a few blocks away and the Empire State Building beyond it were a splendid enough view. "This is brilliant, Rook. A nice touch after the day we've had."

"I have my moments," he said. As they ate, she watched him in the candlelight, thinking, Now what was my issue here? On the street somewhere beneath them a car rolled by blasting classic rock with mega bass. It was before her time, but she knew the Bob Seger song from the clubs. Rook caught her staring at him as the chorus blared out that what they had in common was the fire down below.

"What's wrong, did I overdo the candles?" he asked. "Sometimes I can come off kind of Mephistophelian when lit by flame."

"No, the candle's working." Nikki took a bite of quesadilla and said, "But I do have something serious I need to ask you."

"Sure, but we don't have to do any heavy lifting tonight. I know that was the plan but that can wait. I've almost forgotten how you crushed my spirit this afternoon."

"But I need to know this and I need to know right now."

"OK . . ."

She wiped her hands on her napkin and looked him in the eyes. "Who has black pillowcases?" Before he could answer, she continued, "It's been bugging me since your office. Were those your black pillowcases?"

"First of all, they aren't black."

"So they are yours. I ask again, who has black pillowcases? Besides Hugh Hefner or, I don't know, international arms dealers?"

"They are not black. They are the darkest of dark blue, called Midnight. You'd know that if you had hung around long enough to see my autumn bachelor linens."

She laughed. "Autumn linens?"

"Yes, seasons change. And by the bye, those sheets are eight hundred and twenty thread count."

"I can see what I've been missing."

"I'll bet," he said, dropping the wiseass from his tone. He paused and added, "You know exactly what you've been missing, and so do I."

Nikki studied him. Rook was not looking at her but into her, the candle flame dancing in his eyes.

He pulled the bottle from a bowl of ice and came around beside her to pour. When her glass was full, she rested one hand on his wrist and put the other around the bottle to take it from him and place it on the table. Looking up at him standing over her, Nikki held his gaze as she took his wrist and drew his hand inside her robe. She tensed with a shiver as his cool palm rested on her breast. And held her, warming.

Rook slowly lowered, bending himself to kiss her, but it wasn't fast enough for what was building inside Nikki. She clawed the front of his shirt roughly and pulled him to her. Her excitement made him come alive, and he fell onto her, kissing her deeply and drawing her close.

Nikki moaned, feeling a spreading warmth, and arched backward as she rose up to him. Then, sliding herself off the chair, she laid herself down on her back on the flat of the rooftop. Their tongues reached for each other, searching in some wild, aching desperation. He untied the sash of her robe. She unbuckled his belt. And Nikki Heat softly groaned again and whispered, "Now. *Now* . . . ," and moved herself to the long-past beat of the "Fire Down Below."

EIGHT

Something stirred Rook awake. A siren, likely an ambulance, judging by its chirps and guttural honks, announcing itself at an intersection over on Park Avenue South before fading into the night. It was one part of New York living he never got used to, the noise. For some it became background they could tune out. Not for him. It challenged him in the day when he wrote, and he never got an unbroken night's sleep because this was the city that never did. Somebody should write a song about that, he thought.

With the eye that wasn't buried in the pillow, he read the luminous dial of his watch on the nightstand: 2:34. Three hours more sleep before the alarm. He smiled. Hm. Or maybe two hours. He slid backward across the bed to dock himself skin-to-skin with Nikki. When he reached the middle of the bed, he felt the sheet and her pillow. Both were cool.

Rook found her in the living room, perched on the window seat in a sweatshirt and a pair of Gap drawstring bottoms. He stopped in the hallway entrance and watched her, a catlike silhouette in the bay window with her knees pulled up to her chin and her arms wrapped around her shins, contemplating the street below. "You can come in," she said without turning from her view of the block. "I know you're there."

"Aren't you the trained observer, Detective," he said. He moved behind her and folded his forearms loosely around her neck.

"I heard you the second your feet hit the floor in there. You move about as subtly as a draft horse." Nikki settled back and lounged against him.

"You'll never hear me complain when the comparison involves a horse."

"No?" She turned her face up to his and smiled. "No complaints here, either."

"That's good. And saves me the trouble of leaving a survey card."

Nikki sniffed a little chuckle and turned back to the window, this time resting the back of her head on his abdomen, feeling the warmth of him on her neck.

"You thinking that he's out there somewhere?" asked Rook.

"The Texan? Oh, he is for now. Just for now."

"You worried he'll come here?"

"I hope he does. I'm armed, and if that's not enough, if he'll hold still long enough, you can subdue him with one of your famous nosebleeds." She leaned forward and head-nodded over the sill. "Besides, Captain put a patrol car out front." As Rook leaned over her to see the roof of the blue-and-white, pressing his weight on her shoulders, Nikki added, "Doesn't he know the city's in a budget crisis?"

"Small price to protect his star detective."

A change came over her. She uncoiled her legs and moved from him, sliding herself around to put her back to the window. Rook sat beside her on the cushion. "What?" he said. When she didn't answer, he leaned a shoulder against hers. "What's got you up and sitting here at this hour?"

Nikki reflected a moment and said, "Gossip." She turned her head halfway to him. "I've been thinking about how ugly gossip is. How it victimizes people, but how as much as we say we hate it, we still feed on it like it was crack."

"I hear you. It ate at me every day with Cassidy Towne. They call what she did journalism—hell, I even said it was the other day when I argued with Toby Mills's spin doctor—but, when you get down to it, Cassidy Towne was as much about journalism as the Spanish Inquisition was about justice. Although, Tomás de Torquemada had more friends."

"I'm not talking about Cassidy Towne," said Nikki. "I'm talking about me. And the rumors and gossip I've had to deal with since you put me on the cover of a national magazine. That's what got me all shitty with you in the car today. Someone made a snide comment insinuating that I slept with you for the publicity."

"It was that lawyer, wasn't it?"

"Rook, it doesn't matter who. It's not the first of those I've had to deal with. At least that was an overt remark. Most of what I get are looks or I catch people whispering. Since your article came out I feel like I'm walking around naked. I've spent years building my rep as a professional. It's never been called into question until now."

"I knew that shyster said something to you."

"Did you even hear what I just said?"

"Yes, and my advice is to consider the source, Nik. He's just working on your head to get some sort of psychological leverage in the case. His client's going down. Richmond Vergennes will be an Iron Chef, all right. Ironing in the Sing Sing laundry."

She tucked a knee up and scooted to face him, resting a palm on each of his shoulders. "I want you to listen carefully because this is important. Do I have you?" He nodded. "Good. Because I'm telling you about something that's going on with me that's a big deal, and you're spinning off on your own side road. You think you're with me but you're running parallel. Understand what I mean?"

He nodded again and she said, "You don't."

"I do. You're upset because that lawyer made an unfair crack."

She took her hands off his shoulders and folded them in her lap. "You're not hearing me."

"Hey?" He waited for her to face him. "I am hearing you, and here's what you're feeling. You're feeling like your life was rolling along fine until my article came out, right? And what did I do? I put you where you aren't comfortable—thrust into the spotlight with everybody looking at you and gossiping about you, and not always to your face. And you're frustrated because you tried to tell me it wasn't what you wanted but I had it so in my head it was good for you that I did everything but consider your feelings." He paused and took both her hands in his. "I'm considering them now, Nik. I'm sorry for how I made you feel. I thought I was doing a good job and apologize that I let it get complicated."

She hardly knew what to say, so she just stared at him a moment. At last she said, "So. I guess you were listening."

He nodded to himself and said, "We just had a Dr. Phil thing there, didn't we?"

She laughed. "Sorta, yeah."

"Because it felt sort of like one of those Dr. Phil things."

They smiled and looked into each other a long time. Nikki was starting to wonder, What now? This connection they had just made was unexpected, and she wasn't prepared for what it might mean. So she did what she always did. Decided to not decide. Just to be in the moment.

He may have been in the same place, because in some unspoken ballet of synchronization, the two leaned forward at the same instant, drawn to each other for a tender kiss. When they parted, they smiled again and then just held each other, jaws resting on opposing shoulders, their chests slowly rising and falling as one.

"And so you know, Rook, I'm sorry, too. About this afternoon in the car, being so rough on you."

A full minute passed and he said, "And so you know? I'm good with rough."

Nikki drew back from him and gave him a sly look. "Oh, are you?" She reached down and took him in her hand. "How rough?"

He cupped a palm behind her head, lacing his long fingers through her hair. "Wanna find out?"

She gave him a squeeze that made him gasp and said, "You're on."

And then she gasped as he gathered her up in his arms and carried her to the bedroom. Halfway down the hall, she bit his ear and whispered, "My safe word is 'pineapples.'"

Nikki wanted them to arrive at the Two-Oh separately the next morning. She got up early and, as she left, asked Rook to cab home to change and to take his sweet time before he came to the precinct. She had enough gossip swirling around her without the two of them showing up for work together looking like the poster for *Date Night*.

Heat rolled into the bull pen at five of six and was surprised to find Detectives Raley and Ochoa already there. Raley was on his phone listening to someone and gave her a howdy nod, then resumed his note taking. "Hey, Detective," said Ochoa.

"Gents." She usually got a smile whenever she spoke to one member of the pair as the rep for both. This time, nothing. Ochoa's phone rang, and as he reached for it, she said, "You boys got something against sleep?" Neither one answered her. Ochoa took his call. Raley finished his and passed by on the way to the whiteboard. Nikki had a feeling she knew what these two were up to, and sure enough, when she tailed Raley to the board, she discovered that he and Ochoa had started a new section labeled "The Lone Stranger" in red marking pen.

Rales referred to his notes to update the status report they had begun under the taped-up police sketch of the Texan. As his dry-erase marker squeaked out block capitals on the bright white surface, Heat read over his shoulder: No overnight ER visits with gunshots or broken collarbones from anyone matching his description in Manhattan or the boroughs. Calls pending in Jersey. Checks of all CVSs and Duane Reades south of Canal Street and west of St. James Place came up neg for first-aid shoppers matching Tex. Digital copies of his sketch were blasted out in e-mails to private urgent-care storefronts in case he sought treatment at one of the local doc-in-the-boxes.

Under a section headed "Patrols/Quality of Life" she saw that these two had already contacted all relevant precincts with no hits on any complaints, arrests, or homeless pickups matching her man.

Nikki Heat was standing witness to how cops had one another's back. A sister detective got assaulted, and Roach's stoic response was to come in to the precinct under a setting moon to start turning over all the stones. It wasn't just a code. It was life itself. Because in their city, you just didn't pull that shit and walk.

In any other sort of profession this would be a warm moment leading to a group hug. But these were New York cops, so when Ochoa got off the phone and stood beside her, she said, "This the best you two could come up with?"

Raley, who was bent over writing, capped his marker and turned to face her, keeping an excellent straight face when he said, "Well, seeing how you let the suspect evade capture, there's not much to work with."

"But we all do our best," added Ochoa. Then, for good measure, he threw in, "At least you got a piece of him before you let the yokel slip away, right?"

And that was that. Without a high five or even a fist bump, the three of them had had their say. For one it was, Thanks, guys, I owe you; for the other two it was an emphatic, Got your wing, anytime, anywhere. And then they got back to work before one of them got all misty.

Ochoa said, "That call I just got was Forensics. I've been all over them about the typewriter ribbon you found on the subway platform. Tests are done, they're e-mailing the digital images right now."

"Way to gochoa." A poke of excitement pressed her gut at the prospect of actual evidence to examine as she moved to her computer to log on.

Rook entered with a cheery "Morning" and handed Raley a paper bag blotched with grease stains. "Sorry, all they had left was plain."

Raley squinted at the corner of Rook's mouth. "You got a little something. There."

Rook touched a finger to his face and came away with a blue sprinkle embedded in some icing. "Huh. Well, I didn't say *when* they ran out. Just that they had." He ate the sprinkle and turned to Nikki, selling a bit too hard. "How are you this morning?"

She flicked only the slightest of glances up from her screen. "Busy."

While Heat waited for the server to log her on, Ochoa said, "Remember yesterday at the ME's, you asked me to talk to Lauren Parry about the status of Coyote Man?" She gave him one of her nickname looks and he bobbed his head side to side. "I mean, Mr. Coyote Man? . . . You were right, Padilla's autopsy was stacked. She's going to get on it herself first thing this morning."

"Not so good news on the other Padilla front," said Raley. "Our canvass of residents and businesses where his body was found turned up NG. Same for security cams."

Rook said, "Which reminds me, have you seen today's *Ledger*?"

"*Ledger*'s crap," from Ochoa.

"We'll leave that to the Pulitzer committee," said Rook, "but check this out. About sunset last night they spotted a coyote hiding in Central Park." He held up the front page. Nikki turned from her monitor and recognized the brazen eyes in the grainy picture of the animal peeking out of the shrubs near Belvedere Castle.

"Gotta love the headline," said Raley, who then read it aloud, as if they all couldn't make it out. It was only in the size font they use on the top line of an eye chart. "'<u>Coy</u>-ote.'" He took the paper from Rook to examine it. "They're always doing that, putting some kind of groaner pun with the story."

"Hate that," said Ochoa. "Can I have it?" Rook nodded and Raley passed him the newspaper, which he set aside for later. "Like I said, *Ledger*'s crap. But the price is right."

"Here we go, boys and girls." Detective Heat opened the attachment from Forensics. It was a huge file containing enhanced screen captures of every inch of the typewriter ribbon. Nikki read the accompanying e-mail from the lab technician aloud for the others. "'In case you are not familiar with the low-tech phenomenon known as the typewriter,' great—geek humor," she said, and continued, "'each time a key is touched, the corresponding raised metal letter on the type bar strikes the ribbon, which not only prints the letter on the page but also embosses itself on the ribbon. Each letter strike causes the ribbon to advance one space, allowing us to scan the ribbon like a reverse tickertape, reading the sequence of letters that were printed on the writer's page.'"

"This dude's seen *Avatar* six times," said Raley.

Nikki read on. "'Unfortunately, the owner of this ribbon had rewound and reused the ribbon at the end of each spool, causing overstrikes which have obliterated most of the retrievable text.'"

"Cassidy was cheap," offered Rook. "That's already in my article."

"Is any of this ribbon readable?" asked Ochoa.

"Hang on." Nikki scan-read the rest of the e-mail and summarized. "He says he flagged those images that at least had some promise for us to examine. He's sending the ribbon to get X-rayed to see if more can be read on it. That takes time, but he'll let us know. . . . He's happy to . . ."

"Happy to what?" said Ochoa.

"Live in his parents' basement," suggested Rook.

But Raley read the last line over Nikki's shoulder. "'I am happy to have the privilege of doing any favor I can for the famous Detective Nikki Heat.'"

Nikki caught Rook's grimace but moved on. "Let's split these up and start screening them."

Raley and Ochoa each took a block of screen captures, about fifteen apiece, and brought them up on their desk monitors. This was one area where Jameson Rook's knowledge of the victim would clearly be useful, so Nikki entrusted him with a series of files to examine, too, at the desk he had claimed. The remaining prospects she kept for her own perusal.

The work was tedious and time-consuming. Each image had to be opened separately and looked over carefully for any words or, hopefully, sentences to make sense out of the blur. Raley commented that it was like staring at one of those matrix posters they used to have in malls, where, if you squinted the right way, you might see a seagull or a puppy. Ochoa said it was more like looking for the weeping Virgin on the trunk of a tree or Joaquin Phoenix on a piece of burned toast.

Nikki didn't mind their banter. It made the arduous task merely grueling. As her eyes strained and squinted at her own screen, she reminded them of her tenets of good investigation. Rule #1: The time line is your friend. Rule #2: Some of the best detective work is desk work.

"Right about now, I've got a third rule," called Ochoa from his desk. "Take the early retirement."

"Got something," said Rook. All three detectives gathered behind his chair, glad for the excuse to get away from their own desks and monitors, even if it was for nothing. "It's some decipherable words, anyway. Five words."

Nikki leaned around Rook to bring herself closer to his screen. Her breast grazed his shoulder, an accident. She felt her face flush but soon got pulled from that distraction by the image on his computer.

stab me n th back

"OK, this is frame 0430. 'Stab me in the back.'" Nikki could feel a small release of adrenaline. "Bring up 0429 and 0431."

Raley said, "I think I've got 0429," and hurried back to his desk while Rook brought up 0431, which was garbled and unreadable. They had all gathered behind Raley already by the time he said, "Come look."

His screen, displaying the frame before "stab me in the back," had a name typed on it. And every one of them knew it.

―――――――

Heat and Rook stood against the back wall of the Chelsea rehearsal hall
watching Soleil Gray with six male dancers run through choreography
for her new music video. "Not that I don't enjoy my backstage access,"
said Rook, "but if we know Tex is the killer, why are we bothering
with her?"

"We know Cassidy was writing about Soleil because of the typewriter ribbons. And the Texan stole them, right?"

"So you think Soleil and Tex are connected?"

The detective flexed her lips into an inverted U. "I don't know that
they aren't. Now I have a question for you. Did Cassidy have any tension with our rock star?"

"No more than any other. Which is to say plenty. She tended to
open her columns with Soleil's rehab lapses. Most of it is past history,
though. Things I found in archives when I was doing research. Back in
the day, Soleil had a wilder side and that always made good copy for
'Buzz Rush.'"

Six years ago, when she was twenty-two, Soleil Gray had been a
brooding Emo icon, when Emo was the thing. Although, when the rock
band you front has a couple of gold records and you can fill a summer's
worth of venues in North America, Europe, and Australia—and you're
traveling to them on Citation jets—there's not too much to brood about.
The early songs she wrote and sang lead vocals on, like "Barbed Wire
Heart," "Mixed Massages," and notably, from the band's second CD,
"Virus in Your Soul," made millions and earned reviewer raves. *Rolling Stone* called her the distaff, pre-hype John Mayer, basically looking right past the rest of the band to the pale lead singer who was
perennially staring through a curtain of black sloping bangs with de-
spondent green eyes framed by mascara.

Rumors of drug use gained traction when Soleil started arriving
hours late for concerts and, eventually, missing some altogether. A You-
Tube cell phone video capturing her on stage at Toad's Place in New
Haven went viral, showing her wasted and hoarse, forgetting her own
lyrics even with the audience trying to prompt her. Soleil busted up
Shades of Gray in 2008. She said it was to go solo. It was more like to go

party. The singer-songwriter went a year and a half without writing or recording anything.

Even though clubs and drugs replaced studios and concerts, Soleil stayed in the spotlight after she hooked up with Reed Wakefield, the hot young film actor whose own taste for New York nightlife and ingested substances matched her own. The difference was that Reed Wakefield was able to maintain his career. The couple moved into her East Village apartment after he started shooting *Magnitude Once Removed*, a costume drama in which he played the illegitimate son of Benjamin Franklin. The filming outlasted their affair, which was volatile and punctuated by late-night police visits. Having already broken up her band, Soleil broke up her relationship with Reed and buried her pain in the recording studio with long sessions, creative disputes, and not much output.

The previous May, just days after he had returned to New York from Cannes, where he received a special jury prize for his role as the bastard son of France's first American ambassador, Reed Wakefield pulled a Heath Ledger and died of an accidental drug overdose.

The impact on Soleil was profound. Once again, she stopped working, but this time to go into rehab. She emerged from the Connecticut facility clean and focused. The very day after her release, she was back in the recording studio to lay down tracks for the ballad she had written on her bunk bed in the Fairfield County manor as her farewell to the actor she had loved. "Reed and Weep" got split reviews. Some thought it was a sensitive anthem to the fragility of life and enduring loss. Others called it a shameless derivative of "Fire and Rain" by James Taylor and REM's "Everybody Hurts." But it debuted on the charts in the Top 10. Soleil Gray had officially begun her elusive solo career.

She had also changed how she presented herself to the world. And, as Heat and Rook watched her run through a track from her new CD, *Reboot My Life*, they saw a woman whose career and new hard body had undergone a radical makeover.

The blaring music ended and the choreographer called a five. Soleil protested. "No, let's go again; these guys move like they've got snowshoes on." She went to her first position, her muscles gleaming in the harsh light of the rehearsal room. The male dancers, panting, formed up behind her, but the choreographer shook his head to the playback engineer. "Fine. Remember this, dickweed, when we're shooting and you wonder why it sucks," Soleil said to him and stormed toward the door.

As she drew near, Nikki Heat stepped to intercept her. "Miss Gray?"

Soleil slowed her stride, but only to size up Nikki, as if for a fight. She gave Rook a fleeting appraisal, but concentrated on the detective. "Who the hell are you? This is a closed rehearsal."

Heat showed her badge and introduced herself. "I'd like to ask you a few questions about Cassidy Towne."

"Now?" When Nikki just stared, Soleil dropped an F-bomb. "Whatever your questions are about her, the answer's going to be the same. 'Bitch.' " She went to the small craft services table in the corner and got a bottle of Fiji out of a cooler. She didn't offer one to either of them.

"Your dancing's awesome," said Rook.

"It's crap. Are you a cop? 'Cause you don't look like a cop."

Nikki jumped in to take that one. "He's working with us on this case." No need to freak her out that the press was there.

"You look familiar." Soleil Gray canted her head to one side, appraising Nikki. "You're on that magazine, aren't you?"

Heat ignored that path and said, "I assume you're aware that Cassidy Towne was killed?"

"Yes. A tragic loss for all of us." She cracked the seal on the blue cap and chugged some water. "Why are you talking to me about that dead bee-otch, other than to cheer me up?"

Rook joined in. "Cassidy Towne wrote a lot about you in her column."

"The scumbag printed a ton of lies and gossip about me, if that's what you call writing. She had these anonymous sources and unnamed spies claiming I did everything from snorting lines off a Hammond B3 to groping Clive Davis at the Grammys."

"She also wrote that you fired a .38 at your producer during one of the sessions with your old band," said Rook.

"Not true." Soleil grabbed a towel from a wicker basket near the window. "It was a .44." She wiped the sweat from her face and added, "Good times."

Nikki opened her notebook and a pen, always a means to help folks get serious about conversations. "Did you have any personal contact with Cassidy Towne?"

"What is this? You don't think I had anything to do with her murder, do you? Seriously?"

Nikki stayed on her own track, getting her facts in morsels, accumulating small answers, and, in them, looking for inconsistencies. "Did you have any conversations with her?"

"Not really."

There was a deflection, for sure. "So you never talked to her?"

"Yeah. We went to tea every afternoon and swapped recipes."

Nikki's newfound sensitivity about gossip helped her empathize with the singer's attitude about Cassidy Towne, but her cop sense was telling her this sarcasm was a bluff. Time to move the fences in. "Are you saying you never talked to her?"

Soleil held the cool flat side of the bottle against her neck. "No, I'm not saying never."

"Did you ever see her?"

"Well, sure, I guess so. It's a small town if you're famous, you know?"

Did Nikki ever know. "When was the last time you saw Cassidy Towne, Miss Gray?"

Soleil puffed her cheeks and made a show of looking thoughtful. Nikki felt her acting was on a par with the dog walker from Juilliard—in other words, unconvincing. "I can't remember. Probably a long time ago. Obviously not important to me." She looked over at the dancers coming back from their five. "Look, I have a music video to shoot, and it ain't happening."

"Sure, I understand. Just one more question," said Nikki, with her pen poised. "Can you tell me your whereabouts from one to four A.M. the night Cassidy Towne was killed?" With the Texan as the probable killer, Soleil's alibi—in fact everyone else's alibi on this case—became less significant. Still, Nikki clung to the procedures that always worked for her. The time line was hungry. Feed the time line.

Soleil Gray took a moment to count nights and said, "Yes, I can. I was with Allie, an A & R assistant from my record label."

And you were with her all that time? All night?"

"Um, let me see . . ." Soleil's manner lit up Heat's radar. The searching she was doing carried a whiff of stall. "Yuh, pretty much all night, till about two-thirty."

"May I have the name and a contact number for the assistant, Allie?"

After she gave Heat the information, Soleil quickly added, "Oh, wait. Just remembered. After I was with Allie, I hooked up with Zane, my old keyboard guy from Shades of Gray."

"And what time was that?"

". . . Three, I guess. We had a late bite and I went home to bed about four, four-thirty. Are we done?"

"I have one more question," said Rook. "How do you build upper arms like that? You going to be opening for Madonna?"

"Hey, way things are going? Madge is gonna be opening for me."

———————

The soft elevator chime echoed across the desert-rose marble lobby of Rad Dog Records until the sound was lost in the high, vaulted ceiling. A blonde woman in her early twenties was the only one to step off. She looked up from her BlackBerry, spotted Heat and Rook at the security desk, and walked over to them.

"Hi, I'm Allie," she said while she was still twenty feet away.

After they shook hands and made introductions, Nikki asked her if it was a good time to talk. She said it was, but she could only be away from her desk for five minutes. "Did you see *The Devil Wears Prada*?" asked Allie. "Mine wears Ed Hardy, and he's a guy, but the rest is pretty dead-on." She escorted them across the reception area to a sofa grouping. It was made of hard molded plastic and didn't do much to absorb the sound that bounced around the room. Nikki was struck by how comfortable the sofa was.

Rook settled in opposite them on a large white molded plastic chair. "Looks like we're waiting for the next shuttle to the space station." Then he looked down at the coffee table and saw Nikki's cover on top of a stack of magazines. He picked up a day-old *Variety*, pretended to scan the headline, and tossed it over the *First Press*.

"Is this about the murder, the gossip columnist?" Allie swept her hair behind her ear and then twirled the ends with her fingers.

Nikki had figured word would reach her from Soleil before they got there, and it had. That might account for the assistant's nervous tics. Time to find out. "It is. How did you know?"

Her eyes grew wide and she blurted, "OK, Soleil called me and said you might come." Allie licked her lips, and her tongue looked like it was wearing a pink sock. "I've never dealt with the police like this. At concerts, I have, but they're mostly retired."

"Soleil Gray said you were with her the night Cassidy Towne was killed." Heat got out her reporter's spiral notebook to signal this would be on the record. And waited.

"I . . . was."

Hesitation. Just enough to make Nikki press. "From when to when?" She uncapped her stick pen. "As exact as you can be."

"Um, we got together at eight. Went over to the Music Hall at ten."

"In Brooklyn?" said Rook.

"Yeah, in Williamsburg. Jason Mraz had a secret show. He's not on our label, but we got passes."

Nikki asked, "How long were you there?"

"Jason went on at ten, we left at about eleven-thirty. Is that good?"

"Allie, I need to know what time she left you."

"Is this between us?"

Nikki shrugged. "For now."

She hesitated and said, "That is when she left me. Eleven-thirty." Heat didn't need to look at her notes to know that the times Soleil had given her were bogus. Allie flipped her hair around her ear again. "You won't tell Soleil?"

"That she asked you to lie in a murder investigation?" Allie's lower lip started to tremble and Nikki put a hand on her knee. "Relax, you did the right thing." Allie flashed a quick smile that the detective returned before she continued. "Soleil and Cassidy Towne had some bad blood between them, didn't they?"

"Yeah, that bitch—sorry, but she kept printing all sorts of ugly crap about her. Like if she had one beer. Made Soleil nuts."

"So we understand," said Nikki. "Did you ever hear Soleil say anything threatening about Cassidy Towne?"

"Well, you know, who doesn't say stuff when they're mad? It doesn't mean they did it." Allie could see that she had gotten their interest and looked down, rolling her thumb on the trackball on her BlackBerry just to have something else to do. When her eyes came up and found Nikki scrutinizing her, she set the PDA on the coffee table and waited, knowing what was coming.

"Tell me what you heard her say."

"It was just talk." Allie shrugged it off. Heat simply watched her, waiting.

Rook leaned forward onto his thighs and smiled. "She always wins the staring contests, trust me, I know. You might as well, you know . . ."

Allie made her decision to come clean. "One night last week she took me to dinner. The cool artists do that. They know my salary. Anyway, Soleil wanted Italian so she took me to Babbo." She misread the look that passed between the other two and explained, "You know, Mario Batali's place in Washington Square?"

"Yeah, it's great," said Rook.

"We were eating upstairs, and Soleil has to use the loo, so she excuses herself and goes downstairs. A minute later, I hear all this shouting and a crash. I recognized Soleil's voice so I ran down the steps and there's Cassidy Towne on the floor with her chair tipped over. Just when I got there, Soleil grabs a knife off her table and says . . ." Allie dry-swallowed again. "She says, you like stabbing people in the back? How would you like me to stab you in yours, you frickin' pig."

Nikki walked out of the parking garage off Times Square and found Rook buying two hot dogs from a sidewalk vendor across from the *GMA* studios. "This is why you hopped out of a moving car?" she asked.

"I call that more rolling than moving," he said. "I saw the stand and sprung into my signature hero deployment. Keeps my reflexes sharp. Dog?" He held one out to her.

"No, thanks, job's dangerous enough." As they crossed Broadway Detective Heat made her habitual check for suspicious parked cars, ever mindful of the Crossroads of the World, the New Normal, and life on orange alert. By the time they reached the other side of the street, Rook had finished his first dog.

"Man, I don't know if I can eat two. What the hell, yes, I can." He started in on the other, filling his cheeks like a squirrel, making her laugh as they walked north, weaving between the tourists. Except for the gun on her hip, thought Nikki, they could be a suburban couple themselves.

Between swallows, Rook asked, "Why are we checking Soleil's other alibi? Let's suppose maybe she hired the Texan to stab Cassidy Towne. What's her whereabouts going to tell us?"

"It gives us a chance to talk to people in her life. We follow the leads we have, not the ones we wish we had. Besides, look what the last alibi check gave us."

"We learned Soleil lied to us?"

"Exactly. So let's talk to some more people who might tell us the truth."

Waiting for the cross signal on 45th, Rook followed her gaze to the newsstand where a dozen Nikki Heats hung from clothespins along the roof of the kiosk.

"How many weeks till November?" she said. And then the light changed and they crossed the street to enter the lobby of the Marriott Marquis.

They found Soleil's old keyboardist Zane Taft exactly where his agent had told Nikki he would be, in the Marquis Ballroom on the ninth floor. Nikki had also gotten the musician's cell phone number, but she didn't call ahead. Soleil could have already texted him, as she did Allie, but if she hadn't yet, no reason to give him a heads-up and a chance to call his former lead singer to line up their alibi stories.

He was alone in the ballroom, on a riser overlooking the empty dance floor, doing a sound check on his keyboard. The first thing Nikki noticed about him was his smile, big and open and crammed with perfect teeth. He fished out Diet Cokes from the ice bucket the hotel had left for him, a man glad for the company.

"Got a gig here tonight, a Sweet Sixty."

"Birthday party?" asked Rook.

Zane shrugged. "Life, huh? Four years ago today I'm at the Hollywood Bowl in Shades, playing our second encore, looking out at Sir Paul in the front row and making eye contact with Jessica Alba. And now?" He popped the tab on his aluminum can and Coke fizzed over. "I should have had a business manager. Anyway, tonight I'm getting duked an extra three hundred because birthday boy likes Frankie Valli and the Four Seasons and I know all the songs from *Jersey Boys*." He slurped the overflow from around the rim of the can. "Fact is, Soleil was the band. She gets the fat contract, I get to play 'Do You Like Piña Coladas?' for boomers who are recession-proof enough to afford parties for themselves."

Nikki said, "You don't sound bitter."

"What's that going to get you? And, hey, Soleil's still a pal. She checks on me from time to time, or when she hears about a studio gig, she'll make a call for me. It's cool." He smiled and all those teeth reminded Heat of the keyboard on his Yamaha.

"Have you been in touch with her recently?" Nikki phrased it openly, seeing how he played it.

"Yeah, she called about half an hour ago, telling me to expect a visit from the famous detective, what's-her-name. That's her saying that, not me."

"No problem," she said. "Did Soleil tell you why we're here?"

He nodded and took another hit off his soda. "Here's the truth. Yes, she was with me the other night. You know, when the lady got killed. But not for long. She met up with me at the Brooklyn Diner on Fifty-seventh about midnight. I was only on the first bite of my Fifteen Bite Hot Dog when she got a call and freaked and said she had to go. That's Soleil, though."

"I can never finish those," said Rook. "And I'm a dog eater."

Nikki ignored Rook. "So she was only with you for how long?"

"Ten minutes, if."

"Did she say who the call was from?"

"No, but I heard her say his first name when she answered. Derek. I remember it because I started thinking . . . and the Dominos. You know as in," and then he started riffing the iconic piano solo from "Layla," the coda sounding as authentic as if the band were in the room. Later that night, he'd be playing "Big Girls Don't Cry" for a landscape contractor from Massapequa, Long Island.

As soon as the doors closed to the ballroom, Rook said to Heat, "Know how you've been kidding me, always saying my insider knowledge ain't crap?"

"Who says I was kidding?"

"Well, stop. Because I know who Derek is."

Nikki U-turned herself in the hallway and stepped in front of him. "Seriously? You know who Derek is?"

"I do."

"Who?"

"I don't know." When she moaned and strode to the elevator, he caught up with her. "Hang on, I mean I've never met him. But hear me out—I was with Cassidy Towne when she got a call from a Derek, and I heard his last name when her assistant said he was on the line."

Multiple synapses started firing in Heat's brain at once. "Rook . . . If there's a connection between Soleil and this Derek and Cassidy Towne . . . I don't want to say what it means yet, but I have an idea."

"Me, too," he said. "You first."

"Well, for one, what if he is the Texan?"

"Sure," said Rook. "Timing of the call to Soleil, her reaction . . . Derek could be our killer. Maybe he and Soleil were both involved in that big story Cassidy wouldn't tell me about. And they wanted it and her killed."

"Fine, fine, fine. What's the last name?"

"I forget." She shoved him and he stumbled back into a potted plant. "Hang on, hang on now." He took out his black Moleskine notebook and flipped to some early pages. "Here. It's Snow. Derek Snow."

The address trace didn't take long. A half hour later, Heat was parking the Crown Victoria in front of Derek Snow's fifth-floor walk-up on 8th Street a few blocks east of Astor Place.

She and Rook made the climb of five flights with a squad of heavily armed uniformed cops borrowed from the Ninth Precinct. There was another contingent on the fire escape, both high and low. Their reward for the hike was to knock and get no answer. "It is just past one," said Rook. "He could be at work."

"I suppose I could maybe knock on a few doors to see if anybody knows where he works."

"I don't think that's going to help you."

Nikki gave him a puzzled look. "Why not?"

Rook leaned toward the door and touched his nose. She leaned in and sniffed.

They had a battering ram, but the super was there to unlock the door to the apartment. Nikki entered with one hand over her nose and the other resting on the grip of her service weapon. The uniforms rolled in behind her, then Rook.

The first thing she recognized when she saw Derek Snow's body was that it wasn't the Texan. The young African-American sat slumped forward at the kitchen table with his face down on a place mat. The dried pool of blood on the linoleum underneath him came from a puncture in his white shirt, just below his heart. Heat turned to get the OK signal from the cops who had cleared the other rooms of the apartment, and then she turned back to find Rook on one knee doing what she was about to do, checking out his forearms.

Rook turned to her and said the word just as she was thinking it. "Adhesive."

NINE

Jameson Rook sat off to the side of the bull pen with his back against his squatter's desk while the rest of the detectives from Homicide plus a few familiar faces from Robbery-Burglary and a pair from Vice drew up chairs around the whiteboard. Behind them, through the glass wall, he could see Nikki rising from her meeting with Captain Montrose.

Just as cop humor is laced with dark understatement, cop tension is also between the lines. The veteran reporter in him could hear it in the silence—the way the room fell quiet when Detective Heat came into the pen and stepped up to address them. He saw it in the faces turned to her, all experienced, many showing the world-weariness years on the job had etched into them, but all full of attentiveness.

He had been discreet about his note-taking since his return to the Two-Oh. Rook had an unexpected exclusive that was all going into his Cassidy Towne article, but in deference to Nikki's sensitivity and the fish eyes he had been getting from some of the squad, his MO had been to memorize key words or to scrawl them on scraps of paper or, if something required more jotting than he felt he could sneak, to make an unnecessary trip or two to the men's room. But that day, Rook surrendered to the volume of detail coming at him and began to take written notes in the open. If anybody noticed, he or she didn't seem to care. They were all taking notes, too.

The spine of his black Moleskine answered with a comforting crack as he bent it back so the fresh page would lie flat on his thigh. He heard the throaty tone in Nikki's voice when she said a simple good afternoon to the packed room, and the journalist wrote on the top line in block letters, "Game Changer."

Detective Heat confirmed it with her opening remarks. "I just briefed Captain Montrose to let him know what we all suspect from today's developments. Although the autopsy is pending and CSU is still on the scene of this afternoon's homicide, I have reason to believe we are now dealing with a professional killer." Somebody cleared a throat, but that was the only sound in the room. "What began as a search for a revenge killer, perhaps someone who hired our John Doe Texan to murder Cassidy Towne, it's clear this has ratcheted up to where we have someone who is trying to cover something up and has a pro contractor on the job as a sort of silencer.

"We already had allocated extra resources on this case because of the high-profile nature of the first victim, but due to this change in scope, the Cap has requested, and has received from 1PP, the clearance to bring in extra manpower and lab resources to find our killer." Nikki called on one of the Burglary plainclothes, who had a finger raised. "Rhymer?"

"What do we have on the new vic?"

"Still developing, but here's the rundown I do have." Nikki didn't need notes; she had it all in her head and wrote each item on the new, smaller whiteboard that had been brought in and set up beside Cassidy Towne's. "Prelim TOD is same night as our gossip girl. OCME will give us a time window soon and I'll forward to you. Derek Snow was an African-American male, twenty-seven, according to DMV. No arrests, except for a couple of speeding tickets. Lived alone in a one-bedroom, Lower East, steady tenant, paid his rent, no problems, neighbors loved him. Stable employment, worked since '07 as a concierge at the Dragon-fly House in SoHo. If you aren't familiar, it's a five-star boutique hotel, quiet and discreet, attracts lots of creatives, mostly Euros but Hollywood-friendly, also."

She waited for them to make their notes before she continued. "Rhymer, I'd like you and Roach to head down to his apartment to dig a little deeper with the neighbors, see if one didn't love him. Or if anybody has new thoughts on something they saw or heard.

"I don't know if he liked boys or girls, but see if he had any relationships worth looking at. Check the neighborhood, too. It's one of those blocks where everybody knows your name, so hit the diners and the bodegas."

Ochoa, who was sitting beside Rhymer, a clean-cut Carolina trans-plant, said, "In that neighborhood you can get yourself a nice tat while you're down there, too, Opie. 'Love' and 'Hate' on your knuckles, maybe?"

Nikki seemed glad for Ochoa's tension breaker, and when the laughter settled, she said, "CSU is sweeping his place with a special eye toward any hard connection to Towne or Miss Gray. I'll let you know. And let's not forget our common COD by stabbing and the apparently identical restraints with the duct tape. I'm heading over to OCME now to see the results of Snow's autopsy, but aside from the new arrival of other possible suspects, we are still liking our John Doe Texan, so show his sketch and the picture of Soleil Gray in your files when you make your rounds.

"I also want a team to work the Dragonfly. Malcolm, you and . . . how about Reynolds from Vice? Cover the usual coworker angles, beefs with guests or vendors, the union. But it is a hotel, so look into the vice aspects, too. He was a concierge, and rumor has it some of them actually have been known to procure." She paused again for the chuckles to subside. "But our best connection is through a new person of interest, the rock singer, Soleil Gray, who connects—loosely, so far—to Cassidy Towne and to Derek Snow. Rook, any thoughts on Snow's connection?"

She had startled him from a thought. His Moleskine dropped to the floor, where he left it. He almost stood, but that would be dorky, so he just sat a little straighter, feeling all the cop stares turned his way. "Uh, yeah, actually, I have something very interesting now that I hear he worked at the Dragonfly. Before I knew the specific hotel, I assumed the connection might be he was one of Cassidy Towne's sources. Cassidy paid her sources for their tips. That's unusual. Richard Johnson of 'Page Six' at the *Post* told me he doesn't pay tipsters. Other papers don't have the budget. But she did, and they were mostly in personal service industries. Limo drivers, private trainers, cooks, masseuses, and, of course, hotel employees. Concierges." He started to relax as he saw the nods of understanding from the detectives.

"That's a viable theory, so we'll go with that for now," said Heat, as one of the detectives handed Rook his Moleskine with a nod and a smile.

"I'm not done," Rook said. "That was where I came down before I just heard he worked at the Dragonfly. That's the hotel where Reed Wakefield died last May. Soleil Gray's fiancé."

Heat didn't like to bigfoot Malcolm and Reynolds, but she wanted to check out the Dragonfly herself. Those two detectives could cover the other angles, but she wanted to check out the Reed Wakefield death. Nikki called ahead to Lauren Parry to tell the ME she would be later than planned. While she had her friend on the phone, Heat asked her if she could look up the coroner findings on Wakefield, then she and Rook headed for SoHo. Lauren called back while Nikki was parking in an open space in front of Balthazar, just around the corner from the hotel on Crosby.

"COD was toxic overdose, ruled accidental," said the medical examiner. "Deceased was a habitual user, a self-medicator. Looked from his history like one of those seesaw cases, you know, took something to bring himself up, then something else to level it off, something else to set him down. Blood work and stomach showed high alcohol, plus toxic amounts of cocaine, amyl nitrate, and Ambien."

"I have the file on its way to my office, but I'm on the road. Is there a notation in yours about the inquest?"

"Yeah, of course. And we all talked about it here, too, so I remember it pretty well from the office buzz. They took a close look, especially after Heath Ledger, to cover all the bases. He was depressive, distraught after his engagement broke off, but gave no hints of suicidal thoughts. They interviewed coworkers, family, even the ex."

"Soleil Gray?"

"Right," said Lauren. "Everyone says the same thing. He was pretty much to himself the final month of shooting his last movie. When it wrapped, he went to the hotel in SoHo, basically, to cocoon and shut out the world."

Nikki thanked her for the crib notes and apologized for being late. "If you want, I could just get your Derek Snow report over the phone."

"Not on your life," said Lauren. "You get your happy ass down here when you're done." And then she left it with a cryptic "I promise to make it worth your while."

———

It was a difficult time to visit the Dragonfly. The staff was clearly shaken by the news of the concierge's murder, but, as one of those small hotels with a casual air but impeccable couth, they soldiered on without letting their high-end guests know anything was amiss. Though nobody could miss the accumulation of expensive flower arrangements filling the area around the concierge desk, no doubt from devoted travelers who mourned Derek Snow.

The manager and night manager, who got called in early for the interview, met Heat and Rook in the bamboo-paneled lounge, which had not yet opened. Both had been on duty during the weeks Reed Wakefield stayed there, up to his death. They confirmed what Lauren had conveyed in her synopsis, and it jibed with what Heat, Rook, and most New Yorkers knew about the tragedy. The actor checked in alone, spent most of the time in his room, leaving only occasionally, like when housekeeping needed to service it, or at night. He came and went alone because it was clear that was what he wanted. He was polite but kept to himself. The only complaint he made was to insist housekeeping re-close his drapes and leave the lights off in his room when they were finished.

The night of his death Wakefield did not go out, nor did he have any visitors. When he didn't answer his door the next day—he had specified 11:30 to 12:30 for his service—the housekeeper let herself in and discovered his body in the bed. She mistakenly assumed he was sleeping and left quietly, but then became concerned, and two hours later was when they discovered that he was dead.

"What was his relationship like with Derek Snow?" When the two managers reacted, Nikki said, "I'm sorry. I know this is a difficult time, but these questions need to be asked."

"I understand," said the manager. "The fact is, Derek was quite popular with all our guests. He was so well suited to the job and had a passion for it. He was naturally friendly, discreet, and masterful at bookings for theater or impossible restaurants."

Nikki asked again, "And was he also popular with Reed Wakefield?"

The night manager, a thin young man with pale skin and a British accent, said, "Truth be told, I don't think Mr. Wakefield availed himself extensively of Derek's services during his stay. That's not to say they didn't pass the greetings of the day, but that might be the extent of it."

"Did Soleil Gray ever visit him?" asked Heat.

"Mr. Wakefield?" The manager looked at the night man, and both shook no.

"Not during that period, as far as we recall," said the night manager.

"Did Soleil Gray ever come to this hotel at all?"

"Oh, yes," said the manager. "She was a frequent visitor to this lounge in particular and for certain parties, as well as being a guest of the hotel from time to time."

"Even though she could almost walk here from her apartment?" said Rook.

"Mr. Rook, the Dragonfly is a destination experience for travelers no matter how far they come." The manager smiled. That wasn't the first time he had said that. Probably not the first time that day.

Heat asked, "What was her relationship like with Derek Snow?"

"Same as everyone's, I suppose," said the manager. He turned to the night manager. "Colin?"

"Absolutely. Quite. Nothing out of the ordinary."

His certainty and exuberance seemed a little heavy-handed for Nikki's taste. So she just went for it. "Were they lovers?"

"No, of course not," said the manager. "That would be a breach of policy. Why do you ask that?"

Nikki directed herself to the night manager. "Because you are hiding something." She paused for effect and watched pink splotches surface on his cheeks. "What is it, then, did they fight? Deal in drugs? Arrange cockfights in her room? You can tell me here, or you can tell me Uptown in a more official setting."

The manager looked at his colleague, whose scalp was showing beads of perspiration through his thinning blond hair. "Colin?"

Colin hesitated and said, "We had a bit of . . . an incident . . . involving Miss Gray. You have to understand crossing this line of discretion is very difficult for me."

"We're here for ya, Colly," said Rook. "Let her rip."

Colin withered under his manager's look. "One evening last winter," he began, "Miss Gray was a guest of the hotel and had a lapse in her sobriety. At two-thirty A.M., on my shift, as it happens, she, ah . . . had to be subdued in the lobby. Derek Snow was still about, and I asked him to help me escort her into her room. In the process, a firearm she had in her handbag discharged, and the bullet grazed Derek's thigh."

"Colin?" said the manager, obviously unhappy.

"I admit, we did not adhere to procedure and report this, but the plea was made by Derek not to make a fuss, and, well . . ."

"She paid you guys off," said Heat. Not a question.

"In a word, yes."

"And there's no police report of this." Again, Heat didn't have to ask. When Colin shook his head, she said, "How bad was his wound? Doctors are required to report those to the department."

"It was a graze but enough for several stitches. Miss Gray was acquainted with a physician who gave cast physicals for the film industry, and an arrangement was made."

Now that Detective Heat understood the connection between Soleil Gray and Derek Snow, she asked a few more questions, details that satisfied her and allowed her to check later, and ended the meeting. After she got the contact information for Colin, she showed the police rendering of the Texan. "Have you ever seen this man here?"

They both said no. She asked them to think of him in a different context than as a guest, perhaps on someone's security detail. The answer was still no, although the manager kept the picture.

"That's all for now," said Heat, "except a question about one more person. Has Cassidy Towne ever come here?"

"Please," said the manager. "This is the Dragonfly."

On the walk back to the car, Rook laughed and said, "Or we can talk to you in a . . . 'more official setting.' That goes on my list of Heatisms, along with Zoo Lockup and blast matrix."

"I was showing some refinement. After all, it was the Dragonfly."

Rook said, "So the question for me remains, why was Derek calling Soleil Gray the night of Cassidy's murder?"

"Right there with you," said Heat. "And the freak-out reaction from her."

"I don't suppose that's because the concierge couldn't get her the table she wanted at Per Se."

"Not being a fan of coincidences, I'd say a call with that timing, two bodies with stab wounds, duct-taped to chairs . . . Derek Snow has to be related to Cassidy Towne, but how? And if Soleil wasn't complicit in her murder, is she feeling in some kind of danger herself?"

"Here's a nutty idea. Ask her."

"Yeah, and she'll be straight with me, too." And then she said, "But you know I will."

As Nikki headed north on First Avenue toward the OCME, Rook said, "With or without the lobby gunplay, I'm still going with the premise that Derek was a Cassidy tipster."

"Well, we're pulling his phone records, let's see if you're right." She blew air out between her teeth. "Sordid, isn't it? Thinking people are spying on you for cash. What you ate, what you drank, who you're sleeping with, all so Cassidy Towne can put it out to people in the *Ledger*."

"Most of it was true, though. She told me she got something wrong early on, right after she started her column, about Woody Allen having an affair with Meryl Streep. Her source said he was obsessed with her ever since *Manhattan*. Not true, totally blew it. The other papers pounced on it and called her the Towne Liar. From then on, she said if it wasn't true and verifiable—from two sources—she'd rather let someone else scoop her."

"Noble. For a scumbag."

"Yes, and none of us ever read those columns, do we? Come on, Nikki, the problem is if you take them seriously. They're like the sports section for peeping Toms, which is just about everybody."

"Not I," she said.

"Look, I agree with you that it's scummy. And not just because I am intimidated by your impeccable command of grammar. But, at the same time, she was only covering what people were doing. Nobody made Spitzer mount a call girl in over-the-calf socks. Or Russell Crowe toss a telephone at a hotel night manager. Or Soleil Gray blow a hole in a concierge's pants with a handgun."

"Right. But who says we have to know all that?"

"Then don't read it. But it doesn't make the secrets go away. You know, my mom's been putting together a night of Chekhov readings at the Westport Playhouse. She was rehearsing one last weekend, 'The Lady with the Little Dog.' There's a passage about this guy Gurov that I'm going to excerpt in my article about Cassidy. It goes something like 'He had two lives: one, open, seen and known by all . . . full of relative truth . . . and another life running its course in secret.' "

"And your point?"

"My point, Detective, is that everybody's got a secret, and if you're in the public eye, you're fair game."

They stopped at the light and Nikki turned to him. He could see that for her this was more than just an abstract topic. "But what if you're not used to being in the public eye, or didn't choose to be there? I ended up with the world reading about my mother's murder. That's not a scandal, but it was private. You write stories about Bono, and Sarkozy, and Sir Richard Branson, right? They're equipped for all this intrusion, but does it make it any better that they need to be? Shouldn't some things be allowed to be kept private?"

He nodded. "I agree." And then he couldn't resist. "Which is why I will never again even write the word 'pineapples.' "

––––––––

"Going to give you plenty to reflect on here today, Detective Heat." Lauren Parry's formality with Nikki was only invoked when Heat's BFF was pulling her leg or prepping her for news beyond her workaday coroner reports. Heat could tell from her friend's face that there was no joke coming after that setup.

"What are we dealing with, ME Parry?" she said in matching attitude.

The medical examiner led Heat and Rook to Derek Snow's body

on the table and picked up his chart. "As usual, the tox disclaimer not-withstanding, we have a cause of death from a single thoracic knife wound in the intercostal tissue between ribs, causing perforation of the left ventricle."

"Stabbed in the heart," said Rook. When Lauren gave him an eye roll, he shrugged. "You want layman's terms, or disclaimers about call-ing your physician after four hours, who's your guy?"

Nikki asked, "Did he also have signs of torture?"

Nodding, Lauren beckoned her closer to indicate the victim's left ear. "See the little blood flecks? Same as on Cassidy Towne. I took some ear canal shots for you."

"Dental picks?" said Heat.

"Don't need to explain it to you, do I?" The memory of being ha-rassed herself by the Texan made Nikki wince involuntarily. Lauren said nothing, but put a hand on her shoulder in comfort. Then she took it off and said, "There's more." She flipped back the top page of the chart to indicate the matching adhesive remnants found on both Cassidy Towne and Derek Snow.

Rook said, "Little doubt we're dealing with the same killer, is there?"

"It gets more interesting."

"Wow." Rook rubbed his palms together. "This is like the late-night infomercials. 'But wait, there's more.' "

"You have no idea," said Lauren.

Nikki lifted the sheet to verify the scar on Derek's thigh. When she found it, she joined Rook and Lauren at the ME's lab bench, a stainless-steel surface laden with an array of macabre instruments that were part of dissecting and analyzing the dead. In the center of the long coun-ter, a small white towel covered a tray. The ME set her chart down and folded back the towel halfway, exposing the blade of a plastic knife the color of dried Elmer's glue. "This is a polymer mold I made from Cassidy Towne's stab wound. The killer worked clean, an expert plunge and withdrawal, so I was able to make an excellent cast from her puncture."

Heat recognized it immediately, the arc of the edges coming together dead center at the tip, which was sharpened to a point, and, most distinctive, the fullers, those twin grooves running parallel the full length of the flat. "This was his knife. The Texan's," she said.

"A Robbins and Dudley Knuckle Knife, according to the catalog on the server," said Lauren Parry. "Exactly like"—she peeled back the remaining half of the towel—"this one here." Beside the first cast on the tray rested a mold of the identical blade.

"Get out," said Rook. "If this were a TV show, this is where they'd go to a commercial."

A slight smile showed at the corners of the ME's mouth. It wasn't often that she had the occasion to be a little theatrical, and she was obviously enjoying her moment. The dead ones didn't appreciate her work. "Well, if they ran a commercial now, you'd miss the biggest part."

"I don't know what could be bigger," said Nikki, looking over her shoulder at Derek Snow's corpse. "You just linked Cassidy Towne's exact murder weapon to Derek Snow."

"But I didn't." Lauren waited until both their faces clouded, puzzling. She pointed to the first blade replica. "This knife cast here? Taken from Cassidy Towne." Then she picked up the second one. "This knife cast here? I took from Esteban Padilla."

"No way!" Rook turned a circle and stomped a foot. "Coyote Man?"

All Nikki said was "Lauren . . ."

"Yup."

"The Texan stabbed Coyote Man, too?"

"Well," said Lauren, "his knife did, anyway."

Heat was still processing all this through the haze of her astonishment. "Whatever made you think to take a mold from Padilla?"

"The puncture on both victims had a lot of material displaced at the center, or what we call the neutral axis of the blade. It's negligible, but visible if you're looking. Soon as I saw the similarity, I ran the molds."

"You're a jock," said Nikki.

"Not done yet. When the molds matched, I ran one more test. Know that bloodstain you pointed out to me on the wallpaper at Cassidy Towne's brownstone? It wasn't hers. It was Esteban Padilla's. A perfect match."

"Best autopsy ever," said Rook. "I think I just peed myself a little. Seriously, I did."

TEN

Nikki was not about to let this wait for a meeting back in the bull pen. Momentum on this case was picking up, and even though she wasn't sure where her new clues would lead, she was going to ride it, and hard. The Office of the Chief Medical Examiner was only a few blocks north of the Derek Snow crime scene, so Heat got on her cell phone and called Ochoa to tell him she'd meet him and Raley in the East Village in five minutes for a briefing.

"You sound pumped. Did you get a confirm that Snow had the same killer as our gossip lady?" Ochoa asked.

She looked over at Rook, riding shotgun with her down Second Avenue and said, in her best infomercial announcer voice, "But wait, there's more."

The two detectives were out canvassing Derek Snow's neighborhood when she reached Ochoa, so instead of going to his apartment, they made a plan to meet up at Mud Coffee just off Second. Traffic flow on East 9th was one way the wrong way for her, so Heat bypassed it, pulled into a loading zone on St. Mark's Place, tossed her placard on the dash, and walked it. Rook was a marathon and 10-K runner, but he had to work to keep pace with Nikki.

Mud Coffee was a storefront on a block that had one foot in the old New York City of custom tailor shops, one-of-a-kind dress boutiques, and a Ukrainian soul food restaurant. The other foot was in the newer, more gentrified Manhattan of upscale skin spas, sake bars, and an Eileen Fisher. Raley and Ochoa were waiting at the outside bench with four coffees when they arrived.

"Usually, it's too crowded to score any outdoor seating here," said Raley. "Might have something to do with people's aversion to smelling Le Gar-bahge." Talks between the city and the union had broken off the night before, and a fresh layer of trash had been added to every sidewalk in the borough.

Rook side-glanced to the hedgerow of trash bags lining the curb six feet away. "Getting so I don't even smell it anymore."

"Maybe from spending too much time with your gossip queen," said Ochoa. Instead of a comeback, he got a maybe nod from Rook.

Detective Heat was unable to resist employing Lauren Parry's flair for the dramatic as she stepped out the information she had just gotten at OCME: the Derek Snow cause of death; the cast of the knife used on Cassidy Towne matching the one the Texan attacked her with; and then the kicker—Cassidy Towne's blade cast matching the one that gave Esteban Padilla his mortal wound.

Even cops who thought they had seen and heard it all could be surprised once in a while. This was the second time this case had managed to bring the vets up short. When Heat finished her story, the air was full of whispered holy craps and f-bombs.

"So," Nikki said when it seemed they had taken it in, "setting aside the fireworks, the significance of this forensic news is that we still have a professional killer but we've added a third vic."

"Man, Coyote Man." Ochoa shook his head, still on it, still absorbing the scope of it all. "OK, so if that was Padilla's blood on her wallpaper, what was his deal? Was he with the killer, maybe one of the crew tearing the place up? Something went wrong with the posse?"

Raley picked it right up. "Or was Padilla a Good Samaritan, passing by, heard her scream, and got into something over his head?"

"Or," said Rook, "was he a part of this in a way we can't even see yet? He was a produce driver, right? Did he service Richmond Vergennes's restaurants, perhaps delivering fresh fruits and vegetables and some sweet lovin' on the side? Maybe this was some sort of romantic triangle revenge thing."

Detective Heat turned to Roach. "I need you all over this, guys. That's why I'm pulling you two off this detail and sending you to get aggressive on Esteban Padilla."

"Cool," said Ochoa.

Raley nodded. "On it, Detective."

"Obviously, push the usuals: friends, family, lovers, his job," she said, "but what we need is the connection. That's where daylight's going to come. Find out what the hell the connection was between Cassidy Towne and a produce truck driver."

"And The Texan, and Derek Snow," added Raley.

"And Soleil Gray. She's still in the thick of this somehow. Make sure you flash all four of the pictures I put in your files—you never know." Nikki kicked herself for waiting this long to let the Padilla investigation shift into this mode. Unfortunately, the reality of the job was such that as much as she tried to invest in each case to the eyeballs, at a certain point, it did become a matter of triage. It had to. Cassidy Towne was the high-profile victim, and meanwhile the Esteban Padillas of the world got nicknames like Coyote Man or, worse, slipped through the cracks anonymously. The saving grace, she thought, if there was one, was that Cassidy's murder might be a step to solving his. That kind of justice was better than none. At least that's how, if you were a detective with a conscience like Nikki Heat, you lived with it.

"Lauren give you a TOD for the concierge?" said Ochoa.

"Yes, one more wrinkle."

Raley clutched his heart melodramatically. "I don't know how many shocks I can take, Detective."

"Do your best. Derek Snow's murder was the same night as Cassidy Towne's. Lauren's best window is midnight to three A.M."

"In other words . . . ," said Raley.

"Right," Heat answered. "Roughly an hour or two before Cassidy's."

"And just after his call to Soleil," said Rook.

She stood and swirled the last of her coffee in the cup. "Tell you what I'm going to do. While you get to work on Mr. Padilla, I'm going to go have another chat with Soleil Gray and challenge her on her lack of candor."

"Yes," said Rook, "she has given us quite a song and dance."

The others didn't even bother to groan. They just got up and left him sitting on the bench, alone. A Jack Russell tied to a bike rack, waiting for its owner, looked over at him. Rook said, "Cats, huh? Can't live with 'em, can't seem to catch 'em."

Just minutes later, Heat and Rook approached Soleil Gray's apartment in a slightly more Village-y block of the East Village. To get there, they walked, passing head shops, tattoo parlors, and a vinyl music walk-down. It was that time of evening when there was just enough light left to see the pink jet contrails overhead in the teal of the gloaming. Dozens of small birds chirped as they found roosts for the night in the canopies of trees set in the sidewalk. In the morning the trees would make excellent platforms for garbage swoops. Threading through a crowd waiting on the sidewalk outside La Palapa, Rook spied some mighty inviting margaritas at the window tables and, for one, brief, impulsive flash, wished he could just lace his arm through Nikki's and steer her inside for some serious downtime.

He knew better. More to the point, he knew her better.

A housekeeper answered on the squawk box in the vestibule. "Miss Soleil no here. You come back." Her voice was old, and she sounded sweet and small. Rook imagined that she might even actually be inside the little aluminum panel.

Back down on the sidewalk, Nikki flipped through her notes, found a number, and called Allie, the assistant at Rad Dog Records. After a short conversation, she closed her phone and said as she started walking, "Soleil is at a TV studio rehearsing a set for a guest appearance tonight. Let's surprise her and see what shakes loose."

As they strode by, Rook looked longingly at a deuce that had just opened up in La Palapa. Downtime would have to wait. He hurried to catch up with Nikki, who was already at the corner getting out her car keys.

His brake lights turned the weeds red as Raley backed the Roach Coach into the driveway that went nowhere but a small vacant lot between a taqueria and a three-story row house that was listed as Esteban Padilla's address. "Careful, man, don't hit that shopping cart," from Ochoa.

Raley gophered his neck for a better view in the mirror. "I see it."

When the bumper tapped the cart, his partner laughed. "See, this is why we can't have a nice car."

All the parking spaces on East 115th Street were taken, and there was a beer delivery truck double-parked across the loading zone. The truck couldn't unload in the space because it was occupied by a small beater with a fender made of Bond-O and a windshield full of tickets. So Raley improvised, parking nose out, bridging the sidewalk, front tires on the street, the back ones where the dirt and sparse clumps of grass met concrete.

East Harlem, *El Barrio*, had the highest crime rate in the borough, but that rate also had experienced a huge drop in recent years, roughly 65 to 68 percent, depending on whose figures you liked. Raley and Ochoa felt obvious, looking every inch like cops, even in plainclothes. They also felt safe. Crime rate notwithstanding, this was a community of families. They were experienced enough to know that low income didn't spell danger. Ask people with experience in both places, and you'd be surprised how many felt a lost wallet had a better chance on Marin Boulevard than on Wall Street.

The pleasant warmth of the fall day was siphoning off and the evening was cooling fast. A clank of bottles made them turn. In front of Padilla's place a man his age, about thirty-five, was stacking full black plastic garbage bags on the mound that ran along the street. He clocked the two detectives as they approached, but stayed with his work, keeping an eye on them peripherally as he went.

"*Buenos noches,*" said Ochoa. When the man bent to pick up his next garbage bag without acknowledging him, the detective continued in Spanish, asking him if he lived there.

The man flung the trash bag in a V he had created between his two other bags, and waited to make sure they would stay put. When he was satisfied, he turned to face them. He asked the two cops if there was some sort of trouble.

Ochoa continued in Spanish and told him no, that he was investigating the murder of Esteban Padilla. The man told him Esteban was his cousin and he had no idea who killed him or why. He said it loudly, gesturing with a large double wave of his palms to them. Raley and

Ochoa had seen this many times before. Padilla's cousin was signaling that he was not a snitch, to them and, more importantly, to anyone who was watching.

He knew it was probably futile, but Detective Ochoa told him there was a killer loose who had murdered his cousin, asking if they could just talk about it, inside, in private. The cousin said there was no point; he didn't know anything and neither did anyone else in the family.

Under the harshness of the orange streetlight that hummed above them, Ochoa tried to read the man's face. What he saw there wasn't a dodge, it was theater masking fear. And not necessarily fear of the killer. This was about the eyes and ears that could be taking all this in at that moment on a street in Spanish Harlem. The Stop Snitching code was a more powerful law than any Raley and Ochoa could bring. As the man turned and walked in through the front door of Padilla's house, Ochoa knew it was even stronger than wanting justice for the death of a relative.

Later On with Kirby MacAlister, a talk show in a wrestling match with Craig Ferguson and the Jimmies, Kimmel and Fallon, for the late-night after-crowd, was broadcast live out of a leased studio on West End Avenue. Its first five years on the air, the syndicated show had taped out of a former strip club in Times Square, a spit take from Letterman's shop in the Ed Sullivan Theater. But when one of the daytime dramas moved west to LA, *Later On* jumped at the chance to show off its success by grabbing the soap's stage and modern production offices.

In the lobby window, looking out on West End, Nikki finished her cell phone call and stepped over to join Rook by the security counter. "What's our status?" she asked.

Rook said, "They're sending a production assistant down to take us upstairs to the studio. What was the call?"

"Forensics. They were able to pull a couple of decent fingerprints off the cartridge of that typewriter ribbon I found in the subway."

"Score another one for us. Although, with all the people who must have handled it, how will they know whose is whose?"

"I have a feeling these were the Texan's," she said. "Seeing how they were the only ones with blood on them."

"Hey. You're the detective . . ."

Heat could tell by Soleil Gray's reaction when she and Rook entered the back of the studio that Allie had not called to tip her off they were coming. The performer was running the same routine with the male dancers they had seen her working at the rehearsal hall, only this time she was singing live to the track. The song was a hard-driving rocker called "Navy Brat," Nikki guessed, judging by the repeat of the phrase in the chorus. It would also explain why the boys were in white sailor suits. Soleil's wardrobe was a one-piece sequined white bathing suit with admiral's epaulettes. Hardly regulation, but it had the advantage of showing off her stunning gym-rat figure.

She spun two cartwheels across the stage into the waiting arms of three sailors, but made a sloppy landing. Soleil waved her arms to stop the track, and when it chopped to a halt, she blamed the sailors. Nikki knew it had happened because she was distracted by her.

The stage manager called a crew break. As the camera operators and stagehands left for the exits, Heat and Rook approached Soleil on stage. "I don't have time for this. I'm on live TV at midnight, and in case you didn't notice, this sucks ass."

"I don't know," said Rook. "You've got me counting the days to Fleet Week."

The singer pulled a robe on. "Do we have to do this right now? Here?"

"No, not at all," said Nikki. "If you'd like, we can do this in about a half hour at my precinct."

"In a more official setting," said Rook with a wink to Nikki.

"Might cut into your rehearsal a bit, Soleil. And you're right. You can use it." Heat had decided on the drive over that this was going to be about intimidation and shaking the tree.

"You don't have to be a bitch."

"Then make it so I don't have to be. This is a homicide investigation and I had to come back to you because you lied to me. Starting with saying you were with Allie when in fact you left her early in the night."

Soleil's eyes darted around. She took a step as if to go, but stayed.

"OK, here's the deal. It's a reflex thing. Whenever I have something to handle like a detail thing, I always refer it to the record company."

"That's weak," said Nikki.

"That's the truth. Besides, I told you, I was also with Zane. Did you talk to Zane?"

"Yes, and he said you were with him at the Brooklyn Diner for all of about ten minutes."

Soleil shook her head. "That bastard. So much for having my back."

"Let's forget about where you were, or weren't, that night."

"Fine by me," said the singer.

"Why did you lie to me about not having contact recently with Cassidy Towne?"

"Probably 'cause it was no big deal, didn't register."

"Soleil, you knocked her out of her chair in the middle of a restaurant. You called her a pig and threatened to stab her in the back."

She sighed and rolled her eyes to the ceiling, as if her answer could be found among the suspended rigs holding the stage lighting. "Well," she finally said, "think about how she died. Why do you think I didn't want to tell you what I said to her?"

Heat had to admit there was logic to that, but she responded, "I am trying to find a killer. Every time you lie to me, you're making yourself look more guilty and making me waste valuable time."

"Fine, whatever."

Heat brought out some pictures. "Have you ever seen this man?"

Soleil examined the DMV photo of Esteban Padilla. "Nope."

"What about this man?" She handed her the police sketch of the Texan. "Ever see him?"

"Nuh-uh. Looks like the *Bad Santa* guy." She gave Nikki a smug smile.

"And what about him? Do you know him?" Nikki handed her a head shot of Derek Snow at his autopsy and watched the arrogance melt off her face.

"Oh, my God . . ." She let the picture flutter to the floor.

Heat said, "His name was Derek. The same Derek you popped a cap on in the Dragonfly House last December. Is that the Derek you got a call from when you were with Zane Taft? I'm asking because you left the Brooklyn Diner and this man, Derek Snow, was murdered shortly after that."

"I can't . . . I . . ." Soleil's face went ashen.

"We're talking two people connected to you who were killed that night, Soleil. You think good and hard and tell me what's going on. Was Cassidy Towne writing something about you? And I want the truth, no more lying."

"I have nothing more to say to you."

The crew was coming back onto the set. Soleil Gray pushed through them as she ran out. Rook said, "Aren't you going to try to hold her?"

"For what? I can charge her with lying to a police officer? Go back in time and hit her with illegal discharge of a firearm? That's not getting me anywhere. The record company lawyers would have her out in time to sing on tonight's show. I'd rather save that card for when it would do me some good. Right now, what I want to do is keep pressure on her and let her freak."

"All right. But if she blows that cartwheel tonight, it's on you."

They waited around in their back row seats for rehearsal to resume. In Nikki's experience, sometimes difficult people had changes of heart after she jammed them, and she wanted to give Soleil a breather to reflect and, perhaps, return in a more cooperative mode. But after they'd spent fifteen minutes in the freezing studio, the stage manager called a one-hour meal break and Soleil didn't come forward, so they left.

As they turned the corner into the hallway leading to the elevators, someone called out behind them, "Oh, my God. Is that Nikki Heat?"

She whispered, "I don't need this right now."

Rook said, "Maybe we can outrun this one."

"Nikki?" said the man.

Hearing his voice again, she stopped walking, and Rook watched a look cross over her, the annoyance transforming into dawning surprise. Then Nikki turned and her face lit up into a radiant smile. "Oh, my God!"

Rook twisted to look behind him at the lanky, sandy-haired guy in the V-neck and jeans approaching with his arms spread wide. Nikki ran to him, colliding with him, and they hugged. She squealed with glee and he laughed. And then they rocked each other back and forth, still hugging. Not sure what to do with himself, Rook shoved his hands in his pockets and looked on as the two pulled apart to hold each other at arm's length, beaming.

"Look at you," said Nikki. "With no beard."

"You look the same," he said. "No, better." Rook noticed his "r" had a guttural sound, not a burr like he was Scottish, but definitely an accent.

Then Nikki gave him a kiss. Brief, but—as Rook made note—full on the lips. Finally, still holding him by one arm, she turned to Rook and said, "This is Petar. My old boyfriend from college."

"No kidding." Rook put a hand out and they shook. "I'm Jameson."

"James?" he said.

"Jameson. And you're . . . Peter?" Rook was a man who could be proud of a cheap shot.

"No, Petar. Rhymes with 'guitar.' People make that mistake all the time."

"I can't get over this." Nikki gave Petar a shake with the arm she had around his waist. "I didn't even know you were in New York."

"Yes, I work here as one of the segment producers."

"Petar, that's great. So you're the producer?" she asked.

He looked sheepishly around the hall. "Shh, you'll get me fired. Not the producer, I'm a segment producer."

Rook made himself known. "You book the guests and do the pre-interviews."

"Very good. Jim knows his stuff."

Heat looked at Rook and smiled. "Jim. Love it."

Petar explained, "The pre-interviews are to help Kirby know what to ask his guests. They get about six minutes with him once they hit the chair, so I talk to them before the show and give him a list of suggested topics, maybe some funny story that happened to them."

"Sort of like being a ghost writer," said Rook.

Petar frowned. "Well, better than that. I do get my name in the credits. Listen, I have some time, do you want to come to the green room for something to eat or drink? We could catch up."

Rook tried to get Nikki's eye. "We'd love to but—"

"We'd love to," said Nikki. "We can spare a few minutes."

The show was a live broadcast, so it wasn't on for hours; therefore the green room was all theirs. Rook began to feel, what . . . ? Sullen. He had hoped to take Nikki out to dinner, but there they sat, filling up on Thai chicken skewers and smoked salmon wraps.

"This has turned into a day of good omens. First, five minutes ago, Soleil Gray suddenly canceled for some unknown reason." Heat turned to catch Rook's eye, but he was already doing the same with her. "So with her taking a powder that means one of my backup guests is coming in to take her segment, a feather for me. And now you, Nikki. How many years has it been?"

Nikki swallowed a tiny bite of salmon roll-up and said, "No, no. Let's not start counting years."

"No, let's," said Rook.

She dabbed her mouth with a napkin and said, "I met Petar when I took a semester abroad. I was in Venice studying opera production at the Gran Teatro La Fenice when I met this gorgeous film student from Croatia."

The accent, thought Rook. Rrr.

"We had this mad fling. Or at least I thought it was a fling. But when I came back to the States to resume my classes at Northeastern, who shows up in Boston?"

"Pete?" answered Rook.

Nikki laughed. "I couldn't send him back, could I?"

"No, you couldn't." And Petar laughed, too. Rook just kept himself busy twirling his satay in some peanut sauce.

Nikki and her old flame exchanged phone numbers and promised to get together and catch up. "You know," said Petar, "when I saw your article in that magazine, I thought of looking you up."

"But why didn't you?"

"I don't know, I wasn't sure what your life was. You know."

Rook chimed in. "It's pretty busy. In fact, Detective, we should get going."

"You are working on a big case?"

She looked around to make sure the room was clear and said, "Cassidy Towne."

Petar nodded and shook his head at the same time. Rook started trying to figure out how he did that and then decided not to.

"It was a shock. And then it also wasn't. She didn't have many friends, but I liked her."

"You knew her?" asked Nikki.

"Sure. Hard not to. In my job here I am constantly barraged by columnists, PR folks, book people. Some want to get authors on the show, some want to know who's on or, in Cassidy's case, how they behaved, who they were with, stories I might have heard that didn't make it on the air . . ."

"So you and Cassidy had some sort of relationship?" Rook tried to put just enough stink on it for Nikki to absorb with the most unsavory connotation.

"We had a great relationship," said Petar without equivocation. "Was she the warmest person in the world? No. Did she deal in human weakness? Yes. But I have to tell you, when I started this job, I almost didn't make the cut. Cassidy saw I was foundering and took me under her wing. Took me to boot camp on getting myself organized, hitting deadlines, how to manipulate PR flaks into getting their stars to come on our show first, ways to talk to the celebrities so they would let their guard down for the host interview . . . She saved my ass."

Nikki said, "I'm sorry, Petar, I stopped listening when you said she taught you to be organized."

"And hit deadlines, Nikki, can you believe it?"

While they laughed about some private memory, Rook could picture Petar ten years ago, a bewildered Croatian shuffling around her dorm, wearing her bathrobe, going "Nee-kee, no can find shoose."

When the laughter faded, Petar lowered his voice and moved closer to Nikki, his knee touching hers, Rook noticed. He also noticed she didn't move away. "I heard she was working on something."

"I knew that," said Rook. "Something big, too."

Nikki explained, "Rook was doing a profile of her."

Petar said, "Oh, so then she told you what it was?"

Rook couldn't tell if Petar knew or was fishing for what *he* knew, which could have been less than Petar knew, so he said, "Mm, not in so many words."

"I don't know, either." Petar used his forefinger to poke a caper off Nikki's plate. He stuck it on his tongue and said, "I heard about it from one of my publishing contacts. Cassidy was supposedly working on a tell-all book about someone. She was writing a tattler. And when it came out, some very powerful people were going to go to jail for a very long time."

ELEVEN

Jameson Rook got up at five the next morning to get his life back in order. After he showered and dressed, he ground beans for a pot of strong coffee then carried a broom, dustpan, and bucket of cleaning products down the hallway to his office to confront the shambles created by the Texan two days before. Standing there in the doorway, he paused to assess the post-tornado zone of his cozy writer's workplace: strewn files; emptied desk drawers; broken glass from pictures, awards, and framed magazine covers; banker's boxes of research clawed open and dumped; his own bloodstain dried on the floor; rummaged cabinets; scattered books; lamp shades off-kilter; the writer's chair that had become his prison—OK, he thought, actually, that one wasn't much of a change.

His view was a snapshot of personal violation, both disheartening and overwhelming. Rook couldn't figure out where to begin. So he did the only logical thing. He put the broom, the dustpan, and the cleaning products in the corner and sat down at his computer to Google Petar Matic.

He smiled as he typed in the name. Say it quickly and it sounded like an erotic toy. Best don't go there, he thought. Not if he wanted the morning to be about getting his life in order.

To his surprise, numerous Petar Matics came up. A prominent financial guy, a teacher, a Cleveland firefighter, and so on, but no hits on Nikki Heat's college beau. Not until the second screen page. The sole link was to a dated bio excerpted from a wildlife documentary film he had shot once in Thailand, *New Friends, Old Worlds*. It wasn't much of a mention. "A film student and adventurer from the village of Kamensko in Croatia who had resettled in the United States, Petar Matic was honored to received a grant for a film introducing the world to a host of newly discovered species." So Petar was one of those guys who shot footage of snakes with two tails and birds with hair under their wings.

Next he searched: "Petar Matic Nikki Heat" and was glad for no matches. He was especially relieved there was no link to any film project. He nudged out of his brain the image of Nikki and some Croatian Romeo as haunting green ghosts in some night vision video and started sweeping up broken glass.

About a half hour later his cell phone rang with the *Dragnet* theme. "Notice I'm calling you this time before I show up," said Nikki. "I'm around the corner, and you've got exactly two minutes to shoo the cougars."

"All of them? I'm growing fond of this one. In fact, hang on." He pretended to cover the mouthpiece and said, "Are you trying to seduce me, Mrs. Robinson?"

When he got back on, Nikki said, "Careful there, Rook. You'll give yourself another nosebleed."

She arrived with coffee that even she admitted was no match for his and a bag of warm Zucker's bagels seeing their first sunrise. "I figured I'd stay downtown this morning so we can go visit Cassidy Towne's editor right when the publishing house opens and then head up to the precinct from there." She saw something come across his face and said, "What?"

"Nothing. I just didn't know we'd be going to the publisher together, that's all."

"You don't want to come? Rook, you want to come everywhere. You're like a golden retriever with a Frisbee in your mouth the moment you hear car keys."

"Sure, of course, I want to go. I'm just bummed I didn't make more progress. It's still a FEMA site back there."

She brought her coffee and a gouged-out sesame bagel half to the office for an assessment. "You've hardly made a dent."

"Well, I got started, and then got on the computer and got caught up working on my Cassidy Towne piece."

Nikki looked at his monitor, where the *Big Lebowski* screen saver was engaged—a floating image of the Dude's head on a bowling ball.

Then her gaze drifted to the radio-controlled toy helicopter on the desk. She put her hand on the fuselage. "Still warm," she said.

"The bad guys don't stand a chance with you, Nikki Heat."

They had a half hour before they had to leave for the publisher, so Nikki began collecting loose papers off the floor. Rook found a home for the helicopter on the windowsill and said, as casually as he could make it sound for a man who was fishing, "Must have been bizarre seeing your old boyfriend like that."

"Blew me away, is what it did. Of all the gin joints, you know?" And then she said, "So you think he was one of Cassidy's conquests, do you?"

"What? Huh, I hadn't thought of it." He turned away quickly to scoop pens back into his souvenir mug from the Mark Twain Museum. "Is that what you think?"

"Don't really know. Sometimes it's nice to take someone at face value." She looked at him, and he turned away again, this time on paper clip patrol. "It was a different side to hear about Cassidy, helping someone out like she did for Pet."

Pet. Rook concentrated so he wouldn't roll his eyes. "Well, from what I saw of Cassidy, she was tough but she wasn't a monster. But I wouldn't say she was altruistic, either. I'm sure by helping Pete learn the ropes she was also building a relationship with a TV insider on a solid foundation of 'IOU.' "

"Did she have anybody who you would call a close friend?"

"From what I saw, no. She was wired to be a loner. That's not to say lonely. But her downtime was spent with her flowers, not people. Did you see the porcelain plaque screwed into her wall by the French doors? 'When life disappoints, there's always the garden.' "

"Sounds like Cassidy spent a lot of her time coping with disappointment."

"Still," he said, "you can't fault a person whose passion is for helping living things. Albeit vegetation."

Nikki hefted a pile of recovered papers and evened the corners by tapping them against her tummy. "I don't know where you want these filed, so I'll just make stacks on your credenza. At least you'll be able to walk around in here while you play with your toy chopper."

He worked alongside her, chucking anything that was broken into the kitchen trash can he had put in service. "You know, I like this little bit of shared domestic activity."

"Don't get any ideas," she said. "Although, mm-mm-mm. What says turn-on to a police gal more than cleaning up a crime scene?" The credenza was full, so Nikki set an armful of files on the desktop, and when she did, her arm grazed the space bar on Rook's keyboard, causing the screen saver to vanish. The Dude disappeared, exposing the Google search results for "Petar Matic Nikki Heat."

Rook wasn't sure she saw it, and he closed his laptop, muttering something about getting it out of her way. If she had seen it, she didn't let on. Rook forced himself to wait a few moments, working in silence. After a decent interval, he transitioned to shelving books, then casually dropped in a "Hey, I tried calling you last night but you didn't answer."

"I know" was all she said.

When they left the *Later On* studios the night before, Rook had pushed for a dinner date but she wasn't up for it, telling him that she was exhausted from the evening before.

"You mean our sex?" he had asked.

"Oh, yes, Rook, you wore me out."

"Really?"

"Feel good about you. If you recall, I had an altercation with the Texan right before our night of bliss. Followed by a pretty full day of trooping around on this investigation."

"I did all those things, too."

She crinkled her brow. "Pardon me, but did you actually fight with Tex? I thought it was more like sitting down in a chair and tipping over."

"You wound me, Nikki. You lash me with your mockery."

"No," she had said with undisguised lust, "that was the sash from my robe." It only made him ache all the more to share another night with her. But, as ever, Nikki Heat was protective of her independence. He'd taken a sulking cab ride back to Tribeca, his writer's imagination filling his head with possible consequences of reunited college sweethearts exchanging phone numbers.

He slid a volume of his *Oxford English Dictionary* into its home and said, "I almost didn't call. I was afraid I'd wake you up." He put another blue *OED* next to its companion before he added, "Because you said you were going to sleep."

"Are you checking up on me?"

"Me? Get real."

"I'll tell you if you want to know."

"Nik, I don't need to know."

"Because I wasn't home asleep when you called. I was out." For an avid poker player, he was masking his tells about as well as Roger Rabbit after a swig of whiskey. At last, she said, "I couldn't sleep so I went to the precinct. I wanted to run a check through an FBI database searching specific weapons and duct tape and persons with a history of torture. Sometimes an MO will jump out. I got nowhere last night, but I connected with an agent at the National Center for Analysis of Violent Crime in Quantico who's going to stay on it and see what kicks. I also got them the fingerprint partials we pulled off the typewriter ribbon."

"So all that time you were working?"

"Not *all* that time," she said.

So there it was. She had seen the Google screen. Or maybe she hadn't and she actually had connected with Petar. "Are you trying to torture me, Detective Heat?"

"Is that what you want, Jameson? Do you want me to torture you?" And with that, she finished her coffee and took her cup back to the kitchen.

———

"It's the code, man," said Ochoa. "It's that stupid code that keeps people from helping us." He and his partner Raley sat in the front seat of their unmarked across the street from the Moreno Funeral Parlor at 127th and Lex.

The door to the funeral home was still idle, so Raley let his gaze wander up the block to watch a MetroNorth train on the elevated tracks slowing for the Harlem station, last stop before depositing its freight of morning commuters from Fairfield County at Grand Central. "It makes no sense. Especially when it's family. I mean, they must know we're trying to find whoever killed their own kin."

"Doesn't have to make sense, Rales. The code says you don't snitch, no matter what."

"But whose code? Padilla's family doesn't show any banger ties."

"Don't have to. It's in the culture. It's in the music, it's on the street. Even if snitching doesn't get you whacked, it makes you the lowest. Nobody wants to be that. That's the rule."

"So what can we hope to do then?"

Ochoa shrugged. "I dunno. Maybe find the exception?"

A black van pulled up to the receiving door of the mortuary and honked twice. Both detectives looked at their watches. They knew OCME had released Esteban Padilla's body at eight A.M. It was now a quarter to nine, and they watched silently as the rolling metal door rose and two attendants emerged to offload the gurney and the dark vinyl bag containing the victim's remains.

Just after nine a white '98 Honda pulled up and parked. "Here we go," said Raley. But he cursed when the driver got out and the uncooperative cousin from the night before went inside the building. "So much for finding our exception."

They waited ten minutes without talking, and when nobody else arrived, Raley started the car. "I was thinking the same thing," said his partner as the Roach Coach pulled away from the curb.

Nobody answered their knock at Padilla's row house on East 115th. The detectives were just about to leave when a voice came through the door, asking who it was, in Spanish. Ochoa identified himself and asked if they could have a word. There was a long pause before a security chain slid, a deadbolt shot, and the door opened a crack. A teenage boy asked if he could see badges.

Pablo Padilla brought them to sit in the living room. Although the boy didn't say so, it seemed the invitation was not so much about hospitality as to get them all in off the street. Ochoa reflected on how this no-snitch thing was supposed to be about solidarity, but the eyes of the kid looked more like those of victims of terrorism he had seen. Or the townsfolk in some old Clint Eastwood Western who were scared of the tyrannical outlaw and his boys.

Since he was the Spanish speaker and was going to be doing the talking, Ochoa decided to go gently. "I'm sorry for your loss" was a good place to start.

"Did you find my uncle's killer?" was where the boy started.

"We're working on that, Pablo. That's why we're here. To help find who did this and arrest him so he can be sent away for good." The detective wanted to paint a picture of this person off the streets, impotent as a source of vengeance to anyone who cooperated.

The teenager absorbed that and looked appraisingly at the two cops. Ochoa noticed Raley was keeping a low profile, but was being eyes and ears. His partner seemed especially interested in numerous garment bags hanging on the back of a door. The boy picked up on it, too. "That is my new suit. For my uncle's funeral." The sound of his voice was broken but brave. Ochoa saw the water rimming his eyes and vowed never to call the vic Coyote Man again.

"Pablo, what you tell me here will be between us, understand? Same as if you called an anonymous tip line." The boy didn't respond, so he continued. "Did your uncle Esteban have any enemies? Anybody who wanted to harm him?"

The boy slowly shook his head before he answered. "No, I don't know anyone who would do this. Everybody liked him, he was always happy, a good dude, you know?"

"That's good," said Ochoa, while thinking, That's bad—at least for what he needed—but he smiled, anyway. Pablo seemed to relax a bit, and as the detective delicately asked him the usual questions about his uncle's friends, girlfriends, personal habits like gambling or drugs, the boy answered in the short-form way teenagers do, but he answered. "What about his work?" asked Ochoa. "He was a produce driver?"

"Yes, it wasn't what he liked, but he had experience as a driver, so that was what he got. You know, a job's a job sometimes, even if it's not as good."

Ochoa looked over to Raley, who had no idea what they were saying but could read his partner's look signaling he had hit a point of interest. Ochoa turned back to Pablo and said, "I hear that." Then, "I notice you said 'not as good.'"

"Uh-huh."

"Not as good as what?"

"Well . . . It's sort of embarrassing, but he's dead, so I guess I can say." The boy fidgeted and shoved his hands under his thighs so he was sitting on them. "My uncle had a, you know, classier job before. But a couple of months ago . . . well, he got fired all of a sudden."

Ochoa nodded. "That's too bad. What did he do when he got fired?" Pablo turned when he heard the keys in the front door, and the detective tried to get him back. "Pablo? What job did he get fired from?"

"Um, he was a driver for a limo company."

"And why did he get fired?"

The front door opened and Padilla's cousin, the one they had left at the funeral home came in. "What the hell's going on here?"

Pablo stood up, and his body language needed no translation even for Raley. It said this interview was over.

———

Even though Detective Heat didn't have an appointment, Cassidy Towne's editor at Epimetheus Books did not make her wait. Nikki announced herself in the lobby, and when she and Rook stepped off the elevator onto the sixteenth floor of the publishing house, his assistant was waiting. She keyed the code into the touchpad that opened the frosted glass doors to the offices and escorted them through a brightly lit hallway of white walls with blond wood accents. This was the nonfiction floor, so their path was decorated by framed covers of Epimetheus books, each a biography, exposé, or celebrity-rant best seller encased side by side with a reprint of its peak *New York Times* list.

They reached a bull pen area of three assistants' desks outside three wooden doors that were conspicuously larger than the others they had passed. The center door was open and the assistant led them in to meet the editor.

Mitchell Perkins smiled over a pair of black-rimmed bifocals, dropped them onto his blotter, and came around the desk to shake hands. He was cheerful and much younger than Nikki had expected for a senior editor of nonfiction—in his early forties, but with tired eyes. She quickly understood when she saw the piles of manuscripts spilling out of his étagère and even sprouting up from the floor beside his desk.

He gestured to a conversation area off to one side of his office. Heat and Rook sat on the couch; he took the armchair in front of the window that spanned his whole north wall, giving a spectacular unobstructed view of the Empire State Building. Even for the two visitors who had spent most of their lives in Manhattan, the panorama was awe-inspiring. Nikki almost remarked that the office could be used as a movie set with a backdrop like that, but it wasn't the proper tone for this meeting. First she had to offer condolences for the loss of an author. Then she had to ask him for his dead author's manuscript.

"Thank you for seeing us on short notice, Mr. Perkins," she began.

"Of course. When the police come, would I do anything but?" He turned aside to Rook and added, "These are unusual circumstances, but it's wonderful to meet you. We almost met last May at Sting and Trudie's Rainforest Benefit after-party, but you were in deep conversation with Richard Branson and James Taylor and I was a bit intimidated."

"No need for that. I'm just people."

So Rook, thankfully, provided the ice-breaking laugh, and Nikki could then steer to business. "Mr. Perkins, we're here about Cassidy Towne, and first of all, we're sorry for your loss."

The editor nodded and puckered his cheeks. "That's very thoughtful, certainly, but may I ask how you came to hear we may, or may not, have had some association with her?"

She wouldn't have been much of a detective if she hadn't noticed the thick smoke screen of his word choice. Perkins hadn't come out owning the simple fact that Cassidy was writing a book for him. He'd parsed. Nice guy, perhaps, but he was playing a chess game. So she decided to come straight up the gut. "Cassidy Towne was writing a book for you and I'd like to know what it was about."

The impact was visible. His eyebrows peaked and he recrossed his legs, shifting himself to get comfortable in his soft leather chair. "Well then, the small talk portion is over, I suppose." He smiled, but it lacked heart.

"Mr. Perkins—"

"Mitch. This will strike a more pleasant note for all of us if you'll call me Mitch."

Heat remained cordial but pressed the same theme. "What was her book about?"

He could play that game, too. His non-answer was to turn again to Rook. "I understand you were contracted by *First Press* to do five thousand words on her. Did she say something to you? Is that how we got here today?"

Rook never got a chance to respond. "Excuse me," Nikki said. She maintained the decorum Perkins had established but rose and moved away to lean with her hips on his desk so he had to twist and pivot away from Rook. "I am running an open homicide investigation and that means following every possible lead to find Cassidy Towne's killer. There are a lot of leads and not a lot of time, so—if I may?—how I got my information is how I got my information. How I got here is not your concern. And if striking a more pleasant note is what you want, let's begin with me asking the questions and you being direct and cooperative, all right . . . Mitch?"

He folded his arms across his chest. "Absolutely," he replied. She noted that he closed his eyes briefly as he said the words. Mitch was one of those.

"So can we start over again with my question? And if this helps, I do know she was working on a tattletale book, a tell-all."

He nodded. "Of course, that was her wheelhouse."

"So who or what was the subject?" She sat down again across from him.

"That I don't know." In anticipation of her, he held up a staying palm. "Yes, I can confirm we had a deal for a book with her. Yes, it was to be a tell-all. In fact, Cassidy guaranteed it would be newsworthy across the board, not just the tabloids and ambush TV shows. It would, in the parlance of the Paris Hilton generation, be hot. However." He closed his eyes again and opened them, making Nikki think of barn owls. "However . . . I can only say that I do not know the subject of her exposé."

"You mean you know and won't say," responded Heat.

"We are a major house. We trust our authors and give them great latitude. As such, Cassidy Towne and I operated on blind faith. She assured me she had a blockbuster book, I assured her I would get it to market. Now, sadly, we may never know what the subject was . . . Unless you can locate the manuscript."

Detective Heat smiled. "You know, and you're not telling. Cassidy Towne got a huge advance, and especially in this economy, that doesn't happen without a solid proposal and everybody signing off."

"Forgive me, Detective, but how would you know whether she got any advance, let alone a sizable one?"

Rook weighed in on that issue. "Because it was the only way she would be able to fund her network of tipsters. You know newspapers. She didn't have the budget from the *Ledger* to pay that tab. And she wasn't a wealthy woman."

Nikki added, "I can get into her bank records, and I bet I'll see a deposit from Epimetheus in a sum that says you knew exactly what you were buying."

"If you do, and there is such an advance, the linkage you insinuate is only conjecture." He said no more, and a beat of silence passed between them.

Nikki got out a business card. "Whoever this book was about could be the killer or lead us to the killer. If you change your mind, here's how to reach me."

He took her card and put it in his pocket without reading it. "Thank you. And if I may say, as good as Jameson Rook here is, his article barely did you justice. In fact, I'm starting to think there may even be a book in Nikki Heat."

For her, nothing could have more definitively ended the meeting.

———————

As soon as the elevator door closed, Nikki said, "Shut up."

"I didn't say anything." And then he smiled and added, "About a Nikki Heat book . . ."

The car stopped at the ninth floor and several people got on. Heat noticed that Rook had turned himself to the wall. "You all right?" she asked. He didn't answer, just nodded and scratched something on his forehead, covering half his face for the rest of the ride down.

At the ground floor, he let the elevator clear before he slowly got off.

Nikki was waiting for him. "Did you get bitten on the face by something?"

"No, I'm fine." He turned and speed-walked ahead of her, crossing the lobby at a fast pace. He had just put his hand on the door leading out to Fifth Avenue when Nikki heard a woman's voice echo across the marble.

"Jamie? Jamie Rook, is that you?" She was one of the women from the elevator, and something in the way Rook hesitated before he turned from the door to face her told Heat to hang back and watch this play out from the near distance.

"Terri, hello. Where's my head? I didn't see you." Rook stepped to her and they hugged, and Nikki saw a blush come to his face and blend with the scratch marks he had just excavated on his forehead.

When they separated, the woman said, "What are you doing coming here and not saying hello to your editor?"

"Actually, that's just what I was going to do, but then I got a call for an assignment I'm working on so I figured, next time." He looked up and caught Nikki watching and stepped around, presenting their backs to her.

"You'd better," said the editor. "Listen, I have to run, too. But you saved me an e-mail. Your manuscript is due back from copyediting next week. I'll ship it as an attachment as soon as it comes in, OK?"

"Sure thing." They embraced again, and the woman ran off to join her companions, who were holding a cab at the curb.

When Rook turned back toward Nikki, she was gone. He scanned the lobby, and his stomach tightened as he saw her over by Security, reading the building directory.

"You have an editor here?" she said as he approached. "I see a lot of book publishers in the building, but I don't see a listing for *First Press* magazine."

"Ah, no. They're in the Flatiron."

"No *Vanity Fair*, either."

"They're in the Condé Nast. Off Times Square." He touched her elbow. "We should get up to the precinct, huh?"

Heat ignored his prod. "So why would you have an editor here if it's all book publishers? Do you write books?"

He rocked his head side to side. "In a manner of speaking, yes."

"Now, that woman, Terri—your editor—got on at the ninth floor, as I recall."

"God, Nikki, do you always have to be such a cop?"

"And according to this"—she ran her finger along the glass covering the building directory—"the ninth floor is Ardor Books. What would Ardor Books be?"

The security guard at the counter beside them smiled and said, "Ma'am? Ardor Books is a romance fiction publisher."

Nikki turned back to Rook, but he wasn't there. He was speed-walking to the Fifth Avenue door again, thinking he had a chance in hell to escape.

TWELVE

oming into the bull pen with Rook twenty minutes later, Nikki thought there must be a SWAT operation or another suspicious vehicle discovery the way everyone was crowded around the TV. But that didn't seem likely, because she would have certainly picked up the chatter on the TAC frequencies during the drive up from the publishing house.

"What's the big news?" she asked anyone in the room. "Somebody else get fed up with the strike and set their trash on fire?"

"Oh, major story," said Detective Hinesburg. "All the TV choppers are on it. ACC has a coyote cornered at the north end of Inwood Park."

"That critter gets around," said Raley.

Rook stepped to the back of the circle rimming the TV. "Do they know if it's the same one that went after Coyote Man?"

Ochoa turned his way. "Hey, man, don't call him that, OK?"

Through split screens showing simultaneous aerial and telephoto ground video, they watched live as an animal control officer prepared to fire a tranquilizer dart at the coyote. Nikki, never one to be glued to a TV except for the major shared moments of truly breaking news, experienced an odd moment of being transfixed by the trapped animal, hunkered, peering out of the thicket above Spuyten Duyvil Creek. The ground-level camera was shooting from a distance, so the picture was wavy from air distortion and magnification, but the angle wasn't so different from the one she had had looking at the coyote that one morning in front of Cafe Lalo. That moment, unsettling as it had been, was for Nikki Heat rare contact with something wild, an untamed animal finding its way in a city alone. And, mostly, unseen. Yet here it was now; its life and existence couldn't be more public. Nikki was the one staring at it now, and she understood too well what she saw in its eyes this time.

The coyote shivered when the dart struck its coat, but then it immediately ran off, disappearing in dense brush on the steep hill. The news reporter said the dart hit and either glanced off or didn't stick. The aerial camera panned fruitlessly.

Detective Heat killed the TV with the remote, eliciting mock moans and protests as the squad gathered for the morning update.

Nothing connecting the three victims had yet surfaced from the CSU sweep of Derek Snow's apartment. Forensics was still running prints and samples, just to be sure. Nikki reported on her encounter with Soleil Gray at *Later On*, as well as the confirmation from a segment producer on the show that Cassidy Towne was at work on a tell-all scandal book. Rook cleared his throat, and she gave him a look that said, Don't you dare. She turned back to the squad. "That information was deemed credible based on a meeting Rook and I just had with the book editor. However, he claims not to know the subject of the book and says he doesn't have a manuscript."

"Bullshit," said Hinesburg.

Nikki, who heard enough profanity on the street not to enjoy it in the office, turned to the detective. "Sharon, I believe you're saying what we're all thinking." And then she smiled. "The rest of us had the poise just to think it."

When the laughs died down, Raley asked, "What about a search warrant?"

"I plan to look into that, Rales, but even with some of the more sympathetic judges we know, my gut says that's a tough one to get because of First Amendment issues. The whole idea of police looking through files at a book publisher conjures some unpleasant totalitarian connections for some people, go figure. But I'll try anyway."

Roach made their report on the Padilla ground they had covered. Ochoa said that for something that had looked like it might be nothing but dead ends because nobody would talk, they had ended up finding something pretty intriguing. "Our nobody produce truck driver was actually a former limo driver. Frustrating that it took so long for that to pop. Maybe one day the city can get all the systems so they talk to each other."

"Then what would we do?" said Nikki, her sarcasm eliciting a few chuckles.

"Anyway, we ran him through TLC," continued Raley, "and got the name of his old employer."

Ochoa picked up. "We also got with his produce truck boss. He says that Mr. Padilla had gotten an attorney and filed a wrongful dismissal suit against the limo company. Figured we'd check out the lawyer first before we hit the limousine dudes. That way we'll know what we're walking into."

"Know who the attorney is?" asked Raley. "None other than Ronnie Strong."

The whole room groaned and then began a unison, albeit ragged, chorus of the tagline from the sleazy lawyer's local TV commercials. "Been done wrong? Call Ronnie Strong!"

"Nice work, Roach," Heat said. "Absolutely, get over and see that attorney. Judging from his commercials, I'd bring some hand sanitizer." And as she gathered up her files, she added, "And if either of you comes back here wearing a neck brace, you're dead to me."

———

Detective Heat had a gift waiting for her when she got over to her desk. An encrypted e-mail from the FBI agent at NCAVC in Quantico. It was from the data analyst she had befriended the night before, and when she clicked the e-mail open, the top half of her screen filled with a color photograph of the Texan. The police sketch Nikki had provided was underneath and it was nearly an exact match. She stared at both and then had to remind herself to breathe. Nikki wasn't sure if her reaction was due to the memory of his assault or the excitement of zeroing in on him. Either one was enough to kick her heart rate up a notch.

A brief note from the NCAVC analyst said, "I'd like to take credit for the quick ID, but this is what happens when cops give good data. Your counterparts around the country could take a lesson, Detective

Heat. You can thank me by bringing this one down." Nikki scrolled to read the sheet the agent had put together for her.

His name was Rance Eugene Wolf. "Male, cauc, forty-one. 6'-1", 160. Born/raised in Amarillo, TX, by his father after the disappearance of his mother when subject was in middle school. Local police investigated the mother's sudden miss-pers on a drive to Plainview to visit relatives with the son/subj., who was found alone in a motel room off Hwy 27. Husband was cleared and case went cold as unsolved/runaway. Interesting to note the son/subj. was questioned five times over two years, including by a psychologist. No comments, no disposition.

"Subject's father continued to live/work in Amarillo as a veterinarian. Subject-Rance worked in practice, trained in, and was accredited for surgical assists." Nikki pictured the array of sharp instruments on Rook's counter. She raised her head to look at the whiteboard and the autopsy photos of Cassidy Towne's perforated ear canal. She turned back to read on.

"No connections made at time, but new data search based on Det. Heat info/subj. MO with pick-tools and duct tape shows hits on unsolved animal mutilations in Amarillo vicinity corresponding to subj.'s residence there.

"Subj. enlisted US Army, completing two tours Ft. Lewis/Tacoma, WA, as military police. MP records provided first hit on the fingerprint provided by NYPD-Det. Insp. Heat. Data delayed on link to mutilations (human & animal) in vicinity during service hitch due to duplicate suspect MOs in area—will update." Nikki could imagine what a sadist with a badge could do and expected some hits.

"Following hon. discharge, subj. took security job at Native Am. casino near Olympia, WA, for one year, leading to sim. detail at casino in Reno, NV (6 months), then moved to Las Vegas (4 yrs) working high-end VIP security for major casino [all casino names and employer info listed at end of this memo]. Subj. then recruited as contractor/agent for Hard Line Security of Henderson, NV (see Licensing Commission ID photo, above). Subj. rapidly promoted on basis of personal protection skills and comity with celebrity and VIP clients. OF NOTE: Subj. detained in knife assault upon threat suspect to visiting client Italian communications tycoon. Incident resulted in subj.'s arrest. Charges dropped due to lack of witnesses willing to testify. Alleged weapon was knuckle knife, described in LV police report (attached) but never recovered.

"Immediately following disposition of assault case, subj. left US to freelance in Europe. Current information ends there. Will maintain database search and contact Interpol. Will apprise as new info avail."

Rook finished reading a full minute after Heat did because he wasn't as adept at the police jargon and abbreviations as the detective—but he certainly understood the significance. "This guy made his career working with celebrities and VIP clients. Someone is paying him to cover something up."

"No matter what it takes," Nikki said.

————

Heat immediately made copies of the dispatch and fast-tracked their circulation both in the squad and in the usual places out in the field, including ERs and other medical facilities, like the ones Roach had canvassed the morning after the Texan's escape. She also assigned detectives to recontact previously interviewed witnesses to see if they recognized him now that they had a picture, not just a sketch.

Nikki also spent some time back at the murder board, studying all the names on it. Rook came up behind her and voiced her thoughts. "Time line isn't your friend so much now, is it?"

"No," she said. "Case has been bending the other way for the last thirty-six hours, but now it's pointing in a different direction. With a pro killer on this level we're off alibis and totally onto motives." She tacked up the color photo of Rance Eugene Wolf beside the sketch and stepped away from the whiteboard. "Saddle up. I want to revisit some of these myself," she told Rook.

"You mean the dog walker I heard was such a fan, Miss Heat?"

"No, definitely not that one." And on the way out, she paused at the door and said in a British accent, "The adulation. Sometimes it bores me so."

Cassidy Towne's nosy neighbor was easy to find. Mr. Galway was at his usual post on West 78th, in front of his town house grinding his teeth at the rising wall of uncollected garbage. "Can't you police do something?" he said to Nikki. "This strike is threatening the health and safety of the citizens of this city. Can't you arrest someone?"

"Who?" asked Rook. "The union or the mayor?"

"Both," he snapped. "And you can go in the clink with them for having such a smart mouth."

The old fossil said he never saw the guy in the picture, but asked to keep it in case he showed up again. Back in the car, Rook suggested that Rance Eugene Wolf would have done them all a favor if he had just gone to the wrong address, which earned an arm swat from Nikki.

Chester Ludlow said he had never seen Wolf before, either. Ensconced at his usual corner in the Milmar Club, he didn't even seem to want to touch the photo, let alone keep it. The duration of his observation of the picture barely qualified as a glance.

Heat said, "I think you should take another, more careful look, Mr. Ludlow."

"You know, I preferred when people still called me 'Congressman' Ludlow. With that form of address, they very seldom told me what I could and couldn't do."

"Or, apparently, who," said Rook.

Ludlow narrowed his eyes at him and then smiled thinly. "I see you still roam Manhattan without neckwear."

"Maybe I like borrowed ties. Maybe I like the way they smell."

"I'm not ordering you to do anything, sir." Nikki paused to let him enjoy her white lie of respect. "You did say you retained a private security firm to gather information on Cassidy Towne. Well, this man worked for such a firm, and I would like to know if you ever saw him."

The disgraced politician sighed and took a longer look at Wolf's ID shot. "The answer's the same."

"Have you ever heard the name Rance Wolf?"

"No."

"Maybe he had another name?" she asked. "Talked with a Texas drawl, soft-spoken?"

"No. Y'all."

Nikki took back the photo he was holding out to her. "Did you employ a firm called Hard Line Security for your inquiry?"

He smiled. "With all due respect, Detective, they don't sound expensive enough to be a firm I would hire."

Since it was past noon and they were on the East Side, Rook said lunch was on him at E.A.T. up near 80th and Madison. After she ordered her spinach and chèvre salad and he put in for a meat loaf sandwich, Nikki said, "So you're still not going to talk about it?"

He feigned innocence. "Still not going to talk about what?"

She mocked him: "What? What?" Her iced tea arrived and she peeled the straw wrapper thoughtfully. "Come on, seriously, it's me. You can tell me."

"I'll tell you what. . . . This table is wobbly." He grabbed a sugar packet and ducked under the table, then came up seconds later, testing the adjustment. "Better?"

"Now I understand why you were so hesitant about going with me to the publisher this morning." He shrugged, so she pressed. "Come on. I promise not to judge. Have you seriously been trying to break in as a romance fiction writer?"

"Trying to break in?" He cocked his head and grinned. "Trying? Lady, I am in. I am so in."

"OK . . . how are you in? I've never seen one of your books. I've even Googled your name."

"For shame," he said. "OK, here's the deal. It's not uncommon for magazine writers to supplement their income. Some teach, some rob banks, some do a little ghostwriting here and there. I do mine there."

"At Ardor Books?"

"Yes."

"You write bodice rippers?"

"Romance fiction, please. You might say I make some pretty handy side money as one of their authors."

"I know 'romance fiction' a little bit. What name do you use? Are you Rex Monteeth, Victor Blessing?" She paused and pointed at him. "You're not Andre Falcon, are you?"

Rook leaned forward and beckoned her closer. After a glance side to side at the other tables, he whispered, "Victoria St. Clair."

Nikki shrieked a laugh, causing every head in the place to turn. "Oh, my God! You're Victoria St. Clair?!!"

He hung his head. "It's nice to see that you're not judging."

"You? Victoria St. Clair?"

"No judging here. This is more like straight to the execution."

"Rook, come on. This is big. I've read Victoria St. Clair. There's nothing to be ashamed of." And then she laughed, but covered her mouth with her hand, stopping herself. "Sorry, sorry. I was just thinking about what you said the other day about everybody having a secret life. But you. You're an A-list magazine writer, a war correspondent, you've got two Pulitzers . . . *and* you're Victoria St. Clair? This is so . . . I dunno . . . beyond secret."

Rook turned to the restaurant, to see all the faces staring, and said, "Not so much anymore."

———————

Roach entered the law offices of Ronnie Strong on a floor below the DMV in Herald Square, and both detectives felt as if they had walked into the waiting room of an orthopedic practice. A woman with both hands fully casted so that only the tips of her fingers were visible was dictating instructions to a teenage boy, probably her son, who was helping her fill out an intake form. A man in a wheelchair with no visible injury also completed paperwork. A strapping construction worker whose chair was flanked by two Gristedes bags of receipts and paperwork gave them a sharp look and said, "He ain't here, fellas."

The receptionist was a very pleasant woman in a conservative suit but with a fish hook in her lip. "Gentlemen, have you been done wrong?"

Ochoa turned so he wouldn't laugh and muttered to Raley, "Hell, it's been a while since I was even done."

Raley maintained his composure and asked to see Mr. Strong. The receptionist said he was out of the office, making a new series of commercials, and that they could come back tomorrow. Raley flashed his tin and got the address of the studio.

It wasn't much of a surprise to Roach that Ronnie Strong, Esq., was not in his law offices that day. The joke in the legal profession was that Ronnie Strong might have passed the bar, but he couldn't pass a TV camera.

The production facility he used was a graffitied brick warehouse abutting a Chinese import distribution center in Brooklyn. Situated halfway between the old Navy Yard and the Williamsburg Bridge, it wasn't exactly Hollywood, but then Ronnie Strong wasn't exactly an attorney.

There was nobody stopping Raley and Ochoa, so they just walked in. The front office was empty and smelling of coffee and cigarette smoke that had fused with the water-stained Tahitian-themed wallpaper. Raley called a "Hello?" but when nobody responded, they followed the short hallway to the blaring sound of the same jingle the squad had recited that morning. "Been done wrong? Call Ronnie Strong! Been done wrong? Call Ronnie Strong! Been done wrong? Call Ronnie Strong!"

The door to the stage was wide open. Clearly, these were no sticklers for sound aesthetics. When the detectives walked in, they both took a quick step back. The studio was so small, they were afraid they were going to walk into the shot.

On the set, which was a rented motor boat on a trailer, two buxom models in scant bikinis wore props indicating some sort of accident. One had her arm in a sling; the other stood on crutches, although without a cast. That could have been a budget saver, although more likely it was to keep her legs visible.

"Let's go one more time," said a man in a Hawaiian shirt, chewing an unlit cigar.

Raley whispered to Ochoa, "Bet he's the owner. He matches the wallpaper."

Ochoa said, "It's an unfair world, partner."

"How so . . . this time?"

"Nikki Heat, she goes to a TV studio, it's polished marble and glass in the lobby, green room with hot and cold running canapés, and what do we get?"

"Know what I think, Detective Ochoa? I think we've been wronged."

"And, action!" called the director, and he added for clarity, "Go!"

Both actresses reached down into a bait box and came up with handfuls of cash. There seemed to be no concern that the one in the arm sling had full utility of the limb. She's the one who smiled and said, "Justice is no accident." To which the other held up her loot and shouted, "Been done wrong? Call Ronnie Strong!"

That was when Ronnie Strong himself, who looked something like an overripe pear in a toupee, popped up from the hatch between them and said, "Did somebody call me?" The girls hugged him, each planting a kiss on a cheek as the jingle played, "Been done wrong? Call Ronnie Strong! Been done wrong? Call Ronnie Strong! Been done wrong? Call Ronnie Strong!"

"And we're clear," said the director. And then for good measure, "Stop."

Roach didn't have to get the lawyer's attention. Ronnie Strong had spotted them during the commercial, and both detectives would know when it aired that his side-stage eye line when he said, "Did somebody call me?" was directly to them. Such were the small perks of police work.

While the girls left to change into nurse uniforms, Ronnie Strong beckoned them over to the boat. "You want some help down?" asked Ochoa.

"No, we're doing the next one in the boat, too," he said. "It's a nurses script, but hey, I rented it for the day. You guys are cops, right?"

Roach flashed ID, and the lawyer sat down to rest on the gunwale close to Raley. Rales couldn't stop staring at the orange makeup ringing Strong's white collar, so he concentrated on the hairpiece, which had a sweat curl in the front that was starting to expose the tape.

"You boys ever get hurt on the job? Suffer hearing loss from the firing range, maybe? I can help."

"Thanks just the same, but we're here to talk about one of your clients, Mr. Strong," said Ochoa. "Esteban Padilla."

"Padilla? Oh, sure. What do you want to know? Saw him yesterday, he's still pressing charges."

Ochoa tried not to make eye contact with Raley, but peripherally, he caught his partner turning away to mask a chuckle. "Esteban Padilla is dead, Mr. Strong. He was killed several days ago."

"Wrongful death, I hope? Was he operating any machinery?"

"I know you have a lot of clients, Mr. Strong," offered Raley.

"You bet," said the lawyer. "And they all get personal service."

Raley continued, "I'm sure they do. But let us refresh your memory. Esteban Padilla was a limo driver who got fired last spring. He came to you with his complaint."

"Right, right, and we filed a wrongful dismissal." Ronnie Strong tapped a forefinger on his temple. "It's all in here. Eventually."

"Can you tell us what the grounds were for the case?" asked Ochoa.

"Sure, give me a sec. OK, got it. Esteban Padilla. He's this good kid from Spanish Harlem. Making a nice living, an honest living, driving stretch limos for years. And he did it all, the long ones, the town cars, the Hummers . . . Those stretch Hummers are awesome, aren't they, fellas? Anyway, eight years of loyal service to those rat bastards and they just can him without cause. I asked him if there was some reason, anything. Was he stealing, was he schtupping clients, did he give his boss the finger? Nothing. Eight years and, bam, done.

"I told this kid, 'You've been wronged.' I told him we'd sue them to their socks, clean them out so he'd never have to worry another day in his life."

"What happened to the case?" said Ochoa.

Strong shrugged. "Never got anywhere."

"What?" said Raley. "You decided you didn't have a case?"

"Oh, I had a case. We were ready to rock and roll. Then all of a sudden Padilla comes to me and says drop it, Ronnie. Just drop the whole deal."

Roach made eye contact. Ochoa's nod to his partner told him he could ask it. Raley said, "When he came to you and said to forget the whole thing, did he say why?"

"No."

"Did he seem nervous, agitated, fearful?"

"No. It was weird. He was the most relaxed I'd ever seen him. In fact, I'd even say he seemed happy."

Roach's visit to the Rolling Service Limousine Company in Queens was not as entertaining or half as cordial as the one they had just paid to Ronnie Strong. The surroundings, however, were about as refined.

They made their way through the service bays, past rows of black cars getting buffed and polished in the huge warehouse, until they found the manager's office. It was a squalid glass box in a back corner, next to a toilet with a grimy door sign that had an arrow on it that could be twisted from "occupied" to "occupeed."

The manager made them stand and wait while he took a complaint from a client who'd been left stranded at the curb at Lincoln Center during one of the Fashion Week events and wanted restitution. "What can I say to you?" said the manager, looking right at the detectives, taking his time while he talked. "This was weeks ago and you call just now? And I checked with my driver, and he said you were not there when he came. It's your word against his. If I listened to everyone who said this, I would not have money to do my business."

Ten minutes later, the passive-aggressive tyrant finished and hung up. "Customers," he said.

Raley couldn't resist. "Who needs 'em, right?"

"I hear that," the little man said without irony. "Total pain in the ass. What do you want?"

"We're here to ask you about one of your former drivers, Esteban Padilla." Ochoa watched the skin tighten on the manager's face.

"Padilla doesn't work here anymore. I have nothing to say."

"He was fired, right?" Roach was going to get their ten minutes back and then some.

"I cannot discuss personnel issues."

"You just did with that client," said Raley. "So give it up for us. Why was he fired?"

"These are confidential matters. I don't even remember."

Ochoa said, "Hold on, you've got me confused. Which is it, confidential or no memory? I want to have this right when I go from here to the Taxi and Limousine Commission to get your operating permit reviewed."

The manager sat in his chair, rocking, processing. At last he said, "Esteban Padilla was let go for insubordination to passengers. We made a change, simple as that."

"After eight years, the man was suddenly a problem? Doesn't wash for me," said Ochoa. "Does it wash for you, Detective Raley?"

"Not even a little, partner."

The detectives knew the surest way to make a lie cave in under its own weight was to go for the facts. Nikki Heat had told them it was the subheading for her Rule #1: "The time line is your friend."—"When you get a whiff of BS, go for specifics."

"You see, sir, we're involved in a homicide investigation, and you just gave us some information that one of your clients may have had a grudge against your driver, the murder victim. That's something that sounds to us like cause to ask you who the clients were who complained about Mr. Padilla." Raley folded his arms and waited.

"I don't remember."

"I see," said Raley. "If you thought about it, might you remember?"

"Probably not. It's been a while."

Ochoa decided it was time for more facts. "Here's what I think will help. And I know you want to help. You keep records of your rides, right? I mean, you're required to. And I even see you have the one on your desk from that complaint call you just took, so I know you have them. We're going to ask you to give us all your manifests for all the rides Esteban Padilla booked prior to his dismissal. We'll start with four months' worth. How's that sound to you versus a nasty inspection from the TLC?"

––––––––

Two hours later, back at the precinct, Raley, Ochoa, Heat, and Rook sat at their respective desks poring over the limousine manifests for Esteban Padilla's bookings during the months leading up to his dismissal. It was slightly more exciting than screening Cassidy Towne's reused typewriter ribbon days before. But it was the donkey work, the desk work, that got to the facts. Even though they didn't exactly know what facts they were looking for, the idea was to find something . . . someone . . . that connected to the case.

Ochoa was refilling his coffee, rolling his head to loosen his cramped shoulder muscles, when Raley said, "Got one."

"Whatcha got, Rales?" asked Heat.

"Got a name here for a ride he gave to someone we've talked to." Raley pulled a manifest from the file and went to the center of the room. As the others gathered before him, he held up the sheet in front of him, under his chin, so the others could see the name.

THIRTEEN

In the new Yankee Stadium, on an off day for the Pinstripes, a trainer and a hitting coach stood a few yards behind Toby Mills, watching him make slow swings with a bat weighted by a donut on its barrel. It was an oddity to see Mills holding lumber. Pitchers in the American League seldom appear at the plate—the exceptions being occasional interleague contests like the Subway Series, and, of course, World Series games played at rival parks. With the Bombers on pace to clinch another pennant and invade a National League park soon, it was time for their star pitcher to get some BP. As he made slow, easy arcs, the staff studied him, but not to assess his skills. They wanted to see how his weight was transferring on his legs after his hamstring pull. All they cared about was if he was healthy, if he would be ready.

Two other pairs of eyes were also on Toby Mills. Heat and Rook stood in the first row of seats above the Yankee dugout. "For a pitcher, he's got one helluva swing," said Nikki, not taking her eyes off the player.

Rook watched him take another cut and said, "I don't know how you can tell. I mean, if he hits the ball, fine. I can say, 'Yeah, good hit,' but this . . . To me, it's just mime. Or shadowboxing. How can you know?"

Now she did turn to him. "Rook, did you ever play Little League?" When he answered with a dopey grin, she said, "Ever go to a game?"

"Give me a break. I was raised by a Broadway diva. I can't help it if I'm more *Damn Yankees* than real Yankees. Does that make me less of a person?"

"No. What it makes you is a romance writer."

"Thanks. So glad you're not going to needle me or anything."

"Oh, if you think this is going away, you're living in a dreamworld. A dreamworld set on a turn-of-the-century plantation in Savannah—Miss St. Clair."

"I thought we had an agreement," came the voice behind them. They turned to see Jess Ripton storming down the steps toward them. Toby's manager was still a good ten rows away, but he continued barking as he approached, speaking as if he were right beside them. "Didn't we have an understanding you'd contact me and not ambush my client?"

He was closing in but still far enough away for Rook to mutter an aside to Nikki. "See, this is why I never go to ball games. The element."

"Afternoon, Mr. Ripton," said Heat, putting some lightness on it. "This didn't seem like anything to bother you with. Just a quick question or two for Toby."

"Nuh-uh." Ripton stopped at the rail and they both turned to face him. He was huffing a bit from his effort and had his suit coat draped over one arm. "Nobody messes with him. This is the first day he's had cleats in the grass since the injury."

"You know," said Rook, "for a pitcher, he's got one helluva swing."

"I know all about what he's got." The Firewall bit off the words. He spread his arms wide, symbolically blocking them from his player, living up to his nickname. "Talk to me, that way we can work out your access."

Nikki put a hand on her hip, a pointed gesture aimed at drawing back her blazer, letting him see the badge on her waist. "Mr. Ripton, haven't we already been through this? I'm not ESPN dogging for a crumb. I'm in a murder investigation and I have a question for Toby Mills."

"Who," said The Firewall, "is trying to come back from an injury that has shaken his confidence. You see a sweet swing? Tell you what I see. A kid who may have to put his foot on the rubber in game one of the World Series and he's crapping himself because he's worried he's not a hundred percent. Plus he has to bat. He's so pressured that an hour ago I pushed back an endorsement meet-and-greet with Disney World. I'm not trying to be uncooperative, Detective, but I'm going to ask for some slack here."

Rook couldn't resist. "Wow. You told Mickey and Minnie to chill?"

Just then Toby Mills called over from the on-deck circle. "Everything OK, Jess?"

His manager showed teeth and waved as he hollered back, "All good, Tobe. I think they have money on the game." He laughed. Mills nodded thoughtfully and went back to his swings. Ripton turned back to Heat and dropped his smile. "See what's happening? Why don't you just tell me what you need."

"Have you decided you want to act as his attorney after all?" Nikki put a spin on it, trying to add enough gravity to put the manager in his place. "You did say you were a lawyer. Are you a criminal lawyer?"

"Actually, no. I was house counsel at Levine & Isaacs Public Relations before I started my company. Got tired of bailing out all the Warren Rutlands and Sistah Strifes of the world for a joke of a retainer."

Nikki reflected on Sistah Strife, the rapper-turned-actress who had a nasty habit of forgetting she had loaded firearms in her carry-on at TSA and who had famously settled a sexual battery suit by a roadie out of court, reportedly for eight figures. "I may have new respect for you, Jess. You handled Sistah Strife?"

"Nobody handled Sistah Strife. You handled the mess she left behind in her wake." He softened the edge, even if only slightly. "So how can we both walk away from this meeting happy, Detective?"

"We're working the murder of a former limo driver and Toby Mills's name has come up."

So much for the respite. Nikki had just succeeded in pushing The Firewall's reset button. She could almost hear the servo-motors whir as the defense shield rose again. "Whoa, ho, hold on. You come to us about Cassidy Towne. Now you're back about some dead limo hack? What's going on here? Are you guys on some sort of vendetta against Toby Mills?"

Heat shook her head. "We're simply following a lead."

"This is feeling like harassment."

Nikki pressed forward against his push-back. "The murder victim had been let go for some unspecified altercation with a client. In checking the records, we see that Toby Mills had been one of his riders."

"This is a joke, right? In New York, New York . . . in Manhattan . . .

you are seriously trying to make a connection between a limo driver and a celebrity? Like that's a quirk of some kind? And you pick my guy? Who else is on your list? Are you also going to interview Martha Stewart? Trump? A-Rod? Regis? Word is they take limos sometimes."

"Our interest is strictly in Toby Mills."

"Uh-huh." Jess Ripton did a slight nod. "I get it. What are you doing, Detective Heat, trying to get some more publicity for yourself by pinning every crime you can't manage to solve on my guy?"

There was no percentage going head-to-head with this man. Much as she wanted to lash back, Nikki decided to stay on point and not rise to his emotional bait. Sometimes it sucks to be a pro, she thought. But she said, "Here's exactly what I'm doing. It's my job to find killers, just as it's your job to protect 'your guy.' Now, I don't know how come, but in two murders this week, the name Toby Mills has come up in connection. I'm curious about that. And if I were you? . . . I would be, too."

Jess Ripton grew reflective. He turned to the infield, where Toby was lying on the grass getting his hamstring stretched by the trainer. When he looked again at Nikki Heat, she said, "That's right. Your guy or not—never hurts to keep your eyes open, huh, Mr. Ripton?" She flashed him a smile and turned to go, leaving him there to think about that one for a while.

———

When Heat and Rook returned to the Two-Oh, Detective Hinesburg came to Nikki's desk before she even set down her bag. "Got a reply from CBP on the information you asked for about the Texan."

She handed a printout to Nikki, and Rook stepped close to read over her shoulder. "CBP?" he said. "Cooties, Bugs, and, what? . . . Pests?"

"Customs and Border Protection," said Nikki as she digested it. "I figured if our mutual acquaintance Rance Eugene Wolf left the country to do security work in Europe, there'd be a record of his return to the States . . . assuming he entered legally and used his passport."

"Post-9/11, odds are, right?" asked Rook.

"Not always," Nikki said. "People find a way to get in. But this little piggy came home. Last February 22nd he flew in on a Virgin from London to JFK. And spare me the wisecrack, Rook, I'm already sorry I said it."

"I said nothing."

"No, but you did that little throat-clearing thing you do. I think we're all for the better I headed you off." She handed the sheet back to Hinesburg. "Thanks, Sharon. Now I have another one for you. Start a list for me of Tex's clients before he left for Europe."

The other detective uncapped a stick pen with her teeth and jotted notes on the back of the Customs printout. "You mean like the name of his security employer? We have that, it's Hard Line Security out of Vegas, right?"

"Yeah, but I want you to reach out to them. Make a friend there and find out who he specifically got assigned to do security for. The NCAVC synopsis said he had good relations with clients, I want to find out who they were. And if he freelanced, anything you can get."

"Anything specific I should be looking for?" asked Hinesburg.

"Yes, and write this down." She waited for her to get her pen poised, then said, "Something useful."

"Got it." Hinesburg laughed and moved off to make her call to Nevada.

Nikki picked up a marker and squeaked the date of the Texan's return onto the time line on the whiteboard. When she was done, she took a step back to look at the collage of victim pictures, dates, times, and important events swirling around the three homicides. Rook watched but kept his distance. He knew her and knew from shadowing her on the Matthew Starr murder case that Nikki was undergoing an important ritual in her process . . . quieting all the noise, staring at all the disconnected elements to see if the connection was up there yet . . . sitting on the board, waiting to be seen. He remembered the quote of hers he'd used in his "Crime Wave–Heat Wave" piece: "It only takes one weak thread to make a case unravel, but it also only takes one tiny thread to pull it all together." And as he studied Nikki from behind, words failed him. Then as Rook was enjoying his view, she turned, almost like she knew what he was doing. Busted, he felt his face flush and words failed him again. "Some writer" was the only thought that came to mind.

Nikki's desktop telephone rang, and when she answered, it was a kinder, gentler Jess Ripton than she had crossed sabers with a few hours before at the stadium. "It's Jess Ripton, how you doing?"

"A little busy," said Heat. "You know, fighting crime . . . looking for my next publicity opportunity . . ."

"That was a cheap shot and I apologize for it. Seriously. And think about it. Considering how I make my living, is there any chance I'd see getting whatever exposure you can get as a bad thing?"

"No, I guess not," she said. And then waited. This was his dime and she was curious about his mission. Guys like Ripton didn't do anything just because.

"Anyway, I thought I'd let you know that I talked to Toby about the limo driver you wanted to know about." Nikki actually shook her head at the mentality of handlers like this. Working the wealthier streets of the Upper West Side over the years, she had seen it so many times. The entourages and insulators who think speaking on behalf of an interviewee precludes the need for her to ask the questions herself.

"I wanted you to know Tobe doesn't recall having any beef with a driver. And I believe him."

"Gee," she said, "then what more do I need?"

"All right, all right, I hear you. You're going to want to talk to him yourself, I know that. And, like I said today, we'll work out a time. But I'm trying to not be a dick here. Not so easy, in case you haven't noticed."

"So far, so good." She kept it offhand. No sense engaging The Firewall's firewall.

"I'm trying to get you what you want and, at the same time, get my guy some breathing room to man up for his return to the mound."

"No, I get it. But you're right, Jess, I am still going to want to talk to him myself."

"Sure, and if you can wait a day or two," he said, "I'll be in your debt."

"So what does that get me? Cover of *Time*? Person of the Year issue?"

"I've gotten similar for lesser people." He paused, and then sounding almost human, he said, "Listen, it's been on my mind since you took that parting shot at me at the Stade. About keeping my eyes open about Toby?" This is another place where experience had taught the detective to work the silence. She waited him out and he continued. "I don't worry about him. Like when he says he had no problems with any drivers? I don't blink. He's got that common touch, you know? Drivers, waiters, his house servants, all love him. You should roll with him. Treats them right, big tipper, gives 'em gifts. Toby Mills is just not what I'd call a big trouble guy."

"And where does kicking in Cassidy Towne's door fit on that good-guy scale?"

"Look, we covered that. He lost his temper. He was the lion protecting his cubs. In fact, that's why I'm calling."

Here it was, thought Nikki. Never failed, the cream center in the Oreo cookie of a peacemaker's phone call. "He wanted me to ask where you stood with that stalker of his."

The question, not to mention the thin pretext for the call, irritated her, but Nikki actually sympathized with it. The kid from Broken Arrow, Oklahoma, might be a millionaire, but Toby Mills was a dad whose family was harassed. "I've got a detective assigned to that, and we're working with two other precincts to find him. Tell your client we'll let you know whenever we turn up anything."

"Appreciate that," he said. And, having delivered his message, he made a quick good-bye.

Rook stood in the Observation Room of Interrogation 2, holding two cups. One was steaming and the other was sweating chilled condensation onto his fingers as he looked through the magic glass at Raley and Ochoa, who had commandeered the mini conference table for their paper chase. He set down the cold cup so he could open the door, then made sure to put a smile on and entered to join them.

"Hey, Roach."

The two detectives didn't look up from the phone records spread before them, nor did they address Rook. Instead, Raley said to his partner, "Look who just gets to roam free around the building now, unsupervised."

Ochoa glanced at the visitor. "Not even wearing a leash, what's that about?"

"Well," said Raley, "he *is* paper trained."

"That's funny from you." Ochoa chuckled. "Paper trained. Clever."

Raley looked up from his work, at the other cop across the table. "Clever?"

"Come on, Rales, he's a writer. 'Paper trained'?"

Rook laughed. It sounded a little forced because it was. "My God, is this Interrogation 2, or have I stumbled into the Algonquin Round-table?"

Roach put their noses back into their printouts. "Help you, Rook?" said Ochoa.

"Heard you guys were flogging the paperwork pretty hard, so I brought you some refreshment." He set a cup beside each. "One coffee, hazelnut creamer for you, and for Detective Raley, some sweet tea." He noticed an eye flick from Raley to Ochoa. It transmitted some disdain, low-grade stuff, like the vibe he had gotten from them since his return. After both muttered absent "Thanks, man"s and just kept reading, he almost left. Instead, he sat.

"Want a hand with this? Maybe spell one of you?"

Raley laughed. "Hey, the writer say he wants to *spell* us, that's clever, too."

Ochoa gave him a flat stare. "I don't get it."

"Forget it, just forget it." Raley turned sideways in his chair and stewed.

Ochoa enjoyed his moment of busting his partner's chops and then air slurped his coffee, which was still too hot to drink. He set down his cup and then rubbed his eyes with the heels of both hands. Poring over phone records was just one typical donkey chore in a detective's day.

But Esteban Padilla had had several phones and made a lot more calls than they had anticipated for a produce truck driver, and this task, after so much seatwork looking through limo manifests, was making both cops paper blind. It was why they had moved the chore to Interrogation. Not just for the table space, but for the peace. And now, here was Rook. "OK. Want to tell us what this is about? The waiting on us, the 'Howya doin', Roach,' the offer to help with all this?"

"All right," said Rook. He waited for Raley's attention, which he got. "Yeah, it's sort of . . . Call it an olive branch." When neither detective responded, he continued. "Look, you know and I know there has been an undercurrent of tension since the moment I saw you in the kitchen at Cassidy Towne's. Am I right?"

Ochoa picked up his cup again. "Hey, we're just doing the job, man. As long as that works, I'm cool." He tested the coffee and then took a long sip.

"Come on. Something's going on here and I want to clear the air between us. Now, I'm not insensitive. I know what's different. My article. It's because I didn't give you guys enough credit, is that it?" They didn't say anything. It struck him right then what room he was in and how ironic that here he was interrogating two detectives, trying to get them to talk. So he played his ace card. "I'm not going anywhere until you tell me."

A look passed between them both, but again Ochoa spoke. "OK, since you ask, yeah. But I wouldn't call it getting credit. It's more like, you know, we're a team. Just like you've seen us do it. So it's not about getting our names in more or being made heroes, we don't want any of that. Just how come it wasn't more like it's all of us together, you know? That's all."

Rook nodded. "I thought so. It wasn't intentional, I assure you, and if I had it to do over, I'd write it differently. I'm sorry, guys."

Ochoa studied Rook. "All I can ask." He stuck out his hand, and after they shook, he turned to his partner. "Rales?"

The other detective seemed more tentative, but he said, "Cool," and also shook with the writer.

"Good," said Rook. "Now, my offer still stands. How can I help here?"

Ochoa beckoned him to scoot his chair closer. "What we're doing is going over Padilla's phone records looking for any calls that weren't to friends, family, his boss, whatever."

"You're trying to spot anything out of pattern."

"Yeah. Or a pattern that tells us something." Ochoa handed a phone record to Rook and placed a pink sheet listing the friend and family and work numbers on the table between them. "You see any numbers that don't appear on the pink sheet, hit 'em with the highlighter, got it?"

"Got it." Just as Rook began to scan the first line of calls, he felt Raley's eyes on him and looked up.

"I have to say this, Rook. There is one more thing bugging me, and if I don't get it off my chest, it's just going to keep eating and eating at me."

Rook could see the gravity of this on his face and set down his sheet. "Sure, let me hear it, let's get it all out. What do you want to say to me?"

Raley said, "Sweet Tea."

Puzzled, Rook said, "Help me out here. You don't like the tea?"

"No, not the damn tea. My nickname. Sweet Tea. You put it in the article, and now everybody's calling me that."

Ochoa said, "I haven't noticed that."

"Why would you? You aren't me."

"Again, I apologize," said Rook. "Better?"

Raley shrugged. "Yeah. Now that I unloaded, yeah."

"Who calls you that?" pressed his partner.

Raley fidgeted. "Lots of people. Desk sergeant, a uniform in booking. It doesn't matter how many, I don't like it."

"Can I say something as your friend and your partner? In the scheme of getting over yourself? . . . Get over yourself." And one second after they resumed their work, Ochoa punctuated it with ". . . Sweat Tea."

They studied the records in silence. A few minutes later, on his second printout, Rook asked Ochoa for the highlighter.

"Got one?"

"Yeah." As he took the marker from Ochoa, it registered exactly what he had. "Holy shit."

"What?" said Roach.

Rook highlighted the phone number and held it up. "This number? It's Cassidy Towne's."

———

A half hour later, Detective Heat stood over the array of highlighted phone records Roach had laid out side by side, in chronological order, on her desktop out in the bull pen. "So what do we have?"

"We have a couple things, actually," began Raley. "First, we have the connection we've been looking for between Esteban Padilla and Cassidy Towne. Not just a phone call, but a regular pattern of calls to her."

Ochoa picked up the tour, pointing to a series of highlights on the first pages, the ones on the left side of her desk. "The first calls come here, once or twice a week last winter and into spring. These correspond to the dates he was working the limo. A sure sign Padilla was one of her informants."

"Know what I think?" said Rook. "I'll bet you can look at the dates of those calls to her, check who Padilla had booked that night, and match them to items in her column the next day. Assuming any of the tips were newsworthy."

"Newsworthy?" said Heat.

"OK, gossipworthy."

She nodded. "But I take your point. What else?"

"Here it gets even more interesting," continued Raley. "The calls stop abruptly right here." He tapped the printout for May. "Guess when this was?"

"The month Padilla got fired from the limo company," she said.

"Right. A whole cluster of calls just after that—we'll have to guess what that was about for now—and then nothing for almost a month."

"And then they pick up again here." Ochoa appeared on Nikki's right and used the yellow highlighter cap to show resumption of contacts. "Calls. Lots of calls all of a sudden in mid-June. Four months ago."

Heat asked, "Do we know if he was working another limo company then?"

"We checked that," said Raley. "He started driving the produce deliveries end of May, shortly after he got canned from driving the black cars. So I doubt if he was still giving gossip tips."

"At least not new ones." Rook leaned in past Nikki and spread his fingers to span the gap in calls. "My guess is this hiatus in calls was when Mr. Padilla was not providing daily tips to Ms. Towne. And the resumption of calls in June was all about research for whatever the hell book she was writing. Depending on where she was with her manuscript, as a writer, I'd say that would be about the right timing."

Nikki scanned the highlighted pattern, a time line in its own right, and then turned to face her detectives and Rook. "Great work. This is big. We not only have our connection between Padilla and Towne, but if Rook's right about what the pattern means, it suggests why he was killed. If she was murdered for what she was writing, he could have been murdered for being her snitch."

"Same as Derek Snow?" asked Rook.

"For once, not such a whacko theory, Mr. Rook. But still, only a theory until we can make a similar link. Roach, get on our concierge's phone records first thing in the morning."

As Roach left the bull pen, she heard Raley say in a low voice, "I'm looking forward to some sleep, but whenever I close my eyes, all I see are printouts of phone records."

And Ochoa replied, "Me, too, Sweet Tea."

Nikki was putting on her brown leather jacket when Rook stepped up to the coatrack, closing his messenger bag. "You boys kiss and make up?" she asked.

"How did you know that? Did we have that post-make-up-sex glow?"

"I may be sick," she said. "Actually, I happened to catch you through the glass in Observation."

"That was a private conversation."

"Funny, that's what the bad guys think when they're in that room, too. Everybody forgets it's a two-way mirror." She flicked her eyebrows at him, a full Groucho. "But that was a good thing you did, reaching out to them like that."

"Thanks. Listen, I was thinking . . . I'd love to cash in that rain check for last night."

"Oo . . . sorry. Can't tonight, I've made plans. Petar called."

His gut took the express elevator to the basement, but he maintained an unfazed smile and kept it casual. "Really? A drink after, then?"

"Problem is, I don't know when after will be. We're going to get together on his dinner break. Who knows, I may end up back at the show. I've never seen them shoot one of those things." She checked her watch. "I've got to run or I'll be late. Catch you in the A.M." She made sure the squad room was empty, then kissed his cheek. He started to reach for her but thought better of it in the police station and all.

But as he watched her go out the door, he wished he had put his arms around her. Irresistible as he was, she might have canceled her dinner.

———

Roach came in early the next morning to find Jameson Rook camped out at his commandeered desk. "I was wondering who turned on the lights in here," said Raley. "Rook, did you even go home last night?"

"Yeah, I did. Just thought I'd get here early for a jump on the day."

Ochoa said, "You don't mind me saying so, you look kinda messed up. Like you've been skydiving without goggles."

"Thanks." Rook didn't have a mirror to look at, but he could imagine. "Well, I'm burning that candle, you know? When I leave here, it's off to my night job at the keyboard."

"Uh-huh, I'll bet it's tough." Ochoa gave him a pleasant nod, and the pair moved across the bull pen to log on to their computers.

Ochoa's comment was sympathetic, but it only made Rook feel guilty. Guilty, first, that he'd had the audacity to tell an NYPD homicide detective how difficult life could be in his comfortable Tribeca loft, writing. And guilty, second, because he had not been writing at all. He tried, all right. He had two full days of notes to write up to stay current with his Cassidy Towne article. But he didn't write them up.

It was Nikki. He couldn't let go of Nikki having dinner with her old college lover. He knew it was nuts for him to be so . . . freaked. What he admired in her was her self-sufficiency, her independence. He just didn't like it when she was so independent of him. And with an old boyfriend. Around eleven P.M., unable to concentrate on his work or even watch the news, he had started to wonder if this was how it started with stalkers. And then he started to think maybe he'd do his next article as an investigation of stalkers. But then, he wondered . . . if you do a ride-along with a stalker, are you stalking the stalker?

It all got very weird.

That's when he made a phone call. There was a comedy writer he knew on a late-night talk show in LA who had been in the business forever, and sure enough, this guy had the story on Petar Matic. "Don't you love the name, Rook? Sounds like a product a mohel would sell on an infomercial." Call a comedy writer, get a one-liner. But it was the only laugh Rook got from the conversation.

Comedy writing, especially in late night, was a small circle of frenemies, and Rook's LA guy knew one of the *Later On* comedy writers who had done community service a few years back. "Hold on," said Rook, "why would a comedy writer have to do community service?"

"Beats me. Pitching a Monica Lewinsky joke after 2005? Who knows?"

So while the *Later On* comedy writer was doing his community service at the Bronx Zoo—for DUI, Rook's friend eventually recalled—on the crew with him doing cage cleaning and litter detail was this bright guy from Croatia, a nature documentary shooter. Rook asked if Petar was there for DUI, too.

"No, here's the poetry. Nature filmmaker. Busted for what?" Rook's friend paused for a drumroll. "Smuggling endangered species into the country from Thailand. He did six months of eighteen in jail, got early release for good behavior, and was assigned community service. To the zoo!"

"More poetry," said Rook.

The two hit it off, and at the end of their stint at the zoo, the comedy writer got Petar a gig at *Later On* as a production assistant. "Not quite a step up from shoveling the elephant yard," said the voice from LA, "but entry level, and he did OK. Worked his way up to segment producer pretty quick. My friend says once Petar sets his mind to something, there's no stopping him."

That was the thought that left Rook sleepless, worried about that signature Petar Matic tenacity—plus conflicted over whether he should tell Nikki about her ex's smuggling bust. But suppose he did tell her? That could make it worse, exponentially worse. He made a list of potential fallout. It could damage a perfectly good relationship she enjoyed with an old friend, which Rook would then feel bad about. Sort of. He might inadvertently create greater interest in Petar. Nikki had a naughty side, and maybe the bad boy thing was something she would spark to all the more. And finally, how did it make him look, doing background checks on her old boyfriends? It made him look . . . well, insecure, needy, and threatened. Sure wouldn't want to give that impression. So when he saw her come through the door at the other end of the bull pen, smiling, he knew exactly what to do. Look busy and pretend he didn't know anything.

"Look at you here, all bright-eyed and . . ."—she studied him— ". . . bushy faced."

"I skipped the shave this morning. A little time-saver after a long night. Researching." He waited while she hung up her jacket, and then he added, "And you?"

"Feeling pretty good, actually, thanks." She turned across the room. "Roach? You get Derek Snow's phone records yet?"

"Put in for them," answered Raley. "Should arrive anytime now."

"Call them again. And keep me up on it." She put her bag in her desk file drawer. "Rook, you're hovering."

"Huh? Oh, I'm just wondering . . ." His sentence hung there, suspended between them. What he wanted to ask was about her night. What she did. Where she went. What she did. When it ended. What she did. So many questions. But the one he asked was, "Is there something I can do to be useful this morning?"

Before Nikki could answer, the phone rang on her desk. "Homicide, Detective Heat."

Before Nikki heard the voice, she heard the unmistakable sound of subway wheels squealing to a halt. "Are you there?" She recognized the voice of Mitchell Perkins. But Cassidy Towne's editor didn't sound quietly superior as he had in his office the day before. He was agitated and tight. "Damn cell phone. Hello?"

"I'm here, Mr. Perkins, is something wrong?"

"My wife. I'm on my way to work and my wife just called. She caught someone trying to break in."

"What's the address?" She snapped her fingers to get Roach's attention. Raley picked up the extension, copied the address Perkins gave, uptown on Riverside Drive, and called Dispatch while Heat stayed on with the editor. "We're sending a car now."

She heard him panting, and the background acoustics changed, telling her he had come up from the subway to street level. "I'm almost there. Hurry, God, hurry . . ."

———

Hurrying in Manhattan isn't so easy, even with police lights and a siren, but the traffic flow was downtown at that hour, so Detective Heat made good time up Broadway to West 96th Street. From her TAC frequency Nikki heard that three blue-and-whites were already at Perkins's apartment, so she killed her siren and eased it back slightly after she crossed West End. She looked up the street and chin-nodded to Rook beside her. "What's this?"

Ahead of them, mid-block, two people were kneeling on the sidewalk in front of a car at a garage entrance. A third, a parking attendant to judge by his uniform, saw her flashing light and waved his arms to flag her down. Nikki was on the air calling for paramedics before she even saw the body stretched out on the pavement.

"Perkins?" said Rook.

"Think so." Heat parked to protect the scene from oncoming traffic and left her gumball flashing. When she got out, a blue-and-white was right behind her and she directed the officers to split up. One to direct traffic, the other to hold the witnesses on scene. The detective hurried over to the victim, who was facedown on the car park driveway in front of the TT that had struck him. It was indeed Mitchell Perkins.

She did a check for vitals. He had a pulse and was breathing; both weak, though. "Mr. Perkins, can you hear me?" Nikki leaned an ear down near his face, which was sideways on the concrete, but got nothing back. Not even a moan. As the ambulance siren approached behind her, she said, "It's Detective Heat. The ambulance is here. We're going to take good care of you." And she added, just in case he was semiconscious, "And police are with your wife, so don't worry."

While the EMTs went to work, Heat pieced together what had happened from the trio of citizens on the scene. One of them was a housekeeper who happened by after the incident and wasn't of much use for information. However, the driver of the Audi said he was pulling out of the garage for a trip to Boston when he struck Perkins. Nikki figured the editor was in such a rush from the subway, freaked about his wife, that he wasn't paying attention. But she adhered to her training not to box the story until all the details were in, and never to lead the eyewitnesses with her own guesses. Let them talk.

That's what she did, and the story she got was big. The parking attendant said Perkins wasn't running up the sidewalk when he first saw him. He was in a struggle with somebody, a mugger, trying to get his briefcase. The attendant had gone into his kiosk to call 911, which was right when the TT came up from the underground ramp. The driver said he pulled out just as the mugger ripped away the briefcase. Perkins had been pulling so hard that when he lost his grip he flew back into the front of the car. The driver said he hit his brakes, but there was no way to stop the collision.

Roach rolled up to the scene, and Heat assigned them to separate the witnesses and get more detailed statements and better descriptions of the mugger from them. As often happened in sudden violent crimes, the eyewitnesses had gotten distracted or shocked by the blur of action and missed basic descriptions of the perpetrators. "I already had one of the uniforms put out the APB for a Caucasian, medium build, in sunglasses and dark navy or black hoodie and jeans, but that's pretty vanilla. See what else you can get, and try to get them down to the precinct for a look at photo arrays. I want to make sure we include the Texan and some of our other players in the deck. And while we're at it, line up the sketch artist, too." She looked around for Rook and saw him squatting in the gutter over the spilled contents of the editor's briefcase.

"No, I didn't touch anything," he said as she approached, snapping on gloves. "I'm incorrigible, but trainable. How's he going to be?"

Nikki turned to watch them load Perkins into the back of the ambulance. "Still unconscious, which is not optimal. But he's breathing and they did get a better pulse, so we'll see." She crouched down beside him. "Anything useful here?"

"One very trashed, rather empty briefcase." It was an old-fashioned hard case, a big clamshell gaping open, with business cards and stationery items like black binder clips and Post-its scattered about it. A handheld digital voice recorder lay scuffed a foot away, beside a granola bar. "Although, I do say I admire his taste in fountain pens," he said, indicating a brick-orange-and-black Montblanc Hemingway limited edition nestled in the L where the curb met the gutter. "Those things go for over three grand now. Kind of shoots down the mugger theory."

Nikki wanted to go along with that, but she pushed away the temptation of coming to any conclusions for now. That's not how cases cleared. "Unless the mugger wasn't a writer-slash–fountain pen collector."

Just then Rook startled her by taking her by the wrist. "Come with me, quick."

She almost hesitated, but she went along with him as he drew her across the street with a gentle grip on her forearm. But that didn't stop her from asking, "Rook, what are you doing?"

"Quick, before it flies away." He pointed to a single sheet of white paper fluttering down 96th toward the park on Riverside.

Nikki reached for it, but the wind took it and she had to make another sprint to get ahead of it. When it landed on the pavement at her feet, she pounced and slapped her open palm down to trap it. "Gotcha."

"Nice. Would have done that myself, but you've got the gloves," said Rook. "And the moves."

With her free hand, Heat carefully pinched the corner of the sheet and turned the paper over to read it. Frustrated by her poker face, Rook grew impatient.

"Well?" he said. "What is it?"

Nikki didn't answer. Instead, she turned the page so he could read it himself.

Wasted, Dead or Alive

The Real Story Behind the Death of Reed Wakefield

By

Cassidy Towne

FOURTEEN

Mitchell Perkins, senior editor, nonfiction, Epimetheus Books, opened his eyes in his room on the fourth floor of St. Luke's-Roosevelt to discover Nikki Heat and Jameson Rook sitting in chairs at the end of his bed. The detective rose and stood beside him. "How are you feeling, Mr. Perkins? Do you want me to call the nurse or anything?"

He closed his eyes briefly and shook his head. "Thirsty." She spooned an ice chip from the cup on his rolling tray table and watched him savor it. "Thank you . . . for helping my wife. Before my little nap she told me you had cops there in no time."

"It all worked out, Mr. Perkins. Although you may not feel like that yourself, at this moment." She gave him another plastic spoon of ice without being asked. "Did you see who did this to you?"

He shook his head and registered some pain. "Whoever it was came at me from behind. That's usually a safe neighborhood."

"We're still sorting it all out, but I don't believe this was a random mugging." Nikki set the cup down on the table. "Putting this together with the attempted break-in at your apartment, this could be the same person." Perkins nodded, as if he had been mulling that possibility, too. "We can't be absolutely sure because your wife didn't see the burglar. She said someone forced open a window and the alarm went off. Whoever it was ran off."

"If I were laying money down," said Rook, "I'd bet the route he took was Ninety-sixth Street."

"Lucky me," added Perkins.

Heat arched a skeptical brow. "The perp was the lucky one. The other factor here is that you still have your wallet and watch."

"He grabbed my briefcase."

"Because that's probably what he wanted." Nikki held up the ice cup, and he shook a "No, thanks" then winced. "Somebody has been on a tear to get their hands on that Cassidy Towne manuscript, Mr. Perkins." Heat had been thus far unable to find a judge willing to test the First Amendment by issuing a warrant to search the publisher's files, and she labored to keep the frustration out of her voice. "You know, the one you said you didn't have?"

"I didn't say I didn't have it."

She heard Rook scoff behind her and knew he was thinking exactly what she was thinking: that Perkins must be feeling better, because he was parsing his words again. Put him in a suit, put him in an open-backed hospital johnny, he'd still lay down a smoke screen. She had to figure a way through it. "Fine, you didn't say you didn't have it; you pretended you didn't. Has it occurred to you this may not be a time to mince words?"

The editor didn't answer. He rested his head back on the starched pillow.

"We know what was in your briefcase. We found the cover page. And we know the rest of the manuscript isn't there now." She let that register and decided to make her move. "Whoever did this is still out there. So far, we have useless descriptions to go on, so what we need is anything that can point to a motive." She hated to beat on a guy with a concussion, a broken leg, and three cracked ribs, but that didn't mean she wouldn't. Nikki turned the top card from her deck. It was the fear card. "Now, do you want to help, or do you want to take a chance this person will try something again—when you're not there and your wife may not be so lucky."

He didn't have to think too long. "I'll call my office and have them messenger you a copy of the manuscript right away."

"We'll send someone to get it, if that's OK."

"Whatever you want. You know, I was carrying it with me because I was this close to giving it to you on my way in. This close." The editor's brow clouded briefly. "Could have saved us all this, if only . . ." He let his admission trail off, then shifted uncomfortably, trying to sit up more so he could face her. "You have to believe me when I tell you this, because I would understand if you were skeptical, given our . . . transactional history. But it's the God's truth."

"Go on."

"I don't have the final chapter. I don't. The material I have from her is incomplete. It only covers the backstory of Reed Wakefield's life and the months before his death. Cassidy was holding back the last chapter. She said it was the one that reveals the details of the people responsible for his death."

Rook said, "Wait a minute, that was ruled an accidental overdose. I thought Reed Wakefield died alone."

Perkins shook his head. "Not according to Cassidy Towne."

Of course none of this squared with either the coroner's official findings or the information Nikki had gathered from her recent checks on the Dragonfly House with all the interviewees, including both managers, Derek Snow, and the housekeeper who found the body. Everything pointed to a drug user who accidentally overmedicated and died quietly and alone in his sleep, and who had no visitors the night before, or morning of, his discovery. "Mr. Perkins, did Cassidy Towne say what she meant by 'people responsible'?" asked Heat.

"No."

"Because that could mean a lot of different things if it's true. Like it's whoever sold him the drugs or handed him a prescription bottle."

"Or," said Rook, "if he wasn't alone and the party in his room got out of hand. But that would mean nobody called the cops, nobody called an ambulance, that they just walked away and left him. That's worth covering up."

Heat said, "And Derek Snow worked at that hotel. Was he part of the cover-up? Or an unlucky eyewitness?"

"Or at the party," speculated Rook.

"Unfortunately, we may never know," said the editor. "She never turned in that last chapter."

"Was it because, possibly, she didn't know all of it?" asked the detective.

"No," said Rook. "Knowing Cassidy Towne, she knew what she had and was holding it for ransom."

"Exactly right," Perkins agreed. "She had it all buttoned up in a sensational chapter that she said would reveal everything. And when she delivered the partial manuscript, she said she wanted to reopen negotiations on her deal. You wouldn't believe what she was asking for. The woman was trying to kill us."

"Ironic," said Rook. When Nikki gave him a chastening glance, he shrugged. "Come on, you were thinking it."

———

Minutes later in the bull pen Nikki split Roach up. With Esteban Padilla also killed by whoever killed Cassidy Towne and Derek Snow, she put Ochoa on the task of checking Padilla's limo company for a Reed Wakefield passenger manifest on or before the night he died. She assigned Raley to canvass for surveillance tape of Mitchell Perkins's mugging. Rook ended a phone call and joined them in the middle of the room.

"Just got off with Perkins's assistant at Epimetheus Books. They made a PDF of her manuscript and they're going to e-mail it. Should get here before the hard copy arrives, so we can dive right in."

Nikki's attention drifted to the murder board and the list of names on it in her neat block printing. "If what Perkins says is true and the last chapter is still out there, that means someone is still going to be looking for it." And then, turning to them so they could read her apprehension, she added, "And won't stop at anything to get it."

"The book guy was lucky. How's he doing?" asked Raley.

"Hurting, but he'll make it," answered Heat. "I think a lot of his pain is realizing he could have avoided all this if he had just shared the manuscript when we asked for it."

"Just one more irony," Rook said. "Epimetheus? . . . The Greek god of hindsight." They all stared at him. "True fact. Alex, I'll take 'Moons of Saturn' for a thousand."

———

It was time to get Soleil Gray in a more official setting. But Reed Wake-field's ex-fiancée responded in kind by showing up in Interrogation 1 with her attorney, one of the most aggressive, successful—and, as a result, expensive—criminal lawyers in the city. Detective Heat knew Helen Miksit from days when she was glad to be in the same room with her. She had been a tough prosecutor who collected guilty verdicts like scalps and made cops want to send flowers. But six years ago, Miksit left the DA's office and crossed the aisle for profit. Her wardrobe had changed, but her demeanor hadn't. The Bulldog, as they called her, made her opening move before Heat and Rook even sat down across the table. "This is bullshit, and you know it."

"Nice to see you again, too, Helen." Nikki slid into her chair, unfazed.

"We're past the pleasantries on this one, I'm afraid. My client has filled me in on your serial badgering and I have advised her to say nothing to you." Beside her, Soleil Gray was occupying herself by nibbling at a loose piece of skin on her knuckle. She took her hand away from her mouth and shook her head slightly to indicate she was on the same page, but what Nikki read from the singer wasn't a stonewall. She looked vulnerable rather than cocky. That part was left to the lady in the power suit. "To be clear, we are only at this interview because we have to be. Now, you can save us all a lot of trouble by recognizing the futility of this and calling it a day."

Nikki gave the attorney a smile. "Thank you, Counselor. I have been diligent, I'll admit. You remember what it's like out here, don't you? People get killed, cops gotta ask questions . . . Such a pain."

"Twice you have gone to her place of employment and disrupted the normal course of her business on a witch hunt. You caused her to miss her performance on a late-night show, and now you've got her completely distracted while she's gearing up to shoot a new music video tomorrow. Is this desperation, or are you performing for your next article?" Miksit side-nodded to Rook.

"Oh," he said, "don't worry, there's no sequel. I'm just along because I love the swell folks you meet in police stations."

Nikki jumped in before that escalated. "My repeat visit to Soleil was to get a straight answer from her after getting a series of lies from her the first time. Your client is connected to two homicide victims, and—"

"Means nothing. 'Connections.' " Miksit spat the word. "Come on, Detective."

Nikki was used to the woman's confrontational style, but she had seen it while sitting behind her in a courtroom as an ally, not across the table on the receiving end. Heat had to wrestle to keep this her meeting, and she did so by continuing on her road in spite of the push-back. "And one of those victims, Cassidy Towne, we have just learned, was writing a book about the death of Miss Gray's fiancé."

"Oh, please, this is why you brought us in here?"

Soleil cleared her throat and swallowed hard. Helen Miksit made great theater placing a comforting hand on her forearm. "Is it really necessary to do this? This subject is still an open wound for her."

Nikki spoke quietly. "Soleil, there's little doubt Cassidy Towne was murdered to stop the publication of her book about the circumstances surrounding Reed Wakefield's death." She paused to choose her words carefully, unsure whether the singer was a conspirator or a victim herself. "If you are involved or know about this in any way, this is the time to speak up. The time to hide is over."

Helen Miksit said, "As I told you at the outset, you can have your meeting. It doesn't mean she's going to participate other than to be here."

Nikki leaned toward Soleil. "Is that how you feel? There's nothing you want to say about this?" The singer pondered, looked like she was about to speak, but in the end, she looked at her attorney, shook her head, and went back to chewing at the tiny flap of skin on her knuckle.

"There you have it, Detective Heat. I assume we're finished now?"

Heat gave one last look to Soleil, hoping to bridge the chasm, but she wouldn't give Nikki her eyes. "We're done. For now."

"For now? Oh, no. This ends here. If you want to get yourself in boldface on 'Page Six,' you're going to do it harassing someone else." Miksit stood. "A word of caution? You may find that when the PR machine reverses direction, it isn't always so friendly."

Heat led them out, and as she watched them walk away through the lobby, she felt even more certain that Soleil was into this. She just wasn't sure how.

Nikki returned to the bull pen, where Rook was already at his computer reading the first pages of the PDF of Cassidy's book, which had arrived during the interrogation. She found Detective Hinesburg sitting in Heat's own chair, using Heat's desk, and jotting on Heat's notepad with one of the pens from her pencil cup. "Make yourself comfortable, Sharon." Nikki was still feeling tight from her meeting with Soleil and The Bulldog, and venting a little steam at Hinesburg gave her some relief. She could feel guilty about it later.

"Hey, funny," said the detective, oblivious. Another irritating quality, but at least it would save Nikki an apology. "I was just leaving you a note. I checked on the PI Elizabeth Essex used to snoop on her errant ex-hubby. Local Staten Island guy her lawyer uses. Not our Texan."

Heat wasn't surprised by the news, but at least that loose thread ended there. "What about Rance Wolf's other clients, where are we with that?"

"Spoke to the CEO of Hard Line Security in Vegas. He's cooperating and putting together a list for me. Both corporate and individual clients. I also asked him about Tex's freelances. He said they maintain notes on any freelance jobs their people take on since their company policy is that agents have to disclose to avoid conflict of interest. He'll share that, too. I'll let you know the minute I get it all."

Detail and initiative like that were why Hinesburg was such a great cop. And why Nikki put up with the petty annoyances. "Good work. And, Sharon, sorry if I sounded a little irritable."

Detective Hinesburg said, "When?" and moved off to her desk.

Ochoa checked in from Rolling Service Limousine. In the background of his cell phone call, Nikki could hear a pneumatic wrench and could envision a town car getting a new tire. "Got something weird over here. You ready for weird?"

"A manifest from Reed Wakefield with a suicide note on it?" said Nikki.

"No Reed Wakefield manifest. In fact no manifests at all from the night Wakefield died. I already had Raley check the records we pulled, they're not in with ours, either. We did our survey before the Reed Wakefield deal surfaced, so we assumed it was just Padilla's day off.

But come on, this is all the manifests for this whole company from that night. It's like every one of their drivers took the night off and didn't have one booking. You see what I'm getting at?" Nikki processed the significance of the missing records. The gravity. The reach. The tire gun whirred again. "You still there?"

"So what's the deal over there, Oach? How do they account for that?"

"Manager just gives me a dumb-ass look and says, 'Don't ask me.' Good luck proving anything, these guys are too slick."

"Yeah," she agreed, "they'll claim burglary or one of the drivers did it. Even Padilla himself, out of spite." And then she added, "Just to confirm, it was a night Padilla was working, right?"

"That they confirmed. Just before they canned him."

"So, what? They've just been ripped out of the book?"

"No. Actually, they've been sliced."

———

An hour later, Nikki left Captain Montrose's office after briefing him on all developments so he could turn around and do the same thing with his superiors down at One Police Plaza. He trusted Detective Heat and told her she was covering all the bases he would. The extra briefings were to satisfy the media pressure on 1PP. Mindful of his upcoming promotion review, the skipper made it his hobby to smile and dial, keeping them in the loop almost hourly.

Raley had set up shop at his desk, with digital copies of surveillance cam video from the parking garage where Perkins had been mugged that morning, as well as from camera-equipped stores and residences all along 96th Street. "I've got a long night ahead of me, but if we get lucky, maybe one of these'll give us a pretty picture of the assailant." As he loaded one of the time-coded videos, he asked, "So you don't think it was the Texan?"

"Wouldn't rule anything out, Rales, not on this case," Nikki answered. "But I broke Wolf's collarbone and put one in his shoulder. Perkins is no Ironman, but whoever overpowered him like that had to have some strength. So I'd bet against the walking wounded."

She made her way over to Rook at his squatter's desk across the pen from hers, to get an update on Cassidy Towne's manuscript. She got a strange vibe off him before he even spoke. Nikki dismissed it, chalking it up to more of Rook's schoolboy jealousy over her reunion with Petar. "What are you getting out of this, anything?"

"I'm a quarter of the way in," he said. "All pretty much as Mitchell Perkins advertised. Reed Wakefield's backstory. She's setting the table but no bombshells yet. She could use an editor, though." That strange look crossed his face again.

"What?"

"There's an extra hard copy on your desk. Actually, in. I put it in your file drawer."

"Rook, either you tell me what's on your mind, or I swear, we don't have a Zoo Lockup, but I'll organize one just for you."

He considered a beat then opened his messenger bag and took out a newspaper. It was the afternoon edition of the *New York Ledger*, folded open to the "Buzz Rush" column. The editors had decided the brand-name value of the column had only inflated since Cassidy Towne's murder, so they were keeping it, but with guest columnists until they settled on a permanent choice. That day's "Buzz" was bylined anonymously by someone called The Stinger.

Nikki felt her face flush when she saw the lead item.

HEAT CRAVE

NYPD hottie and cover girl **Nikki Heat** plus magscribe-cum-boyfriend **Jameson Rook** have been arm in arm on another case, this time, trying to solve the murder of this column's founding doyenne, **Cassidy Towne**. Apparently her brief taste of fame gave her a craving for more spotlight because Heat has been taking her act to all the high-viz peeps and places, most notably on a tear to bring down singer **Soleil Gray**. Detective Hot has been tailing the former Shades lead wherever she goes, including rehearsal halls and even a command perf busting up Miss Gray's rehearsal at *Later On* by showing her autopsy photos of stabbing victims! Since Soleil wasn't rehearsing a number from *Sweeney Todd*, you have to wonder, why all the heat? Is a certain detective getting ready for her next close-up, Mr. DeMille?

Heat looked up from the paper and Rook said, "Nikki, I am so sorry." Her head spun. She pictured trucks unloading bound stacks of the *Ledger* curbside to newsstands all over the city. Copies piled on tables in apartment lobbies or landing on doormats . . . Captain Montrose getting a call from 1PP. She also thought back a few hours to her meeting with Soleil Gray and Helen Miksit, and the lawyer's parting words about how the PR machine can turn against you. Nikki was certain that this was a shot across her bow from The Bulldog.

"You OK?" asked Rook. In the tenderness of his tone Nikki heard all the empathy he had for what was swirling inside her, a maelstrom of regret and anger carrying crumpled pages of *First Press* and the *New York Ledger*.

She handed him the newspaper. "I want my fifteen minutes back."

Jameson Rook called a car service to bring him home. Nikki had asked him for a night of quiet, and he respected her desire without question and with only the slightest twinge of paranoia that she might be meeting up with Petar. After she gave Montrose the heads-up about the *Ledger* item, they had each taken a copy of Cassidy Towne's manuscript to read overnight, and Rook promised he would only call if he hit something that jumped out about the case. "E-mail instead," she had said, and he saw in her a need to find an oasis of solitude in her life. Probably starting with some lavender-scented bubbles in that clawfooted cast-iron tub of hers.

After the black car dropped him in Tribeca, he navigated the garbage heaps and approached his front stoop carrying a bag of Chinese takeout in his teeth while he fished for his door key. He thought he heard a foot scrape beside the stairs. There was no traffic on the street. Down the block, Rook watched the taillights of his ride disappear around the corner. Just as he was thinking about the manuscript in his messenger bag and weighing fight or flight, he saw movement in the shadows of the stoop and turned with his fists up as Cassidy Towne's daughter stepped forward.

"Did I scare you?" said Holly Flanders.

"Mno." He took the bag out of his mouth and said, "No."

"I've been waiting here a couple of hours."

He looked around, instinct telling him to be cautious and make sure he wasn't going to be surprised by a companion.

"I'm here alone," she said.

"How did you know where I live?"

"Last week, after I saw you at my mother's a couple of times, I boosted a key for the new lock from JJ's workshop and let myself in again to see who you were. I found your name and address on her receipts for the messenger service."

"Enterprising and creepy all at the same time."

Holly said, "I need to talk to you."

He set a place for her on the L of his kitchen counter so they wouldn't be side by side. He wanted to look at her when they talked. "China Fun," he announced as he unpacked the bag. "I always over-order, so eat up."

She didn't say much at first because she put everything into her eating. Holly Flanders was lean but had the eye circles and complexion of someone who wasn't a slave to the food pyramid. When she finished her plate, he dished over some more pork fried rice. She held up a palm and said, "That's OK."

"Take it all," said Rook. "There are kids starving in Beverly Hills, you know. Of course, that's by choice."

When she'd finished the rest of it, he asked, "What did you want to talk to me about? By the way, that's one of my great qualities as a reporter. Asking the inobvious question."

"Riiight." She chuckled politely and nodded. " 'K, well, I felt like I could do this because you were nice to me when I got busted the other day. And could relate to the no-parent thing."

"Right," he said and then waited, wondering where this was going.

"I know you're going to write this article about my mother, right? And . . ." Holly paused, and he saw light shimmer off the pools forming in her eyes. ". . . And I know everybody is probably telling you how bad she was. And I'm here to tell you, damn, she was all that." Rook drew the mental image of Holly standing over her mother's bed while she slept, holding a handgun on her, a millimeter of finger movement from blowing her away. "But I came to tell you, since you're going to write her story, don't make her all about being a monster."

Holly's lips quaked, taking on lives of their own, and a tear streamed down each cheek. Rook handed her his napkin and she dabbed her cheeks and blew her nose. "I have a lot of anger at her. Maybe more now that she's gone, because I can't work any of this shit out with her now. That's part of why I didn't kill her; we weren't done, you know?"

Rook didn't know, so he just nodded and listened.

She sipped her beer and, when she had settled enough to continue, said, "All of the bad things about her were true. But in the middle of it is one thing. About eight years ago my mother made contact with me. She had some way of tracking me to my foster home and got permission from my family to take me to dinner. We went to this Jackson Hole burger place I liked in my neighborhood, and it was bizarre. She has the waitress take a picture of us like it was my birthday party or something. She doesn't eat, just sits there telling me all this stuff about how tough it was when she found out she was pregnant, and that she thought she would keep me at first, so she didn't have an abortion and then she changed her mind the first month because it wasn't going to work in her life—'it' she said, like I was an 'it.'

"Anyway she goes through this whole blah-blah about why she did it and then she says she had been thinking long and hard about it and feeling so bad—agony, I remember that was what she said she felt, like she was always in agony—and asked what I thought, if maybe we could talk about getting together."

"You mean, like . . ."

"Well, yuh. Like she thought she could just show up and change her mind about *abandoning* me and I would just get in the frickin' Acura with her and live happily ever after."

Rook let a healthy silence pass before he asked, "What did you say to her?"

"I threw my ice water in her face and walked out." Part of Holly Flanders showed proud defiance. Rook imagined she had told that story before to friends or barflies over the years and reveled in her heroic act of maternal repudiation, poetic in its balancing of scales. But he also saw in her the other part of Holly Flanders, the part that had brought her to his doorstep to wait in the dark, the woman who felt the weight of emotions that nest uncomfortably in any soul with a conscience that has to bear the unhealable wound of banishing another person. With ice water, no less.

"Holly, you were what, early teens, then?"

"I didn't come here to be let off the hook, OK? I came because once you found out she had put me out to foster care, I didn't want you to think that was all there was to her. I look back now, older and all, and realize she didn't just wash her hands and walk away, you know?" She finished her beer in a long gulp and set the glass down slowly. "Bad enough I have to deal with this the rest of my life. I didn't want to make it worse by letting you write her story without telling you there was more to her than giving me away."

At the door on her way out she got on her toes to give Rook a kiss. She went for his lips and he turned to present his cheek. "Is that because of what I do?" she asked. "Because I sell it sometimes?"

"That's because I'm sort of with someone else now." And then he smiled. "Well, I'm working on it."

She gave him her cell number, in case he wanted to talk about the article, and left. As Rook went back to the kitchen to clean up the dishes, he lifted her plate. Underneath he found a four-by-six color photo that looked like it had spent some time folded. It was Cassidy Towne and her teenage daughter in their booth at a Jackson Hole. Cassidy was smiling, Holly was enduring. All Rook could look at was the glass of ice water.

————

The next morning, Heat and Rook sat down at her desk to compare notes on the Cassidy Towne manuscript. First, though, he asked her if she'd had any fallout from the item in "Buzz Rush," and she said, "Not yet but the day is young."

"You do know The Bulldog is all over that," he said.

"I doubt she's the author, whoever The Stinger is, but I'm sure Soleil's lawyer worked her contacts to send me a message."

He filled her in on his visit from Holly Flanders and Nikki said,

"That's sweet, Rook. Sort of reinforces the faith I keep investing in humanity."

He said, "Good, then, because I almost didn't tell you."

"Why not tell me?"

"You know. I was afraid you might take it funny. A young woman coming to my place at night when I told you I'd be home alone, reading."

"That is so sweet that you'd think that I'd care." Nikki turned and left him there to sort that out while she got her manuscript.

Heat used paper clips and Rook used Post-it flags, but both had marked only a few passages in the book as pertinent to the case. And none pointed to direct suspicion of anyone as an agent of the gossip columnist's death. And, importantly, there was no concrete indication of anything untoward in Reed's passing. That was all deftly crafted as sly questions and hints of a bombshell payoff buildup by Cassidy Towne.

The passages they had marked were the same. Mostly they were name mentions of Soleil Gray and episodes in their drunken, druggy courtship. Tales from the movie set told of a sometimes morose Reed Wakefield who, after their romantic breakup, immersed himself deeper into the role of Ben Franklin's bastard child. His passion to escape his own life into the character's, many felt, would lead to an Oscar, even posthumously.

Much of the book was material the public had all known about Wakefield, but with insider detail that only Cassidy could have sourced. She didn't spare the actor any blemishes. One of the more damning, albeit minor, stories was attributed to a former costar of three of his films. The ex-costar and now ex-friend said that, after Reed became convinced he had lobbied the director of *Sand Maidens*, a sword-and-sandals CGI epic, to re-edit their battle scene for more close-ups of him than Reed, Wakefield not only wrote him off as a friend but took revenge. Photos captured on a cell phone arrived at the costar's wife's office. They were candids of the costar with his hand up the skirt of one of the hot extras at the wrap party. The message written on the back of one of the photos said, "Don't worry. It ain't love, it's location."

Both Heat and Rook had made a note to discuss that with each other, and both agreed that, even though the touchy-feely costar ended up divorced, it provided no motive for killing Cassidy Towne, since he had been the one to tell her the story.

The bulk was an anecdotal chronicle of a talented, sensitive actor's hard partying, boozing, snorting, popping, and shooting lifestyle. The conclusion Heat and Rook independently drew from reading the book was that if the final, missing chapter fulfilled the hype, the book would be a blockbuster, but from the material they had read, nothing in these pages seemed explosive enough to warrant the murder of the author to cover it up.

But then again, in the second to last chapter, where the manuscript left off, Reed Wakefield was still alive.

Detective Raley, who often cursed his designation as the squad's go-to screener of surveillance video, sealed his fate that morning. While she and Rook followed Ochoa, who had summoned them to Raley's desk, Nikki Heat could see from Raley's expression across the bull pen that he had a righteous freeze on his screen. "What do you have, Rales?" she said as they formed a semicircle around his desk.

"My last video to screen and I hit it, Detective. Parking garage only gave me legs and feet on the perp. Assailant seemed to run east after the attack, and so I worked that block and the one after. Small electronics retailer on the corner of Ninety-sixth and Broadway had this from a sidewalk pass-by, time coded six minutes after the mugging. Matches the description plus our subject is carrying a thick stack of papers, like the manuscript."

"Are you going to let me take a look?" asked Heat.

"By all means." Raley got up from his chair, knocking over one of the three coffee empties on his desk. Nikki came around to look at the freeze frame on his monitor. Rook joined her.

The freeze caught the mugger on a full-face turn to the camera, probably reacting to showing up live on the LED TV screen in the electronics shop window. In spite of the dark hoodie and the aviator sunglasses, there was no mistaking who it was. And further, even in grainy, surveillance-grade black-and-white, the mugger was caught red-handed carrying a stolen half ream of double-spaced manuscript.

"That's bringing it home, Raley." The detective didn't say anything, just beamed through some bleary eyes. "I'll give you the pleasure of cutting the warrant. Ochoa?"

"Ready the Roach Coach?"

"Now would be good," she said. And then when the two left on their assignments, she turned to Rook, unable to suppress a smile. "Ready for my close-up, Mr. DeMille."

FIFTEEN

Detective Heat knew Soleil Gray had a music video shoot that day because her lawyer had mentioned it the afternoon before when she accused Heat of harassing her client at her places of business. Well, she thought, add one to the list. Nikki looked up the number in her interview notes for Allie over at Rad Dog Records and found out where the video was being shot. The record company assistant said it wasn't on a soundstage but on location and gave Heat all the particulars, including where to park.

Fifteen minutes later, after a short drive south on Twelfth Avenue, Heat and Rook pulled up through the chain-link gate and passed a half dozen paparazzi lurking outside, some leaning on their motorcycles. Nikki flashed her shield at the security rent-a-cop and drove into the parking lot of the USS *Intrepid* at Pier 86. On the way there, Rook had asked if Heat was afraid Allie might call and tip off Soleil they were coming. "That would surprise me. I cautioned her not to and told her that this was going to be a felony arrest. I made it clear that if Soleil got tipped off by someone, that person could face charges as an accessory. Allie said not to worry, that she was going to head out for a long lunch and leave her cell phone at her desk. Turned off. She sounded like she'd even cancel her cellular contract."

Heat had caravanned with the Roach Coach behind her and, behind them, a van carrying a half dozen uniforms in case crowd control became an issue. Nikki had learned early on when she worked the organized crime unit that few planned arrests were routine and that it always paid off to take a quiet moment to stop and visualize what you were walking into and not just posse up and ride. On the outside chance there were any Soleil fans hanging out at this event, the last thing she wanted was to try to stuff a handcuffed double-platinum

Grammy nominee into the backseat of her Crown Vic while warding off a swarm of zealous disciples.

They all parked nose-out, poised for a rapid exit. When they got out of their vehicles, each and every one, including Nikki, did the same thing: tilted his or her head far back to look up at the retired navy aircraft carrier looming over them. "Makes you feel small," said Raley.

Ochoa, still craning up at the floating museum, asked, "How tall is that thing, anyway?"

"About six stories," said Rook. "And that's just from the wharf height we're on. From the waterline, add another story or two."

"What's it going to be," said Heat, "tour or arrest?"

They filed past the temporary base camp cordoned off for crew parking, portable dressing rooms, and meals. A caterer cooked split chickens on a huge grill, and the autumn air was filled with a mix of generator exhaust and grill smoke. At the top of the main gangway they were greeted by a young woman in a T-shirt and cargo pants, whose laminated ID said she was an assistant director. When Heat identified herself and asked where the shoot was, the AD pointed up toward the flight deck. She raised her walkie-talkie and said, "I'll tell them you're on your way."

"Don't," said Heat. She left a uniform behind just to make sure and to watch the exit.

After they ascended in the elevator, Heat and Rook stepped out onto the flight deck and were met by the playback track of "Navy Brats" carrying on the breeze from the stern of the flattop. The two of them walked toward the music, and as they came around an A-12 Blackbird, a Cold War spook plane and one of the thirty or so aircraft parked there, they found themselves behind a small army of video crew and its ordnance of props, lighting, miles of cable, and three HD cameras: one on a pedestal; a Steadicam harnessed onto a muscleman with ballet skills; and a boom for getting sweeping overhead shots.

They got there in the middle of a take, and Soleil Gray danced the steps Heat and Rook had seen her rehearse once in Chelsea and again at *Later On*. In her white sequined leotard, she cartwheeled across the set between an F-14 Tomcat and a Chickasaw helicopter, only this time something was different. There was a show intensity to her performance, a crispness and excitement that she had been saving for the cameras, and she unleashed it with abandon as the Steadicam operator backpedaled to track beside her and she flipped end-over-end the width of the deck, until she landed perfectly in the waiting arms of the sailor-suited male dancers.

Rook whispered to Nikki, "I predict one helluva prison talent show up in Taconic."

The director, who had been viewing it all on split screen at a hooded monitor, shouted for a cut, looked to his camera ops, and when he got nods in return, called a reset.

When the fill lights dimmed and the grips started hauling pieces of the set to the next mark, Heat made her move. With Rook following, she strode toward the canvas director chair where, in spite of the brisk fifty-degree air, Soleil Gray dabbed perspiration off her face. Ten feet from reaching her, a jumbo guy with a shaved head and wearing a yellow security windbreaker blocked the path. "Sorry, folks, this is a closed set. Tours resume tomorrow." He wasn't unpleasant, just a guy fulfilling the job description on the back of his jacket.

Nikki kept her voice low, showed her badge, and smiled. "Official police business."

But the singer, alert to everything happening on her set—or perhaps on the alert for something like this—lowered the towel from her face and stared at Nikki with wide eyes. Her makeup artist stepped in to repair the damage from the towel, but Soleil waved her off, keeping her attention on the visitors as she slid out of her chair.

Heat cleared the security man and, on her way to her, said, "Soleil Gray, NYPD. I have a warrant for your—"

And then Soleil turned and ran. Slightly behind her, to the port side of the ship, sat a small changing tent for the extras and, beyond it, a passage leading to a flight of metal stairs. Halfway there, Raley and Ochoa came around from behind the changing tent, followed by three uniformed officers. Soleil turned to make a break the opposite way, toward the hatch where Heat and Rook had come on deck, but another pair of officers was posted at that door. Rook ran into her path and she turned sharply again. Distracted by his move, she didn't notice that Nikki was a half step away. Heat made a lunge for her, but Soleil heard her footfall and spun clear. Heat's momentum carried her into a wardrobe rack, and in the instant it took her to regain her balance, her suspect was bolting across the almost football field–wide deck to the starboard side of the aircraft carrier. Soleil's shooting company—grips, electricians, dancers, the director—all looked on in a stunned zone of inertia and disbelief.

Her training kicked in and Heat drew her gun. A gasp rose from the crew, sharp enough and full of sufficient horror to let Soleil guess what had just happened behind her back. She slowed to a stop at the edge of the flight deck and turned to see Heat approaching, gun up, aimed at her. And then, without hesitation, Soleil Gray turned, and leaped over the edge.

Amid a clamor behind her from the frozen onlookers, Nikki rushed toward the side where the woman had gone over, trying to recall what lay six stories directly below her jump. Parking lot? Pier? The Hudson? And in those quick seconds, she also wondered, could someone survive a fall from that height even into water?

But when she got to the edge and peered over the side, Nikki saw something completely unexpected: Soleil Gray tucking and rolling her way out of a safety net suspended from the deck below. "Soleil, stop!" she called, and took aim again. But it was all for show. Heat certainly wasn't going to open fire on her under these circumstances, and the singer bet on that. Nikki reholstered about the same time she saw two men, stunt coordinators she would learn later, reaching for her suspect and pulling her out of sight onto the deck below, oblivious to what had just taken place above and unwittingly helping her escape.

Heat calculated options, thought of all the places to hide on a ship built to carry over 2,500 sailors, including all the mazes belowdecks. Then she thought of how slow the elevator or the stairs would be. "Roach," she said, "call down and have them seal the exit."

And then Detective Heat holstered her Sig and jumped over the side.

———

The pair of stunt coordinators helped her out of the net but then tried to subdue her. "What are you doing? I'm a cop."

One of them said, "She told us you were a crazed fan trying to kill her."

"Which way did she go?"

They sized up Nikki and pointed to a hatch. Nikki ran for it, taking the door cautiously in case Soleil was waiting on the other side, but she wasn't. Ahead of Nikki stood a long passageway and she went down it at a run. It terminated at a T, and Nikki paused briefly there, imagining, if she were Soleil, the direction she would choose in her scramble to escape. Her instincts made her turn left, rushing toward a stream of daylight and what felt like the direction of the wharf side of the ship.

Heat arrived at an open hatch, the source of all the sunlight. She paused long enough to bob her head through the opening and return it, once again cautious of an ambush. When she got through the hatch, she saw a metal staircase, probably the lower level of the same one Soleil had tried for topside before Roach appeared. She hoisted herself over the rail and descended the steps another level, to where they ended at a small deck near the stern, a semicircular balcony that hung out over the wharf and one of the carrier's power supply or warehouse sheds.

Then she spun, hearing shoes on the steps above her. "Rook?"

"God, you're fast. How do you do it? I'm still dizzy from the jump."

But Nikki wasn't paying attention to him anymore. She'd caught a flash of white and sequins in the sunlight on the pier below. Heat calculated the four-foot leap the singer had made across from the railing to the roof of the support shed and jumped it easily herself. While she ran across the shed's flat top to a metal spiral staircase leading down to the parking lot, she could hear Rook keeping pace behind.

The sole uniform they had left below had sealed off only the gangway, not anticipating a bold rooftop escape like the one Soleil had made, so there was no one to stop her when she came around the far side of the crew parking area, sprinting for the exit on Twelfth Avenue. Fifty yards behind her and gaining, Detective Heat called out to the security guard to stop her, but he was geared to protecting the singer and, instead, looked around for some unseen female assailant to stop, not Soleil herself.

She got out through the gate.

The pop star's curse quickly turned into a blessing when she saw the paparazzi loitering outside the fence, three of them with motorcycles. By now they were snapping her as she ran toward them. Soleil called to one of them by name. "Chuck! I need a ride, fast."

Chuck was already peeling out onto Twelfth with Soleil clinging to his back when Nikki got there. The other two paps with bikes were starting to saddle up to follow, but Heat showed her badge and pointed to the rider on the fastest bike. "You. Off. I need your bike for official police business." The paparazzo hesitated, weighing the legal penalty versus the loss of photo op, but he soon felt Heat's hand clutching his jacket. "Now."

Heat took off in pursuit and the other pap started to follow, but Rook arrived waving his arms, blocking him. He hit the brakes. "Rook?" said the photographer.

"Leonard?" said Rook.

Heat had to work to maintain her tail on Soleil and her paparazzo driver. He was reckless and ballsy, threading the needle between cars and zigzagging across lanes without a care about his series of near misses. As a cop in Manhattan, Nikki had seen how the celebrity shooters had increasingly begun to hunt in packs, often on motorcycles, and the image that always came to her was the pursuit of Diana in that tunnel in Paris. Now she was pursuing one of them and decided to exercise skill over daring so she didn't kill herself or a bystander.

But she was still able to keep up, if not overtake. It was evident that Soleil didn't have a destination; this was purely about evasive maneuvers, losing the tail. The path they took was a pattern of up one street, down another, through Midtown West. At one point, heading east on 50th, Soleil must have tired of the game, because Nikki saw her cast a look back, register Heat was still on their tail, and then shout something in the paparazzo's ear.

At the next corner her paparazzo, with the exclusive he could only have dreamed of, faked a right turn but instead cut a U, not only traveling the wrong direction on the one-way street but bearing down head-on at Nikki. Heat evaded, cutting to her right, and side skidded, nearly setting the bike down in the middle of traffic. But gearing down and steering into the skid, she made a U-turn herself, although almost clipping a parked FedEx truck as she swung her one-eighty.

Going the wrong way herself now, Heat flashed her headlight and used her horn. Fortunately the only close call she had was with a motorcycle driven by one of the other paps, with, she realized in disbelief, Jameson Rook on the back of the saddle, also in pursuit.

When they came to the end of the block, Soleil's driver cut a right and opened it up, racing north on Eleventh Avenue. Nikki kept pace, although she lost time slowing and creeping through the red lights instead of just busting them with impunity like the lead bike did. This was the time Heat wished she had her two-way so she could call in roadblocks or intercepts. But she didn't, so she kept her focus and grabbed speed where she could.

Eleventh Avenue became West End Avenue and shortly thereafter Soleil made another back glance that told Nikki to expect another stunt. It came at 72nd Street. Her driver carved a diagonal across the intersection, nearly getting popped by a bus, and then gunned it toward the Henry Hudson on-ramp. Heat followed cautiously through the intersection and had to lurch to a stop for an elderly woman on a walker, who shuffled into the crosswalk against the light and almost became Nikki's hood ornament. She waited until the yellow tennis balls slid by and then sped onward, but stopped at Riverside Drive and cursed.

She had lost them.

Heat almost got on the northbound Hudson but something stopped her. The traffic was thick, at a crawl. Even with the advantage of a motorcycle to squeeze through, that wouldn't be the escape route she would take. She heard a backfire and turned toward the sound. Behind the Eleanor Roosevelt statue at the opposite corner, a streak of white zoomed down the pedestrian path of the park that ran along the river. Nikki waited for an SUV to pass and then steered herself on a diagonal across the intersection, rode the handicap ramp up onto the sidewalk, and followed them into Riverside Park. Riding past the neighborhood dog run, she got yelled at by some of the pet owners. One of them threatened to call the police and she hoped they would. She sensed movement in her side mirror and knew without looking that Rook was following.

Nikki kept it slow on the paved pathway that ran north along the river. Even though it was mid-afternoon on a chilly day, there were enough joggers, cyclists, and dog walkers to pop out of nowhere, and she felt as long as she could see the motorcycle ahead, she could bide her time and make her move farther upriver, where there was less access to the greenway.

Her break came after the Boat Basin and before the sewage treatment plant in Harlem that had been converted into a state park. The stretch of pathway between the two landmarks ran parallel to train tracks that were fenced in and therefore formed a barrier to pedestrian access. Nikki gunned it. The cycle ahead also took advantage of the open path, but Nikki had the faster machine and was gaining on them. Soleil, looking surreal in the distance, like an apparition in white sequins, kept back-checking and gesturing for her driver to go faster. He shouldn't have.

Just before the state park, the path took a jog to the right, curving sharply away from the river. It was a turn engineered for pedestrians, not speeding motorcycles. Nikki knew the terrain from her weekend runs along this part of the Hudson and slowed before she got to the curve. When she came around it, Heat saw the bike on its side. The paparazzo was sliding his leg from underneath, his forearm bleeding from road rash. Soleil Gray was a short distance off trying to run away, hobbling on one of her legs.

Rook's driver also took the blind curve too fast and Nikki had to goose her bike to avoid getting hit. The other rider careened past her and struggled against a wipeout. Just as it looked like they were going over, he managed to correct and brought the bike to a stop without falling.

"Take care of this one," said Nikki, "he's hurt." And then she drove her motorcycle across the grass after Soleil, who was pulling herself up and over the chain-link fence separating the path from the train tracks.

The West Side Line was historically the conduit for Manhattan freight service with its tracks emerging from a tunnel at 122nd Street and running along the bank of the Hudson River from New York to Albany. Nineteen years before, the line had been taken over by Amtrak for northbound passenger service out of Penn, and as Detective Heat dismounted her motorcycle, the low rumble of a locomotive signaled one of those long passenger trains was coming. Soleil jumped down from the fence and ran across the siding in an attempt to make it onto the other side of the rails before Nikki got there, buying herself getaway time as the Empire Service rolled past and blocked the cop. But the locomotive got there first, and now Soleil was walled in by the long, lumbering train as Nikki also began to climb the fence.

"It stops here, Soleil," she called over the groan of metal and the screech of steel wheels passing behind her suspect. "Get away from the track. Lie down and put your hands behind your head."

"Come closer, I'll jump."

Nikki leaped down from the top of the fence, landing on both feet, and Soleil made a move closer to the track and leaned, canting her body toward the train, making as if she was going to throw herself under its passing wheels. "I'll do it."

Heat stopped. She was thirty feet away. Even though it was a flat surface, the gravel made poor footing and the singer was quick. Nikki couldn't hope to cover that distance and stop her from hurling herself under a wheel. "Soleil, come on, step away from there."

"You're right. It does stop here." She turned to look down at the track, metal rusted and coated with dust and carbon on the sides but gleaming brightly, like a fresh sheet of aluminum foil, on top, where the wheels churned by and friction carried away all grime. When Soleil looked up, Nikki was a few yards closer, and Soleil shouted, "Nuh!" and so she stopped.

"Just be still, then, Soleil. Take a minute, I'll wait." Nikki saw all the signs she didn't like on her. The woman's posture was deflating. Her body was turning in on itself, making her seem small and alien to the show wardrobe she had on. Every bit of arrogance and hardness was gone from the singer's face. Her mouth trembled and Nikki could see red blotches surfacing through her stage makeup. And she kept staring down at those wheels grinding by two feet away from her. "Are you hearing me?" Nikki called over the noise, knowing she was but just trying to pull focus.

Soleil said, in a barely audible voice, "I don't think I can do this."

"Then don't."

"I mean go on anymore."

"You'll work it through." Both of them knew she had to arrest her, but the detective was trying to get her to look past the immediate. Move her out of The Now.

"What happened to that guy? You know, from yesterday morning?"

"He's fine. Be out of the hospital tomorrow." Heat was guessing but told herself this was the time for positive thoughts. She flashed back to Interrogation 1 the day before and the cut on Soleil's knuckle, the one she kept nibbling at. At the time she assumed it came from rehearsal, having seen how physical the routines were. The god of hindsight visited her, and she now saw it as the mugger's battle scar.

"I had to get it. He wouldn't let go, so I had to . . ."

"He's going to be OK. Come on, get away from there."

"I still have nightmares about it." Soleil ignored Nikki; she was off in her own conversation. "I can deal with jail, maybe. But not the nightmares. About what happened to Reed, I mean. I want that night back. It was so stupid." And then she shouted, "*I* was so stupid . . . And now I'll never have him again."

As Soleil broke down in sobs, Heat was torn between wanting her to go on and tell the story of what happened to Wakefield; an obligation to read her her rights so if this turned into a confession she could use it in court; and a human need to not lead Soleil into a place so dark she would take her own life. "Soleil, we can talk about this later. Come on, come to me, let's get you some help, all right?"

"I don't deserve to live. Do you hear me?" Her mood weather vaned from somber to angry. The biting tone Nikki was accustomed to receiving suddenly got turned inward. "I don't deserve to be here. Not after Reed. Not after what I did to him. Fighting, killing our relationship. That was all me. I called off the marriage. I hurt him so bad. . . ." And then the anger gave way to more sobs.

Nikki glanced down the track, wishing to spot the end of the train, but the line of passenger cars extended as far south as she could see. It hadn't gotten to speed yet and its slow roll made its length feel infinite to Heat.

"And then that night. Do you know the guilt I carry around about that night?"

Nikki assumed it was the night of Reed's death, but again she didn't want to tip Soleil over the edge by asking at a time of such vulnerability, so she said, "You won't have to carry it alone anymore. Understand?"

Soleil pondered that, and Nikki began to have hope that at last something she said was reaching her. That's when they both turned toward the noise. Three NYPD motorcycles rolled slowly with lights but no sirens down the path. Nikki turned the other way just as a Parks Department SUV was rolling up beside Rook from the other direction. Heat saw the change in Soleil and called out to Rook, "Tell them to stay back!"

Rook stepped to the driver's window and spoke to the Parks officer, who Nikki watched grab his microphone. Seconds later, the NYPD motorcycles must have gotten his call, because they braked and waited in the near distance, idling, the purr of their engines mixing with the squeaking and moaning of the lumbering train.

"I can't deal with it all, I can't," moaned Soleil. "It's all too much."

Nikki could finally see the end of the train about a hundred yards away and began calculating her rush.

"I just feel . . . hollow. I can't turn off the pain."

Fifty yards to go. "I'll get you through this, Soleil." Now only three more cars. "Will you let me help you?" Nikki extend her arms, hoping her gesture would be felt over the yards that separated them, across the crushed stone of the railroad siding. Soleil straightened her posture, looking like a dancer again. She raised her face to the sun with her eyes closed for a moment, then lowered it to look right at Nikki, smiling at her for the first time ever. And then she threw herself under the last car.

SIXTEEN

NYPD cordoned off a wide area around the scene of Soleil Gray's suicide to keep media and fans at a distance so the medical examiner, Forensics, and the chief's squad from One Police Plaza that routinely investigated any officer-involved death could do their jobs with privacy and focus. Other investigative personnel, including Parks and Rec and representatives from the train company and its insurance carrier were present but would have to wait their turns. To maintain the dignity of the deceased and to give the technicians privacy, a line of portable vinyl screens had been erected on both sides of the train tracks where most of the singer's remains were strewn. Twelfth Avenue had been closed off between West 138th and 135th Streets, but news photographers, paparazzi, and mobile TV newsrooms had staked out elevated vantage points both in Riverbank State Park and on the opposite side of the tracks, on Riverside Drive. OCME deployed a tent fly to mask the scene from the half dozen news choppers that had positioned themselves overhead.

Captain Montrose visited Detective Heat where she waited alone in one of the police personnel vans, still shaken, holding a cup of coffee that had grown cold resting in both her hands. He had just come from a huddle with the chief's unit and told her that their initial interviews of Rook, the two paparazzi, the Parks officer, and the motorcycle cops all corroborated her story that the woman jumped of her own volition and that Heat had done everything she could to diffuse the situation and prevent the suicide.

The skipper offered to let her take a few days off to recover, even though she was not going to get put on leave or desked. Nikki gave it to him straight. She felt deeply upset but knew that this case wasn't closed yet. The cop part of her—the part that could compartmentalize the human tragedy and stuff down the trauma she felt from what she had witnessed two hours before—that part viewed Soleil's death objectively as a loose end. Vital information died with her. Heat knew she had cleared the mugging of the book editor, but many questions remained that she could no longer get answers for out of Soleil Gray. And the Texan, Rance Wolf, who was potentially her accomplice and the lead-pipe cinch to have been the killer of three people, was still at large. And as long as the last chapter of Cassidy Towne's book was unaccounted for, there was every reason to believe he would kill again to get it. Unless the need to do so had also died with Soleil Gray.

"I'm feeling it, Captain, but that part will have to wait." Detective Heat poured her cold coffee out the open door and onto the gravel. "So if that's all, I need to get back to work."

———

Back at the precinct, Heat and Rook had a moment alone for the first time since it had happened. Even though a police cruiser had brought them back to the Two-Oh together, she'd ridden up front in the partner seat in silence; he had the back to himself and spent most of the ride trying to shake the image of what he had seen. Not just the grisly death of Soleil Gray, but the anguish he'd observed in Nikki. Both of them had seen their share of human tragedy in their careers. But whether it was Chechnya or Chelsea, nothing prepared you for witnessing the instant life leaves a body. When he took her elbow and stopped her in the hall on the way to the bull pen, he said to her, "I see the brave front, and we both know why. But just know I'm here, OK?"

Nikki wanted right then to indulge herself in a brief squeeze of his hand, but not at work. And Heat also knew it wouldn't be wise to open the door to her vulnerability just yet. So that was it for sentiment. She nodded and said, "Let's bring this home," and pushed on into her squad room.

———

Detective Heat kept herself in motion, not giving anyone an opening to ask her about how she was doing. She became instead all about doing. Nikki knew she would have to deal with what she had experienced at some point, but not yet. And she reminded herself that, by the way, it was not she but Soleil Gray who had experienced the worst of it.

Detective Hinesburg, ever sensitive and empathic, turned from her computer monitor to ask Heat if she wanted to see the online pics of Soleil's death scene from the Web edition of the *Ledger*. She didn't. Fortunately, the pictures taken by the two paparazzi at the scene hadn't surfaced yet. They were still being reviewed by investigators as corroborative evidence of the sequence of events. No doubt the moment-of-death shot would go up for bidding and be purchased by some British or German webloid for six figures. People would shake their heads in disgust and then surf to see if they had to register to see it.

Heat looked at the board, staring at Soleil's name, hearing the plaintive echo of her voice before her death, lamenting "that night." She called Ochoa's cell phone and caught him en route back to the precinct. "I'm revisiting every loose connection I have here," she told him, "and I can't get past the missing limo manifest for the night of Wakefield's death."

"I'm with you," said Ochoa, "but it's sort of like that last chapter. As long as it's missing, we can only guess."

"Tell Raley to turn that Roach Coach around. I want you guys to go back to Spanish Harlem. Talk to the family again, the coworkers again. Maybe if you ask more specifically about Reed Wakefield something will kick loose. See if Padilla was in service that night and if he confided anything about what he saw or heard, even from the other drivers."

Ochoa paused, and Nikki was afraid he was about to offer her some sort of condolence for her ordeal by the tracks. But he sighed and said, "We'll do it, but I have to tell you, me and my partner have had a bitch of a day today. But you wouldn't know anything about that, would you?"

Yep. A gal could get misty.

———

It was not quite six, and Rook was sliding the strap of his messenger bag over his shoulder. "Knocking off early?" said Nikki.

"Got a text from my editor at *First Press*. Now that this Soleil business has kicked the story up to an international scale, they want me to file by tomorrow so they can get a rush edition into production."

"So you're going to go finish up the article?"

He laughed. "Hell no. I'm going to go start the article."

"I thought that's what you had been doing."

"Shh." He looked around conspiratorially and lowered his voice to a whisper. "So does my editor." Then he added, "Call me later. If you want, you can come over for a beer or something."

"You have a full night ahead of you, mister. You'll be busy . . . with your toy helicopter and all. Besides, the sooner the new edition is on the newsstands, the sooner mine is off, so don't let me slow you down." He started to go, and as he went she said, "Hey, Rook?" He stopped. "I need to tell you how foolish you were following me like that today. First on the carrier and then with that paparazzo on the motorcycle. So first of all, never pull a stunt like that again. And second? Thanks for having my back."

"Sorry and you're welcome," he said as he turned and left.

Roach waited before they got out of the car. They had cruised the block for a space, and when they passed Esteban Padilla's old address, his cousin was just stepping out the front door. "Shall we reach out?" said Raley.

"Know what?" said his partner. "That dude's just a buzz killer. Let's hang back until he's gone and see if the kid's home. We'll start with him."

Twenty minutes later, Esteban Padilla's buzz-killing cousin unlocked his front door and, as he stepped in, called out in Spanish, "Yo, Pablo, I'm back. You ready to roll?" Then he stopped short when he saw that the detectives were once again in his living room with Esteban's teenage nephew.

"You taking some kind of trip, Victor?" asked Ochoa.

Victor gave Pablo a WTF look and the boy looked away.

"This is some nice luggage, man. Quality stuff, all brand-new. This is real Tumi, huh, not that knockoff crap."

"Yeah, well, we're taking some vacation time. Need to chill after the funeral and all," said the cousin, not sounding very convincing, even to Raley, who didn't speak the language.

"That's a lot of luggage for just a vacation. How long you plan to be gone?" When the cousin just stood there with his door keys in one hand

and a CVS bag in the other, Ochoa rose from his chair and walked the line of suitcases. "Let's see, you've got two jumbo sizes here. A garment bag—I guess that's for those new clothes we saw hanging on the door the other day. Another large suitcase. Three carry-ons . . . Homes, you are going to get so hit with baggage fees. And tips. You're going to need to tip that skycap a ton to help with all this. That's going to cost you, my friend. But you can handle that, I guess, right?"

Victor said nothing, just stared at a dead spot in the air somewhere between himself and Ochoa.

"Well, I think you can swing it no sweat. Tips, baggage fees . . . I bet you could even get a limo from your cousin's old boss to drive you to the airport and it still wouldn't make a dent. Not in this." The detective nudged a small sport duffel with the toe of his shoe. The skin on Victor's forehead tightened and his gaze slowly descended to the bag. The top zipper was wide open and the stacks of cash were visible.

"I told you to zip it," Victor said to the boy.

Ochoa wanted to ask whether he meant his mouth or the duffel, but he didn't want to ice the conversation. They had a lot to talk about.

———

Back at the precinct, Heat took a call from Raley, who told her about the carry-on of cash and that they were bringing Victor and Pablo in for questioning. She agreed that since the bag was open and in plain view, spotting the money likely obviated the need for a search warrant, but that he should consult the DA in case any charges came out of this. "How much cash was it?"

"Ninety-one thou." Raley paused before he added, "In twenties."

"Interesting number."

"Yeah, and we ran a check, the cousin's straight. No drug busts, no gambling or gang affiliations. That chunk of change smells like some sort of payoff that's light by about nine thousand. My guess is it went to plane tickets, wardrobe, and luggage."

"A hundred grand just doesn't go as far as it used to, does it, Rales?"

He laughed. "Like I would know."

When Heat hung up, she turned to find Sharon Hinesburg hovering around her desk. "We've got a customer coming."

"Who?" Nikki figured it was too much to hope it would be the Texan, and she was correct.

"Morris Granville. The Toby Mills stalker? They picked him up in Chinatown trying to get on a Fung Wah bus to Boston. He'll be here in thirty minutes. Or you don't pay." Hinesburg handed her Granville's file.

"They're bringing him here?" asked Heat. "Why not the Nineteenth Precinct or CPK? Central Park claimed turf on him, we're just cooperating."

"Except the arresting officers say the guy mentioned you specifically by name. He says he saw you in yesterday's 'Buzz Rush' and has something he wants to talk to you about."

"Know if he said what?"

Detective Hinesburg shook her head. "Maybe it's a desperate attempt to bargain." And then she chuckled. "Hey, I know. Now that you're a big celebrity, maybe he wants to stalk you."

"Hilarious," said Nikki mirthlessly.

Oblivious as ever, Hinesburg said, "Thanks," and moved on.

Nikki wondered if she should call Toby Mills's manager, Jess Ripton, to notify him. Ripton had cooperated by providing photos and details about Granville, but the stalker's specific request to see her was unusual enough to make Heat decide to see what that was about before inviting the brutish distraction of The Firewall into the mix. And to be truthful, she had to admit she was annoyed at the manager for being such a ballbuster every time they encountered each other. Making him wait an hour brought an undeniable passive-aggressive satisfaction she wasn't proud of but could live with. Cops are human, too.

While she reviewed Morris Granville's jacket to prepare for the interview, her phone rang. It was Petar.

"I heard that was you with Soleil Gray today and wanted to see how you were doing."

"Holding up," she said. The mental replay of the singer's dive under the train spooled again in the sickening slow motion unique to traumas. Nikki tried to switch it off before the part with the blood on the white leotard but couldn't. Then she realized Petar was asking her something. "I'm sorry, I missed that. What did you say?"

"I was asking if you wanted to get together on my dinner break."

"Petar, you know, this may not be the best night."

"I probably shouldn't have called," he said.

"No, it's thoughtful of you, thanks. I'm just preoccupied. You can imagine."

"OK then. I know you better than to push."

"Smart boy."

"Hey, if I were that smart, I would have learned that years ago. Anyway, I'm sorry you had to go through what you did today, Nikki. I'm sure you did everything you could."

"I did. But it was in her head to do this. Soleil had something she couldn't live with and found her way to end the pain."

"Did she say what?"

"Unfortunately, no." Heat made it a practice never to discuss details of a case with anyone outside the squad, so she slid by it. "All I do know is there was nothing I could have done." Saying it made her feel a little better, though she knew that if she really believed it, she'd stop the replay and the search for what she could have done differently.

"Nikki," he said, "I know right now isn't the time . . . but I want to . . . see you again." The weight of that notion and the complication it brought was off the charts for her to even consider, especially after her day.

"Petar, listen—"

"Bad timing, sorry. See? I pushed it anyway. When will I learn?" He paused. "What about a coffee or something tomorrow?"

Across the room, Detective Hinesburg appeared in the doorway and gave her a beckoning nod. Nikki picked up Granville's file. "Tomorrow . . . Yeah, maybe we could do that."

"I'll call you in the morning. In the meantime, please know that if you want to talk, I'm here for you."

"Thanks, I appreciate that." After she hung up, she stared at her phone, feeling a little strange about his call and his pushing. Then Detective Heat cleared her head and strode off to Interrogation.

———

In the corridor she met up with Raley, who was outside Interrogation 1. "How's it going with the lottery winners from East Harlem?"

"Ochoa's in there with them now. Nothing yet." He held up a package of peanut butter crackers and a bottle of hideous blue energy water from the vending machine. "The kid's hungry, so I'm springing for dinner."

"I'll be in I2 with Toby Mills's stalker. But let me know if anything breaks."

Nikki stood a few moments in the Observation Room to size up Morris Granville through the glass before she went in. His file said he was forty-one, but in person he looked more like he was in his twenties. In spite of his receding hairline and the first strands of gray showing up in his thick brown curls, he had the look of a man-child. Chubby, short, with a pasty complexion and a slouchy posture that made his neck disappear into his double chin. He was alone and kept looking up at himself in the mirror across the room, but sideways, never facing himself. It was as if he kept checking to see if he would still be there when he looked back.

Granville sat up when Heat entered the room and sat down. His eyes, which had a permanent squint that made him look like he was always smiling, widened and fixed on her in a way that made Nikki feel uncomfortable. Not leered at so much as . . . gawked at with unearned admiration and intimacy.

"I'm Detective Heat." She tossed his file and a pen on the table and sat. "You wanted to talk to me about something?"

He stared at her some more and said, "I loved your magazine article."

"Mr. Granville . . ."

"So formal. Morris is fine. May I call you Nikki?"

"No."

"I saved an issue. Is there any chance I could get you to sign it?"

"Zero." She watched him tilt his head down. His mouth twitched ever so slightly and his dense eyebrows flicked, as if he was having some sort of inner conversation. While he talked to himself, she said, "If you read that article, you'd know I'm a busy person. Do you want to tell me what you've got to say, or shall I call the van so we can get you to Riker's in time for chow?"

"No, don't."

"Then let's hear it."

"I wanted to talk to you because I saw in 'Buzz Rush' yesterday that you were following Soleil Gray around."

Coming from a stalker, that put the *Ledger* item in an entirely different context for Nikki. She thought about The Stinger and understood the enmity celebrities felt for the gossip press. But she came back to Granville and wondered, What was his deal? Was this Hinesburg's insensitive joke coming to pass? Heat knew stalkers had no single profile, but her take from his file was that his "special identification issue" was focused on a single celebrity, Toby Mills. That's where all the complaints derived. And all the trespassing citations and disorderly conducts. At least officially, he didn't have a pattern of obsession with celebrities in general—not Soleil Gray and, hopefully, not cover girl cops.

"What's your interest in Soleil Gray?"

"She was an awesome musician. A great loss."

"That's it? Thank you for the visit, Mr. Granville."

Nikki gathered up her materials to go, and he said, "No, that's not all." She paused but gave him a look under an arched brow that said he'd better bring it. He blinked and lifted his palms off the tabletop, leaving perspiration ghosts in the shape of hands on the surface. "I saw her once. In person."

His look of pride at what he thought was the apparent significance of that fact made her reflect on the psychology of these people, the latch-ons. How they defined themselves by proximity to a stranger. In extreme cases, usually in schizophrenics, they even believed the star was communicating uniquely to them through messages embedded in their songs or talk-show interviews. They obsessed about them to the point that they would go to extraordinary lengths to make themselves relevant in their lives—some even to the point of killing the objects of their infatuation. "Go on," she said. Something in his urgency told her there was no harm in playing it out. "So you saw her, lots of people have."

"She was outside a nightclub one night, actually early morning by then. It was late enough I was the only one out there."

"Where?"

"At Club Thermal down in the Meat Packing District. And Soleil? She was dru-unk, loaded. Really loud and waving her arms all over and having this major fight out on the sidewalk, you know where all the limos line up?"

At the mention of the limos, Heat took the files out of her hands, set them back in front of her, and nodded. "Yeah, I know the place. Tell me what you saw." The irony struck her that, for this shining moment in his twisted life, Granville was relevant, and that she was feeding that very need.

"Like I said, she was loud and really hot—yelling, you know? And when I saw who she was fighting with, I thought, if I can ever get close enough with my cell phone, this picture would make the cover of *People* or *Us*. Or at least the *Ledger*."

"Why couldn't you get closer? Was there security?"

"No. It was past closing. And they were the only other ones on the sidewalk. I didn't get too close because I didn't want them to see me."

Nikki was drawn in. Assuming he wasn't delusional or grandiose, he seemed credible in his own nutty way. She wanted him to be telling the truth. "Who was she fighting with? Why was it such a big deal?"

"Because," he said, "she was fighting with Reed Wakefield the same night he died."

SEVENTEEN

Jameson Rook glanced up across his office from the screen of his laptop and cast a longing look at the helicopter sitting on the windowsill. His orange Walkera Airwolf had survived the violent room toss by the Texan and now beckoned the writer to take a time-out and come play. He could rationalize a break, too. After drafting for hours, the aluminum body of his MacBook Pro was warm to the touch, bearing witness, he told himself, to his laudible work ethic. It reminded him of the way the helicopter fuselage warmed agreeably after it took flight around his loft.

"And lead me not into temptation," he said and went back to his keyboard. A journalist who relied heavily on his personal observations, who liked to get his shoes dirty and his shins bruised, whether it was diving for cover in the rubble of a Grozny high-rise during a Russian air attack, tracking Bono to rural Senegalese hospitals with singer Baaba Maal, or getting a polo lesson in Westchester County from one of the visiting young royals, Rook knew the stories were in the experience, not on the Internet. He had a vivid memory and a notes system that delivered him back into the moment every time he pulled the frayed black ribbon of his Moleskine bookmark to part it to a lined page of quotes remembered and details observed.

He worked rapidly from beginning to end of the articles as he wrote, drafting at first-impression speed, leaving gaps and reserving the fine work to be done later when he would move once again from front to back. He made numerous passes like that but always continuously, without any backtracking, for a sense of flow. He wrote as if he were the reader. It was also how he kept his writing from becoming too cute, which is to say, about him not the subject. Rook was a journalist but strove to be a storyteller, one who let his subjects speak for themselves and stayed out of their way as much as possible.

The voice of Cassidy Towne came back to him, and through him she was once again alive in Times New Roman, in all her lively, bitchy, guffawing, honest, vengeful, and righteous self. As Rook chronicled his days and nights with her, what emerged was a woman for whom everything in life, from getting the best cut of Nova to landing an exclusive with an S&M dominatrix who'd brought a congressman to his knees, was a transaction. Her mission in the world was not to be a conduit but a source of power.

A restlessness came over Rook as he neared the end of his rough draft. The discomfort came from knowing how much was not known about the defining event of her life. Sure, he could fill in the gaps in the middle, there was plenty of color for that, but the piece concluded before it reached the real end of the story. His word count swelled; he had enough for a two-parter (note to call the agent), but the bulk of his article, as soundly as it was coming together, felt like a drumroll without the cymbal crash.

Just like Cassidy Towne's book.

He picked up the helicopter's radio controller, but guilt pangs made him set it down beside his laptop and reach for her unfinished manuscript. Moving from his desk to the easy chair beside the small fireplace filled with candles, he flipped through her text again, wondering what he had missed. What crescendo had she been building to?

The storyteller in him felt like he would be cheating to submit an exclusive profile that concluded with a glaring loose end. Questions, however intriguing, were not satisfying to him and wouldn't be to the reader he respected so much, either.

That's when he went old school. He took out a fresh Circa notepad, found a fountain pen that had some ink in it, and started to freestyle. *What do I want?* To find the ending for my article. *No, you don't.* Then what? *You know.* Do I? *Yes, you know, you just haven't defined it properly yet.* . . .

Every time Rook did this, he thought that if someone found these ramblings in his trash, they would think he was a madman. It was actually a technique he had picked up from a fictional character in one of the Stephen King novels, a writer who, when he needed to sort out a plot, interrogated himself on paper. What seemed like a cool device in a novel got put to use by Rook once, and it worked so well connecting him to his subconscious that he employed it whenever he needed to think through dense terrain. It was like having a writing partner who didn't take a percentage.

. . . *You are defining the wrong goal.* I know my goal, to name her killer in the damned article. And Esteban Padilla's. And Derek Snow's. *You know the killer, it's the Texan.* That's a technicality. *That's right, you want whoever hired him.* Soleil Gray? *Maybe. But now that she's dead, too, it's a guess.* Unless . . . *Unless?* Unless I—Unless I can find that last chapter. *Congratulations, you just defined your goal.* I did? *Pay attention. Don't read your notes looking for clues to the killer. Or even the one who hired him. Read them looking for clues to what Cassidy did with the last chapter.* What if she hadn't written it yet? *Then you're screwed.* Thanks. *No prob.*

As it usually did, his little exercise in dual personality disorder brought him around to something basic and obvious he had overlooked because it had become so familiar. He had been looking for a who, and he needed to shift to a what—and the what was the AWOL chapter. Back at his laptop, Rook opened the Word document of notes he had transcribed from his Moleskine. He scrolled at skim-reading speed looking for something to grab him by the shirt. While he reviewed the notes, he could almost hear Nikki's voice asking him over and over again since they'd reunited, "What is it you have observed about this woman?"

The qualitative things, like her need to control and her compulsion to exercise power, were character traits not to be ignored, but that didn't lead him anywhere specific. So what else did he know about her?

Cassidy slept with a lot of men. He paused to think if he could envision one she seemed to trust enough to hold the critical chapter, and none came to mind. Her neighbors were sources of complaints and feuding, not trust. Her building super was an entertaining character who did good work but was graced with just enough charming larceny that Rook couldn't see her entrusting the chapter to JJ. Rule out Holly, too. Her daughter's kinder feelings after her mother's death didn't seem to have been reciprocated in the last weeks of her life. So that is what he knew about Cassidy Towne and her relationships. They didn't work except transactionally.

On his computer, Rook stopped the scroll on one of the notes, one of the small details of her character he had meant to include but forgotten. The porcelain plaque near the French doors in her office that pretty much summed up her view of relationships. "When life disappoints, there's always the garden."

Rook slowed down his scrolling to read more carefully. He had entered a section of notes of some length because it was about her passion for gardening. If not redeeming, it was at least illuminating. He came across a topic sentence he'd tried out and rejected as too flip after he and Nikki visited Cassidy's belated autopsy and Lauren showed the dirt under the gossip columnist's nails. He had written, "Cassidy Towne died the way she lived, with dirt on her hands." Much as he liked the line, its glibness broke his rule of authorial intrusion.

And yet as a fact instead of as prose, it made him stop and think.

He skimmed ahead to observations he had made about the numerous times he saw her coming and going through those French doors to her garden in the little walled back courtyard. Cassidy would get off a phone call with her editor, and Rook would follow her out there and wait patiently while she deadheaded some of her plants or tested the soil moisture with her fingers. She told him that tiny enclosure was the whole reason she'd chosen that place to live. One evening, when he arrived to accompany her to a Broadway opening party, she greeted him in her cocktail dress holding a clutch purse in one hand and a garden trowel in the other.

Then he stopped again. This time on a quote he planned to use in the article, maybe even in boldface—the one that elegantly tied together her vocation with her avocation. The one when Cassidy said if you are on to something big, "Keep your mouth shut, your eyes open, and your secrets buried."

Rook sat back in his chair and stared at that quote. Then he shook his head, dismissing his thought. He was just about to scroll on when he remembered another quote he had heard recently. From a Detective

Nikki Heat. "We follow the leads we have, not the ones we wish we had."

He looked at his watch and got out his cell phone to call Nikki. But then he hesitated, feeling that if this was some fool's errand he was about to undertake, he didn't want to drag her along, especially after the day she had had. He thought about bagging the idea he was hatching altogether. But then he had another notion. He went to his notebook and thumbed back until he found the number he wanted.

"You're lucky you caught me," said JJ. "I was about to go out to the movies."

"Well that's my good luck." Rook took a step closer to Cassidy Towne's front door, hoping the super would pick up his cue and spare the chatter. And if that move was too subtle, he decided to eliminate ambiguity. "So if you'll just open up, I can do my thing and you can make your show."

"You go to the movies these days?"

"A few."

"Know what bugs me?" asked JJ, not making any move toward the carabiner holding all the keys dangling from his belt. "You pay your money getting in, and it's not cheap, am I right? And you sit down to watch a film, and what do people do during the movie? Talk. They talk and talk and talk. Spoils the whole experience."

"I agree," said Rook. "What film are you going to?"

"*Jackass* in 3D. That is one funny buncha wing nuts, I tell you. And it's in 3D, so you know the laughs are going to be big when those fellas start crashing their shit into light poles and such."

Twenty dollars eventually diverted the super's attention away from social commentary to opening the door. JJ demonstrated how to lock up and left for the cinema. Once inside, Rook locked the door behind him and snapped on lights so he could navigate the clutter in Cassidy Towne's apartment, which was only in a slightly more orderly state of the disarray he had last seen.

He stood in her office long enough to give it one more scan in case there was a clue that spoke now but hadn't had a voice the morning of her murder. Finding none, he stepped to the light switch beside the porcelain plaque, and when he flicked it on, the little courtyard through the French doors became bathed in mellow light.

Holding a flashlight and one of Cassidy's trowels, Rook surveyed the plantings in the terraced rows rising up from the brickwork patio in her cloister. In the subdued lightscape she had created, the colors of the autumn flowers that surrounded him were muted to dark gray tones. Rook switched on his flashlight to illuminate the shadows, shining it around slowly and methodically, passing it over each planter. He wasn't sure what he was looking for. And he certainly wasn't about to turn the whole garden into an archaeological dig. So he employed another Heatism and looked for an odd sock. He didn't know the names of most of what he was looking at, just a few, like pink salvia and New York aster. One variety Cassidy had pointed out to him once was Liatrus, also known as blazing star when it was in the last of its bright summer color. Now it had gone to seed heads and faded to rusty brown.

A quarter hour into his search, Rook brought his light to rest on a chrysanthemum. In his beam its flowers were rich-colored and fall-ish but somehow seemed ordinary for what Cassidy had grown around them. . . . Somewhat of an odd sock. He stepped closer and also noticed that unlike the other flowers and plants, this one was buried in the soil but still in its flowerpot. He clamped the flashlight in his armpit and used the trowel to dig out the pot. He removed it from the soil, tapped the pot on the planter to loosen the packed dirt and roots, and then dumped it all onto the bricks of the patio. It was a large enough pot to hold the curve of a chapter of manuscript, but there was none such inside. To be thorough Rook went back to the cavity left by the pot and poked the bottom of it with the point of the trowel blade, to feel for any stack of buried paper, and found none. But he hit something that felt through the wooden handle like a small rock, which would be unusual given Cassidy's clean, floury soil.

He shined the flashlight into the hole and caught the reflection of a plastic sandwich bag. Rook reached in, pulled it out, and held it in front of his beam. Inside it was a key.

Ten minutes later, after walking every room and closet and examining every cabinet in Cassidy Towne's apartment, he had found no lock that the key fit. Rook sat down at the kitchen table and studied it. It was a small key, not the kind that fits a door lock but the kind that is more suited for padlocks or lockers. It was fairly new, with a crisp edge on its teeth, and embossed into it was a three-digit number: 417.

He took out his iPhone and called Nikki's cell and got voice mail. "Hi, it's Rook. Got a question for you, call me when you can." Then he tried her at the precinct. The desk sergeant picked up. "Detective Heat's busy in interrogation and forwarded her phone. Do you want her voice mail?" Rook said yes and left a similar message.

Cassidy belonged to a gym but he had seen her with her gym bag and noticed the hot pink combination lock clamped on the strap, so scratch that off. The key could belong to a public locker like in a bus station, and Rook thought of how many bus and train terminals with lockers there were in New York City. It was also possible it fit some cubby at the *New York Ledger* offices, but tonight anyway, he wasn't about to visit there and introduce himself. "Hi, Jameson Rook. I have a key. May I . . . ?"

Then he realized he had seen a key like this before. In 2005 Rook had been on assignment for two months in New Orleans after Katrina and lived in a rented RV. Since he moved around the area so much, he had rented a mailbox at a UPS store, and this was the kind of key they had issued him. Wonderful, he thought, now all I have to do is go to every mail drop in New York and hope to get lucky.

Rook rapped the key on the kitchen table and tried to recall if he had seen Cassidy go to or near a mail drop. He couldn't come up with one and wasn't sure if there was one in this neighborhood. And then he remembered her daughter, Holly. Holly Flanders had said she found out where Rook lived by looking on the waybills for the messenger service her mother used to send him material. He couldn't remember the name of the service, and there was no way to find that needle in the haystack of Cassidy Towne's office.

After he locked up, Rook walked to Columbus to hail a cab down to Tribeca, to see if he still had any of the shipping envelopes he had received from Cassidy. As the cab passed West 55th, he had a brain tug that the place was located somewhere in Hell's Kitchen. He did a Google search of messenger services on his phone, and five minutes later the taxi dropped him outside Efficient Mail and Messenger on Tenth Avenue, a storefront squeezed between an Ethiopian restaurant and a small grocer with hot tables and pizza by the slice. The garbage pileup had gobbled the sidewalk outside, and under Efficient's dingy awning some of the letters were sputtering in the neon window sign, which read, "Checks Cashed — Copies — Fax." A little run down, he thought as he went inside, but if the key fits, paradise.

The place smelled of old library and pine disinfectant. A small man in a turban sat on a high stool behind a counter. "You wish to make copy?" Before Rook could say no, the man spoke rapidly in a foreign language to a woman using the sole copy machine. She answered back in a short, angry tone and the man said to Rook, "Be five minute."

"Thanks," said Rook, not wanting to engage or explain. He was already at the wall where the bank of brass mail cubbies ran its length from knee to eyebrow. He scanned them and found number 417.

"You rent mailbox? Monthly special."

"All set." Rook held up the key and inserted it. It went in cleanly, but the lock didn't budge. He waggled it with some force, remembering that the teeth of the key had a freshly cut edge and might need some coaxing. Still nothing. He looked and realized that when the counterman had distracted him he had put the key in 416.

The teeth of the key snagged in 417, then it opened. He got down on one knee to look inside and his heart kicked.

Two minutes later, in another cab to Tribeca, he tried Nikki again. She was still in interrogation. This time Rook didn't leave a message. He slouched back between the seat and back door of the taxi and took the stack of double-spaced, typewritten pages from the envelope. They were curled from having been half-rolled to fit inside the mail cubby, so he flattened them on his thigh and held the paper-clipped packet to the window light to read the chapter title again.

CHAPTER TWENTY

—

FADE OUT

EIGHTEEN

Nikki Heat was big on hands. Sitting in an interrogation room, what she could observe physically about the person across the table was as important as what that person was saying—or not saying. Facial expressions, of course, were key. So were posture, demeanor (restless, fidgety, calm, checked out, and so forth), state of hygiene, and attire. But hands told her a lot. Soleil Gray's hands had been lean and strong from the rigors of her athletic stage dancing. Strong enough, as it turned out, to overpower Mitchell Perkins with such force that people assumed his assailant had been a man. One of the tells Nikki had misjudged when the singer had been sitting at the table with her lawyer just the day before was the cut on her knuckle which the detective had taken to be from the rehearsal hall, not the street mugging.

Now, self-reproach was trying to creep in on Heat, pestering her with the virulent notion that if she had only looked at that hand with a more open view to causes she might have averted a tragedy. She told that idea to have a seat, she'd deal with it later.

Morris Granville's hands were soft and pallid, as if he soaked them daily in bleachy water. He was also a nail biter, although he wasn't doing it in front of her. Swollen domes of irritated skin enveloped the nail stubs at the tip of every finger, and the cuticles that weren't scabbing were raw. She considered those hands and his loner lifestyle and decided to let her projection end right there.

His mind was on Soleil Gray as well, and it wasn't lost on Nikki that her despised moment of fame was the very thing that had brought Morris Granville to her. He had sought out Detective Heat because of her public connection to the now-dead singer, so he could share his moment of special bonding: the night he saw Soleil argue on the sidewalk outside a club with her ex-fiancé, Reed Wakefield.

"And you are certain this was the night Reed Wakefield died?" asked Heat. She had been through this with him and asked that same question in different ways over the last half hour, looking for the slipup. Morris Granville was a bona fide celebrity stalker. For this reason the detective was exercising a high degree of caution. His experience could provide an important missing piece of the puzzle, but Heat didn't want to jump for that candy in a weak moment of wishful thinking.

Nikki had run all her back-channel checks. Asking him what date it was. "May 14." What night of the week that was. "A Friday." What the weather was like. "It was drizzling off and on. I had an umbrella with me." Whether there was security. "I already said there wasn't any. Nobody else was out there." She told him these, as well as the other details he had given her, were all things she could check. He said that was good because then she would believe him. She noted that he seemed to relish the fact that she was writing down his answers. But she was skeptical there, too. Heat knew his need to be at the center of things could be driving that same way it drove everything else in his life.

There was another question she wanted to ask Morris Granville. An obvious one to her, but she held it, wanting to get to the things she didn't assume first, in case he decided to stop talking. "What happened with the fight?"

"It went on a long time."

"In the rain?"

"They didn't seem to care."

"Did it ever get violent?"

"No. Just arguing."

"What did they say?"

"I couldn't hear it all. Remember, I said I didn't want to get too close?"

Heat mentally ticked off one of her consistency cross-checks. "Did you hear anything?"

"It was about their breakup. She said he was only into himself and getting high. He said she was a selfish bitch, stuff like that."

"Did she threaten him?"

"Soleil? No way."

Heat made another mental note that Granville sounded like he had taken on some role as Soleil's defender. She began to wonder if this stalker's outreach was rooted in squaring himself in her legacy somehow. She filed it as a possibility but left herself open. "Did Wakefield threaten her?"

"Not that I heard. And he was out of it, too. He kept holding on to the light post for balance until they were done."

"How did it end?"

"They both cried and then hugged each other."

"And then what?"

"They kissed."

"As in kissed good-bye?"

"As in romantic."

"And after they kissed?"

"They left together."

Nikki double-tapped her pen on her spiral notebook. He was getting to the part she wanted to hear, and she had to make sure to ask in a way that didn't set him up to please her. She kept her question general. "How did they leave?"

"Holding hands."

So she got more specific. "I mean did they walk? Take a taxi? How did they leave?"

"They got in one of the limos. There was one waiting right there."

Heat concentrated on trying to sound detached even though she could feel her pulse rate rising. "Whose limo was it, Morris? The one Soleil came in or Reed Wakefield's, do you know?"

"Neither, I saw them come in cabs."

She tried not to get ahead of herself, although the temptation was strong. She told herself to keep the slate blank, just listen, not project, ask simple questions.

"So it was just there and they flagged it?"

"No."

"What, they helped themselves to someone else's limo?"

"Not at all. He invited them and they got in with him."

Heat pretended to be perusing her notes to keep the gravity out of her next question. The one she had been waiting to ask. She wanted to make it sound offhand so he didn't go defensive on her. "Who invited them for a ride?"

———

Pablo drank the last swallow of the electric-blue energy drink and set the empty bottle on the interrogation room table. Because of his age, Roach wouldn't make the boy sit through the interrogation but had strategically allowed him to have his snack in there to let the stakes sink in on Esteban Padilla's cousin Victor. Raley set the teenager up with an officer from Juvenile to watch TV in the outer area and returned to Interrogation 1.

He could tell by how Victor looked at him when he sat down across the table that Raley and his partner had been right when they planned their strategy. Victor's concern for the boy was their wedge. "Happy as a clam," said Raley.

"*Bueno*," said Ochoa, and then he continued in Spanish. "Victor, I don't get it, man, why won't you talk to me?"

Victor Padilla wasn't as self-assured outside of his neighborhood or his home. He said the words, but they sounded like they were losing steam. "You know how it is. You don't talk, you don't snitch."

"That's noble, man. Stand by some code that protects bangers while some dude that carved up your cousin walks free. I checked you out, Homes, you're not part of that world anyway. Or are you some kind of wannabe?"

Victor wagged his head. "Not me. That's not my life."

"So don't pretend it is."

"Code's the code."

"Bullshit, it's a pose."

The man looked away from Ochoa to Raley and then back to Ochoa. "Sure, you're going to say that."

The detective let that comment rest, and when the air was sufficiently cleansed of innuendo, he head-nodded to the Tumi duffel of money on the table. "Too bad Pablo can't hang on to that while you go away."

The guest chair scraped on the linoleum as Victor slid back an inch and sat upright. His eyes lost their cool remoteness and he said, "Why should I go away anywhere? I haven't done anything."

"Dude, you're a day laborer sitting on almost a hundred Gs in greenbacks. You think you're not going to get dirt on you?"

"I said I haven't done anything."

"Better tell me where this came from is all I can say." He waited him out, watching the knot of muscle flex on Victor's jaw. "Here it is straight up. I can ask the DA about making this problem go away if you just cooperate." Ochoa let that sink in and then added, "Unless you'd rather tell the kid that you're going away but, hey, at least you were loyal to the code."

And when Victor Padilla bowed his head, even Detective Raley could tell that they had him.

———

Twenty minutes later Raley and Ochoa stood up when Detective Heat came into the bull pen. "We did it," they said in an accidental chorus.

She read their excitement and said, "Congratulations, you two. Nice work. I scored a hit, too. In fact, I'm getting a warrant cut right now."

"For who?" asked Raley.

"You first." She sat on her desk to face them. "While I'm waiting for my warrant, why don't you tell me a story?"

While Raley rolled over two desk chairs for them, Ochoa got out his pad to consult as he spoke. "Just like we thought, Victor says his cousin Esteban was making money on the side selling information about his celebrity riders to Cassidy Towne."

Raley said, "Ironic when you consider the big stall was all about some snitch code."

"Anyway, he was spying for pocket money that he got if his tips were hot enough to make her column. Twenty here, fifty there. Adds up, I guess. It's all a beautiful thing until one night last May when some bad shit goes down on one of his rides."

"Reed Wakefield," said Nikki.

"We know that, but here's where Victor swears to God his cousin never told him what happened that night, only that there was some bad business and the less he knew the better."

"Esteban was trying to protect his cousin," said Heat.

"So he says," added Raley.

Ochoa flipped a page. "So whatever exactly went down is still unknown."

Heat knew she could fill in some of that blank, but she wanted to hear their raw story first, so she didn't interrupt.

"Next day cousin Esteban gets canned from his limo job, some vague BS about personality conflict with his clients. So he's out of a gig, gets bad-mouthed in the business, and has to drive lettuce and onions around instead of A-listers and prom queens. He gets all set to sue—"

"Because he's been wronged," interjected Raley, quoting the Ronnie Strong commercial.

"—but drops it because once our gossip columnist hears from him about whatever happened that night—obviously involving Reed Wakefield somehow—she gives him a load of money to drop his suit and chill so he doesn't attract attention to it. Probably she didn't want a leak before her book was done."

Nikki jumped in here. "Cassidy Towne gave him a hundred large?"

"Nope, more like five grand," said Raley. "We're coming to the big payout."

"Esteban wanted more, so he double-dipped. He called up the subject of his tip to Cassidy Towne and said he was going to go public with what he saw that night unless he got a healthy chunk of change. Turns out it wasn't so healthy."

Raley picked it up. "Padilla got himself a hundred grand and then got himself killed the very next day. Cousin Victor freaks but hangs on to the money, figuring to use it to get away someplace where whoever did this can't find him."

"So that's what we got," said Ochoa. "We got some of the story, but we still don't have the name of whoever Padilla was shaking down."

They looked up at Nikki, sitting on her desk grinning.

"But you do, don't you?" said Raley.

———

In the auditorium of the prestigious Stuyvesant High School in Battery Park City, Yankee phenom Toby Mills posed with an oversized prop check for one million dollars, his personal gift to the varsity athletic program of the public school. The audience was packed with students, faculty, administrators, and of course, press—all on their feet for his ovation. Also standing, but not applauding, was Detective Nikki Heat, who looked on from behind the curtain at the side of the stage, watching the pitcher grip 'n' grin with the athletic director, flanked by the Stuy baseball team turned out in uniform for the occasion. Mills smiled broadly, unfazed by the strobe flashes pummeling him, patiently turning to his left then his right, well acquainted with the choreography of the photo op.

Nikki was sorry that Rook couldn't be there. Especially since the school was only a few blocks from his loft, she had hoped that if he hurried he could meet her there to close the loop on his article. She had tried to return his calls on the drive down, but his phone rang out and dumped to voice mail. She knew better than to leave a message with sensitive content, so she said, "So let me get this straight. It's OK for you to bug me when I'm working, but not the other way around? Hey, hope the writing's going well. Got something going on, call me immediately when you get this." He'd be pissed about missing it, but she'd let him interrogate her, a thought that gave Nikki the first smile of her long hard day.

Toby's eye flicked to Heat in one of his turns, and his smile lost some of its luster when he registered her presence. It gave Nikki second thoughts about coming to see him in this venue, especially after her experience that day on the *Intrepid*. But he made no move to flee. In fact, when he finished shaking hands with the team mascot, who was attired in fifteenth-century garb as Peter Stuyvesant, Mills made his good-night wave then strode across the stage directly to her and said, "Did you catch my stalker?"

Without hesitating and without lying, Heat said, "Yes. Let's find a place to talk."

Heat had arranged to have use of a room nearby and she escorted Toby Mills into a computer lab and gestured to a chair. He noticed Raley and the two waiting uniform cops on the way in and got a funny look on his face when one uniform stayed inside while the other closed the door and posted himself outside with his body blocking the little window slit. "What's going on?" he asked.

Nikki replied with a question. "Isn't Jess Ripton here? I'd expect he'd be all over an event like this."

"Right. Well, he was going to come but called to say he had a sponsor fire to put out and to start without him."

"Did he say where he was?" asked the detective. Heat already knew The Firewall wasn't at his office or his apartment.

Mills looked up at the classroom wall clock. "Ten of nine, he's probably having his second dirty martini at Bouley."

Without being told, Detective Raley moved to the door. He gave a soft two-tap as he opened it, and the cop in the hall stepped aside to let him out.

The departure of the plainclothes cop wasn't missed by Toby. "This is starting to weird me out a little here, Detective."

That was pretty much the effect Heat was hoping to have on the pitcher. Her instincts were on alert that Ripton had broken form and wasn't there, but on the plus side it gave her a chance to apply pressure on Mills without the security blanket of his handler. "It's time, Toby."

He looked perplexed. "Time? Time for what?"

"For us to have a talk about Soleil Gray." Nikki paused and, when she saw the blinks come to his eyes, continued. "And Reed Wakefield." She took another beat and, when she could see him dry swallowing, added, "And you."

He tried his best, he truly did. But as sophisticated as were the circles a multimillionaire athlete in Gotham traveled in, Toby Mills was at heart still the kid from Broken Arrow, Oklahoma, and his upbringing made him a poor liar. "What about Soleil Gray and . . . Reed? What have they got to do with this? I thought this was about that creep following me and my family around."

"His name is Morris Granville, Toby."

"I know that. But he's always just 'the creep' to me. Did you get him or not? You said you got him."

"We did." She could see he wanted her to continue, and so she didn't. Toby Mills wasn't a star now, he was her interrogation suspect and she was going to run the board, not he. "Tell me how you knew Soleil Gray and Reed Wakefield."

His eyes darted to the door where the uniform waited, then back to her. And then he studied his shoes, looking in them for the answer to give now that he had no script from The Firewall.

"Soleil and Reed, Toby. Let's hear it."

"What's there to know? I heard about her today. Man . . ." And then he tried out, "I read in the paper you were harassing her. Were you chasing her today, too?"

Heat did not rise to his bait, let alone acknowledge it. "My question remains, how did you know Soleil and Reed?"

He shrugged like a child. "Around, you know? It's New York. You go to parties, you run into people. 'Hey, howarya,' like that."

"Is that all you knew of them, Toby? 'Hey, howarya'? Really?"

He checked the door again and pursed his lips repeatedly the way she had seen him do on TV once when he had walked the ninth man to load the bases and the top of the order was coming up with no outs. He'd need different skills to get himself out of this jam, and Toby wasn't sure he had them; she could smell it on him. So with his confidence flagging, she said, "Let's take a ride. Want to put your hands behind your back for me?"

"Are you serious?" He met her gaze, but it was he who blinked. "I met them around. You know. Parties, like I said. Reed, I guess he played in my charity softball game for the Oklahoma tornado victims in summer '09. Soleil, too, now that I think about it."

"And that's it?"

"Well, not totally. We hung out with each other from time to time. The reason I hesitated to talk about it is because it's embarrassing. I'm past all of it now, but I kinda got a little 'off the chain' when I first hit New York. Hard not to. And maybe I did do some partying with them back then."

Heat remembered Rook saying that Cassidy Towne had written up some of Mills's wild nights in "Buzz Rush." "So you're saying that was a long time ago?"

"Ancient history, yes, ma'am." He said it fast and smooth, as if he had passed the dangerous shoals and come out into calm waters.

"All before your charity game summer before last."

"Right. Way back."

"And you didn't see them after that?"

He started shaking his head for show, even as he pretended to be thinking. "Nope, can't say as I saw much of them later. They broke up, you know."

Nikki seized the opening. "Actually, I heard they got back together. The night Reed died."

Mills kept a game face but couldn't keep the blood in it, and he went a little pale. "Oh, yeah?"

"I'm surprised you didn't know that, Toby. Seeing how you were with them that night."

"With them—I was not!" His shout made the officer at the door straighten up and stare at him. He lowered his voice. "I was never with them. Not that night. Trust me, Detective, I think I'd remember that."

"I have an eyewitness who says otherwise."

"Who?"

"Morris Granville."

"Oh, come on, this is crazy. You're going to take the word of that psycho over mine?"

"When we picked him up, he told me about Club Thermal and how he saw Soleil and Reed." Heat leaned forward in her chair, toward him. "Of course, what I knew in the back of my mind was that the only reason I could think of for Morris Granville to be outside Club Thermal that night was because he was stalking you."

"Sounds like a load of bull. The guy's lying to get some kind of deal or something. He's just lying. The creep can say anything, but without proof, forget it." Toby sat back and crossed his arms, attempting to signal that he was all done.

Heat slid her chair over to the computer beside him and inserted a memory key. "What are you doing?" he asked.

When the thumb drive opened up, she double-clicked on a file, and as it loaded, she said, "I pulled this off Morris Granville's cell phone."

The image loaded. It was amateur cell quality, but the picture told the story. It was a shot of a wet street outside Club Thermal. Reed Wakefield and Soleil Gray were getting inside a stretch limo. Esteban Padilla, dressed in a black suit and red tie, held an umbrella over the open door. And inside the limousine, a giggling Toby Mills held a hand out to help Soleil get in. In his other hand was a joint.

As Mills weakened and his hands began to shake, Heat said, "Cassidy Towne. Derek Snow . . ." When he bowed his head, Nikki tapped lightly on the monitor. When he looked back up at the image, she added, "And think about this, Toby. Everyone here is dead—but you. I want you to tell me what's wrong with this picture."

And then the phenom began to weep.

———

Toby Mills had entered Stuyvesant High that night in the backseat of a black Escalade with a million-dollar check. He left in the backseat of a police car in handcuffs. The charges, for now, would be tokens just to hold him: lying to a police officer; failure to report a death; conspiracy; conspiracy to obstruct justice; bribery. From the confession he had made to her after he broke down and wept, it wasn't clear yet to Detective Heat if meatier charges would be brought. That would be up to a grand jury and the DA. And most importantly, if she could find a way to connect the pitcher to the Texan.

The stalker's cell phone picture would be compelling evidence. In her own way Nikki was in debt to whatever sickness in Morris Granville had taken the picture and kept it since May. When she asked him why he hadn't come forward with it before or tried to capitalize on it, he said he wanted to protect his idol, Toby Mills. So, she had said, that raised the question, "Why show it to a cop now?" To that, Granville said, as if it was obvious, "He had me arrested." And then the stalker smiled and asked, "If he goes to trial, will Toby be there when I testify?" Heat reflected on the stalker mentality and those of them who loved their victims so much that when they couldn't get near, they destroyed them. Some killed them. Apparently others got them arrested. It was all about seeking relevance in an unrequited relationship. Choose your poison.

In Toby Mills's version of the events following Club Thermal, the three of them rode around Manhattan with one objective: partying. Reed and Soleil already had a leg up, and Toby, who wasn't due to pitch until a Monday start at home against the Red Sox, was in the mood that

Friday night to blow it out after a losing road trip that had just ended in Detroit. He laughed at the MLB random drug tests. Mills and many other players either banked or bought urine to keep the commish out of their downtime. Mills had with him a small gym bag full of recreational narcotics and was a generous host. He told Heat that while they were parked briefly at the South Street Seaport, watching the East River, Reed and Soleil started getting serious about their reunion sex, and since everyone was tired of riding around in the car anyway, they all went back to Reed's room at the Dragonfly House to continue the party there. Toby, who in normal circumstances would have been the third wheel, had the drugs, so he was most welcome. He confessed that a part of him was hot for Soleil, and he even said to Nikki that he had thought, "What the hell, who knew where the night would lead?"

Where indeed?

He told Nikki that what happened at the Dragonfly was all an accident. Up in Reed's suite they played a game reciting famous movie titles, substituting the word "penis" for key nouns—*Must Love Penis. ET the Extra Penis. GI Joe: The Rise of the Penis*—while Toby laid out the portable pharmacy on the coffee table. Heat pressed him for details, and he listed pot, cocaine, and some amyl nitrate poppers. Reed had a stash of heroin that didn't interest Toby and a bunch of Ambien he said he used to help him sleep. He also said it was awesome for sex, and he and Soleil both downed some with vodka straight from a bottle they kept jammed into a room service ice bucket.

While Soleil and Reed went into the bedroom, Toby said he put on some music to drown out their screwing and watched ESPN with the sound off.

When he heard Soleil screaming, he thought it was her orgasm at first, but Mills said she ran out into the living room naked, out of control, shouting, "He's not breathing, do something, I think he's dead!"

Toby went in the bedroom with her and flipped on the lights, and Reed was all gray-faced and had saliva bubbles in the corner of his mouth. Toby said they both kept yelling his name and shaking him and got no answer. Toby finally felt his wrist and couldn't find any pulse, and they both freaked.

Toby speed-dialed Jess Ripton and got him out of bed. His handler told him to calm down and to keep quiet and stay put in the room. He told him to turn off the loud music and not to touch anything else and just wait there. When Toby asked if they should call an ambulance, Jess said, "Fuck no," not to call anybody or even think about leaving the room. He amended that, directing him to call his limo driver and tell him to be out front and ready to go when he was, but not to say why or sound upset when he called. Jess said he would get there as soon as he could and would call when he was coming up. He warned Toby not to open the door for anyone else.

But when Toby finished his call with Jess, he went to tell Soleil what was happening and she was hanging up the house phone in the bathroom. Two minutes later Derek Snow came to the door. Toby said not to let him in, but Soleil didn't listen and said the concierge would help, that they knew each other. As Nikki knew, Soleil had shot him in the leg only months before and had paid him off handsomely. Many relationships were built on less.

Derek wanted to call 911, but Toby was insistent and started to think he'd have to do something about this concierge. But Soleil took Derek aside and promised him a lot of money to be cool. When Derek asked what he could do, Toby told him to chill and just wait for his man to get there.

It turned out Derek was cooperative, and while Soleil finished getting dressed—not an easy feat considering all she had ingested—Snow helped Toby pack the drugs back into his gym bag. Twenty minutes later, Toby's cell phone rang. Jess Ripton was on his way up. When he came into the room, he told them it was all going to be OK.

Jess wasn't prepared to find Derek there, but he took him as a fact to deal with and put him to use, ushering Toby and Soleil out of there using the stairwell. On their way out, Jess told Derek that only he should touch doorknobs and to come back up after he delivered them to the limo.

Toby concluded his confession by saying that when they got outside the Dragonfly, Soleil was still freaked and didn't want to ride with him. The last he saw of her she was running off crying into the night.

Then he told the limo driver to take him home to his family in West-chester.

———

On Chambers Street, outside the front door of Stuyvesant High, Heat was about to get into her car when the Roach Coach pulled alongside her and stopped.

"Still no sign of Jess Ripton," said Ochoa out the passenger window. "Not at Bouley, not at Nobu, or Craftbar. We checked all his other usual haunts and watering holes Toby gave us. *Nada.*"

"Think he's helping Jess duck us?" asked Raley.

"Always possible," said Nikki, "but I think Toby wants his Firewall about now, not to have him be MIA like this. A good indicator is that I let him try to call Jess, thinking he'd need his handler."

"Generous of you, Detective Heat," said Ochoa.

"In a self-serving, clever, tricky way. Thanks. Anyway, all Toby got was Ripton's voice mail. We have someone staking out his apartment, but let's also detail somebody else to roam on this overnight. I'll ask Captain Montrose to pull a detective off Burglary who can keep making the rounds to Ripton's usuals. Parking garage, his gym, his office."

Raley said, "But don't you think if Ripton's trying to go off the grid, he's too smart to go to any of those places?"

"Probably. Might be wheel-spinning, but we have to check anyway," said Heat.

Ochoa nodded. "Man, I know somebody's got to do it, but it sounds like a pointless exercise for some poor dude."

Raley laughed. "Give it to Detective Schlemming."

Roach scoffed, shook their heads, and muttered his nickname. "Defective Schlemming."

"Sounds about his speed," said Heat.

Ochoa's face grew serious. "I think we ought to quit picking on Schlemming. I mean, come on, just because a guy rear-ends the mayor's limo trying to shoo a bee out of his car is no reason to— Aw, hell, yes it is."

"Can I tell you something?" said Raley. "All those bodies. It's hard for me to buy Toby Mills as the contract killing type. And I'm a Mets fan."

"Come on, partner, you ought to know one thing by now and that is that you can never know. His Yanks contract, all those endorsements? That's millions of motives for Toby Mills to clamp a lid on that mess."

"Or Ripton," countered Raley. "He has a stake, too. Not just because he was the cleaner at Reed's hotel that night, but Toby's image is his meal ticket also. You agree, Detective?" He leaned over from the steering wheel to look across Ochoa out the side window to Heat. She was busy scrolling on her cell phone. "Detective Heat?"

"Hang on, just reading this e-mail from Hinesburg. It's a forward from Hard Line Security of the list of the Texan's old freelance clients." She continued to scan and then stopped.

"Whatcha got?" said Roach.

"One of his clients? Sistah Strife."

"Should that mean something?" asked Raley.

"It sure does. It means Rance Eugene Wolf and Jess Ripton both worked together for Sistah Strife."

As Raley and Ochoa departed, Heat called in to elevate the search status for Jess Ripton to an APB with an alert that his known associate was a professional killer. Spent and aching from the ordeal of her day, she got into her Crown Victoria and felt her body begin to melt into the driver's seat from fatigue. Tired as she was, she felt bad for Rook that, in his journalistic diligence, he had to miss the Toby takedown. She tried his cell phone one more time to fill him in.

The iPhone sitting on Rook's desk sounded with Nikki Heat's ringtone, the theme from *Dragnet*. The writer sat and stared at it from his chair as it continued to loop its ominous "Dum-dah-dum-dum . . . Dum-dah-dum-dum . . ." The screen header he had entered for her flashed "The Heat," and her ID badge photo filled the screen.

But Rook didn't answer the call. When it finally stopped ringing, a melancholy swept over him as her image faded and the screen went blank. Then he shifted uncomfortably against the duct tape lashing his wrists to the armrests.

NINETEEN

"**Y**ou've got to be one smart aleck putting something like that on your phone," drawled the Texan.

"If you don't like it, cut me loose and I'll change it," said Rook.

Jess Ripton turned from the bookcase he was searching. "Can you button it?"

"I can tape his trap if you want, Jess."

"Then how's he going to tell us where it is?"

"Yes, sir, I hear you," said the Texan. "Just say the word, though."

Jess Ripton and Rance Eugene Wolf continued tossing Rook's loft in another search for the last chapter of Cassidy Towne's manuscript. Across the room, The Firewall was on his knees looking through a built-in that housed DVDs and even some dinosaur VHS tapes that Rook no longer had a machine to play. Ripton clawed them all out of the cabinet onto the floor. When it was empty, he turned to Wolf. "You're absolutely sure you saw him with it?"

"Yes, sir. Got out of the cab and came up with a manila envelope. Same one he brought out of the mail drop."

"You were following me?" said Rook. "How long were you following me?"

Wolf smiled. "Long enough, I figure. Not hard to do. 'Specially if you don't know you're being tailed." He stepped around behind the desk, moving without registering any discomfort, which Rook attributed to heavy painkillers, a high threshold of tolerance, or both. He was dressed in new blue jeans that were tight on his lean frame and a Western-style shirt that had pearl buttons. Wolf had accessorized with a sheathed knuckle knife on his belt and an arm sling that looked like it was from a hospital supply store. Rook also clocked a .25 caliber handgun, holstered on the small of his back, when he turned to clothesline everything but the laptop off of Rook's desk with his good arm. Every item he and Nikki had so painstakingly replaced there—his pencil cup, framed photos, stapler, tape dispenser, copter controller, even his cell phone, hit the rug around his feet.

The Texan then spun the laptop to face him and leaned over to read the draft of Rook's Cassidy Towne article.

Ripton got up off the floor. "Where is it, Rook? The envelope."

"It was from Publishers Clearing House. You wouldn't be interes—" The Texan smacked Rook's mouth with the back of his hand, hard enough to whiplash his neck. Dazed, Rook squeezed his eyes closed a few times and saw kaleidoscoping pinpricks of light. He tasted his own blood and smelled Old Spice. As he came out of his haze, the most disturbing thing to Rook wasn't just the surprise, the quick uncoiling of the violence. What chilled him to the core was that Wolf then went back to reading his computer screen as if nothing had happened.

For a time, Rook sat in silence while Jess Ripton continued ripping apart his office and the Texan scrolled through his article an arm's length away. When Wolf finished, he said to Ripton, "None of the information that would be in that chapter is in here."

"Information about what?" said Rook. When the Texan snapped down the lid of the computer, he flinched.

"You know perfectly well what," said Ripton. He surveyed the mess on the floor and bent over, coming up with the unfinished Cassidy Towne manuscript her editor had supplied. "What's written in the rest of this." He tossed it on the desk in a discarding motion, and the fat rubber band holding it together broke, scattering pages.

"I never got it. Cassidy was holding it back from the publisher."

"We know," said Wolf casually. "She shared that with us a couple of nights back."

Rook didn't have to think hard to imagine the ghastly circumstances of that confession. He pictured the woman strapped to a chair, being tortured, giving only that much up to them before they killed her. He reflected on how her last act was so in character with her life— the power play of giving them the assurance that there was something valuable they wanted, and then denying it to them, taking its whereabouts to her grave.

Ripton signaled Wolf with a head nod. The Texan stepped out of the room and came back in with an old-fashioned black leather physician's satchel. It was weathered and embossed with a caduceus stamped with a "V." Rook remembered the FBI report on Wolf, whose father had been a veterinarian. And that the son liked to torture animals.

"I told you I don't have it."

Jess Ripton squinted at him like he was mulling which of two shirts to buy. "You have it."

Wolf set the satchel on the desk. "A little help?" He couldn't manage the buckle one-handed, and Ripton gave him an assist. "Obliged."

"You just read my article. If I had it, wouldn't the information you want—whatever it is—be in there? How do you prove a negative?"

"I'll tell you how, Mr. Rook." Ripton touched his forefinger to his lips as he chose his words, and then continued. "In fact, I can prove you have it by negatives. One, actually. Ready?"

Rook didn't answer. He just made a fast check of the Texan, who was placing his dental picks in a tidy row on the desktop.

"The negative is as follows. In all the time since my associate and I got here, you never asked one simple question." The Firewall paused for effect. "You never once asked what I was doing here." A burning sensation grew in Rook's gut as the handler continued. "I never got a 'Hey, Jess Ripton, I know this cowboy is involved in all this, but you? You're Toby Mills's guy. What the hell does Toby Mills have to do with all this?' Am I right? You not asking that is what I call negative proof."

Rook's head raced to cover his omission. "That? Well, that's simple. We talked to you a couple of times on this case, of course I wasn't surprised."

"Don't insult my intelligence, Rook. When you and your lady cop checked out Toby, you were fishing with no bait. He was just a name on your list. And you certainly never had anything to connect Toby, ergo me, with Slim here." He waited, but Rook said nothing. "So by not asking, that tells me you know damn well why I am here and what happened that night with Toby and Reed Wakefield. And I want to know where the chapter is that told you that story."

"I already said I don't have it."

"Now, see, you think you're being smart," said Jess. "You think the only thing keeping you alive is that if we kill you, you can't tell us where that chapter is. But, see, here's the thing. In a couple minutes, my friend here is going to get you to tell us anyway. And in between . . . ? You're going to wish you were dead." He turned to Wolf. "Do your thing. I'll go check the bedroom." He went to the doorway and stopped. "Nothing personal, Rook. Given the choice, I don't need to see this."

When he left, Rook struggled against his bonds, bucking in the chair.

"Not gonna help, buddy," said the Texan as he picked up one of his dental tools.

Rook felt something tear near his ankle. He pushed harder and succeeded in ripping one of his legs free of the duct tape. He slammed his foot onto the floor under his desk and shoved off, trying to jam the chair into Wolf. But the man was quick and snatched him in a choke hold with his left arm, trapping Rook's neck in a vise grip between his jaw and his armpit. Wolf still held the dental tool in his left hand, and slowly, trying to keep it steady against Rook's struggling and kicking, he began to curve his wrist inward toward Rook's head. Just as Rook began to feel a sharp graze on the outer rim of his ear canal, he tried another tactic. Instead of pushing back against his assailant, he quickly reversed and threw his torso forward with desperate force.

The dental pick skittered across the blotter, and for the moment, Rook's move worked. The momentum tossed Wolf forward onto the edge of the desk. He landed on his wounded right shoulder and cried out in pain, clutching his collarbone.

The man sat down on the floor, panting like a dog in August. Rook tried to push himself away from between his desk and the wall, but the chair rollers were speed-bumped by debris on the floor. He had started kicking harder, in a futile attempt to get over a three-hole punch and his radio controller, when the Texan rose up to examine the quarter-sized circle of blood ghosting through the shoulder of his shirt. He looked from his reopened wound over to Rook and whispered a curse.

Then he balled a fist hard enough to turn the knuckle skin white and drew back his arm to hit him.

"Freeze it there, Wolf." Nikki Heat stood in the doorway, holding her Sig Sauer on the Texan.

Rook said, "Nikki, careful, Jess Ripton is—"

"Right here," he said as his arm reached in from the hall and he placed the muzzle of his Glock against her temple. "Let it fall, Detective."

Heat had no alternative. With a literal gun to her head, she saw no option but to comply. There was an easy chair between her and the fireplace, and she tossed her gun onto the cushion, hoping to keep it close by.

When Rook hadn't answered his phone the second time, her suspicion had grown and she couldn't shake it. She had never known him not to return a call, and Nikki couldn't get past the concern that there was a disturbance in the Rook Force. Ribbing aside about showing up unannounced, she decided that was exactly what she would do. If it was awkward, let it be awkward. Nikki decided she would rather deal with that than light up the radar with a door buzz if her worries were founded.

After ringing the super downstairs and getting the key, Heat took the stairs rather than the elevator, mindful of the racket it made when it braked at Rook's floor. When she got up there, she put her ear to his front door. That's when she heard the scuffle in the distant reaches of the loft. Normally, she would have followed procedure and taken time to call for backup before she went in, but Nikki's fears for Rook were already spiking and it sounded like time was of the essence. She used the key to let herself in.

And now, for the second time in a week, Heat found herself in Rook's place, in crisis, looking for an opportunity to turn the situation around. As she watched the Texan reach behind to the small of his back and come up with a .25-caliber Beretta, she began reciting her mantra: Assess. Improvise. Adapt. Overcome.

"Move into the room," said Ripton. He gave her a slight nudge away from the easy chair with the Glock. Heat made note that it was the soft push of an amateur. She wasn't sure what to do with that impression other than to underscore her conclusion that between the two, if she ever got the chance, Wolf got her first bullet.

"I've got backup, you know. You're not getting out of here."

"Really?" Since Wolf had her covered with his gun, Ripton stepped to the door and shouted up the hall toward the front door, "Come on in, everybody!" Then he cupped an ear to listen. "Huh . . ."

Nikki's heart sank when Ripton went to the easy chair and picked up her Sig. She watched the handler slip it into his waistband and then she turned to Rook. "How are you doing, OK?" He was staring down at the floor under his desk, fidgeting. "Rook?"

"Sorry, cramp. You'll pardon me if I don't get up."

Wolf spoke. "You know, Jess, maybe now's the time to pull the pin."

Before Ripton could answer, Nikki went for a stall. "We've arrested Toby Mills, you know."

"No, I didn't." He appraised her a beat. "What for?"

"You know."

"You tell me."

Now it was her turn to do some appraisal. Why was Ripton pushing her to answer first? It felt to her like poker games she had been in when it comes down to who's going to be first to show the hand. Translation: He wanted her to reveal what she knew—because he was wondering how much she knew. So Nikki gave up as little as she could in order to keep conversation going and buy time. "Your client was booked for the confession he made about what happened the night Reed Wakefield OD'd at the Dragonfly."

The Firewall nodded slightly to himself. "Interesting."

"Interesting?" she said. "That's all you've got to say about what you've done? 'Interesting'? Sooner or later it's going to come out that Toby had you guys kill the story by killing everyone who knew it, and all of you are going to take the weight."

The ballbuster in Jess Ripton kicked in. "You don't have any idea what you're talking about."

"I don't? I have his confession saying that he and Soleil Gray were there when Wakefield overdosed. Your client gave him the drugs. You snuck Toby out of there. And my take is that when the hush money wasn't enough to keep a lid on this, Toby Mills had you kill the concierge and the limo driver because they were tipping off Cassidy Towne. Who he also had you kill. Tracks for me."

"They'll never make a connection for one simple reason," said Ripton. "Toby Mills had nothing to do with those killings. He doesn't even know I'm involved in all that."

"Sounds like you're making a confession," said Heat.

He shrugged, and in it conveyed his certainty that whatever he said would never go beyond Rook's office. "Truly. Toby doesn't know. He still doesn't even know about Cassidy Towne's book. Or the leaks and the spying by that limo driver and the concierge. All Toby knows is he has a dirty little secret to keep about a party that got out of control."

"Come on, Ripton, I don't think this is the time to be doing your spin. Not after you've killed three people just to save your client's precious endorsement deals."

Wolf was getting anxious to go. "Jess? Ready?"

Rook blurted, "That's not why they killed them." He made a quick glance down at his foot and then looked up again at Nikki. "They didn't kill those people to protect Toby Mills's image. They killed them to cover up the fact that Reed Wakefield's death was not accidental—it was murder."

Heat was taken aback. She had no idea Rook could be so good with a bluff. But then she was floored again because his expression told Nikki he wasn't bluffing. She turned to assess the reactions of Jess Ripton and Rance Wolf. They weren't disagreeing with what he'd said.

"So you *do* have the last chapter," said Ripton. He took a step closer to the desk. "You wouldn't know about the murder unless you did."

Rook shrugged. "I've read it."

"Murder? How is it murder?" said Nikki. "In Toby's confession he said it was an accidental overdose."

"Because Toby still believes it was," answered Rook. "Because Toby and Soleil didn't know it, but Reed Wakefield was still alive when they left that hotel room." Rook punctuated the point by glaring at Ripton. "Right Jess? Then you and Tex here killed him."

"Where is it?" Ripton looked under the desk where Rook had been fidgeting, and when he didn't see the chapter, he said, "You're going to tell me where you hid that chapter."

"Let her go first," Rook said.

"I'm not leaving."

"Damn right." Ripton turned to scan the mess again.

"Nikki. Trying to help you here."

"Where is it, Rook? Last time."

"OK," said Rook. "It's in my pants!"

A brief quiet fell over the room. Rook gestured with his head to his lap and then nodded, affirming.

"Check it out," said Ripton.

The instant Wolf turned and took his gun off Nikki, Rook pressed the toe of his shoe on the radio controller sitting on the floor at his feet. Over on the windowsill behind the Texan, the orange CB180 helicopter whirred to life. As soon as the main rotor began to spin, its tip buzz-sawed against the windowpane, jarring the room with a grating vibration. Wolf twirled around and shot at the copter, shattering the glass. Jess Ripton, who was startled into a frozen state, brought his hands up defensively. Heat threw herself at him, slamming into his side. She grabbed Ripton's forearm and raised it up while, at the same time, sliding both her hands down past his wrist toward his gun.

The Texan spun back around to take aim at her, giving Nikki no time to pull the Glock away from the manager's grip. So Heat slapped both her hands around Ripton's, took her best aim, and using his finger, squeezed off a shot. It missed the mark, puncturing the sling. The Texan moaned and fired.

As Nikki began to fall backward, she gripped harder onto Jess Ripton's hand and squeezed off four more rounds into the left front pocket of Rance Eugene Wolf's Western shirt before she hit the floor.

TWENTY

Almost two hours later, sitting by himself at the counter that separated his kitchen from his great room, Jameson Rook stared at the two streams of bubbles rising in perfect parallel lines from the bottom of his pint glass of Fat Tire. It was his second beer, and he was headed for a third, figuring he wasn't going to get much writing done anyway. It was just past midnight and the OCME and CSU strobes were still flashing up the hall.

Across his loft in the reading den he had partitioned the year before, a cozy enclave with soft furniture and clubby lighting surrounded by shoulder-height bookcases, he could hear the steely voices of the Chief's shooting investigation team. Rook had spent a half hour with them earlier, giving his version of the gunfight; that when it was clear they were about to be assaulted, Rook created a diversion, allowing Detective Heat to seize control of Ripton's weapon and fire once at Wolf, and when the Texan fired the shot that missed her and killed Ripton, she was able to return fire and take him out. Rook made the mistake of thinking they would find it cool that he had created his diversion with a radio-controlled chopper, using his foot and a 2.4-gig transmitter. These were sober dudes doing serious work, and he would have to look elsewhere for his high fives.

Nikki was in with them for her second visit, and though he couldn't make out the words from where he sat, he could tell from the voice tones that the meeting was shifting into a wrap-up cadence.

When the squad finally left, Nikki passed on Rook's beer offer but sat with him. Raley and Ochoa came out from the office, peeling off evidence gloves, and asked her about the ruling. "No disposition yet, not tonight," she said. "Between the lines—as much as the 1PP guys give you—this looks like it will clear just fine. They just need to give it twenty-four because they have to show due diligence since it's my second incident of the day."

"They should give you a rewards card," said Rook, and before they could say anything, he backpedaled. "Jeez, that was insensitive, sorry, sorry. It's the beer talking."

"How do you explain the rest of your day?" said Raley.

But Rook wasn't listening. He was fixed on Nikki, searching her face, which told him she was off in her head somewhere else. "Nikki?" And when she came back, he said, "You did great in there."

"Yeah, well, considering the alternative results, I'm not unhappy."

Ochoa said, "Hey. You dealing OK with, you know . . . ?"

Without having to say more, they all knew he was referring to her killing of Rance Wolf, who—criminal or not—would now lose his nickname and never be the Texan to her again. Unlike some Hollywood versions of the job, taking a life is profoundly affecting to a cop, even when it's the life of a cold, professional killer and the taking is completely justified. Nikki was strong, but she knew she would be coping for a while with the multiple losses of that day. Heat would take the counseling, not because she was weak but because she knew that it was effective. She also knew she'd be all right. Heat answered Ochoa's question with a single nod, and that's all anyone needed.

Raley said, "Hey, man, is it true? You stashed that chapter they wanted in your pants?"

Nodding proudly, Rook replied, "Indeed, I did."

"That answers one question," said Ochoa, dangling his latex gloves. "Why they made us wear these when we handled it."

They didn't laugh. Something unwritten about the decorum that was appropriate for what was happening up the hall kept them from doing that. But they did enjoy Ochoa's barb, all silently bobbing their heads and smirking.

Rook explained that he had just finished reading the chapter and gone to the kitchen to get his cell phone to call Nikki. He had just picked it up off the counter when he heard the elevator groan to a stop. Rook wasn't expecting visitors, and when the picks started shimmying in his lock he ran back to the office, figuring he could get out the fire escape. But his window wouldn't open and he was trapped in that room. Knowing there was a good chance it could be Wolf coming for the chapter, he didn't know where else to hide it, so he jammed it down his pants.

Ochoa shook his head. "That's amazing."

"I know," said Rook, "I'm surprised there was enough room for it." When the others groaned, he added, "What? It's a big chapter."

By that time, all of them but Nikki had read Cassidy's climactic pages, so Rook filled her in on the broad strokes of the narrative. If nothing else, it explained the zeal with which Jess Ripton and Rance Eugene Wolf pursued getting their hands on it. The final chapter was the smoking gun that busted Ripton's client Toby Mills as well as Soleil Gray for a debauched evening culminating in the apparent OD of Reed Wakefield and their cowardly flight from responsibility. The druggy night, celebrities running off and not even calling 911 to get basic medical aid for a companion—that was shocking and sensational by itself. Cassidy had plenty of fireworks right there to guarantee a best seller plus create devastating legal and financial ramifications for all concerned. But the gossip writer took that exposé and shouldered it to the next level. And that level was murder.

Her key was the concierge. Popular with hotel guests, not just for his service but his discretion, Derek Snow was a handler of sorts in his own right. Jess Ripton knew the story of his shooting by Soleil Gray, and therefore saw Derek as a man who took his money and kept his mouth shut. So when Snow came back up to the hotel room from delivering Toby and Soleil to the street, Jess Ripton had reasonable expectation that, for an agreeable sum, Derek Snow would pretend like that night never happened. And Snow, upon accepting the terms, assured The Firewall he needn't worry about him.

When the slim man in the Western wear arrived to assist with the cleaning, Ripton reinforced the need for silence by having the man from Texas plainly threaten to find him wherever he hid and kill him if he talked.

Things got more dicey when the Texan opened his black bag and took out a stethoscope. Derek was in the living room, wiping down knobs and switches with some special wipes they'd given him, when he heard the cowboy's voice from the bedroom say, "Shit, Jess, this man's still alive."

The concierge said at that point he almost fled the room to call 911. But he was frightened by the chilling threat from the Texan and so he didn't. Derek Snow continued his fingerprint wipe-down but moved closer to the bedroom door. He looked in once, and they almost saw him so he stayed back, positioning himself so that he was hidden but could see their reflection in the vanity mirror in the bedroom.

He said they spoke quietly but that he definitely heard Ripton say to the other man, "Do something about him." Tex asked him if he was sure and Ripton said he didn't want Wakefield delirious in some ER telling cops or paramedics what happened and who he was with. "Put the fucker down."

At that, the other guy took some squeeze bottles and vials out of his bag. After he forced some pills down Wakefield's throat, he began spraying large amounts of something into his nose. Then the Texan got out his stethoscope again and listened for a long time. Derek was afraid of getting caught by them, so he moved away to the far side of the living room with a fresh wipe and looked busy. It was quiet in there for a long time, until he heard movement and Ripton say, "Well?" and the other man said, "Put a fork in him, he's done." When they came back out into the living room, the concierge pretended he didn't know what had happened and just kept cleaning. All Ripton said was "Nice job. Do the TV remote once more and then you can go."

What made Derek Snow talk to Cassidy Towne was his guilt. He was no angel; he took her money just as he had taken Ripton's. But sharing with the gossip columnist the details of what really happened, which was the *murder* of Reed Wakefield, became for Derek a quest for absolution. He said he was afraid of the Texan, who had said he would kill him, but he was more afraid of living his life burdened by his own complicity.

Snow also told Cassidy how painfully difficult it was for him to not be truthful with Soleil Gray, who had begun to call him regularly and sob about her guilt over the responsibility she bore for her ex-fiancé's OD. He saw her descending deeper and deeper into an abyss.

He said to Cassidy that when she was done with him for her book, he might contact Soleil and tell her the truth. Towne begged him to wait and he said he would. But not forever. Soleil's pain only added more weight to his own guilt.

Rook asked Nikki, "Do you think that's why Derek was calling Soleil that night when she got that call at Brooklyn Diner?"

"I had the same thought," Heat said. "It was the same night Cassidy Towne was killed. I'll bet Derek spotted Rance Wolf snooping around for him and tried to tell Soleil before it was too late."

"Which it probably was," said Ochoa.

"It's sad," said Nikki. "Soleil not only never got to hear the truth from Derek Snow, but the manuscript she stole was missing the last chapter so that everything she read up to that was an indictment of her behavior, feeding her guilt."

Rook nodded. "The double tragedy for her was that she died not knowing she was off the hook for Reed's death."

Ochoa eyed his partner. "What's got you all twisted up in yourself?"

"What makes you think that?" said Raley.

"Hey, I know you, you're like my wife."

"You mean 'cause I'm not sleeping with you, either?"

"Funny. I mean I know you. What is it?"

Raley said, "OK, about Soleil Gray . . . If Jess Ripton was running all this—I mean the killings—whether it's on Toby's behalf or his own, then how did she figure in? I mean besides being paranoid and guilty about the night of the OD."

Heat said, "Knowing what we know now, I don't think she was involved at all with Ripton or Wolf or Toby. At least not as part of any of the killings."

"And yet she did mug Perkins to get that manuscript," said Raley. "Are you saying she did that coincidentally?"

"No, not coincidentally, simultaneously. There's a difference."

Rook took another pull of his beer. "Well, then what made her suddenly decide to do that?"

"I have an idea," said Nikki. She got off the bar stool and stretched.

"I'll let you know if I'm right tomorrow. After I have a talk with somebody in the morning."

———————

Something was different when Nikki Heat walked along West 82nd from the precinct the next morning. In the distance she detected a low droning sound she hadn't heard in over a week. As she got nearer to Amsterdam, a modest cough of diesel smoke rose and the droning became a brief roar that stopped with the hiss and squeal of air brakes as a city garbage truck came to a halt. Two sanitation workers hopped off and attacked the hill of refuse accumulated there from the strike. First one car and then another pulled up behind the trash truck as it idled, temporarily blocking the street while the men tossed black and green plastic bags into the rear loader. As she walked past, Heat could hear a driver curse through the rolled-up window of his blocked car and shout, "Come on!" Nikki smiled. The garbage strike was over, and now New Yorkers could be frustrated by something else.

It was five after eight. Cafe Lalo had just opened and Petar had been the first one there, waiting for her under one of the large European art posters in the back corner against the brick wall. He gave her a hug. "I'm glad we could do this," he said.

"Yeah, me too." She sat across from him at the white marble table.

"This spot OK?" he asked. "They gave me my choice, but I didn't want to be near the windows. Garbage strike is over and the diesel fumes are back. Man."

"Yes, the trash fumes were so much better."

"Touché, Nikki. I keep forgetting it's always half-full for you."

"Well, at least half the time, it is."

When the waitress came, Nikki said she only wanted a latte, nothing to eat. Petar closed his menu and said to make it two. "You're not hungry?"

"I have to be back at work soon."

A knot of disappointment formed between his brows, but he didn't express it. Instead he soldiered on with his agenda. "You know this is the place they filmed *You've Got Mail*?" Out of nowhere, *You've Got*

Penis popped into Nikki's head, and an unbidden smile opened up her face.

"What?" said Petar.

"Nothing. I think I'm still a bit on the fried side from yesterday is all."

"Where's my head?" he said. "I didn't ask how that's all going."

"It's not so easy, to be honest, but fine." She didn't tell him about her evening ordeal at Rook's loft, but he went right to it.

"It's all over this morning about Toby Mills and Jess Ripton and that other guy. Were you part of any of that?"

Their lattes came, and Nikki waited for the waitress to go before she answered. "Petar, I don't think this is going to be happening for us."

He put down his spoon and gave her a puzzled look. "It's because I'm pressing you, I'm pushing too hard again?"

She had made up her mind to have this conversation, however difficult, and ignored her coffee. "It's not about that. Yes, you are . . . unwavering in your interest."

"Is it because of the writer? You are an item with Jameson Rook?"

He gave her an opening and she seized it. "No, this won't work because I'm not sure I can trust you."

"What? Nikki . . ."

"Let me help you. I've been trying to figure out how Soleil Gray got it in her head to go after Cassidy Towne's book editor." Petar immediately shifted. She could hear a small crack from the stress he put on his bistro chair. When he settled himself, she continued. "That all came on the heels of Soleil's visit to your show. The same night you told me about Cassidy's book."

"You're a friend, of course I told you."

"But you didn't tell me all of it. You didn't tell me who Cassidy was going to expose. But you knew, didn't you? You knew because it wasn't the publisher who told you, it was your mentor. Cassidy Towne told you, didn't she? Maybe not all of it but parts, am I right?" He looked away. "And you told Soleil Gray about it. That's what made her go after the editor to get the manuscript. How else would she know? Tell me it isn't so."

Other customers were coming in, so he leaned forward over the table to lower his voice, which was shaky and hoarse. "After what happened to Cassidy, I thought I should tell Soleil. To warn her."

"Maybe. But you were also star kissing. I'm sure you didn't know what she was going to do, but you couldn't resist working the favor bank. That's how it goes, isn't it? And then you pump me a little, and then details about me showing Soleil autopsy photos at *Later On* end up in print." She paused. "Please tell me you aren't The Stinger."

"Me? No."

"But you know her."

"Him. Yeah."

Heat made sure she had his full attention before she said, "Petar, I don't know what happened to you, maybe it was there in you all along and that's why we split."

"I'm just trying to do the job, Nikki, I'm not a bad person."

Nikki studied him and said, "No, I don't believe you are. I just find you to be a bit morally vague."

Heat put money on the table for her drink and left.

As she crossed to the door, she flashed back to almost ten years ago, the last time she'd walked out on Petar. That time it was on a winter night in a coffeehouse in the West Village and a Bob Dylan song was playing on some rafter speakers. The song came back to her now, echoing her sentiments just as it did then. "Don't Think Twice, It's All Right."

Still steeped in Dylan's blameless melancholy about relationships, Nikki paused on the top step outside Lalo to button her brown leather jacket for the short walk to work. In front of a diner up the street, she saw her friend Lauren Parry getting out of a taxi. Heat was about to call out to her but stopped when she spotted Detective Ochoa getting out of the cab behind her and rushing ahead to get the front door for her. With an exaggerated flourish, he swept his arm, gesturing Lauren inside, and the couple entered laughing for their breakfast date. Or perhaps, thought Nikki, their morning-after brunch. The sight of the two made her forget Dylan for the moment. She breathed in the crisp autumn air and thought—or at least hoped—that maybe once in a while it was better than just all right.

When she stepped down to the sidewalk, Heat paused again, recalling how this was the exact spot where she had encountered the coyote days before. Nikki let her eyes roam the street, running that slide show in her mind.

Then she saw it.

The coyote wasn't where it had been before. This time it was at a distance, sniffing the sidewalk up at the corner of Broadway where the trash had just been collected. She watched it lower its head to the concrete and lick a patch. She continued to watch it silently, and yet part of her wanted to call out a "Hey" or perhaps whistle just to get a reaction. Or to make the connection.

As she was having these thoughts, the animal raised its head. And looked right at her.

The two of them stood there watching each other from a block away. Its narrow face was too far off to make out detail, but in its matted coat and chunky fur Heat could read the story of the week it had had, pursued by copters and cameras. Its head rose a little higher to stare at her, and in that moment she stood naked to its eyes. Then it folded its ears back, and from that gesture Heat felt a sense of what she could only describe as the kinship between two beings that had endured a week out of their element.

She raised her hand tentatively to wave. As she brought it up, a car drove down the street, passing the animal, blocking it for a second from her view.

When the car passed, the coyote was gone.

Nikki lowered her hand and started off back to the precinct. At the corner of Amsterdam, waiting to cross, she looked back the other way just to check, but it was still gone. She understood why. They both knew the need to find cover.

That night Nikki let herself into her apartment, where Rook sat at the din-ing table with his work spread out. "How's the article coming?"

"What? No 'Honey, I'm home'?"

"Never," she said as she went over to stand behind his chair and lace her arms around his neck.

"I knew if I came here I wouldn't get any work done." And then he tilted his face to hers and they kissed.

She moved into the kitchen and called out to him while she fished two beers out of the fridge. "You could always go back to your loft and draw your inspiration from writing at an actual crime scene."

"No, thanks. I'll go back there after the hazmat cleanup tomorrow." He took one of the bottles from her and they clinked. "A double killing is going to wreak havoc on my resale value. I wonder if I have to declare."

"Like you'll ever sell that place," she said.

"Listen, sorry about you and Petar."

She finished a sip of beer and shrugged. "It happens. Sadly, but it happens," she said, keeping it half-full, as ever. "I was hoping we could be friends."

"Yeah, me too."

"Liar."

Rook reflected on what he had unearthed about Petar's smuggling and his jail time, but instead he looked at her and smiled. "I dunno. Seemed like an OK guy."

"Pants on fire," she said as she moved into the living room.

"Hey, where are you going? I was just about to make my move."

She settled onto the couch and said, "You make your move onto that keyboard. Let's hear some clicking over there, Mr. Rook. I want all the Nikki Heats off the newsstands now."

He typed a bit and then said, "You don't feel neglected?"

"No, you go on, I'll just be reading."

"Anything good?"

"Hm," she said, "it's all right, I suppose. Something called *Her Endless Knight*." Rook was already up and out of his chair on his way to her before she could add, "By Victoria St. Clair."

"What do you mean 'It's all right'? That's quality fiction, professionally written."

He sat beside her and she opened to a page, reciting, " 'Her need for him was met in the sanctuary of his long arms and broad shoulders as he enveloped her in the coach.'" She set the book on her lap. "Not terrible."

"I can do better on the next one," Rook said. "All I need is a little inspiration."

"Oh, yeah?"

"Yeah."

Heat put the book on the floor and drew him on top of her, letting herself fall backward onto the couch. Rook kissed her and she rose to him. They tasted each other passionately and deeply. As he began to explore her with his hands, Nikki gave him a simmering look and said, "Go ahead. Rip my bodice."

ACKNOWLEDGMENTS

As a writer, I can think of no greater terror than confronting a blank page, except perhaps the terror of being shot at. This past year I've faced both. Fortunately, I didn't have to face either circumstance alone. When bullets are flying, whether literal or metaphoric, it's good to have trusted friends watching your back.

First and foremost, I'd like to thank the dedicated members of the NYPD's 12th precinct for allowing me access to their world. Many of the details in this book are a direct result of my experiences watching New York's finest in action. Special thanks are due to Detectives Kate Beckett, Javier Esposito, Kevin Ryan and Captain Roy Montgomery for not simply putting up with me, but including me in their professional family.

I'd also like to thank Dr. Lanie Parish and her staff at New York's Office of Chief Medical Examiner for their infinite patience in the face of my endless and no doubt occasionally stupid questions like, "If he's dead, why is he still moving?"

A debt is owed to my associates on the third floor Clune. You guys never cease to amaze me with your imagination and insight. I wouldn't be half the writer I am without your support. Actually, I would be half the writer I am, which would make me too short to ride the rides at Disneyland. Hence my gratitude.

To Terri E. Miller, my co-conspirator, and to Nathan, Stana, Seamus, Jon, Ruben, Molly, Susan and Tamala—your tireless professionalism makes every day a joy.

Thanks to Richard Johnson of the *The New York Post*'s "Page Six" for generously sharing his time and expertise in my background re-search. For the parts of covering the celebrity journalism beat I got right, I owe gratitude to Richard and thank him for his kindness.

Many thanks to my friends at Black Pawn Publishing, especially Gina Cowell for staying on top of me through the final stages of writing. A huge tip of the hat to my editor, Gretchen Young, for her insight and patience, to Elizabeth Sabo Morick and the crew at Hyperion for all their support, and to Melissa Harling-Walendy at ABC for her guidance along the way.

Thanks to my agent, Sloan Harris at ICM. He's taken many a bullet for me in his time, and shot quite a few back, I dare say.

My deepest gratitude goes to my lovely and loving daughter, Alexis. You are my greatest joy and the source of so much of my strength. And thanks to my mother, Martha Rodgers, as well, for providing me with the sort of fiery childhood that inevitably forges novelists.

This book would not be what it is without two very dear friends. Andrew Marlowe guided, led, held both compass and flashlight, and steered me from cliff and ditch. His inspiration is cherished as much as his friendship. Somehow he even managed to make confetti and streamers shower down at the conclusion of that first story conference. And Tom was there early morning and late at night, helping me confront the terror of the blank page and inspiring my pen to work whatever magic is found within these pages.

To the remarkable Jennifer Allen, I can only say it's such a lovely ride-along.

And to you, the fans, my very special appreciation. Your belief and your standards bring the heat to every page.

RC
The Hamptons, July 2010

If you enjoyed *Naked Heat*,
be sure to catch *Frozen Heat*,
Richard Castle's latest Nikki Heat thriller,
available from Hyperion.

An excerpt, Chapter One, follows.

ONE

"Oh, yeah, that's it, Rook," said Nikki Heat. "That's what I want. Just like that." A trickle of sweat rolled down his neck to his heaving chest. He groaned and bit down on his tongue. "Don't stop yet. Keep it going. Yes." She hovered over him, lowering her face just inches from his so she could whisper. "Yes. Work it just like that. Nice, easy rhythm. That's it. How does it feel?" Jameson Rook stared at her intently just before he pinched his eyes into a squint and moaned. Then his muscles went slack and he dropped his head backward. Nikki frowned and brought herself upright. "You can't do that to me. I cannot believe you're stopping."

He let the dumbbells hit the black rubber floor beside the exercise bench and said, "Not stopping." He pulled in a chestful of air and coughed. "Just done."

"You're not done."

"Ten reps, I did ten reps."

"Not by my count."

"That's because your mind wanders. Besides, this rehab is for my own good. Why would I skip reps?"

"Because I turned away once and you thought I wasn't looking."

He scoffed, then asked, ". . . Were you?"

"Yes, and you only did eight. Do you want me to help you do your physical therapy, or be your enabler?"

"I swear I did at least nine."

A member of Rook's exclusive gym slid in behind her for some free weights, and Nikki turned to gauge how much of her and Rook's child-ish exchange he'd picked up. From the tinny music spilling from his earbuds, the only thing the other man heard was the Black Eyed Peas telling him it's gonna be a good night while he stared in the mirror.

Heat couldn't tell what the guy admired more, the row of plugs from his new hair transplants or the snap of his pecs under his designer wife beater.

Rook stood up beside her. "Nice chesticles, huh?"

"Shh, he'll hear you."

"Doubt that. Besides, who do you think taught me the word?"

Chesticle man caught her eye in the mirror and favored her with a wink. Apparently surprised that her knees didn't turn to jelly, he racked his weights and moved on to the tanning beds. Moments like that were precisely why Heat preferred her own gym, a throwback joint down-town with painted cinder-block walls, clanging steam pipes, and a clien-tele there to work instead of preen. When Rook's visiting physical therapist—whom he'd dubbed Gitmo Joe—called in sick for his morn-ing session and Nikki volunteered to spot him in his rehab routine, she had considered using her club instead. But there were negatives there, too. Well, one. Namely Don, her ex–Navy SEAL combat training partner with whom she had a history of grappling in bed, not just on the wrestling mat. Don's trainer-with-benefits days had come and gone, but Rook didn't know about him and she couldn't see the point in forcing an awkward encounter.

"Whew. I don't know about you," said Rook, toweling his face, "but I'm ready for a shower and some breakfast."

"Sounds great." She held out the dumbbells to him. "Right after your next set."

"I have another set?" He maintained the innocent pose as long as he could pull it off, and then snatched the weights from her. "You know, Gitmo Joe may be the spawn of an unholy union between the Marquis de Sade and Darth Vader, but at least he cuts me some slack. And I didn't even take a bullet to save his life."

"One," was all she said.

He paused and then did his first rep, grunting, "One."

They kidded about it, but that night two months before at the sani-tation pier on the Hudson, she thought she had lost him. The ER doc assured her afterward that she indeed almost had. In the blink of an instant after she beat down and disarmed one bad cop in the garbage transfer warehouse, his crooked partner took an ambush shot at her.

Heat never saw it coming, but Rook—damn Rook—who wasn't sup-posed to be there, leaped out and tackled her, taking the slug himself. Over her NYPD career as a uniform and a homicide detective, Nikki Heat had seen many bodies and watched many men die before her, and as the color left him that winter night and she felt his warm blood flow out of his chest across her arms, the vision resonated with all the fragile breaks and hopeless endings she had witnessed. Jameson Rook had saved her life, and now his own survival was nothing less than a miracle.

"Two," she said. "Rook, you're pathetic."

Out on the sidewalk, he took in a long, exaggerated breath. "I love the smell of Tribeca in the morning," he said. "It smells like . . . diesel."

The sun had risen just enough for Nikki to peel off her sweatshirt and enjoy the April air on her bare arms. She caught him looking and said, "Careful, you're one hair plug from becoming chesticle man."

She walked on and he fell in stride with her. "I can't help it. You know, any moment can become romantic. I saw that on a TV commer-cial."

"Let me know if you need me to slow down."

"No, I'm good." Heat gave him a side glance. Sure enough, he was keeping up. "Remember my first shuffles around that hospital corridor? Felt like Tim Conway on the old *Carol Burnett Show*. Now look at me. I'm back to my superhero stride." He demonstrated and powered ahead to the corner.

"Nice. If I ever need help, and Batman or Lone Vengeance are booked, I know who I'll call." As she drew up to him, she asked, "Seri-ously, you doing OK? I didn't tax you too much with that workout?"

"Naw, I'm fine." He placed the tip of her forefinger on his ribs. "I just feel a little tugging sometimes when I stretch." They waited for the light to change, and he added, "Speaking of tugging."

Nikki gave him her best blank expression. "Tugging? I'm sorry, I don't follow." They held each other's gaze until he arched one brow and cracked her up.

Rook laced his arm through hers as they crossed the street. "Detec-tive, I do believe if we skipped breakfast, you could still get to work on time."

"Are you sure you're ready for this? Seriously, I can wait. I'm the queen of delayed gratification."

"Trust me, we've waited long enough."

"Maybe you should double-check with your doctor to see if you're healthy enough for sexual activity."

"Oh," said Rook. "So you've seen the commercials, too."

Instead of stopping for a bite at Kitchenette, they made a sharp turn at the corner and headed toward his loft, arm in arm, picking up the pace as they went.

They kissed deeply in his elevator on the way up, pressing against each other, his back to the wall, and then, suddenly, hers. Then they broke away, resisting or maybe teasing, or maybe a bit of both. Their eyes locked in on each other's, only flicking away to monitor the floor count.

Inside his front door, he reached to kiss her again, but she ducked him and raced through the kitchen, bolted up the hall at a sprint, and leaped at the bed, flying airborne like a club wrestler and landing with a bounce, laughing out a "hurry up" while she kicked off her cross trainers.

He appeared in the doorway, completely naked. At the foot of the bed, he struck a regal pose. "If I am to die, let it be this way."

And then she grabbed him and pulled him on top of her.

The heat took them beyond caution, even beyond play. Lost time, raw emotions, and aching need all cycloned into a swirl of passion with no mind, only frenzy. In minutes the room itself was in motion, not just the bed. Lampshades swayed, books toppled on shelves, even the pencil cup on Rook's nightstand tipped, and a dozen Blackwing 602s rolled onto the floor.

Then it was over and they flopped back, panting, smiling. "Oh you're definitely healthy enough for sex," said Nikki.

All Rook could manage was a dry-throated "That was . . . Whoa." And then he added, "The earth moved."

Nikki laughed. "Feel good about you."

"No, I think it literally moved." He got up on one elbow to look at the room. "I think we just had an earthquake."

By the time she came out from drying her hair, Rook had tidied up the fallen items in his loft and planted himself in front of the TV. "Channel 7 says it was a 5.8 on something called the Ramapo Fault Line, epicenter in Sloatsburg, New York."

Nikki put her empty mug on the counter and checked her cell phone. "I've got service back. No messages or TAC alerts, at least not for me. What's the impact?"

"They're still assessing. No fatalities, some injuries from fallen bricks and whatnot, nothing major, so far. Airports and some subway lines closed as a precaution. Oh, and I won't have to shake the orange juice. Want some?"

She said no and put on her gun. "Who'd have thought? An earthquake in New York City?"

He put his arms around her. "Can't complain about the timing."

"Hard to top."

"Guess we'll just have to try," he said, and they kissed. Her phone rang, and Heat pulled away to answer. Without being asked, he handed her a pen and notepad and she jotted an address. "On my way."

"You know what I think we should do today?"

Nikki slipped her phone into her blazer pocket. "Yes, I do. And as much as I'd love to—believe me, I'd love to—I've got to get to work."

"Go to Hawaii."

"Very funny."

"I'm not joking. Let's just go. Maui. Mmm, Maui."

"You know I can't do that."

"Give me one reason."

"I've got a murder to handle."

"Nikki. If there's one thing I've learned in our time together, it's never let a murder get in the way of a good time."

"So I've noticed. And what about your work? Don't you have some magazine article you should be writing? Some exposé of corruption in the dark corridors of the World Bank? A chronicle of your ride-along with a bin Laden hunter? Your weekend in the Seychelles with Johnny Depp or Sting?"

Rook pondered that and said, "If we left this afternoon, we could be in Lahaina for breakfast. And if you feel guilty, don't. You deserve it after taking care of me for two months." She ignored him and clipped her detective shield onto her waistband. "Come on, Nikki, how many homicides are there in this city in a year, five hundred?"

"More like five thirty."

"All right, that's fewer than two a day. Look, we peace-out to Maui today and come back in a week, you'd miss, maybe, ten murders. And not all of them would be in your precinct anyway."

"You're making a very clear point here, Rook."

He looked at her, mildly taken aback. "I am?"

"Yes. And the point is, I don't care how many Pulitzer Prizes you've won. You still have the brain of a sixteen-year-old."

"So is that a yes?"

"Make that a fifteen-year-old." Nikki kissed him again and cupped him between the legs. "By the way? So worth the wait." And then she went to work.

The crime scene was on her way to the precinct, so instead of going up to the Twentieth first to sign out a car and double back, Heat got off the B train a stop early at 72nd Street to hoof it. The bomb squad had ordered a precautionary traffic shutdown at Columbus Avenue, and Nikki came up the subway steps near the Dakota to witness nightmare gridlock backed up all the way to Central Park. The sooner she finished her investigation, the sooner relief would come to the stuck drivers, so she quickened her stride. But she didn't short her contemplation.

As always, on approach to a body, Detective Heat steeped herself in thoughts of the victim. She didn't need Rook to remind her how many homicides there were in the city every year. But her vow was never to let volume dehumanize a single lost life. Or inure her to the impact on friends and loved ones. For her, this wasn't lip service or some PR tagline. Nikki had come by it honestly years ago when her mother was murdered. Heat's loss not only spurred her to switch college majors to Criminal Justice, it forged the kind of cop she vowed to be. Over ten years later, her mother's case remained unsolved, but the detective remained unbending in her advocacy for each victim, one at a time.

At 72nd and Columbus she picked her way through the knot of spectators who had gathered there, many with their cell phones aloft, documenting their proximity to danger for whatever street cred that gave them on their Facebook pages. She reached down to draw back her blazer and flash her shield to the uniform at the barrier, but he knew the move and gave her the fraternal nod before she even showed it. Emergency lights strobed two blocks ahead of her as she headed south. Nikki could have taken the empty street but kept to the sidewalk; even as a veteran cop, it unsettled her to see a major downtown avenue completely shut in morning rush hour. The sidewalks were vacant, too, except for uni patrols keeping them clear. Sawhorses blocked 71st, also, and a few doors west of them, an ambulance idled in front of a town house that had shed its brick façade in the earthquake. She passed one of the green ash trees growing from the sidewalk planters and looked up through its budding limbs at dozens of rubberneckers leaning out of windows and over fire escapes. Same on the other side of Columbus. As she drew closer to the scene, dispatch calls from the roundup of emergency vehicles echoed off the stone apartment buildings in enveloping unison.

The bomb squad had turned out with its armored mobile containment unit parked in the center lane of the avenue, just in case anything needed detonating. But from twenty yards off, Heat could tell from body language that Emergency Services had pretty much stood down. Elevated above the roofs of vans and blue-and-whites, she caught a glimpse of her friend Lauren Parry walking around inside the open rear cargo door of a delivery truck in her medical examiner coveralls. Then she ducked down and Nikki lost sight of her.

Raley and Ochoa from her squad stepped away from a middle-aged black man in a watch cap and green parka, who they were interviewing beside the Engine 40 fire truck, and met up with her as she arrived. "Detective Heat."

"Detective Roach," she said, using the partners' house nickname that amicably squashed Raley and Ochoa into one handy syllable.

"No trouble getting here," said Raley, not asking, not expecting that she, of all people, would ever have any.

"No, my line's running. I hear the N and the R are down for inspection where they go under the river."

"Same with the Q train coming out of Brooklyn," added Ochoa. "I made it across before it hit. But I'll tell you, Times Square station was unreal. Like a Godzilla movie down there, the way people were screaming and running."

"Did you feel it?" asked Raley.

She replayed the circumstances and said, "Oh, yeah," trying to sound offhanded.

"Where were you when it hit?"

"Exercising." Not a total lie. Heat side nodded to the armored blast container. "What are we working here that warrants the parade of heavy metal?"

"Suspicious package lit things up." Ochoa flipped to the first page of his notepad. "Frozen food delivery driver—that's him over there—"

"—in the green jacket—" chimed in his partner in their usual duet.

"—opens the back of his truck to unload some chicken tenders and burger patties at the deli here." He paused to allow Nikki a beat to eyeball the All In Bun storefront, where a trio of cooks in checked pants and aprons slouched at the window counter waiting out the closure. "He slides a carton aside and finds a suitcase sitting there between the boxes."

"I guess 'See Something, Say Something' is working," Raley said, picking up. "He books it out of there and calls 911."

"Emergency Services Unit deploys and sends Robocop in to check it out." Detective Ochoa beckoned her to walk with him while he led her past the bomb squad's remote control robot. "The 'bot does a sniff and an X-ray. Negative on explosive elements. Their bomb tech was suited up anyway, so—abundance of caution—he pops the lock and finds the body inside the suitcase."

A few feet behind her, she heard Detective Feller. "That's why I go strictly carry-on. Those checked bags'll kill ya." She snapped her head around and saw the surprise on his face, while his audience of two uniforms laughed. He'd been speaking in a low voice, but not low enough. Feller's cheeks reddened as Heat left Raley and Ochoa to cross to him. The unis melted away, leaving him alone with her. "Hey, sorry." Then he tried to charm it away with a preemptive grin and the self-effacing cackle that always reminded her of John Candy. "Don't think you were supposed to hear that."

"Nobody was." She spoke so quietly, so evenly, and so without expression that the casual observer would think they were simply two detectives comparing notes. "Look around, Randy. This is serious as it gets. A murder scene. My murder scene. Not open mic night at Dangerfield's."

He nodded. "Yeah, I know I stepped in it."

"Once again," she noted. Randall Feller, perennial class clown, had a nasty habit of cutting up at crime scenes. It was the one bad habit of one great street detective. The same detective who, along with Rook, had gotten shot saving her life on that sanitation pier. Feller's gallows humor might have fit right in during the years he spent in the Special Operations Division, riding around all night in undercover yellow cabs in the macho, kick-ass, Dodge City world of the NYPD Taxi Unit, but not in her squad. At least not inside the yellow tape. This wasn't their first conversation about it since he'd transferred to her Homicide Unit after his medical leave.

"I know, I know, it just sort of comes out." She could tell he meant it, and there was no point belaboring it. "Inside voice next time, I promise." Heat gave him a short nod and moved off to the delivery truck.

From street level at the rear hatch, Nikki had to tilt her head back to look up at Lauren Parry, who squatted on the floor inside the cargo hold. The stacks of cardboard cartons deeper inside wept with condensation; some even glistened from ice crystals encrusting their sides. Even with the freezer motor off, refrigerated air rolled out cool across Heat's face. At Lauren's knee, a blue-gray hard-side suitcase rested open and flat with the lid clamshelled up, blocking Nikki's view of its contents. She said, "Morning, Dr. Parry."

Her friend pivoted to her and smiled. When she said, "Hey, Detective Heat," Nikki could see puffs of Lauren's breath. "Got a complicated one here."

"When isn't it?"

The ME rocked her head side to side, weighing that and agreeing. "Want the basics?"

"Good a place as any to start." Nikki took out her own notebook, a slender, reporter's cut spiral that fit perfectly in her blazer pocket.

"Female Jane Doe. No ID, no purse, no wallet, no jewelry. Estimating age as early sixties."

"Cause of death?" asked Heat.

Lauren Parry's eyes left her clipboard and settled on her friend's. "Now, how did I guess that would be your question?" She glanced inside the suitcase and continued, "I can't say, except preliminarily."

Nikki echoed back, "Now, how did I guess that would be your answer?"

The ME smiled again, and small trails of vapor floated from her nostrils. "Why don't you come on up here, and I can show you what I'm dealing with."

Detective Heat gloved up as she ascended the corrugated metal ramp sloping from the pavement to the back ledge of the truck. As she stepped aboard, her gaze momentarily stuck on the suitcase, and when it did, her teeth clacked with an icy shiver. Attributing it to crossing climates—leaving behind the mild April morning for a January chill inside the cargo hold—she shook it off.

Lauren stood so Nikki could squeeze by to get a view of the corpse. "I see what you mean," Heat said.

The woman's body was frozen. Ice crystals like the ones shimmering on nearby boxes of ground beef, chicken, and fish sticks glistened on her face. Clothed in a pale gray suit, she had been folded into the fetal position and fit into the suitcase, where she now lay on her side. Lauren gestured with the cap of her pen to the frosty bloodstain covering the back of the suit. "Obviously, this here is our best guess for cause of death. It's a significant puncture delivered laterally to the posterior of the rib cage. Judging from the amount of blood, the knife entered sideways between the ribs and found the heart." Heat experienced that uneasy déjà vu she felt every time she saw one of those wounds. She made no comment though, just nodded and folded her arms to warm the gooseflesh the refrigeration had no doubt raised on them, even through the blazer. "With her frozen like this, I can't do my usual field prelim for you. I can't even unfold her limbs to check for other wounds, trauma, defense marks, lividity, and so forth. I can do all that, of course, just not yet."

Nikki kept her gaze fixed on the stab wound and said, "Even time of death is going to be a challenge, I suppose."

"Oh, for sure, but not to worry. We can still come close when I get a chance to work on her down at Thirtieth Street," said the medical examiner. And then she added, "Assuming I don't get back there to a major situation following the quake."

"From what I hear, it's mostly a small number of treat-and-release injuries."

"That's good." Lauren studied her. "You all right?"

"Fine. Just didn't know I'd need a sweater today."

"Guess I'm more used to the cold, right?" She uncapped her pen. "Why don't I stand aside and make some notes while you do your beginn-y thing?" Parry and Heat had worked enough cases together that they knew each other's moves and needs. For instance, Lauren knew that Nikki had an initial task she performed at each crime scene, which was to survey everything from every possible angle with what Heat called beginner's eyes. The problem with veteran detectives, Heat believed, was that after years and years of cases, even the best investigators became numbed by habit; counterintuitively, experience worked against them by blunting observation skills. Ask a refinery worker how he deals with the stink, and he'll say, "What stink?" But Detective Heat remembered how it felt on her first homicides. How she saw everything and then looked for more. Every bit of input held potential significance. Nothing could be overlooked. Just as the experience of her mother's killing ritualized her empathic approach to the crime scene, her belief in keeping it fresh prevented her survey of it from lapsing into ritual. As she often reminded her squad, it's all about being present in the moment and noticing what you notice.

Detective Heat's eyes told her this truck was not likely the murder scene. Walking the tight area of the cargo section, flashing the beam of her Stinger on the floor between boxes and on the walls, she saw no signs of any blood spatter. Later, after the body removal, the Evidence Collection Unit would offload all the cartons for a thorough inspection, but Nikki was satisfied in her mind that the suitcase had been brought aboard with the victim in it and, possibly, dead already. Time of death and a timeline of the truck's loading and unloading would help button that down. She turned her attention to the victim.

ME Parry's pick of early sixties seemed right. Her hair was flatteringly cut to a shorter business length correct for a woman of that age and, from the roots that were starting to show some gray and dark brown in the part, her honey blond do, subtly streaked with caramel, indicated two things. First, she was a woman with some money who cared enough about her hair to have an expensive cut and a skilled colorist. Second, in spite of that, she was long overdue for a visit. "What kept her away?" wrote Nikki in her notebook. The clothes were similarly tasteful. Petite size. Off the rack, but clearly the rack lived on one of the upscale floors of the department store. The blouse was from the current season and the gray suit was a lightweight wool with some function to it. The feeling Heat got wasn't so much expensive as good quality. Not the uniform of the lady who lunches, but the woman who power lunches. Nikki crouched to look at the one hand that was visible. It was partially closed and tucked up under her chin, so she couldn't see all of it, but what she could see told a story. These were busy hands, toned without being muscular or abused by hard labor. The slender fingers had the kind of strength you see on tennis players and fitness enthusiasts. She noted a small scar on the side of the wrist, which looked years, maybe decades, old. Nikki stood again and looked straight down at her. The body fit the profile of a runner or cyclist. She made another note to have the vic's picture shown at fitness clubs, the New York Road Runners, and cycle shops. Heat squatted again to examine a grimy, dark brown dirt scuff on the knee of the woman's pants, which could say something about her last moments. She made a note of it and scooted around to look more closely at the knife wound. Furthering Heat's notion that the victim had been killed before being put in the truck, the frozen bloodstain formed a wide pond, as if she had bled out facedown. The width of the stain indicated great volume, yet there was not much blood in the satin of the suitcase interior other than from abrasion smears on the lid. Nikki shined her flashlight where the victim's back met the inside hinge of the suitcase and saw only similar bloodstain rub-off, with no evidence of pooling. Again, when they removed her later, better measurements could be taken, but

Heat was getting a picture of a murder not only outside the truck, but outside the luggage.

One more indicator would be to look at the exterior of the suitcase for any major blood collection along the hinges or seams. Taking care not to disturb it, she knelt on both knees, palmed one hand on the cargo deck for balance, and dropped her head, leaning over far enough for her eyebrow to nearly touch the floor. Slowly, methodically, she ran the beam of her flashlight from right to left along the bottom edge of the case.

When her light reached the left corner of the suitcase, Nikki gasped. Her vision fluttered and a vertigo sensation swept over her. The light slipped from her hand and she toppled over onto her side.

Lauren said, "Nikki, you all right?"

She couldn't really see anything in that moment. Hands came on her. Lauren Parry cradled her head off the floor. A pair of EMTs started for the ramp, but by then Nikki had recovered enough to sit herself up and wave them off. "No, no, I'm fine. It's OK." Lauren crouched beside her at eye level to check her out. "Really, I'm OK," said Nikki.

But to her friend, her face said anything but. "You scared me there, Nik. I thought you went over in an aftershock or something."

Heat swung her legs over the back of the truck and let them dangle. Raley and Ochoa approached, followed by Feller. Ochoa said, "What's up, Detective? You look like you saw a ghost."

Nikki shivered. This time, not from the refrigeration. She twisted to look behind her at the suitcase and then slowly turned back to the others.

"Nikki," said Lauren, "what is it?"

"The suitcase." She swallowed hard. "My initials are on it."

The detectives and the ME all looked at one another, puzzled. Finally, Raley said, "I don't get it. Why would your initials be on that suitcase?"

"Because I carved them there when I was a kid." She could see them processing that, but it was taking them too long, so she said, "That suitcase belonged to my mother." And then she added, "Her killer stole it the night she was murdered."

Partners. In crime.

THE COMPLETE FOURTH SEASON

Partners. In crime.

CASTLE

abc

Available On DVD September 11, 2012

CASTLE on abc

Also available:

Visit CastleOnDVD.com

abc studios

ABOUT THE AUTHOR

© American Broadcasting Companies, Inc.

Richard Castle is the author of numerous bestsellers, including *Heat Wave, Naked Heat, Heat Rises,* and the Derrick Storm eBook original trilogy. His first novel, *In a Hail of Bullets,* published while he was still in college, received the Nom DePlume Society's prestigious Tom Straw Award for Mystery Literature. Castle currently lives in Manhattan with his daughter and mother, both of whom infuse his life with humor and inspiration.